Unreliable. I remember that was one of the blemishes you listed against me, when you told me never to darken your door again."

"Your memory is faulty."

"Is it?" He looked down at her from his greater height, but she refused to give ground. "Actually, my memory is rather good. For instance, I remember you agreeing to that bet with me at the Elphinstones'. A kiss if I won or my thumb ring if you did. Is my memory faulty on that detail?"

She hesitated, but he was waiting for her to fib, and she refused to be predictable. "We never finished the game."

"We *could* finish it. Where is the famous Grantham billiard room?" He looked around. "The scene of your many triumphs?"

"I thought we had decided friends do not make wagers that could compromise—"

"You decided that. And I don't think we are friends now. Are we?"

He waited. Her heart was beating quickly, her throat felt tight as she sought for something to say. "I can't take the risk," she blurted out at last. "Not with you. You're the last person I should be friends with."

ALSO BY SARA BENNETT

Dreaming of a Duke Like You

My Secret Duke

SARA BENNETT

FOREVER

New York   Boston

Forever
Hachette Book Group
1290 Avenue of the Americas, New York, NY 10104
read-forever.com
@readforeverpub

First Edition: April 2025

Forever is an imprint of Grand Central Publishing. The Forever name and logo are registered trademarks of Hachette Book Group, Inc.

The publisher is not responsible for websites (or their content) that are not owned by the publisher.

The Hachette Speakers Bureau provides a wide range of authors for speaking events. To find out more, go to hachettespeakersbureau.com or email HachetteSpeakers@hbgusa.com.

Forever books may be purchased in bulk for business, educational, or promotional use. For information, please contact your local bookseller or the Hachette Book Group Special Markets Department at special.markets@hbgusa.com.

ISBNs: 978-1-5387-2383-8 (mass market), 978-1-5387-2384-5 (ebook)

Printed in the United States of America

BVGM

10 9 8 7 6 5 4 3 2 1

For Gill—
thank you for your support
and encouragement over the years.

You'll be missed.

My Secret Duke

Prologue

L ady Olivia Ashton slipped through the door at the back of the room, closing it softly behind her. The Elphinstones' musical evening wasn't the most exciting engagement she had attended since her coming-out ball in May, but she was wearing one of her new, fashionable dresses with a nice string of pearls about her neck. She looked well, she was admired, and after the long years of living neglected at Grantham, that really should have been enough.

Instead, she was on her way to another clandestine rendezvous with Ivo Fitzsimmons, Duke of Northam.

Olivia had danced with him many times now, and looked forward to dancing many more. She watched out for him, and felt disappointed if he wasn't present. He was handsome and charming and paid her extravagant compliments, but exciting as her interactions with him were, she had come to realize he was also the very last person she should be setting her cap at.

This was Olivia's first time in London. Her Season had been delayed, firstly by her father's death, which left them with crushing debts, and then by the revelation that the true heir to the estate—the new Duke of Grantham—was gambling club owner Gabriel Cadieux, meaning the futures of Olivia and her five sisters were in his hands.

Despite their difficult beginning, Olivia had grown to trust and love Gabriel, who was doing his best to bring the Grantham estate back from the brink of financial disaster. But the scandal hadn't helped Olivia's acceptance by the ton.

Olivia had never had to worry about the propriety or lack thereof of her behavior, and it was only now, when things were very different, that she realized how sheltered she had been at Grantham. Here in London, she needed to be the perfect debutante if she was to win over polite society, for her own sake and that of her sisters— it felt unfair, but because she was the eldest, her actions would affect their lives as well as her own. Especially the younger sisters, because the Ashton finances could only stretch so far. A good marriage for Olivia was imperative, and the Duke of Northam was not "good marriage" material. For all he was so handsome and charming, he seemed determined to lead her into even more scandal. And Olivia was finding it difficult to resist him.

Northam was not your ordinary brand of nobleman. He was notorious for his irresponsible behavior, and it was said that nothing was beyond him when it came to winning a wager. His financial situation was, if not quite dire, certainly verging into that territory. He was *not* the sort of gentleman Olivia should be encouraging.

And yet ever since he had danced with her at her coming-out ball, she had not been able to forget him.

She looked up. He was standing at the top of the staircase, leaning his elegant self negligently against the bannister. His corn-colored hair was a little long, and his green eyes sparkled in a mischievous manner.

"There you are," he said. "I was about to start without you."

He was teasing her, but she couldn't give him the satisfaction of winning. *Again.*

She should never have boasted to him about her proficiency at the game of billiards. The subject had come up shortly after her coming-out ball, and she had said something like "I am accounted as quite the expert among my sisters." He had responded that he too was an expert. Before she knew it, he had dared her to play him, and was leading her away from the ballroom and into a billiard room, where he had proceeded to trounce her.

The next time they met, he challenged her to another game, and this time, she won. Perhaps his male pride was piqued, because ever since then, he had been inviting her to take part in a third game. To establish the overall winner.

So far, she had resisted, until tonight when she found her resistance considerably weakened. The musical evening was tedious, the company boring, and she had admitted to herself that nothing here was as exciting as the Duke of Northam.

She began to climb the stairs.

"I think you will find that thrashing your sisters at billiards is not the same as playing a master like me," he said, words designed to incite her into another foolish act.

Olivia glared while at the same time her lips twitched into a reluctant smile. "*I think* you will find yourself completely outclassed, Your Grace."

He chuckled as he opened a door to a dark-paneled room, and said, "Why will you not call me Ivo? Surely we are more than mere acquaintances."

Olivia flicked him a glance as she moved to the green baize table. "Are we?"

The door closed behind her, and her heart gave a little

jump, but Ivo was already reaching for one of the cues and handing it to her with his wicked grin. "Of course. We are friends, are we not?"

The thought warmed her inside. She had never had a male friend, apart from her brother, although Ivo's smile wasn't what she would call brotherly. He flirted with her, which, unlike billiards, was a game she had little experience in, but despite being out of her depth, she greatly enjoyed their lighthearted banter.

"I hope so," she said, feeling color warm her cheeks.

He smiled absently, as if he had already forgotten the question, and set about preparing for their game. He tucked his hair back—the wayward curls had fallen into his eyes—and shrugged off his tightly fitting jacket with a purposeful air. "Last time was beginner's luck," he said.

Olivia laughed scathingly. "Admit it, *Ivo*, I am the better player."

His green eyes narrowed as he put cue to ball. But rather than taking the shot, he suddenly straightened. "If you are so certain of yourself, Olivia, why don't we make a wager on the outcome?"

"A...a wager?" Did he not know the Ashton girls were paupers? Her grandmother had impressed upon her only this morning that in such circumstances, she must find a wealthy match so that her sisters could partake in her good fortune.

"Why yes!" He stepped closer and smiled down at her. Olivia was not tall, and he topped her by several inches. "What shall it be?" He pretended to think, tapping one elegant finger against his chin. "A kiss!"

Olivia stepped back, eyes wide with shock. "Your Grace, I don't think—" she began, but at the same time, there was a flutter in her chest. Was he trying to seduce her?

"On the cheek," he amended. "A peck on the cheek between friends."

He waited for her response, but she didn't know what to say. Surely a kiss between friends was acceptable? But Olivia was wise enough to know that this entire situation was *un*acceptable. She was alone with an unmarried gentleman who was no relative of hers, and now he wanted to *kiss* her?

"I don't think…" she tried again.

He sighed. "Olivia, aren't you confident of winning? I thought you were an expert. You disappoint me."

He was playing games with her, tempting her to take up his wager, and despite knowing it, Olivia couldn't help but be stung by his dismissal of her skill. She *was* good at billiards. She played with her sisters at Grantham and always won. Why shouldn't she win this time, and show Ivo he had seriously underestimated her? She imagined the expression on his face and was persuaded.

"What do *I* get when I win?" she demanded.

His smile tipped up at the corners, showing the dimples in his cheeks. "What do you want, Olivia?"

He was brazen, probably because he was so certain he would be the winner in their game. Well, she would show him…Olivia thought a moment while he waited. Despite his careless manner, he seemed to be holding his breath.

She glanced down at the thumb ring he wore. She had noticed it before, a heavy gold band with a dull red stone set in it. "Your ring," she said.

He gave a crack of surprised laughter and twisted the ring on his thumb. For a moment, it seemed as if he was going to refuse her. What if the ring was valuable, or had sentimental attachment for him? But before she could recant, he shrugged and said, "As you wish. A kiss for me and a ring for you. Shall we begin?"

The game was intense. They played as if their lives depended on the outcome, and Ivo's muffled curse when he missed a shot was echoed by Olivia's groan when she missed another. As she bent over the table, deliberating a complicated maneuver, he came and stood beside her. She could feel the warmth of his body, and as he began to roll up the sleeves of his white shirt, her gaze strayed to his bared forearms. How could a man's arms be so interesting? Lean and muscular, tanned so that the smattering of fair hair was almost invisible.

She was so fixated she did not notice him lean down until his laughing whisper tickled her ear.

"Are you taking your shot, Olivia?"

She jerked her head back to the ball lined up before her cue. "You are trying to distract me," she said, knowing she was blushing again. "It won't work."

He laughed quietly, and she missed the shot.

Then it was his turn.

Olivia studied him as he bent over the table. Hard muscled legs in tight pantaloons, his hip jutting as he leaned in, his broad shoulders shifting as he took aim. A voice in her head told her to leave and return to the music room, but it was as if she was held in place. This was one of the most exciting moments of her life, and she didn't want it to end. Ivo hadn't just challenged her to this game, he was challenging her in other ways too. He was flirtatious and playful, and the obvious admiration in his green eyes was very flattering to a girl who had never had a male admirer.

She considered whether she was courageous enough to use the same tactics Ivo had used on her. Because she couldn't lose. She mustn't lose. No matter how tempting the thought of his lips on her skin was, she suspected he would not be satisfied with something as tame as a kiss on the cheek. She also suspected she might feel the same.

Olivia leaned over the table beside him, so close she could smell clean, laundered clothing and his vanilla pomade. A curl of her dark hair fell forward and brushed his hand. His cue slid off the ball, sending it awry.

"Are you sure you had the angle right?" she whispered.

He turned his head, and his gaze slid over her face, lingering on her eyes and mouth. His smile seemed to suggest things she knew were inappropriate, and her lips tingled. What would it feel like to have his lips brush against hers, to have his hands cup her face so that he could deepen their kiss?

Her imaginings were vivid, making her quite breathless as she moved away and took up her cue once more. But she was having difficulty concentrating, strongly aware of him as he moved about the table, the warm male scent of him tantalizing whenever he stepped closer. He was dangerous, but despite knowing the consequences, she could not seem to help taking the risk.

They were halfway through the match. She already knew she was going to lose when the door opened without warning. Miss Vivienne Tremeer stood staring at her, and at her shoulder was Gabriel. It didn't occur to her then to wonder why Gabriel was alone with Vivienne, something that was as socially unacceptable as Olivia being alone with Ivo, because Gabriel's face turned white with anger, and she forgot everything else.

The next few moments were intense and uncomfortable. Ivo tried to take the blame, but it was no good. No one was listening. Gabriel was gritting his teeth. "Come with me," he said, holding out his arm. She could hardly refuse, even though she wanted to. She let him lead her away from her stupidity. That was when he told her that Northam was probably engaged to Vivienne's cousin, Lady Annette, and while she was struggling to grasp that confusing and disappointing information, they reached the room where all the other guests had been listening to the soprano.

Only to find the music had paused. With nothing else to entertain them, the room as one turned and stared. Vivienne's aunt rose to her feet and positively glared. Olivia wanted to run away—she was no longer feeling brave—but Gabriel led her back to her seat, where she sat with her back stiff and her eyes fixed to the front. When he squeezed her hand, a kind gesture she did not deserve, she had to blink back tears of mortification.

After that, the evening was a blur. Whispers and sneers as supper was served at the end of the performance. Contemptuous glances as guests congregated in groups, even though Ivo and Olivia were now at opposite ends of the room. The Viscountess Monteith, Vivienne's aunt, was busy telling all who would listen that Northam and Olivia had broken her daughter's heart…at least that was what Olivia imagined she was saying. Someone tittered as Olivia walked by, and when she turned her head, startled, the person showed her their back.

Again, Ivo came to apologize. His fair hair looked as if he'd been running his hands through it, and his face was pale and set.

"My apologies," he said in a voice loud enough to be heard by those who were listening. "Completely my fault, Lady Olivia." Then, lowering his voice for her alone, "I promise I will fix this."

She did not answer him. The evening had turned into

a disaster, and it felt as if her faux pas had locked her out of the society she had so longed to enter.

Olivia barely noticed saying goodbye to the Elphinstones, or Gabriel handing her into the coach for the journey home. It wasn't until he spoke that some of her shock wore off.

"Olivia," he sighed. "You have worked so hard. You are beginning to find your place in society. It may not be what you wanted, God knows it isn't what I want, but I thought you were coming to terms with it. You seemed to be enjoying yourself, or was I wrong?"

"No, you weren't wrong," she admitted, her eyes filling with tears. "I *was* enjoying myself. It was so pleasant to be sought after and to dress in pretty things, and I was liking it very much. And now I've ruined it." Her lip wobbled.

Her brother seemed to be choosing his words carefully. Although his expression was stern, there was kindness in his dark eyes. "We are still learning to live within the rules," he said. "Sometimes we can stretch them a little, or even bend them on occasion, but we must never break them."

It was his kindness that threatened to undo her. Her throat almost closed over her anxious reply. "Do you think I have? Broken them?"

"I don't know," he admitted. "You certainly caused a stir. Northam said he would fix things, but how reliable is he, and how can he mend matters? Perhaps people will make allowances for your inexperience."

She expected he actually meant for her headstrong nature and foolish behavior. "I am very sorry. I forgot for a moment where I was and what was at stake. I am trying very hard to be a duke's sister."

"Your life has been turned upside down," Gabriel agreed.

"So has yours. And don't tell me you don't resent it, for I won't believe you," she said when he went to dismiss her words.

"Of course I resent it."

She held her breath. Gabriel had been a gambling club owner, without any encumbrances, and now he was a duke with six unmarried sisters. Could he turn his back on them all and walk away? After tonight, she wouldn't blame him if he did.

His next words soothed that worry.

"I wish it were different, but I understand why I have to change. It's for the sake of you and your sisters. If I had refused to take on the dukedom, then you would have been cast into penury, forced to live with relatives and strangers who had no care for you. How would you have felt about that? The estate was bankrupt, and although I have managed to claw it back to respectable limits, it will take time for us to be truly safe."

Olivia felt the old fears twist in her stomach—memories of her life before Gabriel came to save them. "Do you mean we could still be cast into pen-penury?" she asked and strained to hear the answer to her question over the beating of her heart.

"There is a possibility. However, I will do my utmost not to let that happen. I may be a bad duke," Gabriel said, "but I am an excellent businessman."

Olivia found a shaky laugh. "You're not a bad duke. It was I who messed up. Grandmama will be livid, she is always going on about what is at stake, but I didn't real-ize how bad things could get until now. It's horrible to be treated like that. Especially when I was enjoying myself so much. I don't like it, Gabriel, I really don't."

She *had* been enjoying her new life, and this *had*

been a painful lesson in what she could and could not do if she wanted to keep her reputation and her place in society. Returning to Grantham, to the past, was not an option, and certainly not one she wanted to contemplate.

She finally understood the command she held over her own destiny. Ivo was not the right gentleman for her. Attractive and charismatic he might be, but he was completely wrong when it came to her future. If she was to have any chance of making a good match, if she was to find a wealthy and respectable husband, if she was not to end up where she started, then she must distance herself from him.

She must.

Chapter One

Two weeks later, Ashton House
Mayfair, London

T he girls were huddled together in Olivia and Justina's
bedchamber. Edwina was trying not to bounce on
the feather mattress as her big blue eyes slid from sister to
sister. There were six of them altogether, ranging in age
from twenty to five, and despite the Ashton town house
having many rooms, all six of them were in this one.

"Is Grandmama speaking yet?" one of them asked
Olivia, deferring to her as the eldest sister. They had been
tiptoeing around their grandmother, the Dowager Duchess of Grantham, ever since their half brother, Gabriel,
had rushed off to Cornwall. Apart from one furious out-
burst from the dowager, there had been nothing since but
an icy silence. She kept to her rooms, her meals carried
up on trays by nervous-looking servants, and refused visits from anyone, including her granddaughters.

Especially her granddaughters.

Olivia could understand it. The dowager had discovered the girls had been coconspirators in Gabriel's decision to set off after Miss Vivienne Tremeer, with the goal
of asking her to marry him. The very woman Grandmama
had warned him against because of her tarnished reputation and unsuitable family. The dowager had already

decided that the perfect wife for Gabriel was the Earl of March's daughter, Lady Edeline, and she had believed Gabriel had been convinced. Why should he not be when the beautiful and blue-blooded Edeline would ensure the Ashton family's return to respectability, sweeping their scandals beneath their threadbare carpet?

And their scandals were numerous.

Harry, the former duke, had married his mistress, Eugénie Cadieux, and then kept it hidden when he went on to marry Lady Felicia. Therefore, Gabriel, the "bastard" son of Eugénie, was now the legal heir, while the six daughters of Felicia had no legal standing. Gabriel had agreed to take his half sisters on, as well as an estate that was groaning under the weight of his father's and grandfather's debts. The dowager had thought she could influence him—or bully him—into doing what was best for the family, especially after Olivia created a scandal of her own. But Gabriel was not a man to be forced for long into doing something he didn't want to, and once he fell in love with Vivienne, that was it for him.

"You shouldn't have told him to follow Miss Tremeer to Cornwall," Georgia said in a prim voice. She was eight years old, the youngest sister but one, and a stickler for "doing the right thing."

Olivia's eyes blazed. "What? And let him marry that insipid Edeline? You agreed Vivienne was perfect for him! We all did! And remember how miserable he was, all that walking in his sleep because his mind was disturbed? Besides, he had already decided to go after her, he just needed to know we were on his side. Gabriel will be happy now, and so will Vivienne. And once Grandmama gets to know her properly, I'm sure everything will be comfortable again."

She broke off then because so far, the dowager had shown no signs of softening when it came to Gabriel and his radical choice of wife.

"And to make it worse," observed Justina—at eighteen years, the second-eldest sister—while settling herself comfortably against the bolster at the head of the bed, "Vivienne's aunt has been telling everyone she knew all about their 'romantic' love affair and is looking forward to welcoming the new Duchess of Grantham. And this is after she sent Vivienne away in disgrace!"

The Viscountess Monteith and their grandmother have been enemies for years. The viscountess was also the mother of the woman Northam was supposedly engaged to, Lady Annette.

Roberta, sixteen going on seventeen years old and the third sister, had flung herself backward onto the bed with a groan, but now she sat up, brightening. "But that might be a good thing? Maybe Grandmama will decide she needs to be the one to welcome them home first. To steal a march on the viscountess."

The girls mulled that over in silence. The truth was none of them knew when this situation might begin to right itself. If it ever did. Olivia had only just made her debut into society and had been garnering invitations left, right, and center. Despite her doubts about the whole debut thing, she had been a success, a genuine hit, and then she had accepted a foolish dare from Ivo, the Duke of Northam. The invitations had dried up, and people had begun whispering about her in a manner Olivia had found embarrassing and upsetting. Now that the dowager had forbidden visitors from entering the house, or Olivia from accepting any of her many invitations, she was beginning to wonder if she would ever get another chance.

"I'm going out in the carriage," Roberta announced. "Who wants to come?"

There were several yeses. Their new governess would accompany them. She was far more amenable than their old governess, Pascoe, who Gabriel had sent off to Scotland indefinitely when he discovered just how cruelly she treated his sisters.

"Will Grandmama approve?" Justina asked with a worried frown. "I thought we were all supposed to remain indoors."

"I don't care if she approves or not," Roberta responded valiantly. "I'm tired of being locked up. I want fresh air. I thought we could go up to Hampstead Heath. No one will see us there, and I have a new kite I want to try out."

Roberta was the tomboy of the family, but flying a kite sounded harmless enough. Olivia exchanged a glance with Justina. Since their grandmother had taken over their lives, the rules had been far more rigid. Even before their father died, their mother had not cared much what they did with themselves, as long as they did not bother her. Running wild on the Grantham estate, playing at being highwaymen and pirates, or swimming naked in the pond at the bottom of the garden were just some of the fun things they had liked to do. Not any longer. They were young ladies now, sisters of the duke, and their behavior had to reflect that.

Despite her new resolve to make a success of her position in society—if she was ever given that chance again—Olivia missed being able to behave like a hoyden. Perhaps a run on the heath with the wind in their hair was just what they all needed. She looked up. Five pairs of eyes were focused on her, awaiting her verdict. "I think—" she began, just as there was a tap on the door.

One of the maids peeped in. Her eyes widened when

she saw them all staring back at her. Hastily, she held out a card on a silver tray and stammered, "Th-there is a gentleman come to call on you, Lady Olivia."

Olivia hopped down off the bed. Behind her, she heard Georgia say in that prissy voice, "Grandmama says we aren't allowed visitors."

As usual, they ignored her. Olivia read the name on the card and felt that familiar, unwelcome stutter in her chest, which only seemed to happen when she thought of Ivo. These days, she was trying very hard not to think of him at all.

"Olivia!"

The voice close to her ear made her jump. Justina was standing directly behind her and had read the card over her shoulder. Her sister looked flushed and cross, rare indeed for someone who was always so even-tempered. Justina was the peacemaker of the family, the one who soothed upsets and smoothed over arguments, and she was rarely out of sorts.

"I…" Olivia began, but Justina didn't let her finish.

"What do you think Grandmama will do if she finds out Northam is here?" she whispered. "Aren't we in enough trouble?"

Behind them on the bed, the other girls were loudly bickering about something and taking no notice of their two older sisters. All the same, Olivia leaned in closer. "I did not ask him to come, and I will send him away."

"Tell Humber to send him away," Justina said. She knew about Olivia and Ivo's trysts—Justina was her confidante and the only one of her sisters that Olivia trusted completely.

"If I do that, Humber will tell Grandmama," Olivia hissed. Their butler never did anything without informing their grandmother.

Before Justina could offer more advice, there was a

shriek from the bed, and she hurried over to mediate on whatever this latest brawl was about. Olivia watched in silence, her mind miles away.

Ivo was someone she might have loved. There, she had admitted it! The night she had met him, at her coming-out ball, she had been instantly attracted to him. She had thought…well, she had thought that if she had to marry someone and spend her life with them, then why not him? However, further meetings between them had caused her to doubt he would ever be the sort of man she imagined herself marrying. Someone who would keep her from poverty—despite being a duke, Ivo was not wealthy. Someone who would protect her from scandal—Ivo was reckless by nature and addicted to extreme behavior. And someone who would allow her as much freedom as she wanted—perhaps that last point might work in Ivo's favor, but then again, maybe not. He might be a tyrant in the home. Frustratingly, despite his shortcomings, she had continued to be drawn to him, until the night at the Elphinstones'.

And yet despite all her misgivings, they had become friends. He was someone she spoke to about the matters that troubled her most, and he listened and more often than not teased her out of her megrims. It was his special power. She could forgive him a great deal on account of his kindness.

But when she heard that Ivo was near enough to engaged to Lady Annette, Olivia could no longer make excuses for him. She was angry and disappointed. Because wasn't lying and cheating the reason she and her sisters were in the position they were in now? Her father, Harry, had married his mistress but kept it from his wife, Olivia's mother, and therefore Olivia couldn't abide a man who lied and cheated. That character flaw was bad enough, especially when added to the others, but Ivo must have been aware what would happen when they were discovered together in the billiard room. He was not an innocent like her. He had been on the town for many years, and he must have known Olivia's reputation would be damaged. Didn't he care about her fall from grace?

Painfully, Olivia admitted she was as much to blame as he when it came to their assignation—as the gossips were calling it—at the billiard table. Yes, she had been dazzled by his attentions, but she should have known better. She *did* know better. Justina was right, she should send Ivo away right now without seeing him. But she *needed* to see him face-to-face. To look him in the eye, and ask him to explain himself. And after that, she wanted to tell him to never darken her door again. A little dramatic perhaps, but Olivia was feeling dramatic.

The sisterly brawl was getting noisier, and Olivia left them to it, making her way downstairs. She saw Ivo as soon as she opened the door. He was standing in a patch of sunlight, and everything about him seemed to glow. His hair, the buttons on his jacket, the shine on his boots. He was so handsome; if only his character aligned with his looks. The words she had meant to say dried up in her throat, and she was glad when Ivo spoke first.

"My apologies if I am interrupting you, Lady Olivia, but when you didn't reply to my letter—"

Olivia had thrown it into the fireplace unread, in case she weakened. The reminder was all she needed to regain her composure.

"You shouldn't be here," she said in her coldest voice. "There has been enough gossip about us." There was even one of those dreadful pamphlets with crude drawings of two characters who were meant to be Olivia and Ivo, leering at each other over a billiard table. Olivia had been appalled.

Ivo's gaze remained on her face. Olivia wondered what he saw. A pale young woman with shadows beneath her blue eyes who was under immense strain? Or just another foolish girl falling in love with him?

He took a step forward. "Olivia, I came here to apologize again for my blunder at the Elphinstones'. It was foolish. It was completely my fault."

Olivia opened her mouth to agree with him, but her need for honesty betrayed her. "Not completely. I am impulsive, a character trait I am working hard to correct. It will not happen again."

"I want to—"

But she didn't let him finish. "You are engaged," she blurted out, feeling the heat in her cheeks. "At least my brother told me that you are. If it is true, then it makes your behavior reprehensible as well as reckless, and I would never have spent time alone in your company if I had known."

"I'm not engaged," he assured her in a firm voice. "Lady Annette and I are friends. She is like a sister to me. We were never engaged, and I have spoken to her since that night, and she is perfectly happy not to be engaged to me. Ever. There was a hope, I admit, but it was in the minds of our mothers. Some schoolgirl desire to see our two families united."

He spoke with distaste.

"Perhaps you should have made that clear to your family and hers, before the gossipmongers began to believe it," Olivia replied sharply.

His usually smiling mouth turned down and she saw that there were shadows under his eyes too. He looked serious and oddly uncertain. "You are right, and I was remiss. Again, I apologize. I assure you, I am not engaged. There is no one who holds such a promise from me." He took another step closer and reached out, as if to take her hands in his. Quickly, childishly, she tucked them behind her back.

He frowned. "I had hoped we were friends too."

Olivia spoke angrily. "Would a friend risk the reputation of a single young woman during her first London Season? Would a friend be so careless as to make a wager for a kiss?"

He bit his lip, and then tugged at the ring on his thumb. "You should have this. If we had not been interrupted, you would have won the game."

She stared at him in amazement, and her voice trembled in fury. "I was losing, as you very well know. I don't want your ring. Is that why you are here? To speak of that silly wager? When I cannot leave the house for fear of being whispered about or being depicted as a brainless flirt in one of those detestable gossip rags. I am an object of derision and pity, and you want to speak of *that*?"

He was silent, watching her warily, as if he thought she might explode all over him. "You have quite a temper, Olivia," he said at last. "I can't remember the last time I was abused like this. Perhaps at school when I failed the Latin test."

He was joking. Even now, he was making fun of her. Olivia turned and strode to the window, only to turn around and face him again. "Please go. There is no reason for you to be here. If you were a gentleman…"

That stung him. The amused glimmer in his eyes was gone. "I *am* a gentleman. A single gentleman with no impediments, and that being the case, I am here to correct this situation, which is entirely of my own making. I enjoy your company, Olivia, and I think you enjoy mine. Your birth is not as exemplary as one might wish, but that is hardly your fault. I am sure there are a great many persons whose pasts are riddled with scandal, my own family included. Looked at in that light, ours is a match made in heaven."

She blinked. Did she understand his meaning? Could he be making a declaration? A kernel of warmth flared inside her, and for a moment, she was ablaze with joy. Until she remembered Ivo had thoughtlessly dragged her onto one scandal—yes, it had been her fault too, but she was young and inexperienced, and he was not. He said he was her friend, but he had not behaved like one. And now he wanted to marry her *despite* her unfortunate birth? And then what? They could be disgraceful together?

Her attraction to him gave him the potential to damage her beyond recovery. Olivia had already made up her mind about her future. The misery of her childhood at Grantham, the shock of being rejected by the society she had just begun to be a part of. She was tired of being on the outside, and if she was given another chance to step into the heady world of the ton, then she would snatch it up and hold on tight. No longer would she allow others to treat her with contempt or whisper behind her back. If she had her way, they would not dare. She would be like the phoenix rising anew from the ashes of the past.

Unaware of her profound thoughts, Ivo smiled at her. "Come, Olivia," he coaxed. "You know I'm right. Imagine what fun we could have together, cocking a snook at those gossips you are so worried about. Wouldn't you enjoy that?"

Did he really believe that? She said quietly, "Doesn't it concern you to be the subject of their gossip? When they talk about your curricle races, or the time you jumped into the Thames, or..." She tried to recall some of the more lurid stories about him she had heard.

He laughed. "How many times I could persuade Lady Edeline to dance with me in one evening? Four times, and her father was not happy."

Suddenly stricken, she wondered if he had made a similar bet about her. Her face must have betrayed the thought, because he spoke quickly.

"No, no, I assure you, that was not something I would do to you. Dancing with you was a pleasure, Olivia."

She swallowed. "Have you never considered employing more sober habits?"

"Sober habits?" He frowned, genuinely puzzled. "Why would I? I don't drink to excess."

"I meant...You do not seem to care how thoughtlessly you behave, and how it will affect those around you. Have you never stopped and *thought* before you acted, Ivo?"

He shook his head, and his frown deepened. "Life is to be enjoyed. If I stopped and thought about everything I did before I did it...What a tedious idea! Do you know I rescued a kitten last week? The mother cat had hidden herself away in the attic to have her brood, and this one had wandered up onto the roof. I climbed up and brought it down to her. I suppose if I had thought about it, I would have left it up there to starve rather than risk my neck."

"You're being ridiculous! That's not what..." Olivia's voice grew shaky. "Can't you see that I could never rely on you?"

"I am punctual to a fault!"

Was he joking, or did he genuinely not understand? Either way, any chance of Olivia accepting his proposal died at that moment. "No," she said. "Your actions make it impossible for me to consider your offer. My answer is no, Your Grace."

The puzzled expression was back, as if he found her emphatic refusal completely beyond his comprehension. "I don't think you quite understand me. I want to marry you, Olivia."

"And I don't want to marry you. In fact, I have no desire to see you again, so please do not call or write or contact me in any way. Is that plain enough?"

Was he disappointed? Was he angry? His face was blank, but a moment before, she thought she had seen a shadow in his green eyes. The idea gave her an odd, sour little thrill, before she tamped that down too. Maybe she had been mistaken though, because he was instantly himself again. He even gave a shrug, as if none of it mattered, bowing his farewells, saying the right things. If she had not seen that shadow, she might have believed her refusal meant absolutely nothing to him.

After the door closed, Olivia allowed herself to feel disappointed. Had he really meant to ask for her hand? She was already beginning to wonder if it had all been some silly joke on his part—another of his endless wagers.

"Olivia?"

Justina had come to find her, and now her sister hurried to take her hand, giving it a sympathetic squeeze. Olivia swallowed back the emotion that threatened to spill out in tears, and smiled instead.

"I'm perfectly all right," she said in the carefree manner she had been practicing. "Are we going to Hampstead Heath or not?"

But when she opened the sitting room door, they were confronted with their grandmother. There was an ominous silence. Olivia opened her mouth to say something, she wasn't sure what, because it was obvious the dowager knew exactly who had been with her.

"It wasn't anything—" Justina began.

"I didn't—" Olivia said.

"I don't want to hear any more excuses." Their grandmother's voice was icy. "This is the second occasion you have compromised yourself with the Duke of Northam. Humber says he proposed to you."

The two girls glared at Humber, who was lurking in the background.

"Is it your intention to marry him? A man with as little wisdom as he has money. I grant you he is a handsome specimen, but if he's anything like his father, then you are in for a miserable time of it, my girl. I thought you had better sense."

"If Humber had listened a little longer, he would have known my intention," Olivia said bitterly.

"Don't blame Humber for your own bad behavior," was the cold response. "He was worried you were going to follow your brother's example and elope. Do you enjoy being talked about every time you enter a room? Is that the sort of man you want to marry? Someone who will make you a laughingstock with his antics?" Then, the words that struck Olivia to her very soul. "Have you already forgotten what it is like to be poor and ignored and neglected?"

Olivia's throat ached, and her voice was thick with tears. "No, Grandmama, I have not forgotten, and it is not my intention to marry Northam."

Her grandmother stared at her a moment more and then nodded decisively. "Start packing. We are returning to Grantham forthwith."

Miserably, Olivia and Justina trailed after her. They were going back to the country, back to exile, and who knew if they would ever see London again.

Chapter Two

Ivo had walked to Ashton House, and now he walked home. His family owned a town house in the same exclusive area of London, so it wasn't far, but he took his time. He found he had a great deal to think about, and none of it filled him with joy.

The memory of Lady Olivia Ashton as she had been a moment ago was lodged in his head. Petite, with unfashionable curves, dark hair arranged simply, and the shadows under her glorious blue eyes. She was suffering from the scandal he had caused, and although Ivo had shrugged it off as he did most of his risky adventures, Olivia could not. It was unfair perhaps, but that was the way in which the society they inhabited worked. Rules were very different for gentlemen, and far more censorious for ladies.

She had been angry with him. More than that, she had been disappointed.

Ivo could not remember the last time he had caused someone to be quite that upset. He tried not to hurt anyone when it came to his wagers. They were harmless enough and useful when it came to diverting attention from his other activities. If anyone was hurt, then it was usually himself. Races and cards and japes with his friends and peers. This matter with Olivia was different, and he should have known he needed to tread carefully.

He had been carried away.

From the moment he had seen Olivia at the ball at Ashton House, he had been intrigued, fascinated, and, yes, very tempted. Ivo never pursued respectable young ladies, but something about the sulky curve of Olivia's mouth and the fearless gleam in her eyes would not let him forget her. She had become important to him, and when he was with her, he felt as if he might be something more than the debt-ridden, scandalous Duke of Northam.

Unfortunately, it seemed he had not changed all that much. He had damaged her reputation, she was correct in that, but he had wanted to rectify matters. He had been prepared to give up his freedom and marry her.

Surely, for coming to her rescue like he had with that wretched kitten, he should expect her gratitude. One of those genuine smiles she used to give him. There had been none of that. Instead, she had refused him, but not before asking him to change his life for her benefit.

Have you never considered employing more sober habits?

He shook his head, barely noticing the grand town houses he was passing. Viciously, he kicked aside a pebble. Was it so rash and foolish of him to expect her to accept his generous offer?

Ivo was a duke with an estate in Kent, but the family finances had been declining for years. Olivia was the daughter of a duke, but illegitimate, and her family was also in a financial bother. It wasn't as if Ivo was marrying her for her money, for God's sake! His mother would probably be horrified, but he didn't care about that. He had a right to marry the lady of his choosing, and now that the nonsense with Annette was cleared up, he chose Lady Olivia Ashton.

He had thought…dash it, he had *known* she felt as strongly about him as he did about her. He recognized those looks she sent him. It really would have been a match of two halves of a whole. She was adventurous and audacious, with a spirit almost as daring as his own. They would have had a marvelous time together.

To be rebuffed was not what he had expected. Ivo was the youngest child and only son. He was indulged, and although his mother and two sisters tut-tutted at his "foolish antics," as they called them, they did not censure him. No one ever had. No one ever stayed cross with him for long. He could "charm the birds out of the trees," they told him fondly.

Olivia hadn't been charmed. She had thrown his good intentions back in his face. Ivo tried to tell himself he had had a fortunate escape. Marrying a woman who would have tried to change him into something he was not? A tomcat into a tame house tabby? Impossible!

What should he do now? Well, he would recover, of course he would. He'd soon be himself again. His heart had taken a knock, but it wasn't as if it was broken—more likely just cracked. But for all his inner bluster, Ivo knew he would not be himself in a week or even a month. Those moments with Olivia had shaken him, forced him to think about things he rarely did. He didn't like it. He had the ungentlemanly desire to make her sorry that she'd refused him. To punish her in some as yet indefinable manner for hurting him.

It wasn't pleasant to be thinking that way, but he found he couldn't help it.

By now, Ivo had reached his town house. Just as he placed the toe of one shiny boot upon the bottom step, a gentleman called a greeting, and jarred him out of his uncomfortable thoughts. For a moment, he thought it was a creditor come to collect on one of his many overdue bills. He had promised his mother and sisters some time in London to enjoy the Season, but it had proven damn expensive. Had his sister taken that ridiculously over-priced bonnet back to the milliner as he'd told her?

But the gentleman wasn't a debt collector. It was Charles Wickley.

Charles ran Cadieux's Gambling Club jointly with its owner, the Duke of Grantham, although Ivo had heard that lately, with the duke otherwise occupied, Charles was more or less in complete control.

"Your Grace," Charles said in a droll voice. "I have news of a private nature."

"Mr. Wickley." They exchanged bows. "Walk with me."

Ivo set off through the square, and Charles fell into step beside him.

"There has been a hitch," Charles spoke after a moment. "The spirits and wine that were supposed to be delivered to Cadieux's yesterday did not arrive. I was told by your man Bourne that it was on its way across the channel when a revenue cutter gave chase, and the captain and crew were arrested before they could land the cargo. Which was impounded."

Ivo stopped to stare at him. They were around the same height and build, both with fair hair, although Charles's eyes were blue, and Ivo's were green. If a stranger were to see them together now, they could easily be mistaken for close relatives.

"Arrested?" he repeated. "The cargo impounded?"

"Yes." Charles's usual good humor was missing today; he looked tired and irritable. Complete control of the hell must be taking its toll on him.

Ivo trusted his men, but one never knew what inducements might be offered to those who gave up secrets to the revenue officers. "They aren't aware…?"

"Of your involvement?" That droll mocking note again. "As far as I know, no one else has been arrested, although no doubt the captain and crew are being interrogated as we speak."

"Polgarth." Ivo gave the captain a name. "He has a wife and children in the village. He won't talk."

Portside was the name of the coastal village near Ivo's home, and the place that supplied most of the manpower for the smuggling operation. A smuggling operation that required a great deal of planning. The major ports around Britain's coast were under the close supervision of the government, which made certain the proper amount of tax was paid on imported goods. For those who did not want to pay taxes, it was better to slip in to smaller, unsupervised ports and offload their contraband goods there.

Those goods—brandy and wine, lace and tea, among others—were taken to a safe hiding spot. The next step was to load the goods onto wagons or ponies and deliver them to those who had ordered them. In this case, Charles Wickley at Cadieux's Gambling Club in London.

"The government seems determined to put a stop to us Free Traders," Ivo said. "But we have a great many supporters. Name me one member of parliament who doesn't partake of French brandy in the privacy of his own home."

Charles snorted.

A gentleman walking by paused to give a deferential bow to Ivo and barely a glance to Charles. Charles waited until they were alone again. "I will need to replenish my supplies at the club quickly. If you think it is too dangerous to arrange for another delivery, I will have to find another supplier."

It wasn't a threat, merely a statement of fact. Ivo understood, but he couldn't allow Charles to switch from himself to some other fellow—the smuggling income was the only thing currently keeping his family from becoming beggars.

Ivo hid his panic as he rested his gaze on that uncannily familiar face. "No need, I will deal with it. Do you have a list of your requirements?"

Charles dug a crumpled piece of paper from his pocket, and Ivo gave it a cursory glance. "I will let you know as soon as the delivery is safely across the channel."

With a nod, Charles walked away, and Ivo watched him go before turning back the way he had come. That sense of disquiet he often experienced when he met with Wickley filled him now. It was like looking into a mirror with only a few minor variations. Ivo's father had died when he was fourteen, too long ago to give Ivo answers to his questions, and he didn't expect to hear the truth from his mother or his two sisters; they would never countenance any suggestion that the late duke was not perfect. And yet the rumors implied he had been far from that. He had enjoyed far too many of the village girls for there not to be consequences, and one in particular, Ivo had traced to St. Ninian's Foundling Home for Boys in London. Ivo suspected Charles Wickley was his father's by-blow, but he had never tried to prove it, preferring to simply ignore it.

Why make matters awkward by introducing his suspicions? Theirs was a business arrangement, and it was better to keep it so.

Ivo pushed aside his qualms, and instead turned his mind to the problem of finding someone to fulfill the order for the club. The arrested man—Polgarth—had been reliable, but there were always others keen to make some money even if smuggling was a risky occupation. The government wanted their excise, and the smuggling of items like wine and spirits meant they were missing out on taxes that should rightfully be filling government coffers. And if they were ever to become aware that an important personage such as the Duke of Northam was involved in such an enterprise...

Well, they wouldn't, he assured himself. Polgarth was unlikely to talk, and even if he did, it was doubtful anyone would believe the Duke of Northam was at the head of a band of smugglers. Ivo had been at this game since he was a boy and his father had sat him down with a group of Portside villagers to discuss the details of the next cargo to be smuggled across from France.

Ivo's father had informed the villagers—they were his father's tenants—that his son would be taking over one day, and that it was best he learned the business now. None of them appeared to find anything strange in this, and later Ivo had learned that the smuggling had been going on for centuries, and the Fitzsimmonses had always had a finger in the pie. The Kent coastline and the marshes inland were perfect for hiding and trans-porting contraband. That the Fitzsimmonses had been raised to ducal status did not appear to hamper them in any way when it came to breaking the law. More impor-tantly, the income the smuggling generated was very much needed.

At first, Ivo had simply wanted to make his father proud, but then the craving for risk and danger had crept into his blood. Ivo had often seen the late duke put his horse over fences that no one else would dare to jump, giving his wife palpitations and then laughing loudly when he reached the other side. He never refused a wager, no matter how rash, and he rarely lost. He was a daredevil, and his son had loved and admired him, and wanted to be just like him. When his father had died, Ivo's widowed mother and two sisters had looked to him, and all too soon, his life had been full of weighty decisions about the estate, with the dukedom pressing down upon his young shoulders. He had done his duty and done it well, but it was not something he enjoyed. As well as an important source of income, the smuggling sideline had offered him an exciting diversion, and a test of his skill and courage.

Now, at twenty-seven, Ivo had built up the small Free Trading operation into a business that benefited everyone on his estate. In the past, the smuggled goods had gone to the local community and the local gentry. Now the number of customers he dealt with had blossomed, and he supplied hotels and clubs in his home county of Kent, as well as many more on the road to London and in London itself, including Cadieux's. Yes, it was risky and erratic—he sometimes did not know from one month to the next how much he would be paid—but he was proud of his accomplishment; it was just a pity he could not preen about it to those who thought him a pretty face with little behind it.

He glanced about him at the familiar square, realizing that while he had been lost in his thoughts he'd reached home again. Bourne was probably waiting for him inside and they would need to act immediately if they were to supply the gamblers at Cadieux's with their tipples.

When Ivo entered his town house, his butler, Carlyon, informed him that "scruffy fellow" from Portside was awaiting his pleasure, but he'd thought it best to keep him out of the better areas of the house. Ivo asked he be shown into his study.

Bourne duly arrived, twisting his cap in his hands under the watchful eye of Carlyon. Once the butler had closed the door, Bourne's demeanor changed abruptly from a country bumpkin to someone well aware of his importance in the chain of command.

"Sorry to come uninvited, but I had to see you, sir."

Ivo waved that off. "Charles Wickley was outside. He said Polgarth has been arrested."

"Yes, sir." Bourne was a squat man with broad shoulders and an intelligent glint in his blue eyes. "Locked up tight, they say. He won't talk, or if he does, it will be to lead the revenue astray. As for the crew...I'm hopeful they will take their captain's lead."

"Polgarth should know I will do my utmost to keep him from the hangman's rope or transportation, and in the meantime, I will see that his family is well cared for." Even if it meant canceling the order for his new jacket.

Bourne promised to share that with the captain, adding, "We're all aware of the risks we take."

Ivo offered him brandy from the decanter on his desk, and Bourne accepted the glass. "Why now?" Ivo asked. "Polgarth has been bringing in our goods for two years without anyone the wiser. Who informed?"

Bourne swallowed the nip in one gulp and wiped a hand across his mouth. "There's always those willing to take a bribe," he said wryly. "I'm not saying Polgarth would, nor any of our other men, but these are dangerous times, Your Grace. What with the increase in revenue cutters and riding officers, we need eyes in the back of our heads."

Ivo poured another brandy into the man's glass and watched him down it. During the war, taxes on imported goods had risen beyond the reach of ordinary British men and women. If they wanted their morning cup of tea, they had to pay. But there was a way around it, and that was where Ivo came in.

Bourne spoke again. "There's been more than Polgarth arrested over the past months. Word is it's not safe to set out from France if you're carrying anything liable to raise suspicion. Might be tricky to find someone willing to take the risk so soon. Might be best to lay low for a time."

"And yet we have customers who want their orders filled. I have given my word." And unlike his father, Ivo took pride in keeping his word, and he also couldn't afford to lose any of his customers.

Bourne finished off his brandy and seemed to come to a decision. "There is someone. A new player in the game. His prices are steeper than most, but he seems to have the knack of being able to slip through the revenue net like a ghost."

"Where is he based?" Ivo asked.

"I don't know exactly, but he can be reached through the King's Head down Worthing way. He might be a Frenchman, or he might not. His name is Mystere, and his ship is *The Holly*."

Ivo snorted a laugh. "A mystery Frenchman called Mystere. Are you sure he's genuine?"

"I've heard he gets the job done, and the revenue officers are all running about like headless chickens trying to catch him."

In the circumstances, it seemed worth the risk.

Theirs was an unpredictable profession, and although he would take extra care to keep himself and his men safe, it was not always possible.

"Very well. Find this Mystere and sound him out. Let him know we are in the market for his services. I'll need him to make a run as soon as possible. Keep our names out of it. Is there someone you can use as a middleman?"

"There is, sir."

"Thank you, Bourne. Send word as soon as you know anything."

"I will. I wish you a good day," Bourne said as he left.

A good day? Ivo stood and stared at the closed door. No, it wasn't a good day. Apart from the trouble with his men being arrested and his customers not receiving what they'd paid for, he had had a disappointment of the heart. That pain was new and disagreeable to Ivo, but it was a good lesson. He would guard his heart more carefully next time.

As for Olivia, he thought it only fair she regret her refusal of his offer. She hadn't even fully explained to him why she had said no, apart from his risky character. There must be dozens, no, hundreds, of other girls who would beg for the chance to be leg-shackled to the Duke of Northam, while Olivia would struggle to find even one suitor who lived up to her high ideals.

Her rejection had stung him a great deal. At the same time, beneath his genuine feelings of hurt and anger, there was something else. Something uncomfortable. Something he resolutely refused to examine.

Could some of what Olivia said be true?

Chapter Three

O livia finished dressing and went to the window. Mist engulfed her view of the park and its trees so that she could barely see anything in front of her, just blurred shapes in the swirling white. It felt strangely like her current situation.

True to her word, the dowager duchess had packed her granddaughters up and moved them away from London. It was a strategic move, to allow some of the gossip and rumors to die down, but Olivia wondered if their relocation was permanent. She remembered when she had first learned they were going to London where she was to make her debut. She had been anxious and a little lost in the unfamiliar world of the ton. Now she had tasted life as a duke's sister, and been dressed in pretty clothes and danced in grand ballrooms with handsome gentlemen… Well, it hadn't turned out to be so bad after all.

Olivia was torn.

She had never wanted the structured existence her grandmother planned for her—marriage to a suitable gentleman, children, and a life where appearance was everything—but she couldn't see an alternative. She didn't want the unfettered freedom she'd had before either. While it was nice to do as one wanted, it was difficult to be truly free without the funds to buy food and other essentials. Life at Grantham had been a misery until Gabriel came along. Couldn't she find an indulgent and wealthy gentleman who would give her leeway to enjoy herself? Wasn't it possible to be independent and yet be bound by all the rules that her position in the ton brought with it? And where was love in this equation? The unfortunate truth was, for women in Olivia's problematic position, love was never the most important component of marriage.

Olivia left her bedchamber and made her way toward the stairs, tiptoeing past her mother's rooms. There wasn't a sound from behind the closed door, and there had been no appearance by Felicia when they arrived yesterday. As far as Olivia knew, none of her sisters had ventured nor been invited into their mother's lair. Felicia had become a ghost that existed only in memory.

As soon as they had arrived at Grantham, Roberta had hurried down to the stables, happier than Olivia had seen her for months. Justina had taken a book out into the rose garden, something about a *Wicked Prince* with a lurid description inside the cover. Edwina was playing with her shabby collection of dolls—Grandmama hadn't let her take them all to London—and who knew where Georgia and Antonia were. Olivia wasn't even certain where the dowager was. Was she already plotting her next move in restoring the Ashton family to prominence and respectability, or had she given up on her dreams? She had been furious when word came from Gabriel of his reckless pursuit of Vivienne Tremeer, but the anger had faded, and now she seemed downcast. Her grandmother was such an indomitable figure, Olivia was not used to seeing her like this, and knowing it was partially her fault didn't help.

Is that the sort of man you want to marry? Someone who will make you a laughingstock with his antics?

She cringed every time she remembered her grandmother's words.

By the time Olivia had hurriedly finished her coffee and a piece of toast, the mist was gone, dispersed by the sun. She thought a walk might lift her spirits and set off through the woods along the path to the pond where she and her sisters had been splashing about, naked, on that fateful day when the dowager came upon them. Their father's death had brought his mother back to Grantham, and Olivia had never forgotten the expression on her grandmother's face—a mix of fury and horror and dismay. Seeing the girls running so wild and unsupervised had been the beginning of her plans to set things right.

Grandmama had blamed Felicia. The two women had never liked each other, and the pond incident had only made things worse. The dowager would never forgive her daughter-in-law for neglecting her granddaughters, and if Felicia remained in her rooms forever more, the dowager would probably be ecstatic.

"Olivia!"

She sighed as she turned. Trust Edwina to crash into her peaceful solitude. All the same, it was a relief for her not to have to *think* anymore. Olivia felt as if she had thought enough to last her a lifetime.

"I saw you from the window!" Her youngest sister had an armful of dolls in varying states of undress. Her happy smile turned into a frown. "Georgia says dolls are silly, and I am too old for them."

"Georgia doesn't know what she's talking about."

Georgia was the outlier in the family, or perhaps

being mean was the only role left to her. Whatever the reason for her unpopular behavior, she seemed to relish it.

"Are we going down to the pond?" Edwina asked in a hushed voice, her big blue eyes full of excitement.

"We can. As long as you don't go into the water," Olivia added hastily.

Edwina seemed about to argue, eyeing Olivia a moment as if trying to read her mood. Whatever she saw convinced her not to push her luck. "We can't go into the water, I know that. Perhaps we can walk around the edges and see if there are frogs? Robbie says we should catch one and keep it."

Olivia shuddered. "I don't think that's a good idea either. If Roberta wants a frog, then let her catch it."

They set off through the dappled woods in companionable silence, broken now and again by Edwina chattering with her dolls. Olivia noticed that one of them was now called Vivienne. Her brother's beloved had been an instant hit with the girls, and it was obvious she made Gabriel happy. Although Vivienne was the daughter of a baronet, she was also poor, with a scandal in her past, and the dowager would never have chosen her for her grandson. Fortunately, Gabriel had had other ideas.

They reached the pond, and Olivia found a flattish rock to sit on while Edwina scampered about. Once she tuned out her sister's chatter, it was still peaceful, and her thoughts turned down that well-worn path, at the end of which was the Duke of Northam.

In particular that awkward, painful meeting at Ashton House. When he had asked her to marry him, he had seemed to think he was performing a heroic act by rescuing her from the scandal he had helped create. Yes, her behavior at the Elphinstones' had been reprehensible, but he had encouraged it. There had been a moment, a tiny spark of hope, when she had asked him if he could change…That hope had died when he'd laughed. Because why should he change for her? He saw her as the sort of girl who would join him in his insane antics, and then thumb her nose at the gossips. And Ivo could behave like that because he had nothing to lose.

It was different for Olivia. She had a great deal to lose. She must not let her heart rule her head, not if she wanted to take her rightful place in the world. She needed to stick rigidly to the rules. That was the weight of being the eldest and—now that Gabriel had burned his bridges by running after Vivienne—the only one who could restore the family's good name, according to her grandmother. She had her five sisters to think of—they needed her leadership and the financial security her marriage would bring to the Ashtons. She just had to be clever. Marrying Ivo would not be clever, it would be like someone with a sweet tooth marrying a dessert chef. The two of them together could only make things worse for her family. Olivia had found Ivo's impulsiveness irresistible. Yes, there had been moments when they were alone together or danced together, and it had felt…well, perfect. But then there were the times when he fed into her worst impulses. Her goal must be a secure place in the ton, a wealthy husband who could afford to buy her fashionable clothes and launch her sisters into polite society when the time came. So that none of them would have to worry about being poor and abandoned ever again.

She closed her eyes. His face, when she had refused him, was suddenly very clear to her. It had been as if no one had ever said no to him before, and perhaps they hadn't. He acted the fool, but Olivia knew he was not a fool—behind that handsome face was a clever brain, if only he would use it. Her grandmother seemed to think he was disreputable. Like a coin with two faces. One side, the charming, handsome gentleman who was such good company and to whom every day was a new adventure. And then, when she turned the coin over and looked at the other side...Never knowing from one day to the next what foolishness he might get up to, not being able to rely on him or trust him, the mockery and pity in the eyes of those who were meant to be her peers.

It was not the sort of life she could allow herself, and she should think herself lucky to have escaped in time. If her heart was a little bruised, then at least it was intact.

Dinner at Grantham was a formal affair. The dowager sat at the head of the table, the lines on her face deeply drawn, showing every year of her age. Their current situation had not prevented her from dressing for the occasion, and her black silk gown rustled as she sat down, while her diamond necklace caught the light of the tall candelabra upon the long dining table. The girls followed her lead, sitting in somber silence, and when their grandmother gave a nod to Humber for the meal to be served, the servants went about their tasks with quiet competence.

Olivia dipped her spoon into the bowl of thin chicken broth and was just about to lift it to her lips when there was a gasp. She looked up. Her grandmother was staring at the doorway behind her eldest granddaughter, her expression one of consternation and dismay.

Olivia turned her head to see what new calamity had befallen them.

A woman stood there with her gaze fixed on the dowager as if daring her to deny her a place at their table. Her dark hair, sprinkled with gray, was swept up in a simple style, and her lavender-colored gown hung upon a figure that had previously been curvaceous but was now slim to the point of fragility. Her once-beautiful face lacked its previously smooth, plump cheeks and dimpled chin, but her eyes were the same brilliant blue as her daughters'.

"Felicia," the dowager said.

There was a hush as Olivia's mother approached and sat down at the opposite end of the table from the dowager. Felicia's fingers clenched about her spoon as the servant set a bowl of broth before her. Briefly, she glanced at the amazed expressions on the faces of her daughters.

"You allow the younger girls to dine with you?"

The dowager gave her a considering look. "I thought it was time they learned proper table manners, so yes, we dine as a family unless there are visitors."

Felicia frowned and opened her mouth before changing her mind and focusing her attention on the meal.

Olivia's sisters turned to her now. The weight of their regard reminded her that, as the eldest, she should know what to do with this new development, but Olivia was no wiser than them. She frowned and nodded at their bowls, and so the meal began. But she had only taken a couple of sips of the broth before she threw a surreptitious glance at her mother. How long had it been since Felicia had graced them with her presence at the table? How long since she had left the confines of her bedchamber? Olivia remembered telling Ivo about it. Her mother had always been distant and uninterested in her daughters, so it was no surprise her daughters did not spend a great deal of time thinking of her. But lately, she had been almost entirely forgotten as her husband's disgrace unfolded and engulfed the Ashton family.

What would Ivo think of this latest development? But then Olivia reminded herself that whatever Ivo thought was no longer something she wanted to hear.

The broth was removed, and the next course served, and still no one said a word. Until...

"I received a message today from Gabriel." The dowager's voice broke the heavy silence. She looked about at them as if to assess the effect of her words. "He is returning to Grantham with his new bride."

"They are married then," Olivia said in delight.

"But I wanted to be flower girl!" Edwina burst out, disappointed, and then squeaked when Georgia pinched her.

Their grandmother ignored the interruption. "They married quietly in Cornwall. At least they had the sense to do that." She folded her napkin precisely. "They will be residing here in Sussex for the foreseeable future."

Olivia tried to read her grandmother's thoughts, but apart from a gleam in her dark eyes, there wasn't much to go on. Was she glad, was she angry, was she...? What *was* she thinking?

"I will ready the duke's rooms at once." Humber spoke with satisfaction from his place at the door, where he had been supervising the serving of the meal. Olivia suspected he had never liked the dowager's husband and had liked her son even less. Perhaps he thought Gabriel a better duke than either of them.

The dowager spoke. "There will be much to do when he arrives. I have some thoughts on the matter."

Felicia set down her knife with a genteel clink. Her

face held an expression Olivia had not seen for a very long time. It was the same expression she saw every time Felicia bore another daughter, setting aside her disappointment and preparing to try again for her dearly-longed-for son and heir. *Resolve.*

"I hope I can make my peace with the duke," she said. "I think it is time to put the past behind us."

The dowager looked surprised but also relieved. "I am glad to hear that, Felicia. Our family needs to work together through these difficult times."

"Indeed."

Felicia bowed her head over her meal once more, but Olivia caught the faint curve of her lips. Her mother was smiling, and there was something sly about it. Something shrewd and cunning.

Chapter Four

The Duke of Northam's country estate, Whitmont, was in the county of Kent. The coastline was made up of sand and shingle beaches, and inland was a tidal marshland that strangers could wander for days and still not find their way out of. Not Ivo, he had grown up running free in the marsh, learning of its beauties and its dangers. The nearby village of Portside was ideal for receiving imported goods, and the villagers had been doing so for generations. With the high excise on French luxuries, and despite the government's increasing watchfulness, the lucrative activity didn't seem likely to cease anytime soon. Ivo liked to think smuggling was in his blood, just as Whitmont was in his blood. He could not imagine living anywhere else.

He missed his home—he always did when he was away from it for any length of time—but it was necessary to remain in London a little longer. There was a wager with one of the members of his club, but for some reason, the thought did not energize him as much as usual. He refused to believe his melancholy had anything to do with Olivia. Definitely not. Once he was back at Whitmont, he would feel more the thing, but before he could return home, he needed to pay a visit to Cadieux's.

Bourne had sent him a note to say that his

"invitations" had been sent. It was their code and meant all was in place for the next cargo of smuggled goods to cross the channel to Portside. This time, the cargo would be aboard *The Holly*. Several of Ivo's regular customers had been threatening to move their business elsewhere, and he needed to give the good news to Charles Wickley, in case he was also planning to jump ship to another supplier. He found Charles in the office above the gaming rooms. It was midmorning and the hell was yet to open, but from the shadows under his eyes, it looked as if he had been up for hours.

"So I should expect the delivery in the next few days?" Charles said.

"Yes, after nightfall. The club will be busy, and no one will notice a stray cart or two unloading their wares."

Charles let out a sigh. "This was the last thing I needed." The comment seemed to be aimed at himself rather than Ivo. He nodded at the chair in front of his desk, and Ivo lifted the tails of his elegant coat and seated himself. He couldn't remember ever being invited to linger, and he could only think that Charles must indeed be beleaguered by his new responsibilities to have forgotten their usual formality.

"Gabriel is on his way back from Cornwall." Charles broke the silence, fiddling with the papers on his desk. "Married." He frowned. "You can imagine his grandmother's reaction."

"He pursued his own happiness. I can't fault him for that," Ivo said, pushing aside the thought that not every pursuit of love ended as happily. "I'm sure he was well aware of the consequences." And perhaps his damned imprudence was catching.

Charles didn't seem to hear him. "I am going to buy

him out," he said abruptly. "Cadieux's will be mine. I need capital though. Gabriel won't dun me, I know that, but I'd feel better if I could pay him the bulk of what I owe. Or even if I take on a partner." His frown deepened.

"He's selling the club?" Ivo raised his eyebrows.

That was a surprise. Even after his elevation to the dukedom of Grantham, Gabriel Cadieux had not been willing to give up his gambling hell. He had won it in a game with Sir Hubert Longley, the previous owner, and since then, the club had prospered under Grantham's clever management. Until now, Ivo had assumed it was a piece of the man's past he would never let go. Had Gabriel become comfortable enough in his new skin to finally do so? Then again, rumor had it that Grantham was in dire straits when Gabriel took over—the reckless spending of Harry, the fifth duke, and his father had drained the funds needed to keep the family's holdings in order—so he may have found he didn't have the time to run his gambling club as he sought to turn matters around.

Charles was watching him curiously. "Are you interested? Or are gambling clubs not quite your thing?"

Ivo shook his head. "They aren't." He glanced at the clock on the mantelpiece. "I really should go."

But Charles seemed agitated, and Ivo didn't move, setting himself to wait for the man to say whatever was on his mind.

Charles raked his hands through hair almost the same fair color as his own, while that frown…It was familiar from his looking glass. He could no longer pretend to deny the truth. Charles was a Fitzsimmons. He did not want ironclad proof that his suspicions were correct, so it was better to assume ignorance. Just as well they did not move in the same circles, where the resemblance was likely to be remarked upon and cause all sorts of awkward comments.

"So you wouldn't be interested in financing me?" Charles spoke in a diffident tone. "Or coming in as a partner in the venture?"

Ivo met his eyes.

Charles frowned at whatever he saw there, as if Ivo had already refused him. "If you need references, I can supply them, but I think we have dealt with each other long enough now for you to know what sort of man I am."

He did know. Charles was honest and hardworking, and more than capable of running the hell. Ivo did not doubt it. After all, it had been Charles's idea to bring in the top-notch chef to serve the nightly suppers that attracted guests who usually ended up staying and playing in the gambling area. An innovation that had put Cadieux's outside the normal run of gambling hells and made it something quite special, as well as lucrative. And his high-quality French wines, rather than the swill served at so many other gambling clubs, brought in even more guests with money to spend.

Charles wasn't the reason Ivo had hesitated. He knew the hell was profitable, and he would like nothing better than to invest in it. The problem was that to make money, one needed to have money, and he lacked funds. A place like Cadieux's was probably a whole lot less risky than the smuggling business, and as he supplied the beverages to the club, one might even say it was an extension of said business. The opportunity was too good to pass up; he needed to think of a way he could pull together the necessaries.

"Send me your proposal," he said, to give himself time, and stood up. "I'll take a look at it and get back to you."

Charles nodded, a spark of relief in his weary eyes. "Thank you."

For an awful moment, the words were on the tip of his tongue. *Do you know who your father was?* But thankfully, he was sensible enough not to speak them. Things would become very complicated very quickly. Instead, he gave a nod and made his way out of the room and down the stairs. A hurrying servant glanced at him but showed no interest, and a moment later, Ivo was outside, wondering why he had agreed to something it was unlikely he could follow through on. But he knew why. If he wanted to escape his debts, bring his estate back into the black, and stop disappointing his family by denying them things such as extravagant bonnets, then he needed to find a way to make more money. And everyone knew Cadieux's was a gold mine.

The initial pain would be worth it in the long run… if he could scrape the readies together. He might even be able to support a wife in the style she deserved. Then again, best not to go there.

When he arrived home at the Fitzsimmons town house in Mayfair, he found Lady Annette was paying a visit to his sisters. Upon his entering the room, she looked up, and he was relieved to see that her sweet smile of greeting had not dimmed since their talk about engagements and parental expectations. He now knew that Annette was as reluctant to marry him as he was her, and it was her mother's determination to see her and Ivo leg-shackled that had caused her so much anxiety.

He also felt a twinge of guilt. The truth was that on some level, he had been aware of the talk about him marrying Annette, and he had ignored it. The whispers had kept the ambitious mothers of marriageable-aged daughters at bay, and hopes of having Annette as a daughter-in-law had kept his mother from nagging at Ivo to find a wife. Something that, until recently, he'd had absolutely no desire to do. Well, he had made a mull of it and hurt his childhood friend in the bargain. An example of his selfishness?

Have you never stopped and thought *before you acted, Ivo?* Olivia's words sounded in his head. As much as he wanted to dispute them, he'd come to the uncomfortable conclusion that she may in part have been right.

Ivo looked around for some distraction, and, seeing the cover on the book in his sister Adelina's hands, he teased, "Not that preposterous book."

Evidently, the three of them had been discussing their favorite romances, judging from the pile on the table between them. They were all avid readers, and there had been much excitement last year when a new author had penned a novel that was an instant hit. Ivo had been persuaded to read it, and although it certainly had him turning the pages and wondering what incredible event would happen next, he could not say it bore any resemblance to real life.

"Why do you say that?" Annette asked in a hurt voice. "The hero...the prince, he is—"

"An idiot of the first order," Ivo replied.

There were cries of dissent from the three women, but he refused to be persuaded any sensible man would fall in love so deeply that he would pursue a woman beyond reason. When his cousin Harold arrived to join the fray, he was completely outnumbered, because of course Harold worked for a publishing house and that book was one of theirs.

"Did you know that the Duke of Grantham has

married Miss Tremeer?" Harold asked, when things had settled down a bit.

Annette's blue eyes sparkled at the news. No doubt it was very romantic for a duke to run off with a woman of no fortune and a tarnished reputation, all in the name of love. And of course, Vivienne Tremeer was Annette's cousin and close friend.

"She sent me a brief letter," Annette admitted. "She is deliriously happy, and she deserves to be." She added this decidedly while casting a narrow look at Ivo, as if he might disagree with her. "She is the kindest of cousins, you know, never thinking of herself."

That was as may be, but the runaway marriage had certainly put the cat among the pigeons for the Ashton family.

His older sister, Alexandrina, or Lexy as she was known among friends and family, seemed to be of the same mind. "That family is certainly scandal prone. I heard Lady Olivia has withdrawn to the country." She gave Ivo a pointed look, because of course Olivia's scandal involved him. "I wonder if she will return to London before the end of the Season. Or return at all?"

Annette bit her lip and avoided looking at Ivo. She knew. He had been so careless as to mention to her that he had met someone he liked a great deal, and Annette had put two and two together. She was a softhearted girl; was she feeling sorry for Olivia or for him? He did not want her sympathy, he just wanted to forget all about his momentary madness and move on.

Adelina looked at Harold beseechingly. "Harold, please tell me if the author of *The Wicked Prince and His Stolen Bride* will pen another book. A sequel, perhaps? I would dearly love to know what happened to the prince's brother!"

There were cries of encouragement from the women, but Harold held up his hands with a laugh. He was an affable fellow, with a warm smile and fair hair, like most of the Fitzsimmonses. Ivo had always gotten on well with him. "That, sadly, I cannot tell you," he said. "I have approached a friend of the author's and suggested a sequel would be welcome, but she seems reluctant to write another novel. I shall keep trying, I assure you. We can but hope," he added, with a smile around the room, lingering a moment on Annette.

That moment caught Ivo's attention, and he wondered if there was something between them. The way Annette smiled back, her cheeks pink, made him think there was a partiality. What would the Viscountess Monteith think of Harold as a prospective son-in-law? Sadly, she would probably want a title at the very least, and Harold had none. He may be related to a duke, but his side of the family had inherited neither titles nor fortune, and he worked for his living. While these may be crosses against his suit in the viscountess's eyes, Ivo could see that in temperament, his cousin and Annette were a perfect match.

He had thought himself and Olivia Ashton a perfect match, right up until the moment she rebuffed him. Now he preferred not to think about her at all.

"Ivo?" Adelina was watching him curiously. "Have you eaten something that disagreed with you? You look quite out of sorts."

"Not at all," he replied and shrugged off his mood. "I was just thinking about a wager I made and lost."

Lexy rolled her eyes. "You and your wagers. When are you going to grow up?"

The words rankled more than they should have.

Normally, he would have disregarded them, but he found he could not. He had Olivia to thank for that. "I *am* grown up," he reminded her curtly as he rose to his feet. "And now I must meet with my man of business."

"Boring estate business," Adelina teased.

"Very boring."

With a smile and a bow for Annette, he left them to it. His sisters might think he was never serious about anything, but that wasn't true. Was it? There were times when he played up his role as a pleasure-seeking rascal, just so that people would not look deeper into his affairs. And yes, he admitted that he enjoyed being that man.

But he had his serious side. His secret life. He was a smuggler, and soon, if luck was on his side, someone with shares in a gambling club.

Even if he could scrape together enough money, the imprudence of going into partnership with the man who may be his father's bastard was not lost on Ivo, and still, he rather thought he was going to do it. He found he was looking forward to this new venture. A sensible fellow might invest in something more mundane than a gambling club. Bonds, for instance, or one of those textile mills in the north. Ivo had neither the temperament nor the experience for such things. He would be throwing away money he didn't have. But there was something about a gambling hell that sent that familiar spark of excitement bubbling up inside him.

Perhaps his sister was right after all, and he was yet to grow up. But where was the fun in being sensible and serious all the time? Olivia might demand reliability and sobriety from a prospective husband, but Ivo suspected that she would soon grow bored with such a fellow. A pity he had not thought to tell her so at the time.

Chapter Five

W here are they?" Olivia had hurried downstairs when she heard a coach come rolling up to the front doors of Grantham house. She had been dying of boredom, reduced to playing a game with Edwina and her dolls. Now she could see Humber directing the servants as the luggage was brought in and piled up on the marble floor of the foyer, and already some of it was being taken upstairs to the ducal suite. But there was no sign of the returning travelers.

Justina pulled a face. "Grandmama had them shown into the drawing room. No one else is allowed in."

"That sounds…ominous. What is she going to do? Send them back to Cornwall?"

"I don't think she can do that," Justina said after a moment's serious thought. "After all, Gabriel *is* the duke and the head of the family."

"Have you heard anything? You were listening at the door, weren't you?" Oliva gave her sister a knowing smile.

Justina flushed. "There was no shouting, so I didn't hear anything really, and then Humber saw me and gave me one of his looks."

Humber's "looks" were almost as dread-provoking as the dowager's, but it seemed unfair he should judge Justina for listening at the door after he had eavesdropped on Olivia's conversation with Northam.

Olivia wondered what her grandmother was saying to Gabriel and Vivienne, but she did not have to ponder for long. Just then, the door opened, and the couple in question stepped out. Her heart lifted as she cried out, "Gabriel!"

Her brother turned to her, and his dark eyes warmed. Olivia noticed he was holding Vivienne's hand, although the two of them looked a little shaken. Gabriel and his sister had rarely hugged, but now she couldn't help but throw her arms around him, her eyes stinging with emotion. Gabriel had to bend down, he was so much taller than her, as he gathered her against him. When he moved on to embrace Justina, it was Vivienne's turn, who squeezed her so tightly she could barely breathe.

"I wish I'd been at the wedding," Justina said.

"I'm sorry you weren't," Gabriel replied.

"It was rather chaotic," Vivienne responded with a glance in his direction. "My family is best kept at a distance. Apart from Will." Sir William Tremeer, Vivienne's younger brother, was well known to them all, and well liked.

Gabriel glanced about him. "Where are the others?"

By which Olivia suspected he meant Edwina, her youngest sister—she and Gabriel had a special bond. "Grandmama has them taking lessons with the new governess. No doubt they will seek you out soon. Ever since we heard you were coming home, Edwina's been so excited. We all have," she admitted.

Gabriel met her eyes, and he saw the questions in them. "Has it been awful?" he asked quietly.

Of course it had! Exiled to Grantham with nothing to do but intervene in her sisters' squabbles. But Olivia shrugged, playing it down. "We've been through worse."

"I wish I hadn't left you all to face the music."

"Nonsense. We wanted you to follow your heart." She

smiled reassuringly at Vivienne. "Oh, there is one thing—"
She had meant to tell him about her mother finally leaving
her bed, but they were interrupted by the arrival of a familiar, slightly built gentleman, who bowed before them.

"Your Grace!" It was the family solicitor.

"Arnott?" Gabriel frowned. "What is it?"

"You will recall you are yet to appoint a new estate
manager, sir, so there are some urgent matters that have
been awaiting your return." The unsmiling man began to
rattle on about the fences and tenants and leaking roofs—
why did the tenants' roofs always leak? Olivia tuned him
out, but Gabriel gave his new wife a harassed glance.

"Do you mind, my love? I should at least deal with
the repairs."

Vivienne smiled and waved him away. "Go," she
said. "I'm sure I will be perfectly fine without you to hold
my hand."

All the same, Gabriel reached to brush her cheek with
his thumb in a loving gesture that made Olivia's breath
catch in a strange combination of affection and jealousy. To
love someone so much that you were willing to risk Grandmama's ire and cast yourself adrift from society? These
days, it seemed impossible to Olivia that she would ever do
such a thing. She was determined to be the perfect debutante if she was given a second chance. Plenty of gentlemen
had noticed her before she had experienced the ire of the
ton, and if she had her chance again, there would surely be
a gentleman who would suit her purposes. Someone compatible and affable, wealthy, of course, who would be fond
enough of her to overlook her disgrace and help her sisters.

She pictured him in her mind. A little gray, perhaps,
but still handsome. He would smile at her benignly and fas-
ten sparkly jewelry around her neck. In return, she would be

the perfect wife, run his household and have his children—
she skipped quickly over this part of her plan—and attend
entertainments with him, even the ones she found boring.

And she would never, ever be so foolish as to be
drawn into the company of the wrong sort of gentleman
ever again. An image of Ivo popped into her mind, but
she pushed him out again.

"Will you show me to my room?" Vivienne was
looking between the two sisters, her gray eyes lacking
their usual assurance.

Of course she was feeling lost and uncertain. Unwelcome too, possibly, depending on what the dowager had
said, which was something Olivia was dying to know.

Olivia and Justina set off with her. "Are you very
tired after the journey?" Justina asked, also noticing
Vivienne's discomfort. "We can show you around the
house. It is *your* home now."

"I suppose it is." Her smile was forced. "I do feel
rather daunted at the thought of taking on the role of chatelaine of Grantham."

"Anyone would be daunted," Olivia reassured her.
Especially with her grandmother in residence, and then
her mother, always in the background. Although not so
much in the background these days.

Once they had taken Vivienne to the ducal rooms,
and she had admired them sufficiently, she divested herself of her dusty traveling cloak and changed her shoes,
and they set out to wander over the great house.

Olivia had lived at Grantham all her life, and she was
used to the size and shabby grandeur of the place. However,
Vivienne looked about her at first in amazement and then
growing dismay. Olivia, seeing things through her new
sister-in-law's eyes, noticed for the first time in forever the

damp stains on the ceilings and the crumbling friezes and mold-smudged decorations. Some of the upper rooms in the east wing were closed and had not been opened in years. No one ventured there anymore, and Vivienne could see why.

"No wonder Gabriel is losing sleep over this place," she said at last, her lovely face downcast. "Is it even possible to return Grantham to its former glory?"

Justina shared a look with Olivia. "Perhaps not," she admitted, "but we can fix some of the worst problems. And if anyone can do it, then it is Gabriel. We just need a little more money."

Vivienne's smile at their vote of confidence soon faded. "Gabriel needed an heiress, and instead he chose me."

Justina looked horrified at her words being misconstrued. "N-no, I didn't mean that. We are all very happy he chose you. And even if the east wing falls down, we still have the rest of the house," she added in what was meant to be a cheery tone of voice.

Olivia laughed at her awkwardness, and Vivienne found a smile.

"What did Grandmama say to you both?" Olivia asked. She had hoped Vivienne would volunteer the information, but her curiosity could no longer be contained.

"I do not know the dowager well," Vivienne began thoughtfully. "Before we arrived, Gabriel warned me she could be redoubtable." The girls grimaced. "But apart from a sharp word or two, and a passing mention of ingratitude, she seemed to want to move on."

"She loves him," Olivia said with certainty. "Not that she would ever admit it."

Vivienne's face cleared.

"It's just that they have a very strange way of showing it," Justina added.

Vivienne went on without commenting. "Your grandmother said that she is arranging a welcome home house party here at Grantham. I assume it is because she couldn't host a wedding, and this is the next best thing."

"She has mentioned it." Olivia felt a frisson of excitement at the thought of guests and entertainment. It had been deadly dull so far, and she missed London and wanted to return as soon as possible. Was this the first step in a solution to her problem?

"And I have seen her and Humber plotting together," Justina put in.

"I believe she has a guest list already," Vivienne went on with a shaky smile. "And I am to have a new gown for the event. She is determined that Gabriel's marriage to me will not prevent the Ashtons from retaking their proper place in the ton, and I assured her I will do my best to help in any way I can."

Then she glanced about at the damp, neglected part of the house they were standing in and sighed. "I think I have seen enough for now. I might need a lie down. The dowager told us we will be having a family dinner tonight, to celebrate the beginning of our new lives as Duke and Duchess of Grantham."

Olivia didn't envy her negotiating that rocky road. She had seen the sort of strain her mother had been under all her life, and although she did not agree with the way Felicia had neglected her daughters, she could also appreciate the pressure of keeping up appearances.

They were almost back to the ducal rooms when there was a shriek from the direction of the stairs.

"Vivienne! Gabriel!"

Edwina came galloping toward them, released from the schoolroom above, and there could be no more confidences shared after that. Olivia, who had intended to warn Vivienne that Lady Felicia had risen from her bed, forgot all about it.

It was only later, as they sat down at the dining table resplendent with the best Ashton silver, candles blazing, that she remembered. By then, it was too late. As Gabriel and Vivienne took their seats with the dowager and the six rather subdued sisters, Felicia made her way into the room. Gabriel looked up and frowned, and Vivienne's eyes widened.

The dowager smiled without humor. "Felicia. You have not yet met Harry's son and his wife. Gabriel...Vivienne, this is Lady Felicia Ashton."

In silence, Felicia stared down the table at her husband's bastard son, who had turned out to be the legitimate heir, and who had taken everything from her. Olivia wasn't sure what her mother was thinking, but it was obvious from her expression that her thoughts were not pleasant ones. Tonight, her mother's hair was dressed in a coronet upon her head, and Olivia noticed again how the dark waves were streaked with silver. She had even dressed in one of her more opulent, if sadly out-of-date, gowns. Olivia only knew it was out-of-date because she had lately been in London and had seen the latest fashions for herself.

Felicia paused as she was about to sit and then changed her mind, causing Humber to grip her chair back and shoot a glance at the dowager. But all she said was, "Welcome home," in a voice without inflection.

It was an awkward moment but at least it was over now. Olivia breathed a sigh of relief as the meal was served. Perhaps it would be all right, she told herself. And perhaps this grand welcome home event her grandmother was planning would go off without a hitch and launch Olivia back into the life she so desperately desired.

Chapter Six

I vo glanced across the coach at his mother, the Dowager Duchess of Northam, and his two sisters, Adelina and Lexy. They were close to their destination now: *Grantham*. Ivo shifted restlessly in his seat and straightened the cuffs of his perfectly fitted green jacket. He felt a little guilty for purchasing the garment but had reminded himself that one must look prosperous if one wanted to prosper. His man of business would probably not agree, although their discussion had proven very helpful, and the bank had increased the mortgage on Whitmont. When Ivo saw the figure it now stood at, he had felt rather queasy. But it meant he could buy into Cadieux's, and with the projected profits from the gambling hell and the smuggling, he felt more hopeful than he had in years that he might finally begin to divest himself of the albatross around his neck.

All the same, he'd rather not be on his way to Grantham, the home of the Ashtons. The Fitzsimmonses hadn't always been on the Ashtons' automatic guest list, but these days, the Dowager Duchess of Grantham was furiously throwing out invitations in every direction. And it was an unfortunate circumstance, in Ivo's opinion, that because Annette and Vivienne were cousins, and Annette was a friend of the Fitzsimmonses, his family had been included under the heading of "close friends and family."

They had been promised entertainment. Firstly, tonight there was a dinner for those aforementioned close friends and family, and then on the following night, a celebratory ball. The ball was a "welcome home" event and open to anyone the dowager could entice or cajole into attending—she obviously meant it to be a much-talked-about success. For those who wished to stay on at Grantham after the ball, there was the promise of picnics and shooting parties and other tempting diversions.

The dowager had, in Ivo's opinion, proved amazingly resilient when it came to weathering the family scandals. All the same, he wondered how she expected to recover from Gabriel's marriage to a woman who, although beautiful and no doubt good, was completely ill-chosen. Society was agog about the newlyweds and keen to discover what would happen next. There would always be the sticklers who disapproved, but for others, the Dowager Duchess of Grantham's welcome home ball had shot to the top of their "must attend" list.

Elaine, Ivo's mother, had declared her head was spinning from the Ashton goings-on. All the same, she was quick to accept the invitation. The Viscountess Monteith would be in attendance, and Ivo's mother and the viscountess were bosom bows from their school days, while Annette, the viscountess's daughter, had carried on the tradition by being best friends with Adelina and Lexy. When the invitation was shown to Ivo by his mother, he had tried desperately to think of an excuse not to attend, but even when he came up with several good ones, she had informed him it was a fait accompli. "You will be escorting myself and your sisters to Grantham, and there is the end to it."

Elaine Fitzsimmons had been a widow now for thirteen years. Her husband had been a tall, handsome man with fair hair and a big smile, loved by everyone. Although Ivo's mother played the grieving widow well, he suspected his father's untimely demise may actually have been a relief—not that she would ever have admitted it. Since his death, the duke's reputation as a seducer of women had come to Ivo's attention—some of the older men in the village occasionally let something about his father slip. They had liked him—everyone had—but they hadn't always been happy with his extramarital activities, especially when it involved their womenfolk.

As he was growing up, Ivo had wanted to be just like his father. The late duke had been a daredevil, game for anything, risking his life again and again, until one day he fell as his horse took yet another high fence and broke his neck. Nowadays, Ivo preferred to think he was his own man. The euphoria that came from smuggling goods across the channel and into Portside still had its exhilarating moments, but some days, it was more like hard work. Although he always smiled when he remembered sharing a glass of good French brandy with Lieutenant Harrison, the senior revenue officer stationed in the Portside area. The man had been unaware he was imbibing contraband, and to risk exposure had probably been foolish on Ivo's part. And yet he had done it, and enjoyed the frisson of danger.

Over the centuries, the Fitzsimmons fortunes had waxed and waned. Rumor had it that the first Duke of Northam had earned his title and Whitmont estate by performing some unspecified favor for the monarch of the day, a deed so dark it had been hushed up ever since. Perhaps that was where Ivo's love of intrigue and adventure could be traced back to, along with his desire to lead a double life. It was in his blood. Unfortunately, that early ancestor had ended up on the block with an axe severing his head from his body.

In an abstract way, Ivo accepted that the law of averages suggested he would one day be arrested for smuggling, now that the government was taking a harder line. Yes, the dukes who had gone before him had been lucky, but that luck would one day run out. If he was caught, he would end up being hanged or imprisoned. What would happen to his family after that? The shame would probably send his mother and sisters into isolation.

Yes, one day he would have to stop, but that time was yet to arrive.

"Annette…"

The whispered name caught his attention. His sisters had their heads together on the other side of the coach, sharing secrets. His mother had heard it too, and she now jerked awake from her doze. "What are you two gossiping about?"

"Oh." Adelina shared a look with Lexy. "I was just reminding Lexy how strange Annette's behavior had been recently. She is forever scribbling in her notebooks and barely says a word. Sometimes she looks as if she's a million miles away."

Well, at least she's not pining over me.

His mother must have had the same thought, shooting him a look full of daggers. "I wouldn't be surprised if Harold doesn't pop the question before long," she said. "I shall be very glad to welcome her into our family."

The two sisters agreed. Adelina looked very much like Ivo in coloring, having inherited their father's fair hair and light eyes, but Lexy's locks shone with red highlights, and her eyes were hazel. They were spoken of as a good-looking family, and he knew his mother was proud of her small brood. In appearance, she was nothing like her children, being small and dark-haired with brown eyes, but the Fitzsimmons blood had prevailed when it came to her offspring.

"I hope you will keep your distance from that minx, Lady Olivia Ashton," the dowager went on. "I can't remember that night at the Elphinstones' without a shudder. Poor Jane was beside herself." Jane was Annette's mother, Viscountess Monteith. "The gossips might have quieted down now that they have her brother's misalliance to talk about, but you can be sure that before long, the girl will do something else outrageous. She is nothing but trouble."

Ivo tried not to sigh. He had heard this warning from his mother many times since the musical evening. "It was my fault, Mother, as I have explained over and over again. I apologized to Lady Olivia and then did my best to right matters."

Not that his best was good enough for Olivia.

"All the same." She sniffed. "I believe she has set her cap at you, Ivo. You are a catch, and she is desperately in need of someone like you, someone respectable."

Adelina snorted a laugh, turning it into a cough.

Ivo opened his mouth to protest. Olivia *had* been in need of him, until he had ruined whatever was between them. Before he could speak, and perhaps it was just as well he didn't, his mother carried on.

"If her brother had not run off with that woman and taken center stage, she might have been able to whip the scandalmongers into a frenzy, and then you would have felt obliged to offer for her."

Ivo said nothing. What could he say? *I did propose,*

Mother, but she turned me down. I wasn't good enough for her. He wasn't going to mention that, and he didn't think Olivia would either. He hadn't wanted to visit Grantham, but once he was there, he was determined to ignore Olivia as much as possible. He would not behave like a man scorned. He would be polite and yet completely indifferent. Yes, her words had hurt a great deal, but he would remain proudly aloof. He would show her how little her opinions meant to him.

A fizz of anticipation broke through his melancholy. She might even regret throwing his proposal back in his face.

"Well, the gardeners have been busy!" Elaine exclaimed as they reached their destination. Looking out of the window, Ivo could see that the borders were trimmed, the lawns scythed, and the gravel drive beyond the gatehouse was raked to within an inch of its life. For all the rumors regarding the Ashton family's dire financial straits, Grantham looked very grand indeed. It seemed that the dowager duchess was determined to prove the gossipmongers wrong. As their coach drew up, servants came hurrying down the front stairs, ready to unload their luggage and welcome them inside.

Or, as Ivo whispered to Adelina, prevent them from leaving.

She tapped his arm with a giggle.

Inside the front door, the Dowager Duchess of Grantham was waiting to greet them, and beside her stood Gabriel, with his new wife, Vivienne. The happy couple, Ivo reminded himself, although their smiles appeared somewhat strained, while the dowager was wearing an expression he would have categorized as "determined."

He made his bows and politely congratulated the

duke and duchess, while his mother twittered to the dowager about the gardens as if there had never been a time when they had loathed each other. Gabriel looked as if he'd rather be somewhere else, but a glance at his wife seemed to calm him.

Ivo continued across the marble floor and found himself standing in a dazzling circle of rainbow light. When he stared up, he saw there was a colored glass dome high above, and the light shone through to the floor below. It was impressive. The Fitzsimmons family seat at Whitmont was not nearly as grand as this, and although he told himself his ancestors had preferred comfort to style, the truth was they had never had enough money.

"How do you do, Your Grace?" asked a piping voice.

Ivo blinked and realized he had not finished with the welcoming party. The six sisters stood in a row, and it was Edwina who had spoken. She made a wobbly curtsy, and he couldn't help but smile. There was something about the youngest Ashton girl that lifted his spirits.

The others followed suit, although Olivia barely dipped at all, and her gaze met his but briefly. She looked as glorious as ever in a blue gown that brought out the color of her eyes. When she dropped her gaze, her dark lashes fanned her pale skin, and her plump lips pouted. She had a sullen look that made him want to kiss the life out of her.

He'd missed her, and he hadn't realized how much until now. He'd missed her company and her smiles and their risky trysts. He'd missed spotting her across a room and knowing he would get to talk to her and hold her in his arms as they danced. He'd missed...*her*.

But this was not how he had planned to meet her. Where was his aloof demeanor? Ivo's carefully chosen words stuck in his throat. Urbane, experienced, a gentleman who allowed very little to rattle him, he now found himself at an embarrassing loss.

"Ivo, come along!" The dowager and his sisters were already at the base of the staircase, waiting to be shown to their rooms.

Ivo gave a quick nod. Had any of the sisters noticed his fixation on Olivia? He hoped not. He would really have to do better at this polite indifference, he told himself as he made his way up the stairs.

"There will be dinner tonight, and tomorrow, the dowager has filled the day with diversions before the ball." Elaine was puffing slightly as she climbed.

"What fun!" Adelina said excitedly. "Are there many guests staying?"

"The dowager says there will be a great many coming tomorrow for the ball alone, and some will be staying on. I wonder if there is room to house so many people." She raised her brows. "I don't mean to speak ill," she lowered her voice, with an eye to the servant leading the way, "but the house is rumored to be in a very poor state. The east wing is completely closed off. I do hope our rooms are well aired."

"Is Annette here yet?" Lexy glanced at her sister.

"I don't know. I didn't think to ask," Adelina replied. "I was struck dumb by that glass dome above the foyer. So grand! Why can't we have something like that at Whitmont, Ivo?"

Ivo ignored her. He was thinking that he would be glad of Annette's company, and no doubt, there would be other members of the ton arriving to attend the ball, people he knew and with whom he could be comfortable. Before long, he would be on his way home again, ready to put all of this behind him. Ready to put Olivia Ashton behind him.

And yet for some reason, his assertions rang hollow.

Chapter Seven

There were more guests at Grantham than there had been for as long as Olivia could remember. She found herself hurrying hither and thither, carrying out her grandmother's instructions, but she was glad to keep busy. At least then she wasn't thinking about Ivo staring up at the glass dome in the foyer as if he was spellbound. As always, he'd been perfectly dressed in his beige pantaloons and dark green tailed jacket, his cravat framing his square jaw and cleanly shaven cheeks. His fair hair had caught the ruby light from the colors in the dome, and it had been cut since she saw him last. The wayward curls that had once caused her gaze to linger and her fingers to long to touch were gone, and he now wore a severe Brutus. It didn't matter. His very presence still made her heart flutter as if there were butterflies taking flight in her chest.

She had expected the visit to be a trying one and had been determined to be as focused as the dowager on making the dinner and the ball, and whatever came after, a resounding success. But she wished he wasn't here. Her grandmother had explained that the Fitzsimmonses would not have come without him, which would have made the Monteiths waver. She trusted Olivia to be politely indifferent to him, inspired by the hope of taking the next step in resuming her London Season.

At the same time, seeing Ivo again…It meddled with her, reminding her of the times they had spent together and the way he had seemed to captivate her so effortlessly, and that concerned her. What if she fell back into infatuation with him? Despite their painful conversation after he had proposed, she still dreamed about the Elphinstones' billiard room. Except that in her dreams, he won the wager and kissed her, his warm lips pressing to hers, leaving her reeling and wanting more. He was like a craving she dared not satisfy, because one taste would never be enough. When they were close, there was a frisson, a vibration in the air around them, a sense that it was only a matter of time before something happened. And try as she might, she could not seem to make it stop.

Olivia was carrying a message from her grandmother to the cook, who was busily preparing dishes for tonight's dinner. She had been a recommendation by Gabriel's chef in London, and Olivia couldn't help but wonder how much her grandmother had paid, or cajoled, to get her to come to Grantham. Whatever it was had been worth it, because the smells drifting from the ovens were mouthwateringly delicious. This time, the dowager wanted mock turtle soup added to the menu, and once the message was delivered, Olivia hurried off again.

Edwina had already been scolded for lingering in the vicinity of the kitchen and getting in the way, so as Olivia started up the servants' stairs, she was not surprised to hear her sisters' shrieks of outrage. And there ahead of her was Edwina, in a tussle with Georgia over a cupcake with pink icing. Without a word, she waded in and snatched the prized treat from the girls' greedy hands.

"It's mine!" Edwina cried, her face flushed with fury and her eyes bright.

Georgia smirked. "It was never yours, because you stole it. You're a thief."

"I was hungry!"

"Stop it, both of you!" Olivia had had enough. "Don't you know better than to fight over food like wild animals? What will the guests think? What will Grandmama say?"

Edwina looked sullen. "I don't care," she muttered. "I don't want all these people here anyway. I liked it better when it was just us and we could do what we liked."

Olivia was surprised. Her youngest sister had a different recollection of their past than she did. "Just because we did as we liked doesn't mean it was good for us. I remember you crying yourself to sleep because you were hungry and Mother had sent the servants away again. Your hair was so tangled, Justina had to use scissors to take out the knots, and your clothes were torn and dirty, and when the vicar called, he thought you were a foundling someone had left on our doorstep." She took a breath. "We could not go on like that. Gabriel saved us, and now our lives have changed. We must try our very best to change too."

"You're only saying that because Prince Nikolai is coming to dinner," Georgia retorted, eyes bright with malice.

Olivia went still. "*Who* is coming to dinner?"

"It's a secret." Now Georgia had caught her attention, she made a motion of buttoning her lips.

Olivia was tempted to give the girl a good shake before she noticed Edwina was looking particularly guilty. "Tell me at once," she said sternly. Then, when Edwina shook her head, "Tell me, and I will give you the cupcake."

Georgia began to protest, but Olivia held up a hand

for silence. "Edwina, I'm waiting." She turned the cupcake in her fingertips, admiring its thick icing and tempting cakey smell.

Edwina wriggled, but she could not resist. She never could when it came to food. "Georgia and I heard Grandmama talking to Humber," she burst out. "Prince Nikolai of Holtswig is coming to dinner, and Grandmama is hoping he will fall in love with you and marry you."

Olivia stared. "You're making it up. How does she know this Prince Nikolai of Holtswig?"

"Because she is acquainted with his grandfather, and when she wrote to him, she found out that the prince was in England for…something or other, so she invited him to Grantham."

Olivia handed her the cupcake without a word. Edwina let out a crow of triumph and thumped up the stairs, while Georgia followed, complaining bitterly.

Prince Nikolai of Holtswig? It made sense. The preparations, the attention to detail, the importance her grandmother was placing upon everything being perfect for their guests. Obviously, she hadn't given up on restoring the Ashtons to their former glory and finding Olivia a husband worthy of an Ashton, but a *prince*? Olivia and a prince? Was such a thing even possible? It was certainly a big improvement on her own plan to beguile a slightly gray, wealthy gentleman into proposing to her.

She needed to share this news with someone, so Olivia hurried off to find Justina. She found her sister arranging flowers in numerous vases, while one of the young servants was threading ivy through the bannisters on the stairs. Justina took one look at Olivia and beckoned her into a storage cupboard.

"What is it?" she asked as soon as the door was shut.

They shuffled closer in the gloom and the strong scent of moth-repelling herbs. "Is it Ivo?"

"What do you mean, is it Ivo? Of course it isn't Ivo." Olivia extinguished her flare of anger and took a steadying breath. "Edwina has just told me that Grandmama invited a prince to Grantham to marry me."

"What? Now?"

Olivia snorted a laugh. "No, not now. She is *hoping* he will marry me. He's the grandson of a friend, and when she discovered the prince was visiting England, she sent him an invitation. And he accepted."

Justina considered this information and cut to what she deemed important. "Do you want to marry a prince, Olivia?"

Olivia put her hands over her face. "Would a prince want to marry *me*?"

Justina took her sister's hands and tugged them away. She was taller than Olivia, a slender girl with a gentle and serious nature. "I'm sure you could make him want to marry you. You are beautiful and clever, and gentlemen like you. Look at Ivo."

Olivia groaned. "Please, let us not talk of Ivo."

"Then let us talk about this prince. Olivia, it would be a triumph if you married someone like that. Just think. No one would ever dare to slander you again. Not to your face anyway. No more of those awful pamphlets."

That was true. Olivia needed a respectable husband, wealthy, of course, but also with a character beyond reproach. She would be safe then from the sort of hurtful gossip currently circulating about her. And she could help her sisters too by finding them equally wealthy and respectable gentlemen. A prince each, wouldn't that be wonderful?

"Of course you may loathe him on sight," Justina said

matter-of-factly. "I don't think you should marry him if he does revolting things like chew with his mouth open, or if he never bathes, or if he wears a false hair piece."

"I'm sure his title will sweeten any faults in his character."

"Well then, it is settled." Justina paused as she opened the door. "You will marry this prince, and I will marry…" She bit her lip. "Gabriel said he invited Charles Wickley to dinner. Do you think he will come?"

Olivia had noticed Justina's partiality for Wickley but had kept her feelings about it to herself. Until now. "Justina, you know he can never be suitable as a husband for you. Grandmama would forbid it."

Justina's eyes flashed in a rare show of temper. "I don't care about that. I'm not *saying* I want to marry him, but I…" She glanced down and her voice dropped. "I *like* him."

Olivia patted her shoulder sympathetically, ignoring how her sister flinched away. "I know you do, but it wouldn't work. When I marry the prince, I will find you someone else. Someone better."

Justina's laugh had an unfamiliar, bitter ring to it. "Of course you will."

She opened the door and peered out, and when she saw it was safe, she left Olivia alone in the cupboard.

Olivia told herself that her sister didn't understand. Perhaps, like Edwina, she had forgotten what it had been like at Grantham before Gabriel came along. It was Olivia who had borne the brunt of worrying about her sisters during those times, with the responsibility weighing heavy upon her shoulders. But Justina was a sensible and obedient girl, and she would accept that to marry well was for her own good and the good of her family. She would accept that Charles Wickley was not the man for her.

Chapter Eight

I vo brushed a rose petal from his sleeve. It was late in the afternoon, and now that Annette had arrived with her parents, he had been prevailed upon by his sisters to escort the three ladies around the gardens. Which suited him. Anything to keep him out of the house and away from a possible confrontation with Olivia. There had been a few more arrivals for tonight's dinner, but Annette had informed him that the majority of the guests would be here tomorrow for the ball. Because the London Season was still in full swing, many of those who might have attended already had engagements, and had sent apologies. However, there were still a significant number of guests who intended to come, as well as the local squirearchy.

Perhaps I can think of an excuse to leave? Urgently.

"Vivienne says that her new grandmother-in-law has high hopes of a match between them. Olivia is a very pretty girl, and although she is spirited, recently she has become much more biddable."

Ivo only heard the tail end of the conversation, and he told himself he would not respond. *He would not.* But even as he thought it, he heard himself asking, "Who is this paragon the dowager has in her sights for her grand-daughter?" He had meant to sound light and amused, but there must have been something darker in his tone, because the women shared a furtive glance.

"Prince Nikolai of Holtswig." Annette's blue eyes peered directly into his. "The prince has been persuaded to attend the dinner and the ball. The dowager knows his grandfather. She never stops scheming!"

"A *prince*?" Was that the husband Olivia wanted? And why should it concern him anyway? He ignored the odd sensation in his chest—he had probably eaten something at breakfast that disagreed with him. "I imagine that would solve all of the Ashtons' problems in one fell swoop," he said absently, as if he had far more important things to think of.

"It would certainly be a triumph," Adelina agreed.

Conversation dwindled. They had reached the edge of the gravel drive, where it swept up to the house, when they saw the carriage. It was being drawn by four magnificent grays, but that wasn't what caused the three women to ooh and aah. There was a slim gentleman riding a chestnut stallion beside the carriage. He looked to be about twenty, and his back was as straight as a ramrod, while his glossy dark hair gleamed in the waning sunlight.

"Oh, do you think that's the prince?" Lexy whispered excitedly.

As the gentleman rode past, he must have been able to see them, but did not even turn his head or acknowledge them in any way. It was as if they were beneath his notice. "He's arrogant enough to be one," Ivo said with a frown.

"You seem to have taken an instant dislike to him already." Annette leaned closer. "Why is that, I wonder?"

Ivo did not meet her eyes. He could hear from her

tone of voice that she was amused by him, and if they had been alone, he would have told her that any feelings he may have had for Olivia, and had foolishly expressed aloud, were in the past. As the small group turned back through the garden, the ladies full of speculation, Ivo decided it would be safer to say nothing. If Olivia thought a prince would make her happy, then that was her business and absolutely nothing to do with him. Although if she *were* to ask Ivo…But no, she would never ask. The days when she sought his opinion on anything were gone.

"I may have to leave tomorrow," he said as they reached the house.

The three of them turned to him, eyes wide. "Oh no, Ivo!" Lexy protested. "We need you at the ball! What if there aren't enough gentlemen to dance with? You cannot go tomorrow."

"Besides, Mama will not let you!" Adelina added this last.

"Nonsense, she knows I am very busy. I have, eh, business to attend to." His protest sounded weak, and he wasn't surprised when they refused to accept his excuses.

Annette took his arm in hers and gave it a sympathetic squeeze.

Ivo's sisters had moved ahead, keen to dress for dinner, but he kept his voice low. "It isn't because of…Well, it's nothing to do with Lady Olivia. That is nothing; it never was. It is just that I am particularly busy at the moment."

"Surely not too busy to spend another night at Grantham and dance with your sisters? They will be so disappointed, Ivo."

They would, and they would punish him for it. Ivo heaved a victimized sigh that made Annette's lips twitch. "Very well," he said. "To please you, I will stay."

"Thank you," she said gravely.

"I will dance with you too, as a proxy for my cousin Harold," he added with a smirk.

Annette blushed and did not answer.

Everyone gathered in the drawing room before dinner. Most of the guests were known to Ivo, and in fact, it was a relatively small group consisting of the Viscount and Viscountess Monteith and their daughter, Lady Annette; Sir William Tremeer, who was Vivienne's brother and who was employed at Cadieux's Gambling Club; the Dowager Duchess of Grantham; and Gabriel, the duke; his wife, Vivienne, the duchess; as well as the two elder granddaughters, Lady Olivia and Lady Justina. Ivo, his mother, Elaine, and sisters Lexy and Adelina completed the guest list. Well, apart from the prince.

Although it was Gabriel and Vivienne's recent marriage they were meant to be celebrating, to Ivo, it felt as if Prince Nikolai was the true guest of honor. The prince was the last to arrive, and he strode into the room with a minion scuttling behind him, greeting the dowager with a familiar kiss on her cheek.

"My dear boy," she responded, and promptly began to introduce him to the others, paying particular attention to Olivia. The prince took Olivia's hand in his, and she curtsied low before him, nothing like the slight bob she had greeted Ivo with. Nikolai was a handsome young man, especially when he smiled, and he was smiling now. There was also a gleam in his dark eyes that Ivo recognized only too well.

Attraction. Desire.

Ivo glared at the two of them. For God's sake, the man was looking at Olivia as if she was a particularly delectable dessert!

The prince murmured something flattering to Olivia as she rose gracefully from her curtsy. She was smiling as she met his gaze, a pink blush across her cheeks. Ivo felt that odd tightening in his chest again. Of course, he was annoyed that Olivia had turned her back on all he had to offer, and now here she was, fluttering her eyelashes at a man with far less to recommend him. Well, Ivo supposed he *was* a prince, probably wealthy, with a castle. Thinking about it that way, Ivo couldn't really blame her, and yet he did. Wealth and castles weren't everything. Ivo would have made her happy. Could the same be said for the prince?

He turned away in time to notice Charles Wickley had entered the room. He caught Ivo's gaze and gave a polite nod, before Gabriel moved to take his friend's hand warmly in both of his.

"Thank God," Ivo heard the duke say. "I'm so glad you are here."

Charles chuckled. "That bad, is it?"

"Is Freddie coming?"

"On duty, I'm afraid," Charles replied. Ivo knew that Freddie was the third of the trio of men who had been friends since they were placed in St. Ninian's Foundling Home for Boys.

Whatever else was said was lost in the hubbub as the butler announced that dinner was about to be served.

Ivo escorted his mother into the dining room, where a polished silver candelabra stood guard over sparkling crockery and glassware. It looked as if a year's supply of candles had been lit at once. Olivia's grandmother was certainly going all out to impress, and even Ivo could admit it was effective. He noticed Viscountess Monteith exchange a glance with his mother, eyebrows raised. Neither of them were admirers of the Dowager Duchess of Grantham, but that had not stopped them from accepting her invitation. They were probably hoping for a good supply of gossip to take home with them.

Annette took her place beside him, and leaned in to whisper, "I am so glad you are here, Ivo."

"I tried not to be," he said honestly, "but I was overruled. There are more exciting things I could be doing."

"I don't believe there is anything more exciting than this. I keep waiting for my mother to say something offensive to the Dowager Duchess of Grantham. She still believes you would have married me if it wasn't for the billiard table scandal."

Ivo raised his eyebrows in surprise. "Is that what they're calling it? I would have thought there were more interesting things to talk about by now."

"I shouldn't have spoken of it." Annette searched his face worriedly, and he wondered what she saw.

"No, speak away." He leaned closer. "Do you think they might come to blows by pudding?"

She covered her giggle with her hand.

He grinned back, and then his gaze slid past her, and he realized Olivia was watching them with a little frown between her brows. His expression cooled, and he gave her a polite nod of acknowledgment. Her earrings caught the light as she turned away, and then she stiffened, her hand clenching into a fist on the table top. What on earth…? He followed her gaze to see that someone else had entered the dining room. The others had fallen silent, everyone observing the woman in black widow's weeds as she moved gracefully toward an empty chair.

The dowager's voice was carefully expressionless. "May I introduce Lady Felicia, my late son's…wife." The hesitation was telling.

Felicia shot the dowager a poisonous look, and reached up to fiddle with the black mourning pendant she wore around her neck. Her mouth curved in a cold, supercilious smile as she surveyed the assembled guests. "Welcome to Grantham," she said, as if she was the hostess rather than her mother-in-law.

Ivo exchanged a glance with Annette, who widened her eyes comically. Gabriel and Vivienne looked as if they wished they were anywhere else. Justina, who was seated beside Gabriel, reached over to cover his hand with hers, and he gave her a tense smile. It appeared that the gambling club owner had well and truly redeemed himself in the eyes of his new family. As for Felicia, the outcast wife…Ivo suspected she was enjoying making things as uncomfortable as possible.

"Ah, mock turtle soup! My favorite!" It was the prince who spoke, his usually haughty expression brightening as he recognized what was in the bowl before him. Either he was completely oblivious to the undertone around the table, or he just didn't care.

The dowager smiled fondly. "I hope you enjoy your stay at Grantham, Niki."

The prince's dark gaze slid toward Olivia, who sat opposite him. "I am certain I will."

Olivia blushed again. Or was she simpering?

Ivo barely managed to restrain his snort of disgust, but some part of it must have slipped out, because Olivia looked up abruptly. Whatever she saw in his face caused her eyes to narrow to blue slits. She was furious with him—there had never been anything lukewarm about Olivia.

Ivo admitted he was behaving badly, but he couldn't find it in himself to be sorry. Was he supposed to enjoy seeing her make eyes at another man? If it was up to him, he wouldn't have come to Grantham at all, but he'd thought he would be able to maintain an indifferent veneer. This was torture.

She glared at him a moment longer, as if daring him to say what he was thinking, so he deliberately gave her a big smile. Hectic color flared into her cheeks, and Ivo looked away and unhurriedly began to eat his meal.

Chapter Nine

Despite the lavish spread, Olivia wasn't hungry. She felt shaky, and even more nervous than she had been at her coming-out ball at Ashton House. So much depended upon tonight and tomorrow, and the weight upon her shoulders was immense. She let her gaze slide to the prince, watching him drink his soup with gusto. She had only just realized how clever Grandmama had been to arrange to serve his favorite dish. It was a good start. And Olivia had not missed the admiration in the prince's eyes when they were introduced in the drawing room a moment ago.

It was just a pity that Felicia was here. And to dress in black tonight of all nights, reminding everyone that she was a widow without a husband or a title!

There was someone else Olivia wished wasn't here tonight.

Almost against her will, her gaze moved across the dining table to where Ivo and Annette sat. Their fair heads were close, and they seemed cozy together, as only old friends could be, and Ivo had told her that was all they were—old friends. All the same, their shared smiles and intimate murmurs made Olivia's skin itch. And the look he had just given her! What right had *he* to censure *her*? A man who was notorious for his ridiculous behavior? It was none of his business if she chose to turn her attention to Prince Nikolai. The prince certainly admired her, and she was pleased and flattered that his feelings were already so obvious. Everything was working out perfectly. How dare Ivo try to spoil it for her!

She had been staring too long. Ivo glanced over and caught her at it. For a moment, he looked as if he might smile, a proper smile and not that mocking one he had given her earlier. She felt her own lips twitch in response, which was infuriating when only moments before, she had been incandescent with rage. What was it about Ivo, that he could send her emotions seesawing from one extreme to the other? With a supreme effort, she turned away and stared unseeingly at her next course. It was some sort of fish covered in a rich sauce and served with vegetables. She doubted she could eat more than a bite, but her pride dictated that she at least pretend she was unaffected by Ivo's presence. She picked up her fork, and then dropped it with a clatter as a loud shout came from just outside the dining room.

There were several gasps and a concerned babble of voices as a disheveled-looking man came running into the room. He wore breeches, boots, and a brown jacket, and was obviously some sort of groom—and a very worried one, if his expression was anything to go by. Humber had followed him and grabbed his arm, evidently with the purpose of evicting him, but the man shrugged him off. He quickened his steps, making his way to the prince, who seemed to recognize him and had risen from his chair.

"Sir, it's Leopold! Someone has stolen Leopold!"

"Stolen?" The word exploded from the prince. The controlled young man he had been up until now, very

much aware of his position, was gone, and in his place stood a flushed and angry boy on the verge of tears. "What do you mean, Otto? Explain yourself at once!"

"I went to the stables to feed him his special food, but he has been taken!" Otto was as shaken and worried as his master.

"Taken?" The prince looked about him wildly, as if expecting the thief to jump up from behind a chair.

Humber lingered behind the groom, seemingly at a loss as to what to do. "Your Grace?" he said to the dowager. "Should I...?"

Olivia's grandmother took charge in a calm, authoritative voice. "I am sure this is nothing more than an honest mistake, Niki. Your horse is perfectly safe at Grantham." Then, turning to her butler, "Humber? If you would see to this."

"Yes, Your Grace." Relieved to have something to do, Humber strode purposefully from the room.

"Niki. Nikolai," the dowager addressed the prince, who was still on his feet, "be reassured. I know how much you value your horse."

"Stallion," Nikolai snapped. "Leopold is an Irish stallion. His sire was owned by the Marquess of Waterford and his dam by the Marquess of Donegall. I intend to race him when he is older—he is still too young and not ready to begin his training."

Olivia knew that horses were usually named after their owners, but Nikolai was very precise about Leopold's family tree, and his plans for him. Almost as if Leopold was his favorite child. Annette must have thought the same because she giggled, quickly bowing her head when her mother cast her a look of reproof. Abruptly, Gabriel tossed aside his napkin and rose to his feet. "I will deal with this," he said to his grandmother. He paused to rest his hand on Vivienne's shoulder, before he led the prince and Otto from the room.

A moment later, Charles jumped up too, and with a muttered curse, Viscount Monteith hurried after them. Will Tremeer swallowed his forkful of fish, and then, with an apologetic glance at his sister, followed.

The dowager sighed, Felicia was smirking at her plate, and Olivia had lost what little appetite she'd had. She even considered going after the gentlemen, but her grandmother fixed her with such a stern look that she did not dare. Ivo smiled. "Do not fear, ladies," he said, "I will stay and play the hero and protect you from this ghastly horse thief."

"Stallion," Annette murmured helpfully at his side. "Stallion thief."

"Very amusing, Northam," the dowager said, "but not particularly helpful."

Ivo, not at all chastened, met Olivia's gaze, and his lips quirked. Daring her to say something. It was impossible to resist.

"You mean like the sort of hero who would risk his neck to rescue a kitten?" she queried mildly.

His eyebrows lifted. "Of course! Climbing about on a roof is only one of my many heroic accomplishments."

She wanted to giggle.

It was an echo of their conversation when she had refused his marriage proposal. Until now, she had believed it a painful moment. Were they really making fun of it?

"Whatever you are saying, stop it." The dowager glared at the two of them.

That was when Olivia noticed the confused

expressions on the faces of those around her. She picked up her fork. "This fish is delicious," she said, and this time when Ivo laughed under his breath, she ignored him.

Slowly, the meal progressed, and they had come to an end before Humber returned. He looked a little grim as he approached the dowager and bent to whisper close to her ear. Olivia's grandmother stiffened in her seat in reaction to whatever he had to tell her, and her dark eyes closed briefly. Olivia wondered if she was counting to ten. "Bring her to me in the blue sitting room," she said in a quiet, steely voice.

"Yes, Your Grace."

Everyone was waiting, eyes on the dowager, who seemed to be wrestling with her emotions, before years of training came to the fore and she once more slipped into her role. "If you would like to make yourselves comfortable in the drawing room, coffee and tea will be served. There is a matter that requires my attention."

The guests rose and began to make their way to the drawing room, but Olivia followed her grandmother. When she realized Vivienne was following too, she felt a wave of relief—Vivienne could be relied upon to smooth over a difficult situation, something Olivia had learned when her new sister-in-law had given the six Ashton girls lessons in the proper way to behave in society.

The dowager noticed them trailing after her, but after looking as if she was about to send them off, she chose instead to wait until they entered the sitting room and then closed the door.

"Grandmama, what is it?" Olivia burst out. "The prince's horse—"

"Stallion," her grandmother retorted sourly. "Something you should know about Nikolai is that he is a stickler for protocol. He was brought up by his grandfather after his father died at a young age, and his mother was too busy with her own pleasures."

Olivia thought that sounded a little like her own circumstances, with a dead father and an absent mother. Something she and Nikolai had in common.

There was a tap on the door, and Humber appeared, and when Olivia saw her sixteen-year-old sister, Roberta, at his side, everything became clear. Roberta's dark hair hung down her back in tangled skeins, and her skirts were muddy, as were her boots. There was a scratch on her cheek. But when she lifted her chin and glowered at the three women, it was obvious she was more resentful than apologetic.

"Robbie, what have you done?" The words tumbled out of Olivia's lips.

Her sister's eyes met hers before they darted away again. "I was only gone a moment," she said, as if to excuse herself. "If the stupid stallion hadn't taken me through a thicket, I could have returned him to the stables, and no one would have been the wiser."

"That is not the point," the dowager spoke through bared teeth. "That animal is valuable, and it belongs to Prince Nikolai. You took it without his permission. You will apologize. Immediately."

Roberta looked as if she was about to say something they would all regret, when Vivienne stepped into the fray. "Maybe not immediately, do you think, Your Grace? An apology is always better spoken when it comes from a heart that is sincere. Roberta is not feeling remorse just now. She could do with some reflection." Her gray eyes swept over the younger woman. "And perhaps a wash and a change of clothing. The stallion is not damaged, is he?"

"No!" the girl cried, clearly mortified at the suggestion that she would ever cause such a thing to happen.

"Then tomorrow will do." Vivienne met her grandmother-in-law's gaze head-on. "Both Roberta and the prince will be less...fraught by then. You can set the scene, Your Grace, and I am sure Roberta will be more than happy to follow your instructions to the letter."

It sounded like a solid plan, and Vivienne was right. If Roberta was forced to apologize right now, when she believed she had done nothing wrong, it would only make things worse. Olivia had been embroiled in enough squabbles with her sister to realize that.

After a moment of reflection of her own, her grandmother gave a stiff nod to Vivienne. "Very well. But, Roberta, think on this: You have just added to the gossip about your family and possibly jeopardized my plans for Olivia's future. If Prince Nikolai packs up and leaves tomorrow morning, I will hold you entirely responsible."

She swept out of the room, and Roberta's shoulders sagged. "I didn't mean anything by it," she muttered. "I was just—"

"You never do," Olivia retorted bitterly. "Grandmama is right. If you ruin my chance of making a brilliant marriage, then I will...I will..." But she couldn't think of any punishment bad enough for her sister, and with a huff, she followed her grandmother.

She stopped outside the door, taking deep breaths to try to hold back her temper and her tears. From inside she could hear the murmur of Vivienne's soothing tones interspersed by her sister's complaints. Had she really once been as rebellious as Roberta? So eager to ignore the consequences? What on earth had she been thinking to flout society's rules like that? She had well and truly learned her lesson even before this moment, but if she was ever tempted to backslide, then Roberta's behavior had reminded her of the cost.

She turned toward the drawing room and paused. The guests would be waiting and, no doubt, eager to hear about the latest scandal in the Ashton saga. Olivia couldn't face them. Neither could she face the prince, although he was probably busy with his stallion, and she was unlikely to gain anything by trailing around after him in the muck and mud. And then there was Ivo. How he must be enjoying this Ashton drama after all the things she had accused him of that day!

As if her thoughts had brought him forth, the Duke of Northam stepped through the door and closed it behind him. When he looked up and saw her, Olivia found she had nothing to say.

"Who took the stallion?" he asked, moving toward her. "Everyone is agog." He nodded toward the drawing room. "We thought your prince might order the culprit's head to be chopped off."

He spoke with amusement, but she was in no doubt he was enjoying her discomfiture. She considered brushing the question off, but what was the point? Everyone would know tomorrow anyway.

"Roberta."

He smiled. "Ah, the hoyden sister. You told me about her."

Did she? It seemed she had been very forthcoming during their trysts, but then Ivo had gained her trust. It was something she had liked about him from the first, how he seemed genuinely interested in her. One of his particular skills. Whenever she had been feeling out of her depth in her new role as sister of a duke, she had known she could rely upon him to make her feel better. Or laugh. They had laughed an awful lot during their trysts.

"I assume her head is still attached to her body?"

He was teasing, and the memory of how in alignment they used to be made her feel strangely hollow. Her voice was crotchety when she replied. "Perfectly. Now, if that is all? I have a great deal to do."

His sparkling gaze met hers and cooled. "I thought I would see what's happening in the stables. The ladies are discussing the latest fashions in bonnets, and I have little to contribute."

"I imagine it is very dull here for someone like you. Perhaps you should go back to London."

It wasn't the right thing to say. She knew that at once. She had never been spiteful, but now he was bringing out the worst in her. This close to him, his green eyes were striking as he considered his reply. She thought about making her excuses and leaving him, but that would be cowardly, and anyway, it was too late.

"You seem to believe I am some sort of hell-raiser, Olivia. Unreliable. I remember that was one of the blemishes you listed against me, when you told me never to darken your door again."

"Your memory is faulty."

"Is it?" He looked down at her from his greater height, but she refused to give ground. "Actually, my memory is rather good. For instance, I remember you agreeing to that bet with me at the Elphinstones'. A kiss if I won or my thumb ring if you did. Is my memory faulty on that detail?"

She hesitated, but he was waiting for her to fib, and she refused to be predictable. "We never finished the game."

"We *could* finish it. Where is the famous Grantham billiard room?" He looked around. "The scene of your many triumphs?"

"I thought we had decided friends do not make wagers that could compromise—"

"You decided that. And I don't think we are friends now. Are we?"

He waited. Her heart was beating quickly, her throat felt tight as she sought for something to say. "I can't take the risk," she blurted out at last. "Not with you. You're the last person I should be friends with."

He stilled. "I see. All work and no play when it comes to snaring your prince. I wish you well of him, Olivia, even though I think you are making a mistake." His face transformed into a facsimile of Nikolai's haughty expression, and his next words were spoken with the prince's slight accent. "No one will ever be good enough for him. Except perhaps for Leopold!" He gave her an exaggerated bow and walked briskly away.

She stared after him, and a memory popped into her head.

During one of their illicit meetings, they had found a quiet room to chat in, and she had discovered Ivo had a wicked ability to mimic the more recognizable guests, sending Olivia into whoops. "You should have been on the stage," she had said, wiping her eyes.

He had sent her a sideways glance. "I will tell you a secret. I almost was. Some traveling players came to Portside, and after I saw them perform, I told my mother that was what I wanted to be. I was very disappointed when she explained I was going to be a duke and that was that."

Just now, Ivo had been playing the part of the prince.

He was being cruel, and she had never thought of Ivo as cruel. Had she wounded his pride again? Olivia tried to shrug off the awkwardness of their encounter. What did it matter what Ivo thought? She had made her choice.

She turned toward the stairs.

She had barely taken a step when her eye was caught by a man standing in the shadows of the passage that led to the rear of the house. His back was to her and for a moment—although how could it be?—she thought that fair hair belonged to Ivo. He dipped his head, as if he was…he was…kissing someone? A woman stood in the circle of his arms.

She froze. It was as if her heart was being squeezed. She should have been happy to see Ivo behaving in the manner of a man who cared nothing for others, the sort of man she had accused him of being, but instead, she felt broken into pieces. The error only lasted for a moment, until she heard the murmur of his voice. *Charles Wickley.* Not Ivo after all.

The woman lifted her head. *Justina.* Charles was kissing her sister. After the evening she'd had, it was too much for Olivia.

"No!" she said in a loud voice, making them both jump and hastily step apart. When they saw her, Charles ____ ____ ____ his face as if he didn't know what to say, ____ ____ ____ hair disarranged. Before ____ ____ ____ ____ ____ her sister's arm, pulling her toward the stairs.

"Rather an overreaction," Charles drawled. "I was hardly about to ravish her."

"Olivia," Justina hissed, more angry than embarrassed. "Let me go."

But Olivia ignored them both, continuing up the

stairs with her sister in tow. They reached the top and Justina pulled away, rubbing her arm. "You have no right—" she began.

Olivia spoke over her. "I've had enough of scandals," she said furiously. "First Roberta and now this. Don't you dare create another one!"

Justina glared at her. "Why? You've had your share. Isn't it my turn?"

Olivia did not remember the last time she had fallen out with her sister and closest friend. She could say something now, make it better, but she was too angry to say anything at all. Justina gave her one burning, resentful look before setting off at a run for her bedchamber.

Somewhere, a door banged, and a head peered out from another room. Georgia? It occurred to Olivia that Georgia was in her mother's room, but that couldn't be right. She let the thought slip. Justina was more important.

Olivia knew she should go after her, smooth things over, but she didn't move. It was chilly standing there, and the lamp on the small table fluttered a little in one of the many drafts that plagued Grantham.

I think you are making a mistake.

Suddenly, she felt very much alone—and this time, there was no Justina, and no Ivo, to make her feel better.

Chapter Ten

A fter the excitement of dinner, the new day dawned
still and clear. Ivo lay in bed and viewed the windows with narrowed eyes. He hadn't slept well and was
feeling out of sorts. This visit to Grantham might be
everything his mother, and her best friend, Jane, had
hoped for—they would have lots of gossip to share when
they returned to London—but Ivo wasn't enjoying it. The
scene in the dining room had been unpleasant, with the
arrogant prince demanding to know who had stolen his
stallion, and Olivia's worried face as she watched on. She
was clearly under a great deal of pressure to ensnare Nikolai, although why she would want to was a mystery to him.

He was being disingenuous. Of course he understood why she wanted to marry the prince, although if
she thought she would be happy with him…But perhaps
happiness wasn't the aim. Ivo suspected it wasn't. He
understood well enough the stratagems of marriage in the
upper ranks of the ton and the reasons behind them.

When he had come face-to-face with her outside the
drawing room, he had felt sorry for her. She had looked
lost, and, unselfishly, he had wanted nothing more than to
make her smile. He had started off with good intentions,
but instead, he had ended up picking an argument with
her. In response, she had wielded her tongue like a sword.

You're the last person I should be friends with.

That had certainly stung. No one could blame him for fighting back. Then why did he feel as if he could have done better?

Impatiently, Ivo threw off the covers and rose, thinking a brisk ride would help his mood. He was counting down the hours until he left tomorrow and could return to normalcy. He thought he might spend some time at Whitmont, breathing in the sea air, clearing his head.

Ivo's hopes of having the stables to himself were dashed when he found Prince Nikolai already there, in close conversation with Otto. Leopold the stallion was being walked carefully back and forth over the cobbled yard, while they checked him for any injuries sustained from Roberta's wild ride. The animal didn't look quite as magnificent as he had when Ivo first saw him trot by yesterday. There were scratches on his chestnut hide where he had been ridden through a thicket, and poultices had been applied to the worst of them.

Despite Ivo greeting the prince in his usual polite and friendly fashion, all he got in response was a cool stare. Was Ivo's dislike of the man because of the situation with Olivia? He didn't think so. Nikolai was unpleasant, proud, and rude, and Ivo would have disliked him whoever he was. With an inner shrug, he went to find himself a mount for his ride—he would be glad to be out in the fresh air and away from what was shaping up to be another uncomfortable day.

Gabriel had informed them last night that there were diversions planned today for the guests, to keep them busy.

"Hazard?" Charles had inquired with a smirk.

Will Tremeer had seemed to brighten at the prospect.

"I missed the club while I was in Cornwall," he admitted. "Everything seemed very dull."

Viscount Monteith had then introduced the subject of horseflesh—he owned a racing stable and was a keen bidder at Tattersall's—and that was that. Of course, the prince had his own thoughts on such matters—which he seemed to think were the *only* way to do things—and before long, the two men, having found something in common, were deep in conversation.

Remembering it now, Ivo wondered if Olivia was as horse mad as her hoped-for husband. He didn't believe so, at least she had never mentioned horses to him during their tête-à-têtes, although they had spoken on a wide variety of subjects. A sense of loss flooded him. He missed their conversations. He buoyed himself up with the mischievous thought that if she did marry the prince, she would need to cultivate an equine interest, real or feigned.

The ride did him good, and he returned to the house feeling more his pragmatic self. Breakfast was underway, and after washing and changing out of his riding clothes, he sauntered downstairs to partake. As soon as they saw him, his sisters and Annette looked up guiltily, making him wonder what secrets they were sharing. Olivia sat farther down the table with Justina and a subdued-looking Roberta. None of the sisters appeared to be very happy this morning, and Olivia had that sulky droop to her mouth that…well, Ivo admitted it. Made him want to kiss the life out of her. Not a helpful impulse, under the circumstances.

It wasn't that long ago when he would have hurried to sit at her side. Whispering teasing things in her ear and daring her to meet with him alone. It sounded more improper than it had been. Mostly, they had just talked, or at least Olivia had been the one to talk, usually about her family, and Ivo had listened. He had sensed that she felt rather alone sometimes and needed a confidant, and he enjoyed taking on that role.

His sisters would have laughed at the idea that their feckless brother could offer anyone good advice, but when Olivia had looked to him, he had felt...Well, why deny it? He had felt extraordinary. The soft glow in her eyes, the admiring smile on her lips. It depressed him a little, that it was unlikely she would ever ask him anything again.

Now, he murmured a general greeting and went to fill his plate from the covered dishes laid out on a side table. He was deciding between sausages and bacon, when there was the sound of a scuffle behind him at the door, followed by a quiet reprimand. Two of Olivia's younger sisters and Vivienne had entered the room.

"You shouldn't be here." Olivia had risen to her feet, and her voice was surprisingly harsh. She sounded as if she was on the verge of a temper tantrum. Or tears.

For a moment, Ivo was confused, thinking she was talking to him, that *he* shouldn't be here. After all, she had already told him she couldn't risk being in his company. Again, he felt that dip in his mood, remembering how things used to be, but he quickly pushed it aside when he saw that it was her siblings she was glowering at. Vivienne put her hands on the girls' heads in a protective manner. "They have promised to be good," she said. "Their governess has been seconded by your grandmother to help with preparations for the ball, so they have been left to their own devices."

"Always a dangerous state of affairs." Justina gave a grimace. "Where is Antonia?"

"She is helping set up the archery competition."

"Archery?" Roberta brightened suddenly. "Can I—"

"Not for you," Olivia said in that hard little voice. "Not after yesterday."

Roberta shot her a fulminating look but after an inner struggle said, "I am going to apologize for that."

"An apology does not make it better," her sister retorted, as if that was the end of the matter. She was beginning to sound unnervingly like her grandmother at her most formidable.

"But it helps," Vivienne reminded them as she led the way to the table. "Now, girls, what will you have to eat? Sausage and bacon and eggs? Toast and tea?"

"Black pudding," Roberta murmured, and then laughed softly when her sisters pulled disgusted faces.

"When does the archery start?" Ivo turned and carried his plate to the table, choosing to sit beside his sisters and Annette. That left a nice, safe gap between himself and the Ashton girls.

"At ten," Justina answered him. She gave a little jump, as if Olivia had pinched her under cover of the table, and her expression turned resolute. "I do hope you will be participating, Your Grace. There will be prizes."

Ivo smiled. "Ah, then I will certainly participate. I have not shot an arrow in a contest for some time." Archery had been fashionable among ladies and gentlemen during the last century, but more recently, with the war in France, its popularity had declined.

"Oh, we are all excellent archers," Justina assured him. She slid her sister a sly look. "Especially Olivia. She is a champion."

"Is she now?" Ivo hesitated as he speared a piece of sausage with his fork. "Then I accept the challenge. But do not expect me to let you win, ladies. I am not that much of a gentleman." Olivia had accused him once of not being a gentleman and, as he had hoped, she remembered.

Her head jerked up, and her eyes narrowed. He gave her a bland smile. She was trying so hard to be proper, the perfect wife for the prince, that she may well decide it would be better to bow out of the archery. Which would be a pity. Ivo didn't think that trying to be perfect was making Olivia very happy.

"Are you really going to shoot arrows, Ivo?" Adelina asked doubtfully. "We thought we would go for a walk. There is a nice view from the Grecian folly on the estate, or so I am told."

"It is certainly a pretty outlook," Vivienne said with a smile. "I go there when I want some time to myself."

Ivo suspected the new Duchess of Grantham frequently needed time to contemplate her new relatives.

"Thinking time?" Annette asked brightly, and then seemed to reconsider the question.

He watched as the cousins exchanged a speaking look. What was *that* about? There seemed to be an awful lot of secrets and mystery circulating. Which reminded him that the last thing he should be doing was joining in an archery contest where Olivia was a participant. Not if he wanted to keep secret his own ridiculous obsession with her.

And yet...he couldn't seem to help himself. The memory of her words last night still rankled, but perversely, he had enjoyed seeing her lose control. Perhaps if he could provoke her again, she would admit to herself that the path she had chosen was the wrong one. That Ivo was far more compatible with her than the prince, and she should be sorry she had refused him. So sorry that she may in fact change her mind...?

Hardly the wishes of a gentleman. Better if his hope was to show her how unhappy she would be with Prince Nikolai so she could escape that particular fate and go on to live a more fulfilling life. And if he was an unselfish sort of fellow, *that* would be his goal. Ivo wished he could be better, he really did, but he was not quite there yet.

The contestants in the archery sets were split into two teams, each with a target to shoot at. Ivo, Annette, and his sisters formed one team, while Charles, Gabriel, Olivia, and Justina were on the other team. The older women had decided it was more sensible to rest and chat in one of the sitting rooms, and save their energy for the ball tonight. The viscount was reading the newspaper, while Vivienne was amusing the younger Ashton girls—keeping them out of mischief—with the help of her brother. The prince was who knew where, and frankly, Ivo wasn't sorry for his absence.

The game began in a friendly enough manner. Ivo's team spent a lot of time giggling, while Charles and Gabriel were so deep in conversation that they had to be reminded when it was their turn. Justina blushed whenever Charles looked her way, and blushed even more when he attempted to show her how best to hold the bow. Watching the couple with amusement, Ivo thought Charles was being remarkably patient with the young woman. Gentle. Perhaps the tender feelings he had noticed previously were not just on Justina's part, although seeing Gabriel's frown as he watched them, Ivo wondered if anything more could come of it.

Eventually, the others dropped away, either through choice or disqualification, and the two best archers, or perhaps the only two who were taking the contest seriously, were left to face each other.

Ivo and Olivia.

Ivo supposed he could be a gentleman and bow out, allowing Olivia to win by default. But when the opportunity came and she turned to him, her expression hostile, it felt as if she wished anyone else in the world was facing her, anyone but Ivo. Did she hate him so much? Her behavior irritated and disappointed him, and it made his decision an easy one.

He was not going to be a gentleman.

To decide the winner, they would play one set, with each of them having three arrows to fire at the target. The one with the highest score would be declared the champion. With the first arrow, they both hit the bull's-eye, to the cheers of those who had stayed to watch. On the second shot, Olivia took up her position, focused on the target, and was just about to fire her arrow when a loud voice from behind them called her name. Her shot went astray.

"Lady Olivia!" It was Prince Nikolai, seemingly unaware that he had just caused her to miss. He continued talking. "I thought we could walk in the garden. Your sister has apologized," he added, and then frowned, as if he wasn't quite sure whether Roberta had been truly sorry or not. The girl in question was standing a little way behind him, watching on with a scowl.

Olivia took a deep breath, and Ivo tried not to laugh out loud as he saw her grappling with her desire to tell the prince exactly what she thought of his intrusion. "I'm glad to hear it," she managed with a forced smile.

Olivia was trying so hard to be perfect, but Ivo could

see by the tight line of her mouth, and the flash of irritation in her blue eyes, that it was a losing battle. He decided to encourage her to reveal her true, competitive self.

"You could forfeit," he suggested with a smile as false as hers.

She flashed him a fulminating look. "I am going to win!" Hastily rearranging her features, she turned back to the prince, and spoke in a softer tone of voice. "My apologies, sir, but I need to finish this game. I will be happy to walk with you…soon." She caught sight of her sister lurking near a bush. "Until then, I am sure Roberta will be happy to show you the gardens."

Roberta opened her mouth as if to protest, and then, catching her older sister's eye, swallowed the words. "Of course," she said dutifully.

The prince hesitated, glancing between the two, and then, with a shrug, strolled away with his hands behind his back, Roberta trotting by his side. Just before they disappeared around a bend in the path, she turned back and poked out her tongue.

Olivia wasn't watching. She straightened and drew back her bow string with impressive strength, her eyes narrowed on the target. "Now," she said, "I am going to end this debate between us, Northam, once and for all."

Chapter Eleven

E xcept she didn't.

 Furiously, Olivia kicked at some innocent flowers encroaching on the garden path and strode on toward the house. It occurred to her that she should look for the prince, and repair whatever damage she had done by sending him off with Roberta, but the thought of making polite conversation made her want to scream. The rivalry between herself and Ivo had grown more intense the longer the contest had gone on. It didn't even make sense why she had wanted that victory so much. She had felt as if nothing else mattered. And he hadn't even been apologetic about beating her. He'd laughed in her face and suggested she needed to practice before their next challenge. It seemed that these days, they could not be together without trying to injure each other with their eyes and their words.

 Olivia clenched her hands and wished she *could* scream. The man was infuriating. It was his fault she was behaving in a manner she knew was unbecoming. Right now, she needed to be on her best behavior for Prince Nikolai, and instead, she had palmed him off on her sister. What was it about Ivo that made her act so thoughtlessly?

 But worst of all, and even more confusing, she had felt more *alive* during their game than she had felt for ages. As if he had lit a spark inside her and it was burning bright.

Someone was hurrying up behind her, and with an effort, she arranged her face into a more ladylike expression and turned, only to find it was Ivo again. She scowled.

"What do you want?"

He laughed, as if her foul temper amused him. He didn't seem to care if she was out of sorts, he simply accepted that as a normal part of her character—he accepted *her*—and suddenly, she felt as if she might burst into tears.

"I was going to suggest we play that game of billiards we never finished," he said cheerfully.

Despite knowing that agreeing to such a thing would be a terrible mistake, Olivia hesitated. What she *should* do was go and find the prince. But Ivo was grinning at her, daring her, as if he knew how conflicted she was. How *infuriated*, so that she could hardly think straight. He sent her emotions into a topsy-turvy spin, and she needed to stop it right now.

"No," she bit out.

He looked surprised. Had he really expected her to agree?

"Did you listen to me at all last night?" she said, trying to keep her voice low and level. "I can't risk another scandal. My future depends upon it."

His green eyes searched hers, and she almost believed him to be sincere. "Olivia, you are making a mistake. You are trying to turn yourself into someone who isn't remotely like you."

"How do you know what I'm like?"

"I do know. We have a great deal in common."

She blinked up at him, feeling that odd, teary emotion again.

"Perhaps you do," she said, her voice scratchy. "Perhaps I am a little like you. But I can't let that side of me win, Ivo. You must see that. I must fight it. I can't let my family...my sisters...myself down."

His mouth quirked up into a humorless smile. "And you think marrying Prince Nikolai will give you everything you want?"

"Of course." Could he not see that? "A title, wealth, an entrée into the best houses. Sometimes I remember my life here at Grantham, before Grandmama, before Gabriel...We were hungry, Ivo, we were cold. There was no one who cared. Who knows what would have happened to us if they hadn't come to our rescue? I don't want that time back again."

He took an impulsive step toward her, as if to comfort her, but Olivia took a step back. She shook her head.

"Olivia..."

But she was already hurrying along the path, putting as much distance between them as she could. This was not the time to be close to the man who made her feel so confused and vulnerable. It was far too dangerous.

Once Olivia had tidied herself, washed her face, and gone downstairs again, she found luncheon surprisingly enjoyable. She believed she had redeemed herself with the prince, who had seemed a bit wary of her when they first sat down but was now all smiles and flattering glances. Perhaps turning him down for that walk in the garden had been a good thing—not many people opted to do other than what he wanted, so her refusal to stroll with him made her unique.

"The countryside around Grantham is very pretty," he said, with a glance at her. "But I think you will find Holtswig superior. If…when you visit."

That sounded promising despite his haughtiness. Olivia smiled back. "I would enjoy that, sir."

No more was said, the subject was changed, but Olivia caught her grandmother's approving gaze and felt very pleased with herself.

Vivienne asked her to help with the decorations in the afternoon, and they swathed the staircase and doorways with greenery and took down the draperies over the windows, shook them out, and then replaced them. The orchestra Grandmama had arranged for the occasion was practicing, its music drifting through the house.

"This is a great deal of work for a newlywed," Olivia said with a glance at her sister-in-law, who was trying not to sneeze. "Aren't you a little daunted?"

Vivienne thought for a moment and then smiled. "Not at all," she said. "Well, perhaps a little, but I love being part of your family. It was awful after the lessons were finished and I no longer was. I missed you all so much, and I am so glad that now I belong to you for real."

Olivia shook her head. "How can you say that?" she said in disbelief. "I would like nothing more than to escape Grantham forever."

Vivienne seemed to be considering whether she meant it. "You'd miss your sisters," she replied at last.

"No, I wouldn't," Olivia declared fiercely.

"Not even Justina?"

Justina was still sulking from last night, when Olivia

had dragged her away from Charles's kisses, and so far, Olivia's attempts to repair their relationship had been rebuffed. Just when Olivia needed her favorite sister most, Justina had absented herself.

Vivienne broke into her reverie. "Do you really want to marry Prince Nikolai? You know you don't have to. Gabriel would never allow your grandmother to force you into a marriage you did not want."

Olivia looked at her in surprise. Surely Vivienne wasn't agreeing with Ivo? "But I *do* want to marry him. Don't you see? It would be the solution to everything."

And yet Vivienne still looked as if she wasn't convinced. "Surely not everything?"

Olivia ignored her question and asked one of her own. "What is it like, to be married?"

Vivienne smiled in a soft, dreamy sort of way. "It's wonderful," she said. "Well, it is if you love the person you are married to."

"Not everyone can find a person they love."

"You won't if you don't look."

Olivia thought about responding, but what was the point. Vivienne didn't understand, and Olivia was tired of explaining. Instead, she suggested they begin replacing the candles in their sconces, and the two of them started their new task in silence.

Olivia refused to feel depressed. A moment ago, she had been full of hope for her chosen future. She reminded herself that a great many people didn't love their marriage partners. They married because of other reasons, and surely it was better not to love your partner too much anyway. There were just too many ways to hurt one's beloved and make them miserable, and Olivia had already seen enough of that in her life. Her grandmother had the right idea. Marry for position and wealth, and then live in comfort for the rest of your life.

Then why did the words ring so hollow? Why did she feel as if she had somehow or other stepped off onto the wrong path?

⁂

Supper was served on a tray to her room. She was already dressed for the ball because the maid was run off her feet, and Olivia had offered to be first. Her gown was white, plain but elegant, one of those made by Madame Annabelle, the modiste for Olivia's London Season. Due to that Season being cut short, it had never been worn. Her hair was dressed simply too, with some fresh flowers tucked in among the dark locks, while a single strand of pearls encircled her throat. Unlike her coming-out in May, tonight was all about Gabriel and Vivienne, and she was quite happy to stand back and allow them to be the center of attention.

Once the maid had gone, she took a bite of her supper, and had barely swallowed the first mouthful when there was a tap on the door. Before she could call out, a note was pushed beneath it, and light footsteps hurried away.

Olivia knelt to retrieve the slip of paper and opened it.

Meet me at the archery targets at seven o'clock. I have something of great importance to ask you. And it was signed, *Niki.*

Niki? As in Prince Nikolai? But why…? And then she read it again. *I have something of great importance to ask you.*

Could this be what she had been hoping for? He *had* been very attentive at lunch. And yet it seemed too sudden. Too soon. And definitely too casual for the prince. His proposal would be formal, a stilted recital of his desire to make her his wife, and what he expected from her. Olivia read the note again. She did not even know Nikolai's writing to compare. And yet why would someone else send her such a note? Could her refusal to stroll with the prince this morning really have stung him into action? Olivia wished she could talk to Justina, ask what she thought, but Justina wasn't speaking to her.

She had to go. It was already nearly seven o'clock, and the ball was due to start at eight. She could not be late for that, but if Prince Nikolai—or Niki, as she must learn to call him—was asking her to marry him, then what would being late to the ball matter?

Her mind made up, she found her cloak and wrapped it about her. She tucked her gloves into the pocket just in case she couldn't return to her room in time. But surely she wouldn't be gone that long? Not that anyone would notice, they were all so busy. As she quickly descended the stairs, she tried to ignore the slightly sick feeling in her stomach. Olivia prepared a story about needing to find a maid to sew on a button, but it was unnecessary— she didn't meet anyone. Soon she was making her way along the path through the garden in the direction of the targets. The sky was turning pink and mauve, and as she passed through the perennial border with its scented flowers, there were moths flitting from plant to plant. A bird shrieked and flew up into its tree, which gave her a start. There was another rustle from somewhere behind her, but when she spun around and peered into the shadows, there was nothing to be seen. A fox, she thought, or a hare.

The fright had made her breath come quickly, and she wondered again whether she was doing the right thing. Too late to change her mind now, she was nearly at the archery targets, and yet she lingered. It was as if…as if she didn't want to do this. Didn't want to take that irrevocable step. Which was ridiculous because marriage to the prince was now her goal. Love was all very well, but Olivia was not Vivienne.

Quickening her steps, she turned the bend in the path. Nearly there now. Despite the shadows that stretched long across the lawn where the archery targets were still set up, she could see a figure standing there. Waiting.

Niki?

Her steps stuttered as the man turned to face her. Because this wasn't Prince Nikolai after all. It was the Duke of Northam.

Chapter Twelve

He was formally dressed, although he had removed his tailed coat. He had also forgone the cream breeches worn on formal occasions for a pair of pantaloons, which displayed to advantage the shape of his legs. His fair hair was pomaded into a Brutus, but the plain style suited him, and his face was cleanly shaven above his perfectly tied cravat. There was a jeweled pin in the snowy white cloth which twinkled in the evening light.

He was very handsome.

And she must be in shock, because this was not the moment to be cataloguing Ivo's attributes when she was meant to be meeting Niki. Unless…

"You did this!" Olivia shouted furiously. "You want to ruin my life!"

She moved toward him, not realizing she meant to strike him until he caught her wrist in a firm grip. His eyes blazed into hers.

"Ruin your life? You invited me here. Seven o'clock at the archery targets. A rematch."

She stared up at him, trying to make sense of it. "I didn't…" she croaked. "*You* sent a note to *me*." Or at least Prince Nikolai did.

It was Ivo's turn to stare.

"Didn't you?" she whispered in confusion. As soon

as she'd seen him, she had immediately jumped to the conclusion that this was Ivo's doing. But if it had been he who sent the note, he wouldn't lie about it. And he would have boldly signed his own name. No, reckless he might be, but this was not the sort of underhanded thing Ivo would do.

Ivo drew in a breath. He was still holding her wrist, but now his fingers had slipped down to her hand. Their fingers interlaced as if it was natural for them to do so.

"I sent no note. I was surprised when you changed your mind and wanted to meet me, after you had made it clear to me earlier that you weren't interested. I respected your wishes." She went to object, but he cut her short. "Yes, I know I haven't always respected them. You called me thoughtless, and I am, but to accuse me of ruining your life? Olivia, I won't do that."

Olivia tried to order her thoughts. There was complete sincerity in his face and in his voice. She believed him. But if he hadn't sent the note, and neither had she, then who had? "I don't understand why someone would try to bring us together." She looked about her as if expecting the culprit to step out of the shrubs and declare themselves.

"A joke from one of your sisters?"

That was a possibility, she supposed, but it seemed too malicious, too spiteful.

Ivo said in a low voice, "Whoever did this, I'm glad they did."

Olivia lost track of her thoughts. "You're *glad*?"

"I want to talk to you. Every time I try to talk, we argue or are interrupted." He gave her an intense, searching look, awareness in those green depths. "I do not agree with your motives when it comes to the prince, but I will accept your choices. I understand, Olivia. I just don't…"

He lifted her hand and to her surprise brushed his lips across her knuckles. His voice deepened when he spoke. "I don't like it."

Olivia found it difficult to breathe. The light was fading, and the world had gone still apart from the birds calling softly as they settled for the night. "Why? Why don't you like it?"

"Because he is *wrong* for you. He'll make you miserable. So miserable that all the furs and diamonds in the world will not remedy it. I know you, Olivia."

"These days, I hardly know myself," she whispered.

"You need someone who can make you smile when you have the megrims. Someone who understands you can't be sensible all the time. The prince is…" He paused, his shoulders straightening, his face taking on a familiar, haughty expression.

Laughter bubbled up inside her, along with a connection to him she struggled to resist. He made her feel as if she was caught in a tidal rip, being dragged in his direction despite all of her resolutions. "Don't," she said sharply.

"Why not?" His mouth twitched up into a wry smile. "You used to find my impressions amusing."

"Yes, but now I need to be sensible and serious. I need to think of a future that will benefit my whole family."

"Rather than one that will make you happy?" His eyes searched hers. "Do you know, you hurt me when you rejected my offer of marriage."

She was softening toward him, and she must not. "Ivo, please—"

"No, let me say it." He shifted awkwardly, and she realized he was feeling uncomfortable. "Afterward, I was hurt, and I wanted to hurt you too. Childish, but there it is." Why hadn't he spoken like this to her the day of his proposal? Honestly and frankly. "But I do understand why you think Prince Nikolai is the right choice. You see happiness as a small price to pay for all the good his wealth and prestige will bring to you. You have five sisters. I understand, I really do. I have only two sisters, and I find the expense of supporting them and keeping them in bonnets keeps me awake most nights."

He had made her laugh despite herself.

His voice became serious again. "But you cannot live your life for your sisters, Olivia. It would be such a waste."

That hurt. There was a hollow ache in her chest, and she found herself wrestling with the longing to throw herself into his arms, and that would never do. "Nikolai might have hidden depths," she managed in a voice that tried to be indifferent.

"Ask Leopold. If anyone knows about the prince's hidden depths, then it is his stallion."

This time, she shook her head and covered her face with her hands. "Olivia," he murmured, the wretch, and drew her into his arms.

She could feel the steady beat of his heart and smell the vanilla scent of his pomade. She felt dizzy. He lifted her chin and gazed down at her, and she felt helpless to resist him. The pull of him was drawing her inexorably closer. How did he do this to her? What was it about him that meant that all her good intentions could be overturned in a moment?

He cupped her cheek in his palm, and his warm breath touched her lips. "I want to kiss you," he said, his voice deep with longing. "Will you let me?"

No, she thought. *Definitely not*. And at the same time, Olivia stood up on her tiptoes as she slipped her arms around his neck and brushed her lips against his.

He froze, as if her forwardness had surprised him, but it was only for a moment and then he capitulated. Ivo leaned in, pressing his lips to hers more firmly. His tongue slid along her bottom lip, and he tugged gently with his teeth. She gasped, and he moaned, as if he were as powerless as she. His mouth caressed hers, and it felt amazing. A million emotions swam up inside her, while her blood caught fire, and her legs trembled so that she wondered if she would fall without him holding her up. This was like nothing she had ever experienced before, and yet the warning signs had been there. Some part of her had known from the moment they first met that he could be her downfall.

"I want you," he said, nuzzling against her, peppering her with little kisses, as if he would cover her entirely.

"I want you too." And right now, she did want him.

The words were barely out of her mouth when there was a shout.

"Olivia!"

Gabriel came striding from the shadows so suddenly that Olivia struggled to understand exactly what was happening. The heat and the desire that had her head spinning received a dash of cold water, and common sense came rushing back.

"Gabriel," she managed to speak as he reached them. She had not seen her brother this angry since the night of the billiards match. For a moment, she was seized by a cowardly urge to turn and run, hide herself in the lush foliage that surrounded the clearing, and wait until this was over. It was a lily-livered impulse, and Olivia was never that, so she stood her ground. Her fingers were being crushed in a viselike grip, and that was when she realized she and Ivo were still holding hands. With a wordless cry, she pulled away, putting distance between them.

Ivo cleared his throat, giving Olivia an apologetic glance before he spoke. "It isn't as you think, Grantham."

"What do I think, Northam?" Gabriel glared at Ivo, disgust in every line of him. "That you have indulged in another of your ridiculous wagers? What was it this time? Ruin Olivia? Oh wait, you already tried that."

Ivo straightened. He sounded as if he was trying to keep his anger under control. "Someone sent us both notes with a time and a place for a meeting. Mine was signed Olivia, and Olivia's...?" He looked to her as if realizing he did not know the answer.

"Prince Nikolai," she said.

Gabriel waved a hand to dismiss their excuses. "You were kissing!" he roared. He seemed to recollect himself and took a breath. "You were kissing," he said more quietly. "Don't you realize how serious this is? Anyone could have seen you. What a wonderful piece of gossip it would be. Word would spread like a spark in dry kindling, and before we knew it, you'd be utterly and completely ruined."

He was right. Olivia knew he was right. A vision flashed into her head, another of those dreadful cartoons depicting herself and Ivo, clasped together. She had tried so hard to be good, to do as she knew she ought, and in a single, rash moment, all of her efforts had been consigned to oblivion.

"I am sincerely sorry," Ivo said, and his voice sounded shakier than she had ever heard it. "This is my fault." He shot a glance at Olivia, and she had the awful feeling he was going to ask her to marry him. Again. And she would have to refuse him. Again.

Gabriel barely gave him a glance, his voice gruff with restrained fury. "I wish to speak to my sister alone, Northam. Perhaps you could escort Georgia back to the house and make an appearance at the ball before everyone notices you're both missing. I will deal with you later."

Georgia.

Of course! Her most disliked sister. That explained the sensation that someone was following her through the garden. Georgia would have loved running to fetch Gabriel and tell him her tales. Olivia peered into the gloom and saw the girl, hovering at the edge of the clearing. "You will be sorry—" she began.

"Stop it," Gabriel barked. "Georgia has done nothing wrong. Unlike you." Then, with barely a glance at Ivo, "Are you still here?"

Anyone else would have left immediately, and yet Ivo remained. "Olivia, do you want me to stay?" he asked quietly.

She supposed it was courageous of him, but it would only make matters worse. "No," she said. "Please, go. The ball will have started…What if people wonder where we are?"

There was no answer to that. Ivo gave a somber nod, and set off toward the path, where Georgia waited.

Olivia spoke before Gabriel could. "Did…Do you think anyone noticed?"

"Of course they did! It was your mother who drew everyone's attention to the fact you were missing."

Olivia stared back at him. Her *mother* had drawn

attention to her absence. In normal circumstances, one could assume Felicia was worried, but Olivia did not think that was the case. Mischievous was more likely. Manipulative. Olivia could well be ruined because of it. But no, Olivia had done this to herself. All of her hard work, all of her promises, and after a few moments alone with Ivo, this was the result.

"Well, have you nothing to say?"

Olivia's voice broke. "Gabriel, I truly am sorry. So sorry. I don't know what…why…Is it over? My last chance?"

He shook his head, then looked to the heavens as if he could find an answer to her behavior there. The stars twinkled down in silence. Gabriel held out his arm to her. "I don't know," he said, "but we need to get back." She slid her trembling fingers into the crook of his elbow. "Don't despair yet. I'll make up some nonsense," he went on as they walked back through the garden. "I thought you had learned your lesson, but Northam seems to bring out the worst in you." They took the path to the side of the house, farthest away from the chatter of the guests and the music from the orchestra.

"I don't understand it either," she said in a bewildered way because she truly was bemused by her behavior. It was as if that fire Ivo had lit in her was impossible to put out, and no matter how hard she tried, it kept reigniting. Was this her life from now on? Would she become an outcast from the society she had so longed to inhabit? Her spirits sank with each step she took.

"My advice is to stay away from him."

He wanted to believe this was all Ivo's fault. She would have shown him the note, but it was in her room, and besides, he'd probably think Ivo wrote it to deceive her.

Gabriel had stopped. "Well?" he said bleakly. "This really will be your final chance, Olivia. I don't have the time or the patience to keep digging you out of these holes. You have five sisters who need my help. Your actions reflect on them. You *know* this."

"Yes. Please. I promise never to do this again. I'm so, so sorry."

He nodded, but his expression didn't soften. "Unfortunately, your mother made her concerns about your absence known to Prince Nikolai. She didn't exactly say that you and Northam were an item, but one could easily draw that conclusion. As you know, the prince is a stickler for the rules, and to be embroiled in scandal would send him off on that stallion of his at a gallop."

That was too much to take in. Her mother had spoken to the prince, and Olivia may well have lost her chance to win him.

"Look, Vivienne seems to think you want to marry the man, Olivia, but if you don't, you have only to say. Don't let our grandmother bully you into doing something you don't want to do. I know how that feels. But no more scandals, do you hear me?" He had turned to her, and despite the shadows, she knew he was watching her keenly.

If anyone knew about being pressured into marriage against one's wishes, it was Gabriel. For a time, he had believed it his duty to ignore his heart, but thankfully, he had woken up.

"It's not as simple as that," she said.

"Olivia, it is. Something I have learned the hard way. It is very simple—you just have to make the choice that is right for you. As long as it isn't Northam. I draw the line there."

She found her voice again. "I *do* want to marry the prince. I'm sorry, Gabriel. It will not happen again."

He raised his eyebrows as if he didn't believe her, which in the circumstances was understandable. "If you genuinely mean it, then you will need to repair the damage your mother has caused. Perhaps it was well meant." But he didn't sound as if he entirely believed that.

"My mother hates you," Olivia interrupted urgently. "I saw her watching you during dinner last night and... Don't trust her, Gabriel. I think she is up to something."

He frowned. "Up to what, exactly?"

But Olivia didn't know the answer. Had her mother been responsible for the notes that had brought Ivo and Olivia together? Was she intentionally trying to obstruct the Ashtons' bid to return to their rightful place in the ton? A bitter revenge for all she had suffered? They had reached the side door into the house, and Gabriel opened it. The noise grew louder as they approached the ballroom, which was brightly lit, with guests whirling, fine clothing rippling, and jewelry twinkling. They looked like actors on a stage, and Olivia felt anxious and on edge. She had to join them and play her part. Her very last chance, Gabriel had said, and she had to take it. Gabriel paused just beyond the reach of the candles. "Ready?"

She managed a feeble smile. "Will you dance with me?"

"Of course I will," he said, and led her into the ballroom.

Chapter Thirteen

The first face Olivia saw through the blur of well-dressed guests was her mother, wearing that little satisfied smile that caused her eldest daughter so much consternation. The second was Prince Nikolai's, and his expression was the epitome of disgust, his nostrils flaring as if he had scented a mate who was disappointing. Her heart sank, but before she could react, her grandmother bustled toward them, shooting a questioning glance at Gabriel, which he answered with a nod.

"There you are, Gabriel," she said, completely ignoring Olivia. "Vivienne, where are you?"

Hearing her name, Vivienne glanced up from her conversation with her cousin. She was particularly beautiful tonight in an apricot silk gown, her hair arranged simply, and the famous Ashton emeralds about her neck. She looked more like a duchess every day. When the dowager beckoned her impatiently, she sent Gabriel a wry look before moving to join them.

The dowager took their hands in both of hers and raised her voice. "Everyone! Everyone, please pay attention!"

The music had stopped, and now there was a murmur of anticipation before silence fell. Servants hurriedly carried around trays of champagne for the toast.

"We are gathered here tonight to celebrate the marriage

of my grandson, Gabriel, the Duke of Grantham, to his duchess, Vivienne. Let us wish them every happiness." She joined their hands together before stepping away.

There was a rousing cheer. Olivia joined in, and Gabriel put his arm around his wife's waist and leaned down to kiss her chastely on the lips. They shared a look that made Olivia's chest ache a little, because it said so much about their feelings for each other. It made her wonder if such happiness could ever be hers before she reminded herself that she wasn't looking for that sort of happiness. She had made her choice—if she hadn't botched it up.

The prince stood alone with a champagne glass in his hand. He was looking bored. She needed to speak to him, she needed to…Her disobedient gaze slid to Ivo. He was with his mother and sisters, all raising their glasses to the happy couple. But he wasn't looking at Gabriel and Vivienne. Instead, he was watching her, a frown upon his handsome face. He seemed to be asking her if everything was all right. Her lips tingled, reliving that kiss, and something about the sudden gleam in his green eyes made her think he was remembering it too.

Her arm was taken in a painful grip.

"Ouch!"

Her grandmother was beside her, and there was no doubting her displeasure. As the orchestra struck up again, Gabriel and Vivienne began to dance before the interested eyes of the guests. Once everyone was otherwise occupied, the dowager tugged Olivia away into a private alcove by the windows.

"Don't you realize the chance I have given you?" Her whisper was low and angry, as if even in the midst of her fury, she was conscious of listening ears and potential gossip. "Don't you care that you will end up as soiled goods? That no gentleman will offer for you? That you will be abandoned by society and grow old and alone?"

The picture she painted came from Olivia's worst nightmares, and she suspected it was meant to. She felt ill as she forced herself to meet those dark eyes. "I am so sorry, Grandmama. I apologize. I…It won't happen again."

Her grandmother pinned her with a look that would have sent most people to their knees. "Are you sure? Because it seems to me you have an unhealthy obsession with Northam, and he has done nothing to dissuade you. He is a reckless fellow, just like his father. I remember the late duke well; he was a notorious seducer. Do you really think the son is any different? And Ivo will probably die the same way, thrown from his mount while trying to win some ridiculous wager."

Olivia swallowed. "I'll stay away from him," she spoke through dry lips.

The dowager glared. "No. I don't want it said the two of you acted like guilty children. You will dance with him, one dance, and you will behave as if it is nothing more than a duty dance. Appear as if you are bored. Do you understand?"

"Yes," she replied. "I'm sorry—"

But the dowager hadn't finished. "I will not be here forever to guide the family in the right direction, and I had hoped that when the time came, you would take over my role, Olivia. Do not disappoint me again."

Tears burned Olivia's eyes. "I won't," she whispered in a wobbly voice.

"Speak up!"

She lifted her chin and straightened her back. "I won't," she said firmly. The tears were gone.

"Very well." The dowager's gaze swept over her, and now it was approving. "Return to the ball and play your part, child."

On shaky legs, Olivia did as she was told.

By now, Gabriel and Vivienne had finished their dance, and the ballroom was once more full of elegantly dressed guests enjoying themselves. "Olivia!" A loud and excited whisper came from the gallery above, and Olivia spied her younger sisters, enjoying the scene below. Roberta was there too, a far more subdued Roberta than usual, and Olivia discovered she had some fellow feeling for her tonight. It seemed that the Ashton girls were forever destined to muck up. Well, she reminded herself, that was in the past now, and she had much work to do to redeem herself in the prince's eyes.

With her smile firmly in place, she moved toward the prince, who was now in conversation with Viscount Monteith. About horses, no doubt. She reminded herself to make a study of horses and the sport of racing so that she could converse intelligently about it. Perhaps Roberta could help her? She seemed to live and breathe the creatures.

At her approach, the prince looked up, his face politely blank. He was very proud, she already knew that, and very aware of his consequence. His wife must never put a foot wrong. She would need to stay within his strict guidelines and deport herself as one of those lucky few who belonged to the very upper echelons of society. Could Olivia be that woman?

You will be abandoned by society and grow old and alone.

Her grandmother's words made her even more determined to rise to the occasion.

"Sir," she said, curtsying low. "I do hope you are enjoying the music."

"Music?" He looked about as if he had forgotten he was attending a ball, and wasn't particularly pleased to be hunted down in this manner. "Ah, yes, it is very, eh…" Clearly the prince knew as much about music as Olivia knew about horses.

Monteith, bless him, clapped the younger man on

the shoulder. "Dance with the beautiful Lady Olivia, sir. Enjoy yourself. We can talk later."

The prince seemed on the verge of refusing, but slighting her before her family and friends would have been both callous and rude, and she did not think protocol would allow him to be either of those things. He bowed stiffly and held out his hand. "May I?" he asked.

With a relieved smile, Olivia placed her gloved fingers in his.

He was a handsome young man and a good dancer, every step precise and practiced. All the same, there was something unemotional about the prince's performance—as if it was just that, a performance, made because it was necessary and not with any pleasure.

When the silence between them had lasted longer than she could bear, Olivia sought to make conversation. "Are you enjoying your visit? Apart from my sister purloining your stallion."

His lips twisted up slightly, as if her plain speaking amused him. "Apart from that, yes, I am enjoying my visit. Your family is very hospitable."

"Is yours not hospitable too?"

"My father died when I was young, and my mother is rarely at home, but I prefer my own company."

Should she say she was sorry to hear that? It didn't sound as if he wanted her pity.

"I ride a great deal when I am at home. It is my solace."

"Are there mountains?" Olivia realized as she said it that he probably did not ride up and down mountains, but although he raised his eyebrows, the prince did not ridicule her question.

"There are mountains, yes, but my home is surrounded by forests."

He seemed to relax further as he described the countryside in Holtswig. It sounded chilly, but Olivia nodded and smiled enthusiastically, and by the time the dance had ended, the prince was once more sending her those flattering glances.

Relieved, she left him with his next partner and made her way to Gabriel and Vivienne, only to find Ivo bowing before her, and asking her to dance.

A duty dance, she reminded herself as she agreed, to kill off the speculation. As he took her in his arms, his hands were firm and warm, his steps fluid and elegant. This time, it was Olivia who was stiff and ill at ease in her partner's arms. Then he smiled at her. A warm, genuine smile. She could not help but smile back, until she remembered the part she was meant to be playing, and hastily wiped it from her face. Perhaps it was better not to look at him at all. She fixed her gaze on the dancers over his shoulder, and she spotted Justina in the arms of Charles Wickley.

"No!"

The word was muffled, but Ivo heard her and glanced around. "Whatever has made you look so fierce?" he asked curiously.

"I think my sister has a tendre for Charles Wickley." Olivia answered before she could think to stop herself.

"And that is something to be discouraged?" Ivo asked in a puzzled voice.

"I know he is Gabriel's friend, but he has nothing else to recommend him. And he has a reputation. Justina is too silly to realize he is playing with her."

At that moment, a smiling and blushing Justina noticed her sister was watching her. She leaned in to speak with Charles. He promptly whirled them away through the crowd and out of sight. Olivia sighed. She needed to mend her fences with Justina, but she didn't know how. Without her sister to share confidences with, and with Ivo forbidden to her, she felt very alone.

"I apologize for earlier." Ivo's soft words interrupted her thoughts.

"It wasn't your fault. Someone was trying to make trouble for us. Well, me."

"Georgia looked a little guilty when I escorted her back to the house," he offered.

Nothing would surprise her about Georgia, but to be fair, her sister could not have done this alone. The letters, the assignation…

"Georgia is a puppet, and someone else is pulling the strings." And Olivia thought she knew who that "someone" was.

"That sounds very ominous. Who is this puppet master?"

"My mother," she blurted out. "At least I think so."

"Ah." He frowned down at her. "Can I help?"

Surprised, she met his eyes and was momentarily dazzled by their green depths. "No. Thank you. Though that is very generous of you, after…" After his treatment at Gabriel's hands, and her own.

"I am a very generous person." He was laughing at her. His mouth twitched, and she tried not to remember kissing those lips. The way he had tugged on her lip so gently, causing an ache of need deep in her belly. It was still there, and this wasn't helping. The feel of her hand in his, the closeness of his body, the tilt of his head… Dancing with him had been a mistake. She opened her mouth to make some excuse, but he was already speaking.

"Have you repaired matters with the prince? I noticed him giving me dangerous looks."

Olivia almost tripped, forgetting to concentrate on

her steps, but Ivo was such a good dancer, he smoothed over her fumble. "What do you mean?"

"He's jealous," Ivo said. "Or at least he thinks he is. Maybe he's the possessive type."

"I don't…" Olivia was about to say, "I don't know him well enough to tell," but she guessed what Ivo would think of that.

"Did your grandmother scold you?"

"She reminded me of my priorities."

Ivo tightened his grip on her hand. "Well, you're safe for the moment."

It was an odd thing to say, and yet it was the truth. With him, she did feel safe. Ivo lifted her spirits, made the world a not-so-alarming place. She knew she needed to push him away once and for all because her future was with the prince in chilly Holtswig. Although she would make certain that they spent a good part of the year in London, because what was the point in marrying well if one could not show off one's good fortune?

Just for a moment, she saw herself in the future, snuggled in a fur-lined cloak with diamonds at her throat and the prince at her side—although he was far more at ease than he was now. Perhaps he had even put on a little weight and was laughing jovially.

"You are plotting something, Olivia," Ivo spoke close to her ear, his warm breath stirring the curls that lay against her cheek. "You have that dreamy look that bodes ill for someone."

Olivia gave a brittle laugh. "You have a vivid imagination, Northam."

He smiled down at her, not believing her for a moment, and once again, she remembered their kisses. It really wasn't fair that he had this effect on her. And why did he have that warm, intimate note in his voice? As if despite this room full of people, they were the only ones in it?

A glance about showed her that her grandmother was watching. Another glance, and she saw Prince Nikolai was watching too.

Olivia knew she needed to put an end to the sense of intimacy that was developing between Ivo and herself. She needed to stop it once and for all.

Desperately, she said, "If you must know, I was wondering what the prince's castle in Holtswig is like. Castles, I should say, because I believe he has several. I imagine they are quite luxurious."

His smile faded, and the warmth left his handsome face. "Is that really what you want, Olivia? A luxurious castle and a cold husband?"

He made it sound wretched, but her smile grew brighter. "Nothing would please me more!" she said enthusiastically.

His gaze delved into hers, as if he was trying to discover whether she was being truthful, and then he nodded decisively.

"Then I wish you luck. I fear you will need it."

The music ended and he stepped back with a polite bow before walking away. She watched his back, aware of an aching emptiness inside at his departure. Sensing someone's gaze upon her, she turned, and once again, there was her grandmother. The dowager nodded her head in warm approval.

Olivia did not remember anyone ever showing her that sort of approval. Not her mother or her father, and not her grandmother until recently. It felt good. As if she was doing something right at last. She was determined to keep winning those looks from the dowager. And eventually, she hoped, that hollow ache in her chest would go away.

Chapter Fourteen

Ivo found it difficult to sleep. He knew he should not have said what he said to Olivia, even if it was true. He should have offered her encouragement and support. But how could he? He knew marrying Prince Nikolai would be a dreadful mistake. Yes, the prince might be rich and well connected, but Ivo believed that if she leg-shackled herself to that man, the bright, adventurous spirit inside her would wither and die. She would be forced into a mold that she did not fit, and it would eventually destroy her.

At the age of twenty-seven, Ivo had had his share of liaisons. For a time, he had even kept a mistress, but that had ended when she had up and married. It hadn't been love—Ivo did not think he had ever been in love—which was why this "feeling" he had for Olivia Ashton was so bloody confusing. After his proposal to her, he had thought his turbulent emotions would eventually settle, and he could be comfortable again. So far, that hadn't happened, and he suspected it wouldn't until he could have a good, long period of time without being in her presence. Kissing her and dancing with her only made things worse, and he was guiltily aware they had made things worse for her too.

Ivo groaned. What had he been thinking during those times they met together, before the disaster of the

Elphinstones' musical evening? He admitted he hadn't been thinking much at all. He had wanted to be with Olivia. Her company was like a bright star in his day, and yes, he had probably had ideas of kissing her and seeing where that led, but he had swiftly decided he did not want to hurt her. When he was with her, Ivo grew a conscience, which was very much at odds with his usual reckless behavior. He even felt ashamed of some of the foolish things he had done in the past, although he had refused to admit it.

Until now.

When they had kissed in the garden, it had felt like he had come home. But the precious moment with her in his arms did not seem to have meant as much to Olivia— she had shrugged it off easily enough with her talk of castles. Her decision was made, and he must accept it. He must not interfere in her life anymore. Tomorrow, he would make his excuses and go back to Whitmont. When he was once again embroiled in his own busy affairs, he would be able to put his disappointment behind him.

He recalled he had made a bet at his club. A horse race out into the country between himself and another gentleman, with the loser to be ducked into a pond at a nearby inn. It had seemed like an amusing thing to do at the time, but now... it made him feel uncomfortable. He could be doing something else far more important. He was the Duke of Northam, for God's sake!

He should be tending to his estate and running his smuggling operation. His man of business had sent Charles Wickley a formal agreement over the partnership in Cadieux's, and he should be thinking of that too, and how he could make the most of what promised to be an unexpected windfall.

Were his days as a risk-taker over? No, he didn't think so. He would always be that man, but it was time to restrain those selfish, more precarious impulses and look to a steadier future.

Eventually, he fell into a restless slumber, but the next morning he woke bleary-eyed and morose. Not his usual cheerful and charming self. At breakfast, his sisters eyed him with dismay, and Annette asked him if he was quite well.

"We can't all be little rays of sunshine," he said, which made her laugh. It was nice to be on good terms again with Annette. Apart from his sisters and his mother—and they were family—Ivo did not have many close female friends, and he had missed their conversations. For a time, Olivia had seemed like a friend, more than a friend, and their moments together were some of his most memorable. But he was determined to shut that door.

"I'm glad you are coming on the excursion today," Lexy said. "Mama is resting, but the viscountess will be braving the outdoors with us."

Annette blanched. "She still hasn't accepted we are not destined to marry," she said, dropping her voice. "She thinks that at some point, we will realize we are meant to be."

Ivo was aware that Viscountess Monteith was notoriously critical, her standards impossibly high, especially when it came to her daughter. Last night, he had told himself he would make some excuse and leave this morning, but could he really leave his friend when she needed him most?

"I will divert her attention," he said bravely, and received beaming smiles from the three women.

"Good morning."

Charles Wickley had arrived, looking as if *his* sleep last night had been fresh and worry-free. Seeing him now reminded Ivo that last night during their dance, Olivia had been concerned about her sister falling under Charles's spell.

Ivo could well understand that concern. Charles would not be the only gentleman to indulge in a fondness for the ladies, but if he was Ivo's half brother, then he may well have inherited their father's nasty habit of seducing every female who crossed his path. It didn't take much imagination for Ivo to see what would happen if Charles broke Justina's heart. Or worse, ruined her reputation. More turmoil for the Ashtons. But Ivo wasn't only thinking of Olivia's feelings; it would be awkward for him too. Charles was his associate in the smuggling venture, and soon to be his partner in a gambling club. It made sense for Ivo to warn him off before things became more complicated.

Ivo was deep in his thoughts, and it took a moment for him to realize that there was a heated discussion going on about where they should go for their excursion today. The weather promised to be good, and there were a number of beauty spots in the vicinity. The choice was between the coast, where the beaches were attractive contenders, or inland, where just beyond the borders of the Grantham estate was a well-known lookout, with stunning views over the surrounding area.

By the time Ivo rose from the table, the lookout appeared to have won. As he passed behind Charles, who was tucking into a hearty breakfast, he bent and spoke in a low voice. "Come and find me when you're done. We need to speak."

He didn't give the man a chance to reply but went on

his way. He would change into his riding outfit, wander down to the stables, and wait for the others.

☙

"Good morning."

Once again, Prince Nikolai was in the stable yard, watching as Otto walked the prize stallion back and forth. He looked up in surprise at Ivo's greeting, before giving him a brief nod of acknowledgment and turning back to whatever it was about the animal that was causing him to frown.

"Is he lame?" Ivo asked curiously, pausing by the prince's side.

Nikolai stiffened as though he had been sworn at. "No," he said in a sharp voice. "I think just a little soreness. That wretched girl rode him hard."

"That wretched girl" being Roberta. Despite her apology, it seemed that the prince had not forgiven her.

"Are you coming on the excursion?" Ivo asked. "You could ride Leopold. He might just need a leisurely trot to sort out his problems."

The prince ignored him as if Ivo wasn't worth the bother. *Charming!* Ivo gave up on the rude fellow and made his way into the stables to find his own mount. The others would be here soon, but he hoped Charles would reach him first so that they could have their "chat."

Ivo greeted the horses they had brought with them from Whitmont. He had been worried he might have to sell some of them but perhaps now he wouldn't have to. Just as he was making his choice of a suitable mount, he heard Charles speak his name.

The man looked as unruffled as he had earlier. He was dressed in a plain dark coat but with a colorful waistcoat beneath it, which seemed to be an idiosyncrasy, and his fair hair shone in the light from the stable doors.

"You wanted a word?" Charles asked with a smile, and raised an inquiring eyebrow.

For a moment, Ivo could only stare because that gesture was so familiar. He did it himself, but it was something his father also used to do. Ivo cleared his throat and gave a surreptitious glance about them to make sure there was no one within listening distance.

"I noticed at the ball you were dancing with Lady Justina. And at the archery contest, you seemed...close."

Charles's smile faded, and the friendliness left his eyes.

Ivo carried on. "I hope you have considered the disparity between her situation and yours."

"You don't think I'm good enough for her." It wasn't a question, and now there was a flush on the other man's cheeks. A sign of either anger or embarrassment.

"No, that is not what I meant. Justina is young and vulnerable, and you are a man with a certain reputation. You must see how your attentions to her could be misconstrued?"

"Misconstrued?" Charles echoed. Those familiar blue eyes were fixed on him with such intensity that Ivo, who rarely felt uncomfortable, wanted to squirm. He reminded himself that he was quite within his rights to talk of these things. Or was Charles such a cad that he would refuse to listen?

"Must I explain myself further?" Ivo said impatiently. "Surely you can see how Justina could take your attentions more seriously than they are intended. You would be wise to remove yourself from Grantham before matters cross that line. Put some distance between the two of you."

Because that was what Ivo would be doing.

Charles's eyes narrowed. His hands clenched into fists at his side. "Why are you telling me this?" he said in a muffled tone, very unlike his usual voice. "Are you Justina's protector? Isn't it up to Gabriel—who is my best friend, by the way—to remind me of my lowly position?" He was angry but containing it.

Ivo suspected he had pressed upon a tender spot. "I did not mean," he began awkwardly, forced into the unfamiliar position of explaining his high-handedness.

But Charles had heard enough. "Perhaps you should look to your own house before you start rummaging through mine," he said loudly enough to startle the nearby horses. "By my reckoning, you have twice jeopardized Olivia's chances of reentering society and making a decent match. You are in no position to throw stones, *Your Grace*."

Ivo flushed angrily. This was not going at all as he had expected. It was as if he and Charles were engaged in swordplay, and their words were drawing blood. "My actions are none of your business," he said through clenched teeth.

"Oh, are they not? And yet *my* life is *your* business?" Charles regarded Ivo quizzically, and that damned eyebrow lifted again.

Ivo took a calming breath. "I am simply trying to prevent another scandal. Haven't the Ashtons had enough of them lately? I know Olivia is concerned—"

"Oh, *Olivia* is concerned? So she has sent you like some sort of knight in rusty armor to dispatch me."

Charles shook his head in disgust, and then, with a mocking sketch of a bow, turned on his heel.

Knight in rusty armor?

Ivo was left standing there, fuming, while the rest of the party for the excursion began to arrive. Forced to push down his emotions, he plastered a smile on his face and endeavored to make polite conversation.

The excursion had turned into a picnic—Vivienne's bright idea—and there was a delay while everything was prepared and packed. When they set off at last, most of the men were on horseback, while the rest of the party had taken advantage of the comfortable conveyances. Slower carts were carrying the servants and the picnic paraphernalia. This may be an outdoor meal, but no one was expecting to "rough it." As they rode along, the prince dawdled by the carriage, paying special attention to Olivia.

Ivo pretended not to notice because, as Charles had reminded him, he had done enough damage already.

According to Gabriel, Charles had bowed out of their expedition, claiming he had business to attend to, and although Ivo thought that was a wise move, he couldn't help noting Justina's long face. As he had suspected, the girl's hopes had already been raised by Charles's careless attentions, and he'd be surprised if Gabriel had not noticed and raised the matter with his best friend.

They were passing through woods, and the conversation melded into the sounds of nature. Birds twittered, and the breeze stirred the leaves on the ancient trees. It was all very pleasant, unlike his thoughts. He wasn't sure whether he was angry, insulted, or discomforted by Charles's dressing-down. Unwelcome as it had been, it had given him food for thought.

At the heart of his discomposure was the knowledge that the man was right. He had added to Olivia's disgrace. And yet would she have kissed him like that if she did not like him?

I want you too.

She had said that, and now the memory of her soft lips beneath his, and the warmth of her body molded to his, made him shift uncomfortably in his saddle. He desired her, there was no doubt about that. He knew what desire felt like. But this was more than a mere physical attraction, because whenever they were together it felt *right*, and he could not understand why she did not admit to feeling it too. And then he remembered how clear-sighted she had been when she'd told Ivo that life with him was not what she wanted. How marrying a prince would benefit her far more, certainly financially but also how it would secure her future. She had looked at Ivo's character and prospects and rejected him. How could she be so passionate and imprudent on the one hand, and so cool and pragmatic on the other? And why in God's name was he thinking about her when he had said he would not!

"Not far now!" Gabriel called as they began to ascend the track to the lookout spot. The woods were left behind, and the countryside opened up. Adelina had just commented that soon they may be able to glimpse the sea, when there was a shout behind them. The vehicles and horses came to a halt, and heads turned.

A rider was galloping toward them, and Ivo frowned when he recognized Charles Wickley. Had he decided to join the party after all? Surely this seemed rather dramatic.

Charles brought his mount closer to Ivo, and now he addressed him formally. "Your Grace. Your mother has sent me. You are wanted at Whitmont. Immediately."

Ivo stared at him in confusion, ignoring the questions being thrown at them. "Is someone ill?" Ivo asked. Despite the sun, he felt a sudden chill at the thought.

"Your mother has received a message from your butler." Charles reached into his waistcoat, pulled out a crumpled piece of paper, and handed it across.

What on earth...? Viscountess Monteith demanded to know what was happening as Ivo unfolded the single sheet, but he concentrated on the message. He heard Lexy ask him what was wrong, and Adelina's reply that it must be something urgent.

Ivo, Lieutenant Harrison and his men are camping at Whitmont, and Carlyon says he is threatening to turn the house upside down! You need to return home immediately and put a stop to it. Carlyon says that although he has locked and bolted the doors, he is not sure he can keep them out much longer.

His heart was jumping, and his blood pumping, but there was nothing in his calm demeanor to show it. The revenue officer and his men were at Whitmont, nosing about, and there could only be one reason for it. He crumpled the paper into a ball and squeezed it in his fist. The smile he gave to the others was as near to genuine as he could manage. "Nothing to worry about," he said. "Just some tedious matter I need to see to at home. I'll have to leave immediately and forgo the pleasure of our picnic. My apologies."

Despite his best intentions, his gaze passed over the surprised and curious faces, and paused at Olivia. She looked as concerned as the others and also a little...disappointed? There was no time to reflect on that, because his sisters and the viscountess were demanding to know what had happened at home, and once again, he assured them it was nothing to worry about.

"Do not let this spoil your day," he said. And to the others, "I apologize for leaving so abruptly."

As he kicked his mount into a gallop, heading back the way he'd just come, his mind was already turning over the questions to be answered: Why were Lieutenant Harrison and his men demanding to search his house? What did they expect to find? What *would* they find?

It wasn't until he had almost reached Grantham that he noticed Charles had not stayed behind with the others, but instead had accompanied him back. Perhaps he had even spoken once or twice, but Ivo hadn't heard him, being too deep in his own thoughts.

"Is this what I think it is?" Charles was serious, with none of the usual laughter in his eyes.

Ivo shot him a glance. "You read the message then?"

"Of course." That eyebrow again. "If you are arrested, then I will be next. I am coming with you to Whitmont."

"Won't that raise Harrison's suspicions?"

"Why? They don't know I run a gambling club in London, do they? I will say we are friends. You never know, Northam, you may be in need of a friend if the revenue officers find what they're looking for."

Ivo opened his mouth to refuse the offer—more of a fait accompli—only to change his mind. He wouldn't admit it aloud, but he *was* relieved to have the other man's company. Ivo may have some issues with Charles, not least his parentage, but knowing he would be there, by his side, when he faced Harrison, was strangely comforting.

Chapter Fifteen

O nce they had arrived at the lookout site, the servants set up the picnic in a sheltered dip on the hillside. The meal was served, and afterward, the guests reclined comfortably on blankets and cushions. Even the viscountess was persuaded to lounge a little. Now she was half dozing while the others conversed quietly together.

The view from the lookout was beautiful. Olivia had grown up at Grantham, but today, it felt as if she was seeing this place through new eyes and therefore appreciating it more. She regarded the green slopes, where white and purple flowers peeked out from the grass, while the woods that bordered the Grantham estate were far below them. The sprawl of the grand house was plain to see, with its many chimneys, and from here, one would never guess how desperately in need of repair her home was.

Yes, she admitted to herself, it was beautiful, and yet, for some reason she preferred not to delve into, the view lost its magic because Ivo wasn't here. How did one man's absence dull her pleasure in the day?

Vivienne's voice brought her back to the picnic. "Roberta was desperate to come with us." She had tucked her stockinged feet beneath her skirts, and still looked very elegant. "I had to promise her all sorts of things to pacify her in case she followed us despite the dowager's strictures. I am still rather worried that I'll see her puffing up this hill toward us. Earlier, when Charles caught us up, I thought for a moment it was Roberta."

Gabriel gave her a fond smile as he reached to take her hand in his, playing with her fingers. "You are very good with her," he said, and his dark eyes were warm as they lingered on hers.

"It's not difficult to empathize. I remember what it was like to be young and longing to do all sorts of exciting things."

"Or one can just read a novel and pretend." Annette joined the conversation. "How freeing to be a novelist and able to write exactly what one wishes to say and do."

The viscountess lifted her head. "A ridiculous waste of time," she said. Everyone else ignored her.

Adelina was determined to support her friend's point of view. "In a book, one can visit foreign countries and perform daring deeds, and all from the comfort of a chair."

"I do love a good romance," Lexy sighed.

"One would do better to put aside fantasy when it comes to real life." The viscountess was not to be ignored.

The conversation continued in a similar vein, with the fans of romance novels pointing out the benefits, while the viscountess tried to quash their enthusiasm.

"Olivia?"

Justina's voice brought her out of her thoughts. When she turned, she found her sister was kneeling at her side, holding out a cup and saucer. Tea, of course. One could not have a picnic without tea.

"Do you think it was really business that called Northam home? He and Charles appeared rather worried. Didn't you think so?"

Olivia was surprised her sister was talking to her again, and especially surprised she was talking about Charles. She noticed there was a flush in Justina's cheeks, and she was fiddling with a flounce on her skirt. She didn't seem to be enjoying the picnic either.

She opened her mouth to remind Justina that Charles was not the man for her, and instead heard herself say, "Northam seemed keen to have us believe it was nothing out of the ordinary."

Justina met her eyes, her own clear and bright. "Exactly! They were trying to flimflam us, don't you think?"

Olivia found herself smiling. "Perhaps it is another of Northam's wagers. He had to rush off and race his curricle around London."

Even as she said it, she felt a little guilty, a little disloyal. She was relieved when Justina took up the baton. "And Charles is to be his tiger!"

Olivia laughed at that. A tiger was a small man or boy, small enough to fit on the compact seat on the rear of the curricle. Charles would be far too big for such a position. Justina smiled back, although a little cautiously, as if she was apprehensive Olivia might turn on her again.

"Whatever it was that took them away, I refuse to allow it to spoil our day," she said doggedly.

Justina sighed. "Me too."

Olivia set down her teacup and saucer and reached to take her sister's hand. As much as the reminder of Charles's unsuitability was on the tip of her tongue, she did not speak the words. She just wanted everything to go back to the way it was.

"I'm glad you are yourself again," Justina said.

Olivia stared. "I am always myself."

"No. You've been truly horrible since the prince arrived."

Justina was not normally so blunt. Didn't her sister understand Olivia was only trying to help? "Don't you remember how awful life was? I mean, before," she said in a rush, when Justina gave her a curious look. "I just don't want us to go back there. I want you all to be safe. If I marry well, then we'll never have to go back to those days again."

Her sister looked thoughtful. "I try to remember the fun we had and not the horrible parts." Justina hesitated as Olivia stayed silent, and her tone gentled. "I know it was harder for you, as the oldest. You felt as if the world was on your shoulders, and you worried endlessly. I haven't told you how much your care meant to us. To me. You are the best of sisters."

Olivia's face felt hot and her eyes stung. She blinked hard, aware she might begin to cry, and this was not the place for tears.

Justina squeezed her hand. "But those days are gone. We have Gabriel and Vivienne, and the Ashtons will march on, somehow. Perhaps not quite as Grandmama would like us to—we are rather a ragtag lot—but she is stuck in the past. She put aside her happiness for the family, and I don't think any of us can do that. Or should want to." A frown wrinkled her brow. "I wouldn't like to think you were turning your back on happiness because you believed it would help us. That would make me feel quite sick. I…We can make our own choices, and our own mistakes. Can you imagine Robbie thanking you for marrying her off to some rich old man just to keep her *safe*?"

Olivia swallowed. She felt confused, her thoughts floundering, as if the earth was rocking beneath her. "But surely if I…" *If I marry the prince and make us rich, it would be a blessing to all of us.* That was what she meant to say, but Justina stopped her.

"I would hate to think of you being miserable because you thought it was what we wanted, Olivia. I would be very cross if you did anything like that."

Olivia stared back at her. Was it possible Justina was right? As awful as their lives had been, Gabriel was here now, and he had already told her he would not allow grandmother to push her into marrying a man she did not want to marry. Just as he had not married a woman he did not love. That did not mean he would not be grateful if she married a man with wealth and standing. Olivia was well aware that Gabriel's finances would only stretch so far when it came to six sisters. But her sisters weren't the only reason she had set her rather feverish sights on the prince. There had been the pain of being gossiped about and mocked, and her desire to return to London and finish her Season. It was the life she craved, and if she could help her sisters along the way…

Although now she thought about it, Grandmama had been happy to allow her to believe she was the only one who could save the family. Indeed, she had built on those beliefs, and Olivia's dark memories of the past, until she was quite…frantic. But Olivia didn't blame her grandmother. The dowager thought she was doing the right thing, just as she had always done what she thought was the right thing. Self-sacrifice was in her blood. Olivia admitted she had been rather flattered that her grandmother saw her as her replacement. The chatelaine of Grantham.

It had a nice ring to it. "*What* did you say?"

Olivia came out of her reverie with a start. Her companions, whose conversation had become nothing but background noise to her private thoughts, had fallen strangely silent after the viscountess's furious question.

All eyes were on Vivienne, and her usually calm face had taken on a strained, pinched look. At the same time, Gabriel was staring at her in disbelief, and Annette had risen to her feet, her hand over her mouth and her eyes wide. Her gaze flickered to her mother and away again, as if whatever she saw was too frightening to be borne.

"I'm so sorry," she whispered, and with a shake of her head, she turned and walked away. Behind her, the viscountess struggled to her feet, her face puce with anger, and stumbled after her daughter.

Olivia clutched hold of Justina's arm and leaned in close to whisper, "What? What just happened?"

Justina looked as pale and shocked as the others as she put her lips to her sister's ear. "The viscountess kept saying that only fools read romances, and even bigger fools write them, and suddenly, Annette blurted out that she must be a fool, and so must Vivienne, because they wrote that book. The one about the *Wicked Prince* that everyone is talking about. As soon as she said it, she tried to take it back, but it was too late."

"*They* wrote it?" Olivia hissed. "Did Gabriel know?"

"I don't think so. He doesn't look as if he did."

No he didn't. Her brother looked as white and as shocked as the rest. Vivienne had written that silly book? And Annette had helped her? It seemed too ridiculous to be true, but Olivia could see from the guilt in Vivienne's eyes, and Annette's rigid back as she stood by the carriages being berated by her mother, that it was indeed the truth.

"Is that the only novel?" Lexy asked, agog at the idea. "Have you written any more, Vivienne?"

"No," Vivienne gasped, seeming overwhelmed. "Oh please, can we not talk about it?"

Abruptly, Gabriel stood, beckoning to the servants to

begin packing up. Any sense of lazy relaxation was gone as the others also stood. There would be no more picnic today.

"I had no idea," Justina said, eyes wide on Olivia's. "Did you?"

"No. It never occurred to me. Although…" The cousins were best friends, and there had been moments…hints, that there was some secret between them. But who would have thought it was something like that? And why on earth hadn't Vivienne told Gabriel before they married?

"I doubt he would have cared," Justina responded, when Olivia asked the question in a whisper. "He loves her more than anything."

Well, that was true, although at the moment he didn't appear to be very loving. But if Vivienne had said something, warned them, then they might have avoided what had just happened.

Another scandal. What did the prince think about a duchess writing romance novels? Would he laugh and shrug it off?

Maybe he had not heard?

But when she looked over at him, it was apparent he had. His face had that haughty look, and his mouth was a hard line of disapproval.

What must he think of them, a family that was embroiled in scandal after scandal? Olivia was sorry for Vivienne, she truly was, and she would be very upset if Gabriel and his new wife fell out over this. Her brother and Vivienne were a love story she felt she had had a part in, and seeing them happy together gave her hope that one day, perhaps, she could be happy too. But as she watched Nikolai swing himself up onto his stallion and set off back to Grantham without a word to anyone, she rather thought she had enough problems of her own.

"Oh no, they're arguing!" Justina nudged her.

Gabriel was saying something in a hushed, angry voice, and Vivienne was responding apologetically, on the verge of tears.

As if by mutual agreement, everyone had moved away to allow them some privacy. As Olivia approached the carriage, she saw that Annette was seated, her shoulders bowed, while the viscountess continued to berate her.

"Maybe we should tell her the book was a hit?" Justina said.

"I doubt it would matter. In the 'real world,' ladies of quality do not do such things."

Justina looked flustered and cross. "It was a wonderful book. I loved it. I can't tell you how many times I have read it. Instead of telling Vivienne and Annette off, Gabriel and the viscountess should be telling them how proud they are."

Olivia gaped at her. Clearly her sister did not understand the consequences of such an action, or perhaps she just didn't care.

Justina was wearing a dreamy look and then she giggled. "That part where the prince tries to ravish her! Oh dear, imagine Vivienne and Annette writing *that*?"

Olivia decided she would rather not think about any of it. If only she could pretend it had never happened, but she feared she was going to hear a great deal more about Vivienne and Annette's book before the day was out.

After a journey spent in chilly silence, the subdued party arrived back at Grantham. Gabriel and Vivienne retired to their suite, while Annette disappeared to her room with her mother still in hot pursuit. Olivia saw her grandmother and Humber with their heads close together—of course the servants had overheard, and the news had spread. There was no hope of keeping matters en famille.

"What a to-do!"

Olivia had not noticed Felicia sidle up to her, but from her mother's expression, she was overjoyed with this new family disgrace.

"The dowager must be beside herself," she added, and now there was no hiding her smile. "You know that Prince Nikolai has left?"

Olivia stared. "What do you mean?" It occurred to her to demand to know if her mother had been behind those notes, but Felicia was already speaking again in that excited manner. As if it was impossible for her to hold the words in.

"He came back from the picnic, packed up his things, and returned to London. Your grandmother was incandescent with rage. Do you know she and the prince's grandfather had an affair once? There was even talk of divorce."

"Divorce?" Olivia stammered. "But that is—"

"Disgraceful?" Felicia said the word with relish. "Your grandmother was not always as beyond reproach as she would have you believe. I've wondered about that sanctimonious Humber too. Who knows what goes on between the two of them when the bedchamber door is closed?"

"Stop it," Olivia hissed. "How dare you talk about Grandmama in that hateful way."

Felicia's smile fell, and right then, she looked dangerous. As if she was capable of anything. "How dare *she* replace Harry with his bastard and push me aside? I won't put up with it, not any longer."

And with that, she left the room.

Olivia stared after her, wondering if she should follow and demand to know what her mother was planning, but her head was aching, and suddenly, it was all too much. She made her own escape into the garden.

For a time, she simply walked, letting the smells and sights of nature soothe her. Without meaning to, she found herself once more at the archery targets. If she closed her eyes, she could still feel Ivo's lips on hers, and his arms clasping her tight. It felt like a dream, and it may as well have been one. Ivo had gone back to Whitmont to do heaven knew what, and the prince had left without her being able to secure his affections, or his promise. Olivia should be in despair, but rather to her own surprise, she found she wasn't.

It was as if this recent disaster had only solidified the decision she had been working toward.

She didn't need to go to Holtswig after all. There were plenty of eligible gentlemen in London, and at the time she had made her debut, there had been plenty of interest in her. She had felt a little giddy at all the attention, as if she could take her pick, and if it hadn't been for Ivo distracting her, she might well have done so.

Why couldn't she finish her Season and make a sensible choice this time? The prince would not propose now—why had she pinned all her hopes on him? Besides, trying to keep him in a good mood was exhausting. She had other options, and knowing that filled her with new hope.

She wasn't going to languish here at Grantham. She was tired of others deciding how she should live her life. Tired of trying to shoehorn herself into a future that didn't fit.

Olivia wondered if she could discover a path that was particular to her. Follow it and find, at the end...Well, she wasn't sure what she would find. Happiness, maybe. Contentment, perhaps. But whatever she found, whichever direction she went in, was for her to determine, and no one else.

Chapter Sixteen

When Ivo and Charles arrived at Whitmont, the evening shadows were stretching long over the lawn, while the water from the fountain with its mermaid statue shone in golden droplets. The setting sun turned the many windows on the Tudor house to gold, and the smell of cut grass was in the air. It was home to Ivo, and had been home to his ancestors for hundreds of years, and yet right now, the place seemed unnervingly quiet. Unfamiliar. Ivo felt that tickle of unease increase as he and Charles dismounted.

A servant came to take their horses, and a moment later, Carlyon hobbled down the stairs.

"Sir, sir, I tried to stop them!" he wailed. "I said they had no right, but there was a document—"

Close behind him was Lieutenant Harrison, neat as a pin in his uniform, with a smirk on his face. He called out in an almost jaunty voice, "We had permission, Your Grace. The law was behind us."

"What does he think he's doing?" Ivo growled. On the journey from Grantham to Whitmont, he had been worried, but now he was angry. Harrison's disrespectful behavior was not something he was used to, and it left him feeling worried and discomposed.

Charles put a hand on his arm, and Ivo swung to face

him, hasty words on the tip of his tongue. Charles raised an eyebrow.

"Think before you speak," he said in a low, urgent tone. "Indignation and bluster are good—you *are* a duke after all—but don't allow yourself to be pushed into a corner."

Ivo wondered who Charles imagined he was speaking to—certainly not a man who had been in the smuggling game since he was twelve years old. All the same, it was a timely reminder. Charles had as much to lose as Ivo. Since he was not a duke, then possibly more. They were in this together.

Harrison came to a stop before them. "Your Grace," he said, with the smallest of bows. "My apologies for cutting short your social engagement. Your man," with a dismissive glance at Carlyon, "thought it imperative you be present while we searched your house."

"I tried to stop them!" Carlyon wailed again, wringing his hands.

"You searched my home?" Ivo asked in a voice trembling with outrage. "This is beyond impertinent. What right have you to do such a thing, Lieutenant?"

Harrison might have flushed—the light was getting dimmer by the moment—but he didn't back down. He had always been a stickler for the letter of the law as he saw it. Ivo might mock his unbending manner, but it meant Harrison was unlikely to turn aside if he saw something happening that he considered irregular. That made him even more dangerous.

"I have an order from Lord Ralph Anderson that permits me to search your home. Sir."

Ivo glared at him while his mind galloped like a runaway horse. Lord Ralph was the magistrate in the Portside area, and he was not a friend of the Fitzsimmonses. He had long bemoaned the illegal behavior that went on in the Kent marshes and, several times in Ivo's hearing, had declared that one day he would put a stop to it. Ivo didn't think his lordship knew for certain that the Fitzsimmonses were involved, but anyone who lived in this part of Kent must have their suspicions.

Carlyon was shuffling a few steps behind the lieutenant, and Ivo met the butler's gaze. It was hard to tell in the fading light, but he thought the old man looked paler than usual, and there was an unease in his eyes that worried Ivo. This was Carlyon, who had been a rock throughout Ivo's childhood, and a dependable retainer over many years' service. That he looked anxious was a concern.

"Indeed," Ivo said, his voice icy, turning back to Harrison. "Show me this order, Lieutenant, and *I* will decide whether or not it is valid."

Harrison undid a couple of the buttons on his jacket and reached inside. He took out a crisp fold of papers and handed them to Ivo. But by now, the evening had turned to near darkness and he could not read whatever was on the documents, or even recognize the signature. With a huff of frustration, he took the stairs two at a time and strode into his house, aware of the others trailing behind him.

"Get me a light!" he roared as he made his way to his study.

One was produced—he noted that Carlyon did it himself, and the old man's hands were shaking. He gave the butler a sharp glance, and Carlyon straightened, his expression reverting to its usual impassiveness. Satisfied, Ivo turned to the order.

Lord Ralph had signed it. A quick scan of the wording showed that the revenue men were allowed to be at Whitmont. They were also allowed to search the house for any "items of contraband," and then there was a list that included spirits, wine, tea, chocolate, soap, etcetera, etcetera.

"What makes you think I have any of this?" he asked, maintaining his anger.

Harrison was staring at Charles with a frown, but now he turned back to Ivo again. "We have credible information from a witness that you are involved in the smuggling trade, sir."

Ivo huffed a laugh and shook his head. "Apart from the complete preposterousness of anyone saying such a thing, and of you believing them, have you found any of these items in my house?"

Harrison nodded, a glint of satisfaction in his eye. "A bottle of brandy, sir. French brandy."

Ivo stared, and then he laughed. "Show me any house in England, and I will show you some French spirits! That was a gift, I'll have you know. You have searched my house, dragged me home from my visit to Grantham, and all for this?" He dropped his voice into a low growl. "I am seriously angry, Lieutenant."

"Our witness is credible, sir." Harrison seemed unmoved. "And you offered me a glass of this same brandy one evening when I was here. You offered smuggled goods to an officer of the crown."

"And very pleased with it you were, if I recall," he mocked.

Harrison's eyes narrowed. He did not like to be made a fool of.

Ivo turned to Charles but saw that Wickley was staring over his shoulder. Something about the man's rigid stance made Ivo turn, and he realized Charles's gaze was fixed on the portrait of the late duke in his younger days. Ivo was aware he looked very like his father…but so did Charles.

Harrison was watching them both, and perhaps he had seen the resemblance too. He asked, with a nod at Charles, "Who is this?"

Charles turned to him, and Ivo was relieved to see he was his usual affable self, as if nothing was the matter, though Ivo didn't think that was true. "Charles Wickley, at your service. I accompanied Northam here from the house party at Grantham. I am on my way home to London."

Harrison frowned and opened his mouth to question him further, but Ivo intervened. "You have searched my house and found nothing of consequence. I think it is time you left."

But again, the lieutenant was unfazed, as if his belief that he was in the right trumped all else. "I believe you are involved in smuggling along this coast—our informant has told us so, and he has nothing to gain by denouncing you. Indeed, he has much to lose."

"You arrogant fellow!" Ivo growled. "Who is this informant? Have you a name?"

"He does not wish his name known. He tells me Portside is a hive of miscreants, and if his identity were known, his business would suffer, as well as himself."

"No name, and yet you would believe this liar over me, a duke?"

Harrison continued, though he was speaking more quickly now, aware Ivo had reached the limit of his patience. "You should not expect to escape the full force of the law just because you are a peer. I intend to do my duty without fear or favor. Good evening, sir." And with another glance at Charles, he turned and marched out, chivvying his men before him. Carlyon, whom Ivo saw was also gazing at the portrait, gave a start and hurried after them, probably to make sure they hadn't pocketed anything valuable.

With the door closed, Ivo took a breath and stared down at

the order, now clenched in his fist. "Damn him," he said. "Damn the man to hell." Anger rippled through him, but concern followed soon after. In all his years as master of Whitmont, and his father's before him, nothing like this had ever happened. Why now? Was his family's luck finally running out?

When he looked up, he found Charles was watching him, and his urbane persona had been shed like a cloak.

"Who is this informer?" Ivo asked, not expecting an answer. "Who would inform on me?"

Charles appeared to give it some serious thought. "I know you expect absolute loyalty from your people, but could it be one of them? They might need to make some money in a hurry, or they might feel you're not treating them with the proper respect. They might hold a secret grudge against you or your family. There are many reasons a person might turn to informing on you."

"A grudge?"

"These are but a few possibilities, Northam."

Ivo swallowed back his protests. Charles was right. He tried to think of anyone who resented him enough to ruin him. Although he did his best for the people on his estate and in the village of Portside, there would always be those who believed they were entitled to more. Usually, that showed itself in a few grumbles, or a sour look as Ivo passed by, but more than that…? No names came to him; he needed to talk to Bourne.

Charles spoke in a considered way. "Perhaps it is the same person who informed on the boats crossing the channel from France. Polgarth is in gaol, might he be the one?"

"No, not Polgarth," Ivo said quickly. "I can't believe he would do that. He's always been loyal." Polgarth knew the risks of his profession, and he knew Ivo would help him and his family to the best of his ability.

"Then what of this new shipmaster? Mystere? Could it be him? He has benefited from the revenue arresting his rivals. What do you know about him?"

Ivo ran a weary hand through his hair. "Not as much as I want to," he admitted. "I need to speak to Bourne. He knows every smuggler along this coast."

Charles nodded, and then looked about him. "What did Harrison expect to find here?" he asked, puzzled. "Did he have something in mind, or was he just hoping for a piece of evidence he could use? Or he could just mean to rattle you into doing something reckless."

Ivo frowned. "I'm never reckless when it comes to my business."

Charles stared in disbelief. "I'm sorry to disagree, but what of the many wagers you take part in? Some of them—"

"That's pleasure," Ivo snapped. "This is business. I am never reckless in business. That is why I have never been arrested."

Up to now. The words hung over them.

"Well," said Charles, breaking the moment. "I should start for London."

Ivo shook his head. "It grows late. Stay here and start afresh in the morning. You never know who you might meet on the roads at night."

Charles hesitated before he gave a nod. "Thank you."

"Perhaps we can share a glass of my smuggled brandy," Ivo added with a wry smile.

Charles smiled back, but his easygoing manner was missing. Ivo wasn't sure whether it was the lieutenant's visit and concern over the informant, or something else. He thought, as Charles's gaze slid once more to the late duke's portrait, that it was something else.

Chapter Seventeen

B reakfast was far from a pleasant meal despite everyone being at the table. The tension in the room was tangible. Gabriel was speaking in monosyllables, and Vivienne was listless. Felicia was relishing their falling-out, a satisfied smirk on her lips as she watched them over the brim of her cup.

"Such a pity the prince had to leave so suddenly," she said with insincere dismay. "I wonder if he will return?"

The dowager shot her daughter-in-law a look of dislike. "Eat your breakfast, Felicia." She looked as if she would have liked to say more but restrained herself, viciously slicing her toast into smaller pieces.

Last night, Olivia had sought out Vivienne to offer her the support the other woman had always given to her. Vivienne had been upset about the damage to the relationship with her husband. "I should have told him," she admitted. "He feels I have deceived him, but...everything was going so well. I didn't want to cause any upsets. Especially after the awfulness of my family and then coming to live at Grantham. We had enough to contend with, or so I thought. I was always going to tell him; the right time just never presented itself."

Olivia had comforted her. "Gabriel will understand. He probably read your book and loved it. He is a great reader of romances."

Vivienne gave a wan smile. "He *has* read it. I saw it on his bookshelf at Cadieux's."

Olivia had chuckled, and then Vivienne had giggled.

"It will be all right," Olivia had said as she gave Vivienne a hug. "Gabriel loves you so much. He'll realize this is but a minor bump in the road."

However, at breakfast, she had to wonder just how wide the rift between them really was. Her brother was hurt—he did not like secrets. Well, he would just have to get over it. Matters were much worse for Annette. She had left first thing this morning with her parents for their home in Devon, the viscount and viscountess grim-faced while their daughter's eyes were red from weeping. Olivia hoped things would calm down, but while she had sympathy for Annette, surely it was her own fault for blurting out the truth about the book's authorship in front of everyone.

The dowager finished mangling her toast and seemed to come to a decision. She looked up, her gaze traveling around the table at the subdued breakfasters.

"I have decided I will return to London."

There was a gasp. Olivia's fingers closed so tightly on her teacup she feared it might crack. London? Was her grandmother going alone? *Please, please, take me!* She bit her lip before the words could escape.

The dowager was continuing. "Gabriel and Vivienne will remain here with the younger girls. Gabriel tells me he has estate matters to deal with, and Vivienne has much to learn about running a household like Grantham."

Vivienne's shoulders stiffened, but she did not respond. Grandmama's gaze found Olivia.

"Olivia and Justina will come with me."

Olivia set down her teacup with a clatter, but no one seemed to notice.

"It is time Olivia resumed her Season, and..." The dowager bit back a sigh. "I had hoped that Olivia would be settled before Justina had her coming-out, but that now seems unlikely." Her dark eyes rested censoriously on her eldest granddaughter, and Olivia, remembering the approval she had so recently basked in, tried not to flinch.

"So I will be coming out?" Justina said, eyes wide with trepidation.

"I see no reason for us to wait any longer," the dowager retorted. "Unless..." She looked questioningly at her grandson. "Gabriel? Can we afford another debutante ball so soon after the house party?"

Gabriel cleared his throat. "We can. A small one." He grimaced at Justina. "I'm sorry, the coffers are running low. There is never enough to do everything I want to do at Grantham."

He sounded downhearted, and Vivienne placed her hand over his. Gabriel seemed surprised. Olivia held her breath, hoping he would not pull away. Gabriel's eyes met Vivienne's, delving deep, and then suddenly, they were both smiling. The relief around the table was palpable.

Justina's smile was undimmed. "I don't mind, Gabriel. As long as the people I love the most are at my coming-out, I will be happy. Oh, and if I have a new dress for the occasion."

Gabriel's dark eyes were warm. "Then you will have your wish."

"What about me?"

Roberta's question shattered the harmonious moment. All attention turned to her, but she only lifted her chin and stared back, unfazed. "You have mentioned everyone else, Grandmama, but what about me?"

Olivia gave an inner sigh as she looked properly at her sister. Roberta's hair was hastily bundled up into a chignon, wisps falling everywhere, and her dress had a stain on the sleeve. She had probably been down at the stables already this morning—the girl seemed to live there.

"How old are you?" their grandmother demanded.

"She'll be seventeen in two days' time," Vivienne replied mildly, with a smile for Roberta. "She is no longer a child."

"Despite behaving like one," the dowager said. Then, in a testy voice, "Very well, she will come with me to London, and if she misbehaves at all, if she disobeys even one of my directives, then she will be sent home in disgrace."

Roberta bit her lip and tried hard not to smile.

Olivia couldn't help but smile too. She felt like skipping around the room. London! There would be *some* invitations, surely? And even if she received only one, she would use it to win everybody over so that soon there would be more. Olivia would be sensible and serious, she would make the most of this chance, but she was also going to enjoy herself like there was no tomorrow, because with Roberta accompanying them, there may very well not be.

The dowager was issuing orders. The governess would remain here at Grantham with the younger members of the family, while the companion, Miss Starky, was to come with them to Ashton House. Their companion was young and amiable, although she was understandably anxious when in the company of their grandmother.

Rides and strolls in the park would be in order. Visits to their dressmaker, and the theater, and all the other entertainments London had to offer. So much to look forward to. Olivia could hardly wait. Finally, she would be able to resume her Season. She hadn't realized quite how low her spirits had fallen until they started to lift. And no, she refused to believe that had anything to do with Ivo's hasty departure.

With breakfast finished, the three girls went upstairs to pack. Justina was still wide-eyed from the news of her coming-out, while Roberta was dancing as she climbed the stairs, swirling her skirts around her until she stumbled and nearly fell over the bannister.

"You realize you will not be able to walk around looking as if you've been dragged through a bush backward," Olivia said, catching hold of her sister's arm to hold her upright.

Justina shot her a worried look and, startled, Olivia realized her voice had sounded as testy as Grandmama's. Was she being horrible again?

Roberta seemed to think so, her eyes flashing. "I can be a lady," she retorted, and curtsied low. "See? There's nothing to it."

Olivia shrugged. "Passable, I suppose."

Roberta curtsied again, and skipped away to her room, her untidy hair tumbling down around her.

Justina caught Olivia's hand in hers and gave it a squeeze. "She *does* try. She's just so...so—"

"Annoying?" Olivia finished for her.

Justina gave a little smile, and her eyes sparkled. "Prince Nikolai didn't know what to make of her. We were walking in the garden with him, and suddenly, she turned a cartwheel. Right in front of him!"

Olivia stared in horror. "Her skirts..."

"She was wearing pantaloons. We all saw them. The prince turned as red as a beet and almost ran away."

Olivia didn't mean to laugh. It shouldn't have been funny, but the feeling bubbled up inside her, and a moment later Justina joined her. Until the thought of such a thing happening in Hyde Park terrified her into silence.

Justina seemed to read her mind. "We'll just have to keep her in check."

Easier said than done, but she made a sound of agreement. It was so nice to be on good terms with Justina again—it was to be hoped nothing else occurred to cause them to fall out.

Charles Wickley, for instance. Olivia had restrained herself from mentioning him, but his wicked reputation was still on her mind. If he *dared* to hurt her favorite sister…

But for now, she set aside her fears. It was a time for celebration. Life was good, and if Olivia had her way, this would be the first step on the pathway to her new life.

Chapter Eighteen

Bourne had arrived at the house before breakfast, and so Charles had once again delayed his departure for London and the club. Will Tremeer was back at Cadieux's, in temporary charge, and Ivo could tell that Charles trusted the younger man implicitly.

Ivo could not be sure whether or not Lieutenant Harrison's men were watching Whitmont, but even if they were, there was no reason for them to suspect Bourne of carrying secret messages. He was a regular visitor to the house, as well as being a Portside tenant, who acted as spokesman for the other tenants.

Of course, the villagers had heard of the revenue men's visit, and they were naturally concerned. Ivo spent some time reassuring Bourne that he was doing all in his power to keep everyone safe, before finally moving on to the main reason for his summons.

"Tell me what you know about this Mystere." Ivo poured Bourne a brandy as they sat together in the study. Charles, who already had a glass, stood leaning against the wall near the portrait of the late duke. Ivo tried not to look over there because the resemblance was making him feel deeply uncomfortable.

Bourne took a sip and thoughtfully rolled the brandy around in his mouth before he swallowed. "I don't know much," he admitted. "We needed someone to bring our goods over from France in a hurry after Polgarth was arrested, and Mystere was the only option. It was a risk, I admit, but a calculated one. If you leave a message at the inn on the waterfront at Worth, he will respond, though as far as I'm aware, no one has seen him face-to-face. The goods we ordered were delivered from his sloop into waiting boats near the coast off Portside, but no one saw him, or if they did, they did not know it was him."

"A mystery man indeed," Ivo murmured. "Why would he inform on me to the Revenue Service? Surely that would be counterproductive if he wants to make a living from my business."

"A grudge?" Charles said. "Some past misdeed? Does anything occur to you?"

Ivo huffed a laugh. "This again! Where would I start? But no, seriously, nothing that would cause a man like Mystere to want to revenge himself on me."

"What about other family members?" Charles mused. "Your father, for instance?"

Was there a probing note in his voice? Ivo paused, trying to read the other man's expression, but Charles was very good at hiding his thoughts.

And it was true that Ivo's father *did* have a past that might cause someone to want retribution. Or was it Ivo who had been the reason for revenge? Bourne caught his eye, and Ivo knew he was thinking the same thing. A memory, something he had almost forgotten, rose to the surface. "There was someone…"

"Jacob Rendall," Bourne said. "I haven't seen him for years, but he left Portside under a cloud. If I remember rightly, he swore vengeance on you."

"Vengeance? For what?" Charles asked curiously.

Ivo felt a ripple of shame. He didn't want to talk about it, especially in front of Charles, but Bourne was watching him, and Bourne had been there too. "My father had just died, and this Jacob arrived as I was taking my place as leader of the Portside men. I was young, and it was of huge importance for me to show everyone, to show myself, that I was up to the task. Then Jacob turned up and announced he was my brother. Half brother. He said we should share, him and me. He didn't seem to understand that wasn't going to happen, and he wouldn't shut up about it. In the end, I told him he was no brother of mine, and he left." He looked to Bourne in preference to looking at Charles. "Was there any more to it? Surely it was a tempest in a teacup."

Bourne crossed his arms. "You told him that no one who was a dim-witted, ugly monster like him could possibly be a member of your family. He had something wrong with his eye. He did not take your words well."

Oh God, he remembered it now. He had been rather unfeeling about Jacob and his walleye, but at the time, he'd had a great deal to prove. "You all laughed at him," he reminded Bourne.

"We laughed because you were our new leader. Jacob was one of us, and then he wasn't. I did not see him again after that day."

Ivo pushed his guilt away. There were plenty of other things he had done in his twenty-seven years that he regretted, ridiculous and idiotic things that had probably had consequences far beyond himself. He just hadn't cared at the time. Jacob was but one of them. "Perhaps you can find him," he said at last. "Is his family still in the village?"

"His mother died of fever. He comforted himself

with the belief that he and you were half brothers. It was probably the sort of fantasy a lonely boy might tell himself. No one believed him," Bourne added hastily, with an apologetic grimace. "You were right to send him away."

Was he? It was too late now to make amends, and he had other matters to deal with if he was not to lose everything.

"There was talk that he went off to join the army. I'll ask around. Someone might know." Bourne finished his brandy and stood up. "I'll ask about Mystere too, and see what else I can find out," he said. "If the Frenchman has turned traitor, then others must know of it. And then there is the question of why he is the last smuggler remaining along our stretch of coast, after Polgarth and the others were arrested. Why haven't they arrested him too?"

"Someone out there must have answers." Ivo also stood up. "Apologies, but there can be no more orders from us to Mystere until this puzzle has been solved." He held up his hands when Bourne began to protest. "I know, I know, it is not what either of us wants to hear, but reassure your men that I will assist them in any way I can. No one will go without, and more importantly, no one will go to prison."

Ivo just hoped he could keep his promise as the debts began to pile up.

When Bourne had left them alone, silence fell over the room.

Ivo felt a weight settle on his shoulders. He couldn't ignore it anymore. Charles, standing right beside his father's portrait, was drawing his attention to the plain truth. He had to speak.

But he had waited too long, because it was Charles who spoke first.

"Your father," he began and then stopped.

Ivo sighed. "My father," he agreed. "I admired him when I was a boy, wanted to be just like him, but then I discovered he had another side. A darker side." He looked at Charles. "Do you know anything about your parents?"

Charles didn't seem surprised to be asked that or by the seeming change of subject.

"I was brought up at St. Ninian's, same as Gabriel and Freddie. Someone handed me in as a newborn, and for a time, things were dicey. I was sickly." He shrugged. "But I fought off the usual childhood illnesses, and here I am."

Ivo nodded, waiting, but Charles was waiting too. He raised an eyebrow in that way that irritated Ivo at the same time as it caused a painful sensation in his chest.

"I think you know what I am asking," Ivo said, his impatience leaking into his voice. "Have you ever heard mention of your father?"

"No," Charles replied, "but lately, I have wondered if…" He shrugged, suddenly uncomfortable. "The late duke was a renowned womanizer, or so I have heard, and the only information I did manage to glean from St. Ninian's was that my mother came from Kent. She died soon after my birth, or so I was told, but perhaps they tell all foundlings that."

Ivo let out a breath. "There were always rumors about my father and the village women, which is probably why Jacob got it into his head that he was my half brother. But there was one rumor in particular that seemed based in truth. A child was born and taken to St. Ninian's, far enough away, it was hoped, to stop any gossip from reaching my mother's ears. How old are you?"

"Twenty-six years, I believe."

"I am twenty-seven." Ivo played with his glass a

moment with a frown. "There can be no doubting the resemblance between you and my father," he said, nodding at the portrait, "or you and myself. I think you were the baby, which means…you are a Fitzsimmons."

Charles looked shaken. He gave a jerky nod. "Others have mentioned the likeness between us, but I dismissed it, but then when I saw your father's portrait…" He swallowed. "It is hard to deny that we share the same blood."

"I'm not denying it, although it's damned awkward."

Charles frowned. "I have no claim on you or your family, and I will make none. I have made my own way in the world and have no intention of altering that. If you no longer wish to join me in the Cadieux's venture, then I release you from it."

Ivo could see he'd struck a nerve, but he had simply spoken aloud the concerns he had had for some time. He gave a harsh laugh. "The partnership with you is the only thing likely to keep me afloat." The words were out before he could stop them.

Charles's eyes widened comically. "Are you bankrupt?"

"Not yet. I still hope to turn matters about. When it comes to the Cadieux's venture…" He gave an uncomfortable shrug. "It's I who should be thanking you."

Charles shook his head. "I would never have guessed."

"The Fitzsimmonses are good at putting on a front. Don't worry though. I have the blunt to buy into your business. And I have every intention of making a profit for us both. I only meant, with the resemblance between us, that there will be questions asked," he said frankly, "and we can't ignore them forever. I'm surprised Gabriel hasn't already asked them."

Charles huffed a laugh. "Gabriel and I have known each other for so long, he no longer sees me as anything but a friend. Maybe he's noticed the resemblance in passing, but unless I point it out to him, he won't say anything. You're right, though. There will be others with sharper eyes. If you and I are partners at Cadieux's, we'll need to decide what to say to them."

That was true, but Ivo didn't want to announce the relationship immediately. Especially with Harrison sniffing around. "Maybe a vague reference to a family connection?" he suggested at last. "Everyone knows the Fitzsimmonses have a certain look. A strong resemblance to each other." He waved his hand at Charles and then at his father's portrait.

Charles shrugged. "As you wish," he said. "I will not speak of your father's indiscretion unless I am asked directly, and I doubt anyone will be rude enough to do that. Although Freddie…" He smiled at the thought of one of his best friends.

"I think Gabriel should know first. And then there is the question of Justina…"

Charles's gaze sharpened and his carefree manner hardened. "You warned me off her," he said slowly, as if he was seeing things from a different perspective now. "I think I see why. Is it that you believe I have inherited my father's…*your* father's predilection for seduction? I was angry at the time. I thought you considered me too many rungs below her on the social ladder, and that was why—"

"Not at all," Ivo assured him. "My father was a likable man, a charming man, and I loved him dearly. I did not know about the procession of women until I was older. And as you also have a reputation with the ladies…" He gave Charles a challenging stare.

Again, Charles gave that huff of laughter. "I like women, I admit it, and there was a time when I found myself in their company a great deal. But since I began to help Gabriel with

Cadieux's, I haven't had time for carousing. And now I have met Justina and," his smile was almost sweet, "I do not want to spend time with any woman but her."

Ivo believed him, and besides, why would he lie? It wasn't even as if Ivo was related to Justina and was therefore bound to protect her. But Gabriel was. Ivo suspected Charles would have a job persuading the Duke of Grantham of his sincerity. Things could get awkward, but Ivo did not doubt Charles would fight for her.

"You are in love with her," he said.

Charles blushed, and it was heartening to see him lose that confidence again.

"Yes, I love her. And I am sincere in my desire to marry her, but Gabriel may view things differently. We grew up together, and he has seen me at my worst. Persuading him I am in earnest may take a little time, but Justina is a treasure, and I will do all in my power to gain Gabriel's permission to marry her."

Ivo stared a moment longer, but Charles did not drop his gaze. "Very well. I believe you. If you decide to approach Gabriel and you need my support, I will give it."

Charles seemed surprised by that, and then he smiled. "Thank you," he said. "I may well need your support, knowing how fiercely Gabriel protects his sisters." He stepped away from the portrait and came to sit opposite Ivo. "Right now, I think we have a more pressing matter. Mystere."

"We do not know he is the traitor in our ranks."

"No, but I think it more likely than not. I mean, would this Jacob fellow still be holding a grudge against you after all these years?"

Ivo hoped that was true. They needed to discover what Mystere was up to. Before Lieutenant Harrison and his revenue men made another attempt to arrest him.

Chapter Nineteen

Ashton House
Mayfair, London

They had arrived in London, and Olivia was bubbling with anticipation. The dowager had declared she needed to lie down to recover from traveling with a coachload of boisterous girls. She meant Roberta, everyone knew that, but Olivia restrained herself from saying so.

And to the surprise of everyone, Olivia's mother had announced she was coming to London too. There were times when she felt sorry for Felicia—the woman had lost a great deal because of a turn of events that was not her fault. But her mother had never asked for Olivia's help or understanding. She had never tried to befriend her, or form a bond with her, or to get to know any of her six daughters. The simple truth was Felicia had wanted a son, and nothing and no one else had mattered.

Being replaced by Gabriel had hurt the former duchess deeply. What was left for an ambitious woman like her? At first, Felicia had wallowed in her despair, refusing to come out of her room, but something had changed. She was reentering life at Grantham, and Olivia wasn't sure whether to be pleased about that or worried.

"Are we going for a walk in the park?" Roberta

peered around the door, bouncing with excitement. She was still very much a child and there were times when Olivia envied her joie de vivre.

"Grandmama is resting."

"We can take Miss Starky as chaperone. That is what she is here for. Please, can we?"

Olivia couldn't help but laugh. "Very well," she said. "See if Justina wants to come."

Alone again, she took a deep breath. This would be her first foray into the polite world since the scandal at the Elphinstones' musical evening, not to mention the matter of Gabriel eloping with Vivienne. She could expect knowing looks and whispers behind hands, and even to be cut by those who had previously welcomed her. She needed to be prepared. Yes, the memory of the pamphlet with the cartoon depictions of herself and Ivo still stung, but she was the daughter of a duke. She was no longer going to allow a few cruel comments to drive her from her rightful place in society.

A stroll in the park would be the perfect way to begin this new phase of her life. With a determined air, Olivia went to unpack her trunk and find the perfect outfit.

The park was full of people perambulating and vehicles and horses slowly circling about, with frequent stops for the greeting of acquaintances. It was a fine day, and although Roberta declared she would rather have been on a horse, they enjoyed themselves. Several people paused to inquire after the dowager's health, but what they really wanted was the latest gossip. Olivia was glad they had not heard about Vivienne and Annette's novel writing venture—not yet anyway. She didn't fool herself that it would not happen eventually. A whisper here and a whisper there, and word would begin to spread.

She was pleased with her muslin walking dress, the skirt was a cream color, and the bodice and sleeves a shade of blue that matched her eyes. The current fashion was for waistlines to be very high, and bodices much smaller than she preferred, but Madame Annabelle, their dressmaker, had made allowance for Olivia's abundant "charms." Her bonnet was tied under her chin with a ribbon the same blue as the dress, and decorated with an attractive set of feathers that bobbed and waved as she turned her head. Overall, she felt as if she compared very favorably with the fashionable ladies there.

"Oh, look!" Justina's exclamation brought her attention to a large, stationary group just ahead of them. "Who is that they're all staring at, Olivia? Some famous person?"

"Perhaps it is the Prince of Wales," Roberta said. "Is it true that his father is mad?"

"Robbie!" Justina reprimanded her, glancing about in case they were overheard—which, thankfully, they weren't. "That is not something you should be speaking about in public."

"Why not? It's true, isn't it? Grandmama says it's true."

While her sisters bickered, Olivia tried to see through the crowd of sightseers. The focus of their attention seemed to be a gentleman at the very center. And, unfortunately, it was a gentleman she recognized.

"Don't look. It is Prince Nikolai of Holtswig," she said dully.

Of course, she had known she would be seeing him at some point, but she had hoped to avoid that moment as long as possible. After everything that had happened at Grantham, she no longer imagined he would ever want to propose to her. That ship had sailed, and she would be lucky if he did not give her the cut.

However, any hopes Olivia had of strolling by unobserved were crushed when Roberta raised her hand and waved, calling out the prince's name as if they were the best of friends. Olivia cringed, and Justina gasped, but it was too late to escape.

The prince's head jerked up, his aristocratic nostrils flaring, and his admirers turned to see who had the audacity to behave in such a vulgar manner.

"He won't recognize us," Olivia babbled. "I mean, of course he will *recognize* us, but he will pretend not to."

But not only did the prince nod politely to them, his entourage was forced to part as he made his way toward the three Ashton sisters.

"You don't have Leopold," Roberta informed him, obviously disappointed.

Nikolai frowned in that manner he seemed to reserve only for her—as if he was irritated and puzzled at the same time. "No, I don't. He is not fond of crowds. Why? Are you intending to steal him again?"

The tone was sharp for the socially appropriate prince, but Roberta laughed. "No, I am on my best behavior," she assured him.

Olivia tried not to let her doubts about that show on her face.

The prince's frown deepened, and he turned his attention to Olivia. "You are back in London? Will you be remaining for the rest of the Season?"

His interest in her answer seemed more than polite—there was a hint of concern. Did he think their disgrace was like a cold? Catching?

"I hope so," Olivia said brightly, as if she didn't have a care in the world. "Perhaps we will see you at some of our engagements, sir?"

Justina shot her a look that said *What engagements?* but Olivia ignored it. The trick was to put on an act, to pretend to be popular and busy, even if one was not. It was a lesson her grandmother had taught her.

The prince's manner was guarded as he murmured, "Indeed." He bowed politely, signaling their conversation was at an end.

The sisters curtsied and went on their way. In hindsight, Olivia was relieved they had bumped into the prince. It had taken away some of the awkwardness that might have occurred if they had met at one of those fictious engagements.

Roberta was watching her curiously. "Do you still want to marry him?" she blurted out.

"Shush," Olivia hissed angrily. "He will hear you."

Roberta shrugged and looked away, but there was something in the way her shoulders stiffened, and the pugnacious jut of her chin, that made Olivia wonder what her sister was thinking. Was she annoyed? Jealous? Or did she want the prince as her brother-in-law so that she could ride his horses? Olivia did not understand it, and then she decided not to bother trying. Roberta was just being Roberta. Besides, it was unlikely she would see the prince again, not in a social setting anyway, because although Justina would soon be "out," Roberta would not.

They had almost reached the gate and their waiting coach when a familiar voice called Olivia's name.

Just for a moment, she thought about quickening her steps, leaping into the safety of the vehicle, and shouting for the driver to speed away. It might still have been possible to ignore him...until Justina turned with a smile of greeting. Then Roberta turned too, and was skipping toward the approaching couple before remembering herself and, with an "oops" glance back at Olivia, slowed to a sedate walk.

Ivo had his sister Adelina on his arm, wearing a pretty bonnet to protect her complexion. His smile faded slightly when he caught sight of Olivia's unwelcoming expression, but any hope she had that he might pass them by was checked by Adelina, who clasped Justina's hand and began a long conversation with her.

Roberta shot Olivia a sly look. "I think I will wait in the coach," she said. "I am tired."

It was so obviously untrue that Ivo raised an eyebrow, but Roberta was already gone, and Olivia's voice came out sharper than was polite. "Our grandmother has brought Roberta to London to gain some polish."

"And is it working?" Ivo asked.

"So far today, she has called out to Prince Nikolai to ask him about his horse...sorry, *stallion*. And now she has rudely declared herself too tired to speak."

"The prince is here?" Ivo's gaze was on her face.

Before she could answer, Adelina said, "Roberta is still young. I can remember being lamentably self-centered at that age."

Olivia doubted anyone was as self-centered as Roberta. She looked to Ivo again, but he was staring into the distance now, as if the conversation bored him.

Soon, Justina and Adelina were chatting about the latest fashions, and unless Olivia wanted to stand in silence, or join Roberta in the coach, she had to speak to Ivo. Even if she felt oddly tongue-tied. A quick glance at him showed him to be his typically handsome, perfectly dressed self, and if that ache in the vicinity of her heart would just go away…

But memories of their rendezvous at the archery targets were already crowding her head. The warm evening and the fading light. The press of his lips on hers and the deep murmur of his voice as he held her close. He had stayed with her despite Gabriel's insistence that he go, because he was concerned for her. He had tried to tell her that the prince was wrong for her, because he knew she would be miserable, and she had refused to listen.

Ivo wasn't perfect, she wasn't pretending he was, but he had been her friend. She just hadn't realized how much she valued that friendship until she pushed him away. But could they be friends again without those other tangled emotions getting in the way?

When the silence had dragged on far too long, Ivo said politely, "I was sorry to miss the picnic at Grantham."

"Were you? It was very uncomfortable after Annette—" She stopped, aware he looked puzzled. "Didn't Viscountess Monteith spread the news to your mother? I was sure it would have reached London by now."

Bemused, he shook his head. "The viscountess is in Devon, I believe, and as far as I know, my mother has not heard from her since. Is there something I should know?"

Olivia twisted her fingers in the cord of her reticule. "It was nothing. I shouldn't have mentioned it." Time for a change of subject. "Did you complete your business at Whitmont? You and Mr. Wickley left in such a hurry."

Ivo's practiced smile faded, replaced by an expression she did not see often on his handsome face. Serious.

Grave. It was the same expression he had worn at the ball, when their dance finished, and she had rejected him. Again.

This time, it was Ivo who changed the subject. "Charles Wickley and I are going into partnership. We are purchasing your brother's gambling club."

Olivia's eyes widened. It was the first time she had heard of such a thing. "I did not know," she said. "My brother does not talk to us about his club. Although once, when we were having dancing lessons, he mentioned he had been in a fistfight with one of the more unruly patrons. My sisters were very impressed."

No need to mention she was too.

Ivo laughed, and out of the blue, it occurred to her that Prince Nikolai would never have laughed at such a disclosure. He would have looked at her as if he'd smelled something bad. "I cannot say I have been in a fistfight at a club," Ivo said, "but I do enjoy boxing at Gentleman Jackson's club."

"Perhaps that will come in handy when you are the owner of Cadieux's."

"Part owner," he corrected her. "And I think I will let Charles look after that side of things. In fact, I am going to be a silent partner, which means I will supply the funds and he will do the work."

He had meant her to be amused, so she smiled, but now it occurred to Olivia to wonder what Ivo actually *did*. Apart from being a duke and indulging in ridiculous wagers. He must spend a great deal of time at his tailor's—he was always fashionably dressed, but not outrageously so. And she supposed looking after Whitmont took up his time, unless he had someone he paid to do that. Probably he was like other titled gentlemen who did very much as they pleased. That was the impression she'd had of her father, although by the end of his life, his funds had all but dried up. Which reminded her of Gabriel working so hard to make Grantham pay, so perhaps not all titled gentlemen were idle.

"You have never been to Whitmont," Ivo said, breaking her silence.

Her attention, which had strayed, returned to his face. His eyes were very green, the sort of green that reminded her of the mossy pool at Grantham. The one in which she had swum naked. And now she was back to remembering Ivo's lips on hers.

Her answer was slightly breathless. "No, I have never been to Whitmont."

Ivo's expression softened, as if he was visualizing his home and what he saw pleased him very much. "It is not as grand as Grantham. The house was built in the days of Elizabeth I, with my ancestor given the task of keeping the Kentish coast secure from foreign invaders."

"And have you?" she asked curiously. "Kept the coast safe?"

"Indeed we have." A note of arrogance entered his voice. "From the Spanish to the French, we have kept England safe. Not that many strangers would venture into the salt marshes that lay at our doorstep. They are treacherous, and you need to watch the tides, but we Fitzsimmonses are taught from childhood how to cross them safely."

"Do you often walk in the marshes? It sounds like somewhere you should stay away from."

"It is home," he said simply. "I suppose some might call the landscape uninviting. When the weather is foul, it can be gray and sullen, and dangerous if you are a stranger. When I was young, my father told me that our surroundings have shaped our character. We Fitzsimmonses are strong, no-nonsense people, who refuse to be broken by life's ups and downs. The world outside Whitmont may mock us, or gossip about us, but we don't care because we are secure in the knowledge that there is no other family quite like ours."

He stopped, as if realizing he had disclosed more than he had intended. His smile was wry. "I suspect I am boring you."

His description had been unexpected, and rather moving. It explained so much of his character—confident and secure in his place in the world, and arrogant enough not to care what others thought. But as well as that, he had created an image of Whitmont in her head, and suddenly, she longed to see it and the dangerous salt marshes and the bleak, gray sea. That he genuinely loved the place she did not doubt, and his affection for his home added yet another facet to his personality. Which she was beginning to realize was far more complex than she had imagined.

"Olivia?" Justina was watching her curiously. "We should return to the house. Grandmama will be waiting for us."

Olivia shook herself out of her introspection, and when she smiled at Ivo, she felt almost like the shy, naïve girl she had been when he first asked her to dance. "No, you were not boring me. Whitmont sounds perfect. Perhaps one day you will invite us all to visit so we can see it for ourselves."

Adelina clapped her hands excitedly. "Oh yes, Ivo, let's!"

He didn't respond beyond one of his polite smiles,

and the intimate moment was gone. She had meant it
when she'd said she wanted to see Whitmont, but it was
painfully obvious that he did not want her there. She supposed she could not blame him.

"Olivia!" Justina called from the coach.

Ivo leaned closer so that his words were heard by her
alone, but he spoke in a kind way. "I'm sure you would
find Holtswig far more to your taste. Goodbye, Olivia."

She stared after him as he walked away. Did he still
think she had her sights set on the prince? Well, of course
he did! She had not told him otherwise, and the last he
knew was when they had danced at the ball and she had
told him how much she was looking forward to being
Nikolai's wife.

The kindness in his voice…and that goodbye. She
realized he was letting her go, removing himself from
any emotional ties that may have been between them. It
was what she had told herself she wanted, so why did it
hurt so much?

Chapter Twenty

It did not take long for Ivo to hear about the romance novel Vivienne and Annette had written. His sister was hardly through the door before his question was answered and Adelina gave him all the latest gossip on the Ashton family. He suggested they keep this tidbit to themselves, and that the Ashtons had enough to deal with, and he was pleased when she agreed.

The suggestion had been for Olivia's sake. Earlier, at the park, when he'd called out to her and she'd turned to him, she had a look on her face…As if she expected the worst possible news. He shouldn't have called out, but when he'd seen her, he'd felt so…well, so happy. In that moment, he had forgotten he could no longer be friends with her. He'd just wanted to look into her eyes and see her smile up at him. All of those memories of other times had rushed back to him: when the first person he had looked for at a ball was Olivia, and all he had thought about was how to have some time alone with her.

Well, times had changed, and he wouldn't forget it next time. In fact, there wouldn't be a next time. Enough was enough. He had sworn to keep his distance, and so he would, and eventually these ridiculous emotions would begin to subside.

"You like her," Adelina said quietly.

Ivo was startled out of his thoughts. "Her?"

"Lady Olivia Ashton. Don't pretend you don't know who I mean. It's obvious you are in lo…that you like her. Lexy and Mother have both commented on it. Mother is not particularly happy about such a connection, but I think if you are happy, then so will she be."

Ivo shook his head. "As pleasant as your fairy tale sounds, Adelina, I am not about to propose to Olivia Ashton." *Certainly not again.* "She has an entirely different future in mind, with a prince of our acquaintance."

"The prince left Grantham after Annette blurted out her secret. I don't think he was very pleased by yet another scandal brewing."

This was news to Ivo, and he wondered for a moment whether the chance of an engagement between Olivia and the prince was at an end. Not that it would make any difference to how he was feeling now. She would no doubt find some other wealthy gentleman to set her sights on, cheered along by her bloody grandmother. When he put this idea to his sister, she pooh-poohed it.

"Girls change their minds all the time, Ivo! You should know that; you have two sisters. I don't think you should give up on Olivia just yet. Maybe you should invite her to Whitmont."

Ivo said nothing—he didn't want to encourage Adelina—but he remembered very well the conversation with Olivia about Whitmont. He had found himself carried away, partly because she was listening with such rapt attention. It had seemed more than mere politeness on her part. Perhaps the wild aspect of his home appealed to her? In that moment, he'd had a desperate desire to take her there and show her his favorite places. To stand with her while the salty wind tossed their hair, and wax lyrical about his boyhood. Ridiculous, really.

Besides, what would Olivia think if she knew Whitmont had been searched by revenue officers looking for contraband? She already believed him a lost cause. She would rightly put even more distance between them in case it damaged her prospects.

No, despite what Adelina believed, he was not going to languish over a girl who did not want him.

The Season continued, still in full swing, and in his role as bachelor about town, Ivo accepted the more interesting invitations. One of them was Justina Ashton's coming-out, which he only agreed to because his mother and sisters insisted. It would be a test, Ivo told himself, to see if he was finally over Olivia. He was rather pleased that he hadn't dreamed about her for at least a fortnight.

In the meantime, he put himself at the disposal of his mother, whenever she ventured out into the fashionable world. There were a number of balls where partners were always gratefully received, as well as visits to the theater and late-night suppers. In the past, he would have been busy carousing at his club, but what had once seemed exciting to him no longer appealed. He hadn't made a reckless wager in quite some time, and he found he didn't miss them. In the meantime, the formal purchase of Cadieux's had gone ahead, with papers signed and bank drafts arranged. Gabriel had been more than happy to hand his club over to his best friend, Charles, with Ivo as his partner. And Cadieux's kept Ivo engaged. He had meant to be a silent partner, but Charles seemed to need his input more than expected, and the nightly antics at the gaming club fulfilled any yearning he had for excitement.

He saw Olivia Ashton at a great many entertainments, smiling and being charming—a far cry from the girl who had struggled to take her rightful place in society. If her grandmother had had any concerns about her granddaughter being openly ostracized when they returned to London, then they should by now have been laid to rest. There were still whispers, there always would be, but Olivia appeared to take them in her stride. Sometimes, at the less formal events, Justina was present, and once he even saw Roberta frolicking at a picnic with some younger girls.

Ivo kept his distance from Olivia Ashton. It was easier, despite what Adelina had said; he had no intention of resurrecting whatever had been between them. And he truly believed that, until one evening.

Olivia was dancing with a young gentleman, who was blushing and stammering out his words—at least Ivo guessed he was stammering from the look of him. Olivia was smiling, but her expression seemed uncomfortable. As the dance went on, Ivo found himself turning to watch them again and again, so distracted from the conversation he had been having with a very pretty lady that she must have thought him a bore.

The dance finished, Olivia curtsied, and the gentleman bowed, but before he could lead her back to her place beside her grandmother, another woman came to take his arm. She smiled at Olivia, but it was so obviously false that it raised Ivo's hackles. Then she caught hold of the man's sleeve and tugged him away. Ivo could see the red flags in her cheeks and her mouth moving as she spoke close to the fellow's ear. It was a disturbing display of bad manners.

Olivia had been left standing in the middle of the room, and there were some curious glances sent her way. She seemed deep in her own thoughts, and Ivo knew he shouldn't, he really shouldn't, but he couldn't help himself. He was already strolling toward her.

Just as he reached her, Olivia abruptly turned and almost ran into him. "Oh!" Briefly, he grasped her upper arms to steady her as she blinked up at him. "Ivo?"

He made himself smile politely as he bowed. "Lady Olivia." The music was beginning again, and the dancers were taking their places. "I think we should move out of the way before we get trampled. Who is your next partner?"

"I…" She fumbled with her dance card. "I don't have one."

"How surprising," he said evenly, "and how fortunate for me. Come and sit with me for a moment."

She hesitated and then gave a wry smile and a little nod before tucking her gloved hand into the crook of his elbow.

Ivo had meant to take her back to her grandmother, but instead, he found himself leading her past the dowager duchess—who appeared to be dozing anyway—and found one of those semi-secluded alcoves that seemed to abound at social gatherings. The flimsy curtains were fastened to the sides so that it was open to public scrutiny, but it also gave them a measure of privacy. Olivia sat down without a word, and he joined her on the cushioned sofa that was tucked into the space.

"What was that about?" he asked bluntly.

She frowned at him, and then her expression grew

haughty. "You mean Lord Hollingsworth? I doubt it is any of your business, Your Grace, but he was asking my permission to call upon me at Ashton House. I don't think it was a proposal, but he was rather incoherent."

Ivo's surprise must have shown, because her frown returned.

"You seem shocked that an eligible gentleman should want to call upon me."

There was something in her statement that made him want to dig deeper into her feelings and his, but he resisted. "No, not at all. I just…" He cleared his throat. "Was that his mother who dragged him away? It looked as if she was rescuing him from peril."

She gave an unwilling laugh. "Something like that. I overheard a little of what she said. I am, evidently, an unacceptable prospect for him, and she wanted him to keep his distance in case I 'ensnared' him with my 'wiles.'"

She was making a joke of it, but Ivo knew her too well to miss the distress in her blue eyes. "You're well rid of him," he said roughly. "If he needs his mother's permission to call upon someone—"

"Ivo, I know you are trying to make me feel better, but I understand. I do. I am not an acceptable prospect for many of these people. The Ashtons are scandal-ridden, and we are in debt. I'm not sure my dowry will attract the likes of Lord Hollingsworth or if I even *have* a dowry. I haven't discussed it with Gabriel or Grandmama. I suppose I should, in case—"

He had been eyeing her curiously as she gabbled, but now he broke in. "Have you had many gentleman callers?"

"No one I am desperate to marry, if that's what you

mean. One or two rakes who think I am easy pickings." Her smile turned into a grimace. "Grandmama sent them off with fleas in their ears. I've had some widowers who believe I'd make the perfect stepmother for their children, but I think they are probably as desperate as I am. There has been no one I am inclined to marry."

"The prince…"

"No, he has not proposed, nor will he. That is over."

He waited a beat. "You are very matter-of-fact about it all."

"I have learned to be. I know I must marry, and to someone who can help my sisters when they are out, but I am prepared to wait until the right man comes along."

Ivo felt a wave of feeling crash over him. He wasn't sure what it was. Hope? The desire to take her in his arms and crush her to him was definitely there, but perhaps he was just feeling protective. "You know," he said quietly, "you can always seek me out if you need some company."

Her face brightened. "You mean chat like we used to?" She hesitated. "I didn't think you wanted to be friends anymore."

"I didn't think you did!"

They smiled at each other. Olivia seemed to collect herself, and glanced about. "I should go back to Grandmama." Then, as she went to rise, "Are you still wagering on everything and anything? I haven't heard of any of your antics recently."

"That's because there haven't been any. I am busy with the club, and when I'm not there, I am squiring my mother and sisters about."

"Don't you miss it?" She was watching him curiously.

"I miss the dares I made with you."

She dropped her gaze and then flashed him a look

from under her lashes. "What dare would you make with me? If you could?"

It was on the tip of his tongue to suggest another billiards match, but then his gaze caught the gangly figure of Lord Hollingsworth not far away. He hesitated, but only for a moment. "I dare you to drop your handkerchief in front of Hollingsworth. If he picks it up and returns it to you, then you win. If he picks it up but doesn't return it, then I win."

"Why wouldn't he return it? It seems rather childish…"

"That's half the fun of a dare, Olivia."

She thought about it and then smiled. "Very well. What will I win?"

"The knowledge that you are a beautiful young woman and irresistible even to a mother's boy like Hollingsworth."

That made her laugh. "And what will you win?"

"I have already won," he said gallantly. "I have my friend back again."

She seemed too surprised to answer, and then her face softened. "Thank you," she whispered before she turned away.

Ivo sat and watched as she made her way toward the Hollingsworths. She cunningly let her handkerchief flutter just as she passed them, and the young man immediately retrieved it. But instead of returning it, he gave a sneaky glance about him, and when no one seemed to have noticed, he tucked it into the breast pocket of his jacket.

Ivo smothered a snort of laughter. Olivia had taken several more steps, and now she turned and looked across the room at him. Ivo mimed what Hollingsworth had done, and saw her eyebrows rise. Then she grinned at him in a manner he had not seen for months, and continued on her way.

Chapter Twenty-One

O livia discovered that everything felt lighter, as if a weight had been lifted from her. It was puzzling because she still had the same old problems to beset her. Although she was invited everywhere, she was not flooded with suitors—her only actual proposals had come from a harassed-looking gentleman with seven children and a dead wife, and an ancient gentleman without two pennies to rub together. She had no desire to play mother, having already done that with her sisters, nor did she want to be nurse to the old man.

She was having more fun than she would have believed possible after the scandals that had sent her scurrying back to Grantham. If it wasn't for the niggling anxiety of making a suitable marriage, she would have been perfectly content, and sure that the right partner would come along soon.

In the meantime, Ivo was her friend again. Who would have thought having him once more in her life would make her so happy? And yet it did.

They were being careful though. A conversation in a quiet corner, or a dance where they could chat. He made her laugh and poked fun at some of the other guests, and she found herself doing the same. And if she sometimes worried they were being rude, she reminded herself that plenty of them had spoken cruelly about her, so why not return the favor?

During one of their dances, she told him about the ancient gentleman's proposal. Ivo was amused. "If he had married every lady he ever asked, then he would have a harem by now," he'd said.

Olivia knew what a harem was. "I'd prefer to be the only wife in my husband's life," she said dryly. A memory popped into her head, and she remembered how, when she was twelve, she had planned to run away to London and become a courtesan.

When she told Ivo, he had sputtered with laughter.

"I didn't know what a . . . a courtesan was of course," she admitted. "I had overheard my parents talking, and it sounded like it was an exciting thing to be."

"But they stopped you?" Ivo's green eyes were dancing.

"Yes. They found out from one of my sisters, and I was sent to my room without supper."

There was a comfortable silence before he asked, "Has Lord Hollingsworth called?"

"No. Sadly, I didn't come up to scratch in his mother's eyes."

"Poor Lord Hollingsworth," he replied, mock-seriously. "Is he doomed to be single forever?"

"Surely she will find him someone who comes up to the mark?" she said, aware that her cheeks were warm. She was enjoying herself, and Ivo's eyes were sparkling.

"Only if she can do the choosing."

"You mean like soldiers on parade? Would she line them all up and then inspect them?" She made her voice sound like Lady Hollingsworth's. "Too short, too tall, too forward, smiles too much…"

He fought his laughter, his chest shaking. "I thought I was the mimic," he managed at last.

"Are you coming to Justina's debut?" Olivia changed the subject once more as their dance finished.

"Yes, we are all coming. As long as you promise there will be some juicy scandal."

Olivia grimaced. "I hope not. I want her to enjoy herself. It will be a small affair, but she doesn't mind. Gabriel cannot afford—" She bit her lip.

"Olivia," he said softly, leading her away from the dancers. "None of us are flush with the readies."

She nodded and then sighed. "I know. Why did my father have to be such a spendthrift? Things would be so much more comfortable if we were wealthy."

"I do not plan to always be poor," he said quietly.

There was something meaningful in his expression, which Olivia chose to ignore. Instead, she smiled at him. "Do you have a dare for me? I am bored with polite chitchat."

"A dare?" He met her gaze, and she could see the thoughts turning in his head. And then he said, "I think it's your turn. What dare will you give me?"

Instantly, her mind flooded with possibilities, most of them completely out of the question. *Take me into the garden and kiss me. Dance with me again and again. Hold me close and tell me...*But no, none of them were doable, even though she wanted them to be. She was aware of those old, foolish urges rising up inside her, the longing to do something completely wild and unacceptable despite all of the very good reasons she knew she should not. *Could* not.

She looked about for inspiration, and her eye fell on a young girl she had noticed earlier. She sat against the wall, shoulders a little hunched, looking completely miserable. A stern, matronly woman sat beside her, glowering at anyone who passed in a protective but unhelpful manner. Olivia turned to Ivo with a wicked grin.

"Ask her to dance."

"Her? Who?" He was looking about.

"*Her*. You will make her evening, Ivo. She will go to sleep tonight remembering every moment of the dance, every word you say, every smile you give her." She knew that, because that was how Olivia had felt the first time Ivo had asked *her* to dance.

He gave her a dubious look but set off as instructed. Olivia watched as he approached the girl, smiling at the matron and then bowing. There was a brief conversation, and then the older woman nodded regally, as if she was bestowing something very precious upon him, and the girl stood up. She was smiling, blushing, wondering if this was really happening. That the handsomest gentleman in the room—and a duke to boot—was asking her to stand up with him.

Olivia couldn't help smiling too as the music swelled and the dance began. She might have watched the whole thing, but she was aware of the way in which people gossiped, and her face must be food for plenty of speculation right now. She made her way back to the dowager, and found Adelina and Lexy there with Ivo's mother. They were making stilted conversation and looked relieved to see her.

When the polite greetings had been made, Adelina leaned in close and said, "Ivo is dancing with a wall-flower. Do you see? That is very kind of him."

"And very unlike him," Lexy added.

Their mother was quick to her son's defense. "Nonsense! Ivo was always a kind boy."

"What if her chaperone decides he is going to marry her?" Adelina asked mischievously.

Her mother's face changed. "No, he is not marrying her," she said sharply. "I know her family, and they are as poor as church mice." Then, remembering the company she was in, "I'm sure he is just being kind."

There was an awkward silence. Olivia was well aware of how debt-ridden Ivo's family was, just like hers. Another reason for her to never allow herself to accept a proposal from him, even if he asked her again. Which he wouldn't. That was over. But it brought up the question of Ivo's choice of wife. He needed to marry someone wealthy, just as she did.

And yet, as she turned to watch Ivo dance, charming the young girl into conversing with him, Olivia admitted that if matters were different…*I do not plan to always be poor*.

The dance had finished, and Ivo returned his partner to her chaperone. A glance about the room found his family and Olivia, and he made his way toward them. He had barely reached them when his mother launched into a warning about the wallflower's lack of fortune.

"Good heavens, Mother, I was dancing with the chit, not marrying her," he said, with a sideways glance at Olivia.

"Viscount Marchant's daughter is free," his mother pointed out. "She has a large dowry. Dance with her, Ivo."

Ivo sighed. "I have danced with her. She giggles at everything I say, and then I run out of conversation."

"You should consider the dowry rather than the conversation," his mother said firmly.

It sounded *cold*. Olivia wondered if her grandmother's conversations to her about marriage and money sounded just as cold. More than likely. But then, marriages among members of the ton were business arrangements, something she needed to keep reminding herself.

"I did not reject the Duke of Grantham because of his lack of conversation," Grandmama jumped in, as if reading Olivia's mind. "One did what one was told. These young people read too many silly books about love and romance." She stopped and frowned, no doubt remembering that her own granddaughter-in-law had been the author of just such a book.

Ivo's mother tried very hard not to smile. Adelina and Lexy exchanged glances. Ivo caught Olivia's gaze and raised his eyebrow. A friend of his sisters' had come up to chat with them, and he took the opportunity to lean into Olivia. "How is your brother and his wife?"

"Busy," Olivia replied. "Grantham keeps him constantly occupied, and Vivienne is in charge of the younger girls, as well as learning to manage such a large house. I do not envy them."

"Are you not trained in the art of housekeeping? I can imagine you inspecting the furniture for dust and poring over menus."

Olivia wondered whether she dared to tell him what she really thought about that, but it was Ivo, so she did. "I was never trained in any of the tasks a wife is supposed to be trained in. Most of my time was spent running wild with my sisters, or trying to find ways to entertain them so they would not realize how horrible our lives were. And when I tried to cook, I usually burned whatever it was I was trying to make palatable."

His eyes had widened. "Good God," he said quietly, "you put me to shame, Olivia. Are you *trying* to make me feel guilty? I feel like I should have some dreadful story of my own to share, but the truth is my childhood was quite pleasant. I had my parents and my sisters, who spoiled me terribly, I admit. Which is one of the reasons I plan to do everything in my power to be a good duke and make their lives more comfortable."

"Ivo, you shouldn't apologize for—" she began earnestly but was interrupted.

"What are you two whispering about?" Her grandmother's voice was sharp. "Olivia, here is Mr. Scott come to claim his dance."

Olivia realized it was true. Mr. Scott was standing, patiently waiting. She apologized as she went to meet him, trying to ignore his woolly eyebrows. He was twenty years her senior, and she suspected he had learned to dance by counting his steps, but then who was she to talk? Her dancing was all very well now, but that had not always been the case. During their last encounter, he had told her about the assemblies he attended in Bristol.

"There is always some amusement or other. London is all very well, but give me Bristol any day," he had said.

Mr. Scott was the dowager's latest marital hope for Olivia. He was a shipping company owner, and although he had not a trace of blue blood in him, he was wealthy. That he was a far cry from Prince Nikolai just showed how desperate her grandmother had become.

"He needs a wife." The dowager seemed to know everything about him. "He isn't too picky about a dowry. He wants someone pretty and biddable."

"I doubt that's me. Everyone knows about—"

"Let him know you are grateful for his attentions. And think about your sisters! He will have wealthy friends. Justina and Roberta can partake of your good fortune and find husbands of their own."

As she danced and conversed and was as charming as Grandmama wanted her to be, she tried to like Mr. Scott, she really did. And he was pleasant enough, rather grave when stating his opinions, and although he listened to hers politely, Olivia didn't feel as if he was really listening. She was so much younger than he, so his being dismissive was understandable, she supposed. And there were good points to him. Her grandmother's plan was a sound one, but when she imagined herself being married to him…She was not filled with elation. Instead, she felt a twisting anxiety in her stomach, a sense that she would be making a terrible mistake if she gave away her life, her future, to a man she could not love.

It was the final straw when he told her he did not really enjoy parties "and the like" and would prefer his wife not to gad about. "Home is where a wife should be," he told her firmly. "I would expect my dinner on the table at the same time every day."

Olivia only just managed to bite back her retort, but by then, her mind was made up. She did not care how wealthy Mr. Scott was. She didn't want to marry him. She didn't want to marry any of the men who had so far shown an interest in marrying her. And the ones who had had no intention of offering her marriage but seemed to enjoy her company were of no use to her either. She was growing tired of rejecting one suitor, only to have her grandmother bring forth another. Why did the Season have to be all about her marrying? Why couldn't she just enjoy herself and think about the future later?

The dance finished, and the first thing she did was look about for Ivo. He was standing with his family, watching her with a sympathetic expression. As if he had read exactly what she was thinking and concurred.

As friends, they seemed so perfectly matched. He was not the dangerously reckless duke he used to be. He had changed. When he was with her, he was more cautious—of her feelings and her reputation. Seeing him with his mother and sisters reinforced for her just how much he cared about them, how much he wanted to succeed for their sakes and for the sake of his estate at Whitmont. He did not enjoy lacking a fortune any more than she did, but he was trying to rectify that by buying into Cadieux's. What was she doing? Marrying a man she did not love for his money and her sisters' sakes, and hoping she would not be too miserable.

It felt wrong.

But she did not know how to make it right.

Chapter Twenty-Two

Ivo had accompanied his mother and sisters to a dinner at the Monteiths' town house in London. Jane, Viscountess Monteith, had arrived home from Devon with some exciting news, and Ivo's mother spent a great deal of time trying to guess what it was. His cousin Harold was there, and Adelina had prevailed upon Ivo to escort one of her old school friends, who was staying with them, and who had recently suffered a disappointment in love. Miss Fenwick was a pretty girl with dark hair, blue eyes, and a serious demeanor, and as she hardly said two words together and didn't giggle at his every utterance, accompanying her was no hardship for Ivo. He had told his sister not to expect anything more from him, but she had assured him that "poor Daphne" was too shattered to even think of another gentleman after her true love jilted her.

"She has sworn off men," his sister had added teasingly, "so don't fear she will come between you and Lady Olivia."

The Ashtons were there as well—the dowager, Justina, and Olivia—and Ivo ignored the flare of warmth in his chest at the thought of her company. He must not make his partiality too obvious or there would be talk, and nothing was more likely to drive Olivia away. Having just gotten her friendship back, he did not want to lose it again.

Vivienne, the new duchess, was still at Grantham, but there was a whisper that the viscountess had not invited Vivienne's mother, her sister-in-law, to make the journey from Cornwall. For some reason, the prince was also present, and Ivo wondered when it had been decided he was part of their clique of friends. He suspected the Dowager Duchess of Grantham had something to do with that. Even though Olivia had insisted she and Nikolai were not an item, it didn't mean her grandmother thought the same. She would be doing everything in her power to bring about the union of the Season. What if an announcement was made tonight? It might be a good thing Ivo had the jilted Miss Fenwick at his side—didn't misery love company? And he admitted to himself that if Olivia married the prince, he would be miserable indeed. Frankly, whoever she married would send him into a state of melancholy.

Viscountess Monteith called everyone together before dinner, and Ivo could see from her flushed face that she was bursting with exciting news. She insisted on complete quiet before she launched into a rather breathless speech.

Ivo felt rather sick, but he reminded himself that if Olivia was marrying, then the dowager would hardly allow anyone else to broadcast the news.

"You have been invited here to share in this happy occasion. I have an announcement! Annette is engaged! We are very pleased to welcome the fortunate gentleman into our family. Indeed, he already feels like one of us. Harold, where are you?"

Harold! Of course. Ridiculously relieved, Ivo watched

as his cousin slipped through the chattering crowd, a beaming smile on his face. Although Ivo had been aware his cousin and Annette seemed to be close, and he had suspected for some time they were ideally suited, it was still a surprise. A nice one. Harold reached for Annette's hand and turned that smile on his intended. A smile she returned with tears in her eyes.

Ivo went to congratulate them. "You sneaky devil," he said to Harold. "When did this happen?"

Harold laughed and drew him to one side. "It was hush-hush. I went down to Devon after Annette sent me a rather fraught note and…well," he said with a slight grimace. "The viscountess wasn't exactly thrilled at first, but she's come around. And I love her."

"The viscountess?" Ivo raised a skeptical eyebrow.

"Annette, you idiot!"

Ivo's expression softened. "I know you do. And she loves you too, and I suspect she has for quite some time." He did not need to explain to Harold that Ivo and Annette had never been more than friends, and there had never been any intention by either of them to marry.

"Thank you, Ivo. You will be my best man, won't you?"

Ivo agreed. "And just think," he added, sotto voce, "your wife will be able to pen as many romantic novels as she wants, and you can publish them for her."

Harold grinned. "I'm counting on it."

As if by magic, servants had appeared with champagne, and a toast was drunk, before everyone was ushered into the dining room for a celebratory dinner.

The Monteiths had outdone themselves with the meal. The table was groaning with course after course. Ivo wondered if he would be able to walk by the time it came to retire to the drawing room, where there was to be dancing for those capable of it, and conversation for those who weren't.

Adelina, Lexy, and Justina were whispering secrets with Annette, and his mother had her head close to the viscountess's. He had caught his mother's glance once or twice over the meal and knew what it meant. When they arrived home, she would be asking him when he was going to marry and give her some Fitzsimmons grandchildren, and he would smile and say he had yet to meet the right woman. It was a theme they revisited whenever someone announced an engagement, but lately, his mother had been getting more determined.

Olivia and the prince were conversing in low voices. When Ivo found himself staring, trying to guess what they were saying, he made himself look away. Miss Fenwick sat mute by his side, twisting her fingers in her lap, so Ivo bestirred himself to find a topic of conversation that might interest her.

"Are you enjoying your stay in London? Adelina did not say whether or not you had been here before," he said kindly.

"I am trying to enjoy myself, but I keep thinking of all the things *we* were going to do. Before…" Her lip wobbled, and she bit it before meeting his gaze. "Adelina says you have suffered a disappointment too, Your Grace?"

"Did she? The little wretch!" Ivo said before he could stop himself.

Daphne looked shocked, and then she chuckled, and suddenly she was much more appealing to him.

Someone had gotten up from their chair and moved across the room, and only then did he notice it was Olivia.

Miss Fenwick was speaking again. "Adelina says I

should turn my mind to other matters, but it is difficult when memories of him consume me."

She had a dramatic turn of phrase, but Ivo understood what she meant.

"When I go home, I expect I will be thrown into his company again. He is a neighbor, so I cannot avoid him," she added with a sigh. "I am hoping that if I treat him as if he were any other casual acquaintance, it will become the truth."

"Does he feel no guilt for the way he has treated you?" Ivo asked softly.

"He's head over heels in love. With somebody else. He told me he didn't understand what love was until then."

Love. It was an emotion Ivo had not believed in before Olivia, and he still wasn't sure that was what he felt for her. At first, he had thought it an infatuation, a longing for the company of someone like-minded, and he had mourned the loss of her. Lately, being her friend seemed to be enough, although if he were honest, when she was not at the same entertainment as himself, he felt a degree of disappointment that seemed out of all proportion. As if she held his happiness in her smile. As if she held his heart in the palm of her hand.

The realization gave him a nasty shock. Maybe he and "poor Daphne" made a good pair after all!

Just then, Adelina called to Daphne to join her and mediate on some point of fashion. Ivo looked about for Harold, hoping for a distraction from his thoughts, but his cousin was in serious discussion with the viscount and the prince. Harold would have to learn about horses if he was to hold his own there. Maybe there was an equine instruction manual at his publishing house? The Dowager

Duchess of Grantham's head was nodding as she sat in the most comfortable chair in the room, not quite snoring but almost.

And Olivia?

She had tucked herself away at the piano, although she was not playing. Could she play? Ivo knew if he was falling in love with her, then he should stay away, but as was often the case with self-destructive behavior, the tug of his feelings was too strong. Besides, what had Miss Fenwick just said? *If I treat him as if he were any other casual acquaintance, it will become the truth.* He would have a word or two with Olivia, and then leave her be. Surely there could be no harm in that? A polite word, that was all.

If he could do that and walk away, then he could continue to be her friend without hurt to himself, or to her. Ivo took a breath, set his shoulders, and strolled toward the piano.

Chapter Twenty-Three

O livia was out of sorts. Not that she wasn't happy for Annette and Harold, who seemed ridiculously in love, and no doubt planning their next romance novel— although hopefully they would keep Vivienne out of it. She was happy for them because happiness seemed in short supply in the world she lived in, and it was good to see that some people at least could capture that elusive emotion.

And yet she felt restless and irritable.

She could not complain about her time in London so far. She had had invitations, and she was grateful. And she had played her part, pretending to be perfectly at ease despite sometimes encountering knowing looks and spiteful whispers. She had wanted to complete her Season, and she was accomplishing that. It would be better once Justina could accompany her, but that would not happen until her sister was "out." Not long now though. The preparations were in place, which was why their grandmother was so tired she was asleep in the Monteiths' armchair. Felicia had not lifted a finger to help, but sadly, none of her daughters were surprised by that.

Olivia sat down at the piano and wished she could play. Perhaps music would have been a solace at a time like this. But she had never learned, none of them had, and it wasn't one of the things Vivienne or her grand-mother could fix without a lot of practice. At least after Vivienne's lessons, Olivia could truthfully say she painted…"a little."

The cozy murmur of Ivo's tête-à-tête with Miss Fenwick had reached her even here. Olivia had thought the piano would be far enough away, but perhaps her ears were attuned to his voice. Adelina had said Miss Fenwick was an old school friend, but from the way Ivo's mother was watching her son and the girl, Olivia thought she was hoping something more would develop between them.

Which was why she was over here at the piano. She had discovered she could not abide the thought of Ivo falling in love with a woman who wasn't her. This realization had not happened in a heartbeat. It was some-thing that had been growing inside her for some time. She knew her jealousy was at odds with everything that Olivia had mapped out for her future, but she couldn't help it. Since their first meeting at her coming-out when she had fallen under his spell, their relationship had been like a golden light in a dark room, and she a very fool-ish moth. Even when she clearly saw all of his faults, there was a strong attraction between them. A closeness and understanding she had felt for no other man. Now, despite the changes she had been through, the growing up she had done, she was still aware of his allure. And they were friends again, and that was a wonderful thing, and she should want him to find someone who could make him happy. But she didn't. Seeing him smiling and whispering with Miss Fenwick did not give her an ounce of pleasure.

Was Miss Fenwick to be the next Duchess of Northam? Perhaps Olivia really was the horrible person her sisters thought her to be, if she preferred Ivo to be miserable like her rather than find contentment with another woman. Because she *was* miserable. Miserable at the very thought of being married to Mr. Scott or some other suitable gentleman, while forever yearning for Ivo.

Scars from her unhappy childhood had driven her to seek security and stability, and yet the idea of being held hostage to her past, as if she was some sort of martyr, was equally appalling. Olivia had been searching for her path in life, and she had thought she'd found it. A sensible path. A boring path. Marry Mr. Scott or someone like him and go quietly into domestic drudgery. She'd be able to help her sisters, but it turned out they didn't want her help. Even Gabriel had advised her against marrying someone she didn't love, and he should know.

Acknowledging the truth of her feelings, of her nature, was an immense relief. She knew that eventually, some wealthy gentleman would come along, and she would not be able to find fault with him, and she would probably have to marry him. Ivo might be married by then too, to some rich miss. But that was in the future, and right now, she needed to be herself again. The girl Ivo had told her he knew so well…

"Are you going to play a tune?"

That familiar voice made Olivia jump. She took a shaky breath, ignoring the flutter in her chest. He couldn't read her mind, could he? "Unfortunately, no," she said calmly, resting her fingers on the keys. "What about you, Northam? Can you play?"

Ivo shrugged. "A little," he said, which made her laugh. "What?" he demanded, and this time, she did look. His green eyes were sparkling, and his lips were curled in a mocking little smile above his smoothly shaven jaw and his perfectly tied cravat.

"You can't play at all, can you?" she said.

He shrugged. "No, not a single note. My sisters can, but I never learned. And before you say it, yes, I was too busy riding horses and racing my curricle."

Olivia shook her head. "What is this fascination with horses? I will never understand it."

Ivo followed her glance to the prince and his two companions. "Harold can sympathize with you, I think. You will have to ask Roberta to teach you so that you can hold your own."

"What if I don't want to?" Olivia retorted. "Big, smelly beasts liable to nip your fingers even when you are handing them a juicy apple. Not that I am afraid of them," she denied quickly.

"Ah." He didn't appear to know what to say to that. He glanced back toward the others, and Olivia wondered if he was keen to return to Miss Fenwick. The thought made her prattle on, just to keep him by her side.

"Roberta seems very fond of them. Horses, I mean. Whenever she is melancholy, she goes out riding and comes back in a better mood. Justina is the same with her books. Edwina with her dolls. I wish there was something I looked forward to." Her voice drifted off.

His gaze sharpened, as if he'd suddenly become aware of her low spirits. That knowing look in his eyes made her feel exposed and uncomfortable. That he should see her so clearly! But then he always had. Before she could draw her prickly defenses around her, he spoke again.

"If I wasn't a changed man, I'd…" He bit his lip.

"You'd what?" She stared back at him.

He looked over his shoulder again, and, frustrated, Olivia hurried to recapture his attention. "What were you going to say, Ivo? What would you do if you weren't a changed man?"

Ivo raised his eyebrows, studying her. "I would give you a challenge. A dare."

She tried to read his expression. "But we have already dared each other, have we not? There was Lord Hollingsworth and the girl you asked to dance."

"Rather lukewarm dares, Olivia," he said with a wry smile. "Not the sort I used to make."

It was true, he had been careful with her, heedful not to do anything that might damage her reputation. She had enjoyed their games, yes, but they hadn't exactly gotten her heart pumping with excitement.

"What were you going to say? I want to hear this risky challenge, Ivo."

"Do you?" he asked quietly. "Very well. I was going to dare you to a race. With horses."

Olivia's eyes widened. "A curricle race?"

"No, a horse race. Through Hyde Park."

Her laugh was half shock and half excitement. Her heart was pumping now, all of those feelings she had ignored for so long rushing back like a river in flood. It felt...*wonderful*.

"Impossible!" she declared.

"Why? Are you afraid? You just said you weren't. It would have to be in the early morning with few people about, and it would be a race between just the two of us." He dropped his voice and leaned down, his arm resting on top of the piano.

Olivia couldn't help noticing his hair had grown out of the severe cut he had worn at Grantham, and the ends were beginning to curl again. The waves looked soft and silky, and she squeezed her hands together, resisting the urge to reach out and touch.

"Come, Olivia, are you not even a little bit tempted? You know you want to beat me. You always want to. What about the archery contest? Do you only accept my riskier challenges when you know you can win?"

"Nonsense," she said automatically. "And this is a hypothetical dare, because you are a changed man."

"I am as changed as you want me to be," he replied cryptically. "Do you really want me to be browbeaten like Lord Hollingsworth? Or that other smug fellow with the monstrous eyebrows?" He moved his own brows up and down.

Olivia snorted an unladylike laugh.

"You want the excitement, the risk. I know you do. You thrive on it. Let me give that to you. Tomorrow, some eligible gentleman with his pockets full of gold might sweep you off your feet, and you'll be gone. So let's enjoy ourselves while we can."

It was very much what she had been thinking herself, and she wondered if he could read her mind after all.

She pictured herself riding a horse through Hyde Park with Ivo at her side. It didn't sound all that terrible. Lots of ladies rode in Hyde Park with gentlemen of their acquaintance. But a *race*…What would her grandmother say? It didn't bear *thinking*…Just as well it wasn't going to happen.

And yet, as soon as she reminded herself this was all make-believe, she felt her spirits sink again.

Unaware of her inner conflict, Ivo's knowing green eyes slid up and down her, and he said thoughtfully, "You would need a disguise. Just in case one of those annoying pamphleteers was up and about despite the early hour."

"You make it sound almost possible," she said, a little catch in her voice.

He leaned closer, his breath warm on her cheek. "It is possible. Anything is possible, Olivia, if you embrace it."

So tempting. As much as she enjoyed their friendship, Olivia still longed for something more. That spark that seemed to light up inside her whenever they were together.

"I miss the old Ivo. Sometimes," she blurted.

"Do you?"

He wasn't looking over his shoulder now. He was entirely focused on Olivia.

"Sometimes life seems very boring without you."

He hesitated, then spoke in a rush. "Say yes, Olivia. Let us cut through those restrictions society and family have placed upon us and pretend we are free to do as we please, for just one day."

Her heart was beating so fast and hard in her breast that she put her hand to it, as if to hold it in. If she was in disguise, who would know? Only Ivo. This would be something far more exciting than anything she had done for ages. She shouldn't do it, but she wanted to. Desperately. Surely she deserved one day of freedom out of all the days she had tried so hard to be good?

"When would this ridiculous dare take place?" she asked as evenly as she could manage.

He stiffened, suddenly alert, as if that was the last thing he had expected. His smile was dazzling and slightly predatory. "This day a fortnight hence. Five o'clock in the morning, meet at Hyde Park Corner and—why not?—race along Rotten Row. I don't know if your intentions are genuine, Olivia, or if you're playing games with me. But if you want to go ahead with this, then a simple nod to me the next time we meet will be sufficient to let me know."

When she had nothing to say to that, he gave a polite bow and walked away. Olivia watched him return to the others, her mind still a chaotic jumble. Miss Fenwick looked up at him with a smile as he stopped by her chair.

Olivia had sworn to live her own life, but why did it have to be a life that made her want to scream at the tedium? The prospect of racing Ivo and beating him at something he considered his strong suit made her senses come alive. They were buzzing, but she tried to think calmly.

What if she was caught? What would happen then? Banishment to Grantham probably. This was her last chance, and if she went ahead and indulged in the sort of reckless behavior she had vowed to correct in herself, then she only had herself to blame.

The alternative? Stability, marrying sensibly, playing the bountiful sister…A boring life with a man she couldn't love. Well, all of that was still ahead of her in some form or another. She was not wealthy enough to travel the world or become an eccentric spinster thumbing her nose at convention. And if she was honest, she wouldn't want to. She *was* conventional, in the sense that she wanted love and marriage and a family.

But before she bowed to the inevitable, she wanted some fun.

There was another problem, and it was a huge impediment: she could barely ride. Certainly not well enough to race someone down Rotten Row! Was it an insurmountable problem? Many would say it was, but they were not Olivia Ashton.

Roberta *could* ride. Olivia sometimes thought her

sister was half horse! Roberta could teach her the rudiments of horsemanship, or at least enough so that she would not fall off and make a complete fool of herself. And Roberta could be persuaded to keep it a secret, or, if necessary, be bribed to do so.

A fortnight hence was also Justina's coming-out, but that was in the evening, and she would race Ivo at five o'clock in the morning. Plenty of time to recover. No one would be the wiser. It was feasible.

She admitted then that this pretense at weighing up the pros and cons was just that: a pretense. She was going to accept. Just imagining the look on his face when she joined him at Hyde Park Corner—the amazement and *delight*. Ivo wanted her to say yes, he wanted their relationship to return to what it had been in the beginning. And if she won, he would find pleasure in that and tell her so. He might even kiss her.

Olivia's heart gave a heavy knock against her ribs. The soft press of his lips, the warmth of his breath, and the hard shape of his body against hers. The very thought of it made her quite dizzy. Her fingers itched to slide through the hair at his nape, while the scent of his pomade only heightened her longing.

If you want to go ahead with this, then a simple nod to me the next time we meet will be sufficient to let me know.

Olivia scanned the room.

Ivo was standing with the others, busy smiling and chatting as if he had forgotten all about her. He probably thought she would refuse, or make some paltry excuse to wriggle out of it. He'd probably given up on her altogether and was about to dare Miss Fenwick to do something outrageous instead.

At that moment, the dowager, still sleeping in her chair, woke with a start—which everyone pretended not to notice. In a loud voice, she announced that it was time they were leaving. Obediently, Olivia hurried to her side, but as they donned their outdoor clothing while the coach was brought around, she finally caught Ivo's eye. He was watching her intently, and she read a degree of doubt in those green eyes. Had *he* changed his mind?

She nodded her head firmly, just once, and watched his eyes widen and his mouth curve up in a wicked grin. She had surprised him, but she had pleased him too.

As they made their way out to the coach, her heart continued to beat that wild tattoo. No backing out now. The Olivia of recent months would have been shocked at such an irresponsible decision, but this Olivia wasn't. Instead, she took a deep breath of the cool evening air and felt a wonderful sense of freedom. As if she had thrown aside the expectations that had recently plagued her. As if she had burned her bridges and said to hell with everything. As if she was herself again.

Just for a little while.

Chapter Twenty-Four

Ivo may have played down his concern. He might have put on a brave face, assuming the familiar role of an amusing, devil-may-care gentleman, but beneath that façade, he was worried. He had yet to discover why Mystere—if the culprit was the mysterious Frenchman—would wish him ill. Even the reliable Bourne had failed to turn up any secrets about the smuggler or about Jacob Rendall with his walleye, who seemed to have disappeared completely. During a visit to see Ivo in London, Bourne had informed him that Lieutenant Harrison and his revenue underlings had been in Portside, asking questions of the villagers and sniffing around for evidence. They seemed more determined than ever to bring Ivo to justice.

And if Ivo's right-hand man was troubled, when Bourne was rarely troubled, then matters were dire indeed.

In better news, Cadieux's was doing very well, but there was still the question of Charles's identity. Ivo was yet to decide how he was going to broach the subject with his family. Was it even necessary at this point? His mother would be distraught. All these years, she had pretended the late duke was the perfect, faithful husband, and Adelina and Lexy had followed her lead. To tell them about Charles's parentage would force them to confront the cold truth.

After careful thought, Ivo decided it would be better

to leave the matter be for now. Charles didn't seem to be in a hurry to let the world know. But there would come a point when the truth must come out, and he certainly wasn't looking forward to the turmoil that would ensue. And speaking of turmoil…

He had gone and embroiled himself in yet another ridiculous dare with Olivia Ashton.

Ivo should be more appalled with himself, but honestly, he could not regret making the challenge. It was the only bright spot in his life. Olivia had looked so miserable that night at the Monteiths', brooding over the piano keys as if she was carrying the weight of the world upon her shoulders. He'd recognized how her mouth was turned down in that sulky way that always made him want to kiss the life out of her. Instead of kissing her, he'd thrown out that outrageous challenge. Well, it had certainly shaken her out of her melancholy.

Ivo hadn't been at all certain she would take him up on this latest nonsense—he'd expected her to fire up and tell him off. Accusing him of all manner of things. Hard to believe that when he had walked over to the piano, he had only been going to be there for a polite moment. Instead, seeing her unhappy had made Ivo ache inside. He wanted her. He suspected he *was* in love with her. The only problem was she did not love him, and if she was still determined to marry whoever her grandmother wheeled out next, then Ivo was only going to suffer more heartbreak. In temperament, he and Olivia were perfectly matched. In Ivo's opinion she was far too worried about what other people thought, but he suspected she would say he wasn't worried enough. There was just the little matter of her need for a wealthy suitor and Ivo being in debt. He wanted her to see that he was dealing with that, and the future was looking brighter—*if* he could escape the clutches of the Revenue Service and Mystere.

Ivo sighed. Who was he kidding? She would never agree to marry him. It stung because nothing felt as right, as perfect, as having Olivia in his arms. If they ever did more than kiss, he was sure their passion would light up the world.

Maybe he should call off this latest dare? A horse race! He had been riding since he was a child, and being astride a horse was as natural to him as walking, while Olivia was far from a confident rider. In fact, he could not ever remember seeing her riding a horse.

What was she going to do when she realized this time besting him was beyond her? Send Roberta in her place?

The idea made Ivo smile, and then grimace.

He was being honest when he had assured her the risk to her reputation was small, but if he was a *gentleman*, he would allow her to back out of his challenge in a graceful manner. Perhaps he could even make up some prior appointment that precluded him from taking her up on the race? Or maybe she would swallow her pride and accept the impossibility of her winning. Surely a tumble from a horse would do more damage to her pride than admitting that this time she had overextended herself.

But Ivo already knew he was not going to forfeit, and he was almost positive that neither was Olivia. They were both too stubborn, and the sense of anticipation too heady. And he was looking forward to their encounter. Every time he thought of it, his heart lifted, and he found himself smiling. Life with Olivia would never be dull. If only she would love him back.

Unbeknownst to Ivo, Oliva was at that very moment attempting to master the art of horse riding. She sat on top of Mable, the quietest and oldest animal in the Ashton House stable, trying to concentrate on maintaining her seat.

It wasn't as easy as she'd hoped.

"You look like you're riding a tumbrel," Roberta said in disgust. "Going to have your head chopped off."

"Why is it so difficult?" Olivia complained. "This silly sidesaddle. It must have been invented by a man. I bet if a man sat on it for even five minutes, he would declare it illegal."

Roberta frowned as she walked around Mable, no doubt mentally criticizing Olivia's seat again.

She was not used to her younger sister giggling at her mistakes or huffing impatiently at her questions. The horsey smell was bad enough, but to have Roberta—three years her junior—making her feel small. Was she really such a poor riding student, or was Roberta just making the most of her role as expert?

If Olivia hadn't been so determined to win Ivo's dare, she would have given up by now. Where was the pleasure in riding a horse anyway? Why would anyone want to when there were so many better things to do?

"Wouldn't it be easier if I rode astride the horse?" Olivia wriggled as she perched uncomfortably on the sidesaddle.

"Yes, and it is, but do you really want to be pointed at and gossiped about? Ladies ride sidesaddle—or at least they do when they're in company. I prefer to ride astride when I am at Grantham where nobody can see me. Nobody who matters, that is."

Olivia thought about that. Should she conform to

society's norms and lose the race? Because she already knew she could never ride along Rotten Row like this. Such a silly idea. And winning was what mattered, wasn't it? She remembered Ivo suggesting a disguise, and at the time she had imagined herself in her maid's clothing. But why dress as a woman at all? Why not dress as a boy? A groom? Breeches and boots made so much more sense if one was on a horse, and then she could ride astride without anyone caring a jot.

"I don't think it *will* matter," she said. "Not for my purposes."

Roberta peered up at her suspiciously, and Olivia could tell she was dying to know what this was all about. Thus far, Olivia had fobbed her off with vague notions of learning to ride so that she could join an excursion into the countryside to which she had been invited. But Roberta would not be fobbed off for long. She knew Olivia was telling fibs, and if she was to get the intensive training she needed, Olivia would need to be honest.

"*You* want to ride astride?" Roberta sounded as if Olivia had suggested she dance naked at Justina's coming-out.

"Someone dared me," she replied uncomfortably, and then closed her eyes in pain as Roberta gave a shriek.

They were alone in the stables in the mews at the back of Ashton House, but all the same, she didn't want everyone to know what they were up to. She had already bribed the groom and stableboy to go away for a couple of hours.

"Who?" Roberta demanded, eyes gleaming with excitement. "Oh, do tell, Olivia! Who dared you to ride a horse?"

Olivia gritted her teeth. "The Duke of Northam."

This time, Roberta covered her mouth with both hands to muffle her shriek. She danced around in a circle, her dark hair loose and flying about her, evidently overcome with mirth.

Olivia glared at her. "It isn't that funny."

When Roberta had herself under control, she removed the hands and grinned at her sister. "I knew it! Well, I didn't *know it* know it, but I suspected it was something to do with Northam. It always is!"

Olivia sniffed. "Well, your suspicions have been proven correct, Roberta. Congratulations. Now, let's get back to riding this horse. I have a race to ride, and it is imperative I win. He won't be expecting me to. He thinks I can't even ride."

Roberta seemed to have a lot to say in reply to that, but contented herself with, "You can't. Ride, I mean."

"That's why you're teaching me, Roberta."

Roberta looked smug. "And if anyone can teach you, it is me," she agreed. "Now, let's have a look at your seat again. Astride this time."

Once Roberta had removed the offending saddle, Olivia climbed back onto Mable with a groan. She swung her leg over the mare's wide flank, feeling uncomfortable and looking disheveled, and tried to pretend she knew what she was doing. Her sister didn't appear to be impressed.

"Where is this race taking place?" Roberta asked as she arranged Olivia's foot more securely in the stirrup.

"Hyde Park. We are racing along Rotten Row."

Roberta stared up at her, shocked into silence. But it didn't last for long. A laugh bubbled out of her, and she clamped a hand over her mouth. Her words were muffled. "But…that's more than a mile! Won't people see you?"

"I'm hardly going as Lady Godiva. It will be at five o'clock in the morning, before anyone is about, and I will be in disguise."

"Oh…well…" Roberta chewed on her lip. "I'm not sure that makes it all right, Olivia. Do you really think that is correct behavior?"

Roberta was definitely being sarcastic, repeating her sister's words back to her. She was no doubt remembering those many times recently when Olivia had told her off for behaving improperly.

"Of course it is not correct behavior," she hissed. "But the important thing is, no one will know. Unless you decide to tell them, that is. Will you?"

Instead of replying to the question, Roberta gave a huge sigh of relief. "I thought you were set on being a model of respectability! It was so boring. No one could ever live up to those exacting standards, Olivia. I'm so glad you're back to your normal self again."

Olivia narrowed her eyes. This wasn't the first time she'd been told she'd turned into a stickler for the rules. Had she really been such a pain? She had certainly been wretched while she was trying to be Miss Perfect in order to secure Prince Nikolai's hand. It had been exhausting. Although she still felt the need to help her sisters, to make their lives better, she kept reminding herself that they had Gabriel and Vivienne now. She really didn't have to play the martyr.

Another thought occurred to her, and she made her voice stern. "Don't think for a moment you can do something like this…this race. You will be sent back to Grantham forever."

Roberta tossed her head. "I'm not a fool. I know I must behave myself until I'm properly out. I have plans too, Olivia. You're not the only one."

Olivia wanted to ask questions, but she was afraid of Roberta's answers. Sometimes her sister was a mystery to her, and perhaps it was better that way.

They carried on with the lesson. Olivia urged Mable to walk around the stable, making use of the reins and the muscles in her thighs to turn the tranquil old mare. After a time, she got the hang of it, and even Roberta stopped finding fault. This wasn't nearly as difficult as she had feared, and by the time they finished, she was feeling quite cocksure.

Roberta removed the saddle, saying over her shoulder, "Next we need to practice cantering, and after that, galloping."

Olivia's confidence drained away. "How will we do that?" she said. "Surely there isn't enough room in here. And people will see us in the street."

"Don't be silly," Roberta said in a scornful voice. "We'll have to get up early and ride in the park. You can practice. You'll need to wear your disguise, but I find the regular riders don't take any notice. There are a lot of grooms exercising horses, as well as their owners."

It was Olivia's turn to stare. "*You find...?* Robbie, do *you* go out riding alone?"

Her sister flushed and gave a toss of her head. Perhaps she really was half horse. "So what if I do? I don't think you can reprimand me in the circumstances."

Olivia opened her mouth, then remembered she needed Roberta's help, and bit back her reproof. "And I can ride Mable?" she asked instead.

"Yes. For now."

"But when I race Ivo," Olivia insisted. "I can ride Mable?" She thought she already knew the answer, even before Roberta snorted a mocking laugh.

"You can ride Mable if you want to lose. Or stop halfway down. Mable might want to take a rest and chew some daisies." She shook her head. "No, Olivia, of course you won't be riding Mable. You will be riding Arrow."

Shocked speechless, Olivia turned her head. Arrow's stall was just behind her, and as if he had understood Roberta's words, he was staring at her over the door. He was a chestnut gelding with a white mark on his forehead that resembled an arrow. But that wasn't why he was called Arrow. The name was due to his speed. He was Roberta's favorite, and as far as Olivia was aware, no one else ever rode him.

Now, as she continued to stare, he stamped his hooves restlessly, and tossed his head in a similar fashion to Roberta. It was as if he was daring Olivia to try to ride him, and she was filled with dread. Perhaps she should just send Ivo a note, crying off, make up some excuse…? She had caught a cold. She was too busy. She had to leave the country. She was on her deathbed!

She jumped when a warm hand closed around hers. Roberta was watching her with something close to sympathy, apart from the amused gleam in her blue eyes. "It will be all right," she assured her. "You just have to hold on tight while Arrow does the work. He understands all about racing. Practice not falling off. Unless…" Her eyes narrowed. "Have you changed your mind? Do you still want to go ahead with it? You know that Northam will think you a craven coward if you cry off now."

Olivia attempted to order her shaky thoughts. Roberta was right, Ivo would think that. He would pretend to commiserate with her, but wouldn't she fall in his estimation? No, they were friends, and he wouldn't deride her, although he might tease her. She was still the girl he admired—she felt his admiration like a warm cloak, protection against the chill she often felt from the ton. Besides, she wasn't going to let the Miss Fenwicks of the world show her up. That glimmer of excitement began to grow inside her. Yes, she would race him and probably lose, but she would do it! Because the alternative was accepting the tedium that lay before her.

Olivia took a deep breath, ignoring the smell of horse, and spoke with resolution. "I am going to ride Arrow. I am going to race Northam. And I am going to win."

Roberta's answering smile was full of pity. "Of course you are."

Chapter Twenty-Five

A visit to Madame Annabelle's dressmaking establishment was always something to look forward to. Today, they were to have the final fittings for Justina's debut. Justina was so excited about her grand event that she hadn't even noticed those times over the past week when Olivia and Roberta had slipped away together. Normally, she would have demanded to know what they were up to, but her head was full of hemlines, dance steps, and hairstyles.

Olivia's horse riding skills were coming along nicely. She could confidently push Mable into a shuffling canter during their misty mornings in the park, and was no longer terrified she would fall off. She was even getting used to the other riders exercising their horses before the day properly began, although she was careful to duck her head if anyone looked at her in her groom's disguise. But Arrow would not be as amiable as Mable. And when it came to racing with Ivo, there would be no time to remind herself of all the little things Roberta was always telling her to do. Sit up straight, tighten your leg muscles, push down into the stirrups, just to name a few. There would be no time for anything except trying to stay on Arrow's back.

Roberta was already endeavoring to bring her around to face the fact that she would lose.

At least you will have been brave and made the attempt, Olivia. It's admirable, really. You should be proud of yourself.

But Olivia was, by character, a competitive girl. Being satisfied with runner-up, no matter how brave she was being, wasn't in her nature. She knew that once the race started, she would be doing her very best to win it.

The dowager had a slight cold and had decided to rest at home rather than brave today's chilly weather, so she had sent the girls' companion, Miss Starky, with them to Madame Annabelle's. Olivia was pleased that her grandmother was trusting her granddaughters more and more, while at the same time she still felt a twinge of guilt when she thought about the dare. It helped to remind herself that no one would ever know. She had stopped listening to that inner voice that cautioned her of the consequences of another scandal.

Justina's dress fitting took a long time. As well as the variety of garments she needed for the remainder of the Season, there was her debut gown. It was of simple design, as befitted the occasion, and the pale pink color suited Justina's complexion. The high-waisted bell shape flattered her slim figure, and she had matching slippers. On the night, her hair was to be curled and adorned with a mixture of silk and real flowers.

While Madame Annabelle made the necessary alterations, Olivia and Roberta prowled about the shop. They were listlessly examining a box of ribbons when Roberta leaned in closer and spoke in a loud whisper. "I followed Mama the other day."

Olivia gave her an astonished look. "Whatever for?"

Roberta flushed. "Don't you ever wonder what she does all day? She wanted to come to London with us, but she never joins in when we go out anywhere. She takes most of her meals in her room. If I hadn't been paying particular attention, I would have thought she spent all of her time staring out of the window."

"Doesn't she?"

"No." Roberta's eyes sparkled. "Several times, I've seen her sneaking out of the house in her outdoor clothing, and yesterday, I decided to follow her."

"Where did she go?"

Roberta grinned. "She walked in the park." Olivia tried not to think about Roberta indulging in the sort of behavior she would have expected from the Bow Street Runners. "She met a man. Well, a gentleman, I suppose. She seemed to know him, and they strolled about for a bit. And then she went home."

"Hardly earth-shattering," Olivia said. "What did this gentleman look like? Old, young, in between?"

Roberta considered the question. "About Mama's age, I suppose. He seemed very solicitous, asking if she was warm enough and if she wanted him to take her home in his carriage."

"You were close enough to hear their conversation?"

"Well, yes. There were trees to hide behind."

Olivia pondered on the matter further. "I think we should ask who she was visiting."

Roberta's voice rose. "Then Mama will know it was me who was spying on her!"

That was true enough, and Felicia could be coldly intimidating. All the same, Olivia didn't trust her mother. Could this solicitous gentleman be a relative? They knew little about their mother's life before she married their father—as far as they were aware, her parents were long dead.

"It is a little strange," Olivia said.

Before Roberta could answer, their tête-à-tête was interrupted by Justina, smiling brightly and looking beautiful in her coming-out gown. "What do you think?" she asked, making a twirl.

"Oh, you look so pretty!" Roberta responded.

"You look beautiful," Olivia assured her favorite sister, and squeezed her hands as she reached up to kiss her cheek. "All of the gentlemen will want to dance with you, and Gabriel will glower at them. You know how he is."

Justina laughed. She looked as if she wanted to say something, but she bit her lip instead.

"I hope they will dance with me." Roberta sounded mournful. "When you had your coming-out, Olivia, I had to stay upstairs. It's so dull being a younger sister."

Olivia rolled her eyes. "Think how Edwina must feel then."

"I wonder if you will both be married by then," Roberta mused. "I'm sure Olivia will be," she added with a certainty Olivia did not feel. "You're so pretty that the gentlemen follow you with their eyes. And, Justina, you have your admirers too." She clasped her hands under her chin. "I am not going to get married. I want to be a bareback rider in a circus, and every evening, I will perform to rapturous applause."

Olivia choked as Justina burst out with, "How on earth will you manage that? Grandmama would march in and drag you home."

"I'd just have to call myself by a different name. The Amazing Robbie! Or the Spectacular Berta!"

Justina and Olivia exchanged looks.

Their companion had been chatting with one of the seamstresses, but now she came to join them. Olivia was relieved to put an end to the conversation. Did Roberta really mean the things she said? It was a horrifying thought, and with the Ashton propensity for scandal, she could see trouble ahead. She imagined her sister riding bareback under a circus tent, and gave a shudder.

"Please don't mention this to Grandmama," she said.

Roberta shot her a look, and for a moment, Olivia feared she was going to blurt out her own secret. Her dare with Ivo was all very thrilling, but she didn't want the whole world to know. Thankfully, Roberta thought better of it and gave a shrug.

"I am far from being a fool, Olivia. One day you will see just how clever I am."

Chapter Twenty-Six

The sun was yet to rise when Ivo set out. As expected, there was nobody of consequence about. A few traders preparing for the day ahead, their shops still in darkness, while servants hurried to the market to fetch breakfast for the household. One inebriated gentleman was zigzagging his way home after a long night out, his stumbling steps almost sending him sprawling onto the cobbles. Ivo's gray horse, Star, moved restlessly as the gent staggered away, but Ivo controlled him with the ease of long practice. They were both impatient to be getting on with things.

The mist was knee-deep in the park, encircling the tree trunks and giving an eerie feeling to the place. A number of riders exercising their horses passed him, barely giving him a glance. They were grooms from a nearby stable, calling to each other and sharing tales of the night before.

Was she coming? Yesterday, pricked by his conscience, Ivo had sent a note to Olivia, asking if she would rather defer their "arrangement." It would give her a chance to bow out without losing face. But instead of grabbing hold of his offer with both hands, Olivia had sent him a swift reply that brought a smile to his lips.

Definitely not!

He was glad she was going ahead with the race, even if he was certain to win. Thinking about their dare had made his days brighter, not just distracting him from his worries about Mystere and Lieutenant Harrison, but giving him hope that feelings between himself and Olivia might deepen. Having her as his friend was a great deal better than not having her at all, but if he was honest, then "friendship" was not what he wanted.

He wanted to see her every day across the breakfast table, and kiss that sulky droop from her lips. He wanted to lie in bed with her and hold her, protect her—yes, sometimes from herself—and live each day with her by his side.

To imagine her marrying the prince or anyone else filled him with an urgent need to win her for himself before it was too late. His heart didn't appear to be swayed by the obstacles before it. Olivia was perfect for him, and him for her, and if that made him an arrogant ass, then so be it.

Star tossed his head again, whinnying as he sensed another rider approaching. Alert, Ivo spotted movement from the street, although the mist was still thick enough to make it difficult to make anything out. Slowly, one rider appeared, and then another. He did not recognize them at first, but as they drew closer, his eyes widened, and he chuckled.

One of the riders was definitely Olivia dressed in mannish attire. He would know her anywhere, despite the voluminous coat covering her pocket Venus curves, and her hair bundled up under a cap. The other rider was also disguised as a man, but it was only when she lifted her head to meet his gaze that he realized it was Roberta.

Olivia was riding what Ivo called a "plodder." An

old mare who could barely manage a shuffle. Surely she wasn't intending to race him on *that*? He'd reach the finish line before she had barely started. His gaze turned to Roberta's mount, and he eyed it admiringly. That was more the thing. Was Roberta going to race him instead of her sister? That would be disappointing, but he was willing to be accommodating, since Olivia had come to their rendezvous.

"Ladies!" he greeted them in a cheery voice as they stopped in front of him.

Olivia glanced up, her blue eyes wary. "Northam," she replied, and self-consciously tucked a loose strand of hair back in place. She darted a nervous glance about her. Was she expecting to see some disapproving members of the ton lined up at the starting line? He wished he could teach her not to care so much about others' opinions, because she really would be much happier if she did as she pleased and forgot about the so-called rule makers.

"Northam." Roberta was grinning at him from beneath her own cap, as if they were about to embark on a wonderful adventure. She cast an admiring glance over Star. "Is he fast?" she asked.

"Very."

"Never mind," she said, with a quick glance at Olivia. "He can't be as fast as Arrow."

Ivo shifted his gaze to Olivia's animal and raised his eyebrows.

Roberta scoffed. "That's not Arrow! That's Mable."

Olivia glared at both of them and gave the old mare a loving pat. "Shh, she'll hear you."

Ivo bit his lip, refraining from asking if a creature that old could hear much at all.

Roberta dismounted with practiced ease, while

Olivia dismounted with awkward effort. The two women moved close to confer, and Ivo waited patiently, amused at the sight. A woman rider on a black mare trotted by, and she gave them a curious glance.

"We need to get on," he said. "We do not want an audience."

The two sisters exchanged a glance, and then Olivia reluctantly moved away from patient old Mable and came to stand by Arrow. But Roberta had a firm hold of the reins and couldn't help her sister to mount the much bigger animal. Seeing the problem, Ivo jumped down.

"Here," he said, and made a step with his joined hands.

Olivia gave him a look he found hard to interpret, though fear and trepidation seemed to be two of the components. She needed a distraction, and he was happy to supply it. The coat only hid so much of her body, and she was wearing tight breeches. A bolt of lust went through him as he let himself enjoy the swell of her hips, the nip of her waist, and the plump globes of her breasts beneath her white shirt.

"Very fetching," he said, his voice dropping to a husky growl.

She narrowed her eyes and jammed her booted foot into the grip of his hands. The next moment, she was in the saddle. Arrow gave a nervous dance, but Roberta's calming murmurs settled him again. She handed her sister the reins, keeping a tight grip on the halter. Olivia took a deep breath, wriggling to get comfortable.

"Olivia," Ivo said, no longer able to keep his doubts to himself, "are you sure you want to—"

She shot him a look full of daggers as she cut him off. "Ready, Northam?"

Ivo remounted Star, and they made their way to the start of the popular riding track called Rotten Row. There was a low wooden fence on either side of the prepared surface, with plenty of room for them to ride abreast. During the day, there were often curious strollers standing outside the fence, watching the toffs showing off on their pedigreed animals. Not this early though. Even the grooms had moved on. The place was empty.

Roberta gave her sister her final instructions. "Remember what I told you. Hold on. That's all you need to do. Hold on. Arrow will do the rest."

Olivia nodded jerkily, her face pale beneath her cap. She swallowed, her eyes flicking to Ivo, and he gave her what he hoped was an encouraging smile.

"Are we ready?" Roberta said with a frown for her sister. "Will I start you off?"

"Count down from five," Ivo suggested.

Arrow moved uneasily beneath his inexperienced rider. Olivia's knuckles were white where she had twisted her fingers into the horse's mane. Roberta had barely started the count when Arrow took off, and Olivia was flying down the thoroughfare, her borrowed coat flapping like wings.

With a shout of laughter, Ivo gave Star his head, and whatever Roberta called out after him was lost in the excitement of the moment.

Arrow was fast. Roberta was right about that, and now he had been given his head, there was no stopping him. Ivo wondered if the two women had thought about what would happen when Olivia reached the end of the race. Was she going to jump the fence into Kensington Palace? At least, from the way she was lying flat against Arrow's back, clinging on to him like a limpet, there was no chance of her falling off.

The greenery to the side whizzed past, but there could have been a marching band playing in their honor, and Ivo would have paid it no heed. He only had eyes for Olivia, her small body was pressed tight to the large horse, and he wanted to call out to tell her how wonderful she was. How brave and beautiful. But she wouldn't have heard him anyway.

Mist eddied about the horses' hooves as they thundered along Rotten Row. They were neck and neck. He heard himself laughing with delight, because right now, there was nothing more exciting than pitting himself against this girl. He didn't care whether he won or lost. All he wanted was to have Olivia in his life.

The end of the riding track was in sight. Their horses were still abreast, and Ivo knew they would need to slow very soon. Olivia had more than fulfilled her part of the challenge, but she showed no sign of pulling up, and Arrow was not going to stop on his own, so Ivo edged closer and reached across the gap between them. He fumbled for Arrow's reins. When their hands touched, Olivia gave a breathy gasp and turned to stare at him, her eyes huge in her white face.

"It's over." He raised his voice to be heard.

As Arrow began to slow, Olivia sat up straighter and looked around her, as if realizing for the first time where they were. Had her eyes been closed for the entire race? Ivo drew the horses up, and finally, they came to a halt, their sides heaving. Ivo was flushed and breathless. It had been one of the most exciting experiences of his life, and he had had a few.

"You're amazing," he said, and his smile was so broad that it hurt his cheeks. Her eyes clung to his, bluer than he had ever seen them. "You're brave and—and wonderful!"

"I was scared witless," she admitted with a grimace.

Ivo edged closer, wanting to touch her but holding back.

"At least Arrow has finally stopped," she went on. "Roberta said he was fast, but I had no idea."

Ivo laughed, and they continued to stare at each other, the excitement bubbling in their veins. It was as if they were meeting for the first time but without hiding their true feelings.

"Is it always like this?" she asked him, a little shyly. "Do you always feel like this?"

He shook his head in wonderment. "No. Never like this."

She didn't seem to know how to answer that. Her hair had come loose, and she tried to push it back under her cap. Then, as if suddenly remembering what the race was all about, she said, "Ivo, did I win?"

Chapter Twenty-Seven

I vo thought her question funny. He threw back his head and laughed in delight, the sound disturbing some birds in a nearby tree so that they flew up into the sky, squawking irritably. Puzzled, Olivia smiled too. Now the surge of excitement was fading, she was feeling shaky. Her hands trembled, her heart was thudding, and she wondered if she would be able to stand up if she climbed down from Arrow. She might fall in a heap on the ground.

Her disguise, which had felt so daring as they set off this morning, was now uncomfortable and poking in places it had no right to. Her hair had come down from the pins she had used to keep it up, and the cap was making her scalp itch. But apart from those mundane matters, the race had been unlike anything else she had ever taken part in before. She didn't even know how to describe it, or the look on Ivo's face just now, and the ache of response from her body. Her skin tingled. It was as if he was calling to her and she was answering.

Ivo was still holding Arrow's reins. Olivia wondered if she should ask for them back, but she preferred not to. She wasn't sure she would ever want to ride a beast like this again—Mable was a different matter though. She had grown quite fond of Mable.

She turned to look back down Rotten Row, but there

was no sign of Roberta. There was no sign of anyone else either, although she was aware that this might change at any moment. Only yesterday, she and Roberta had been here practicing, although if she had known how little skill it took to race Arrow, then she may not have bothered.

Roberta had been right when she'd said that all Olivia needed to do was to hang on tight.

Ivo swung himself down from his horse, running his hands through his windblown hair with another laugh, and led the horses from the track and into the park proper. The mist was finally beginning to disperse, and the tired animals dropped their heads and began to graze on the succulent grass. Ivo reached up to clasp Olivia about the waist and help her down. She slid off Arrow, thankful for the support because, as she had feared, her legs felt so boneless they threatened to crumple. With a gasp, she fell against him. He steadied her, and she was suddenly very conscious that her hair had come out of her cap and was all over the place, while the tight breeches and man's shirt clung to her very feminine figure.

Ivo was holding her closer than she thought strictly necessary, but she didn't complain. It was good to be in his arms again. And then he pulled her even closer, pressing his face to her hair so that his voice was muffled. "You rode like the wind. I'll never forget it."

"So I *did* win?" She tilted her head back to peer up at him.

His cheeks were flushed, his green eyes sparkling, and she couldn't mistake his expression. She had seen that look before. Her heart, which had begun to slow down, speeded up again.

"I think we both won," he murmured. Then his lips brushed hers, softly, teasingly. That wasn't enough though, and she flung her arms around his neck and pulled him down for a more substantial kiss. Every inch of them seemed to be pressed together, and when he ran his tongue along the seam of her lips, she gasped.

He gave them an inch of space. "God, you're amazing," he said, just as they heard the pounding of hooves coming toward them from the track.

Olivia stepped back, and Ivo moved in front of her to shield her. Whoever was approaching cursed loudly as he pulled his horse to a halt. Peeping over Ivo's shoulder, Olivia could see it was a gentleman in a green riding coat. A stranger, to her at least.

But not, it seemed, to Ivo. "Northam! You're out early."

"Seemed a shame to waste the morning lying in bed," Ivo said easily, as if there was nothing unusual happening.

The man tried to see past him, and then pointed with his riding crop. "Who do you have with you? Your groom, is it?"

Olivia had used the distraction of the conversation to tuck her hair into the back of her coat, and now she dragged the garment about her, digging her hands into the pockets and staring at the ground. "Mornin', sir," she mumbled, trying to sound like one of the Ashton grooms.

"He's from the stables over there," Ivo said, pointing. "Looking for a lost horse. You haven't seen the beast, have you?"

The gentleman snorted a laugh. "Saw an ancient mare shuffling along. But no, nothing else."

"Ne'er mind, guv," Olivia lowered her voice in what she hoped was a manly growl. "He'll find 'is way 'ome."

Ivo shrugged. The rider said something about getting home himself, and then he was gone. They waited a moment until he was entirely out of sight, and then Ivo turned to her and pulled her into his arms once more.

He was shaking with laughter, and so was she as they clung together. And then they were kissing again, passionately, desire sending shivers throughout her body. She could feel his hard muscles locked against her softer curves, and when he slid his arms beneath the coat and shirt, his palms felt warm against her cooling flesh.

Olivia tangled her hands in his hair, tugging him even closer, her lips clinging to his. This was what she wanted. What she *needed*. Him and her, together.

She could pretend it was the excitement of the race, but in truth, it was Ivo. It had always been Ivo. The more she had tried to distance herself from him the more out of sorts she had felt. How could she even think of marrying another man, of giving herself to him intimately, when he was not Ivo?

He kissed her again, deeply now, his tongue sweeping in to claim her mouth until her head was spinning. He groaned softly against her, then nuzzled into the flesh at her throat. It felt as if he couldn't get enough of her, and she certainly couldn't get enough of him. When his hand closed around the soft warmth of her breast, her nipple peaked, painfully hard. She whimpered, and his thumb rubbed back and forth over the aching nub.

"Beautiful," he whispered. "I want to see you naked. I want to kiss every inch of you. I want you…"

He did want her—she could feel the hard ridge of him against her belly. She ached to have him between her thighs, soothing that fierce heat. Desire overcame whatever common sense she had left. In a moment, her back would be against a tree, and she would have her thighs wrapped around him. And she needed that. So much.

The sound of a throat being cleared came from close by.

Olivia jumped back with a cry. Too late, she remembered they were in a public place. The gentleman from earlier might have returned. What would he think of the flushed cheeks and swollen lips of someone who was obviously not a groom? Ivo looked equally flushed and distracted, as they turned wildly to see who had come upon them.

It was Roberta. She was seated on Mable, watching them with a grin. "Sorry to interrupt, but there is a riding party on their way here."

Olivia tried to find some composure, but her body was still fizzing from Ivo's kisses and his touch. Her breast was aching for his hand, but she tightened her coat about herself and ignored it. "We need to get home," she said in a subdued voice. "I don't want to be missed."

Roberta slid off Mable, her eyes alight with curiosity as she led the old mare over to them. "Who won?"

Ivo smiled. "It was a draw."

"At least you didn't fall off." Roberta was clearly relieved. "If it was a draw, are you planning on another race to settle the question?"

"Certainly not," Olivia said airily. "Next time, I will drive a curricle."

"I believe you would too." Ivo laughed in that delighted way that made her smile back. As if everything she said was enchanting. They might have kept smiling at each other indefinitely, but Roberta broke the moment with a reminder of what the rest of the day held.

"It's Justina's coming-out ball tonight. She will be in a flap, and there's still lots to do."

The day would be a busy one, but suddenly, all Olivia wanted to do was curl up and sleep. Curl up with Ivo.

If Roberta hadn't interrupted them, she wondered what would have happened. Not a great deal, probably, but if they had been alone…What would it be like to sleep in his bed, in his arms? To be his in every way?

She glanced at him from under her lashes. "I shall see you tonight then," she said. "You are coming?"

He smiled, green eyes gleaming wickedly. "Wild horses wouldn't keep me away," he assured her.

Olivia needed assistance to mount the mare, but when Ivo helped her up, his hands didn't linger. He was suddenly the perfect gentleman, and she wasn't sure how she felt about that. Roberta didn't need his help but leaped up onto Arrow, flaunting her prowess. Then the two of them set off at a leisurely pace across the park in the direction of home.

⁂

"Are you sure you are all right?" Roberta asked, when Olivia groaned softly for the tenth time.

"My muscles are sore. My legs feel like jelly and custard. I never want to do that again, no matter how much I enjoyed it."

"*Did* you enjoy it?" her sister asked curiously. "You were shaking like a leaf before the race."

"I was afraid, but once it started, there wasn't time to be afraid."

"Northam thought you very brave," Roberta said slyly. "The expression on his face!" She sniggered. "He couldn't keep his eyes off you in those breeches."

Olivia gave her a glare, but she secretly agreed. Ivo had seemed very appreciative of her male attire. Perhaps, if they were alone one day, she could…

But Roberta was speaking again. "What was it like, kissing Northam?"

Instead of telling her to mind her own business, Olivia pondered the question. What had it been like kissing Ivo, and being in his arms? Pleasurable, certainly, but she suspected being kissed and held by any attractive man might be pleasurable. Ivo was different, and being kissed by him lifted the act above mere pleasure. It was...

"Heavenly," she said. "When we are together, it feels right. As if it was meant to be. All the reasons I told myself I couldn't get close to him suddenly seemed silly. Well, not all of them." She frowned. "He was never good for my reputation, and because of him, my Season was cut short."

"Grandmama is always afraid of the gossips and fears upsetting the old biddies in the ton. I think she worries too much. We could be perfectly behaved and still be miserable, so what's the point? Why not be happy instead? If you are in love with Ivo, then I think you should follow your heart."

Startled, Olivia stared at her sister. "In *love* with him? I'm not in love with him."

Roberta rolled her eyes. "If you say so."

"Why do you think I am?"

Roberta didn't even have to give it any thought. "The way you light up when he enters a room, the way you look at each other as if there's no one else. The way you tease each other—it's as if you have a secret language the rest of us can't understand. The air fizzes around you both, Olivia, until I wonder if you are going to start shouting at each other...or kiss."

Olivia swallowed. She suspected she had been falling in love with Ivo from the first moment they danced together at her coming-out ball. But she had put a stop to that, hadn't she? And yet she did seem to think about him an awful lot. He was her friend, but today, she admitted it was more than that. Today, he had felt like her other half.

"That's easy for you to say," she said grumpily.

But her sister wasn't finished. "You have been simply *awful* these past months. Cross and miserable, and making us miserable too. *I* think you've been unhappy because you're trying to be someone you're not, Olivia."

Olivia closed her eyes a moment, as a wave of emotion washed over her. "I was determined to marry well, but not just for myself. I wanted to help all of you, and I thought that my marrying someone rich would give me a better chance of finding you rich husbands."

Roberta gave her a long look and then shook her head. "It wouldn't have worked. Even if you did find someone who you thought was everything we needed, it doesn't mean we would marry him. We Ashtons like to make up our own minds about things like that. We're not like other young ladies, Olivia."

Despite not wanting to admit Roberta was right, Olivia thought she was. It was what Justina had said to her at the picnic, and surely both of her sisters could not be wrong.

Roberta looked away, her newfound maturity deserting her as she stumbled over her next question. "So, is it over? Between you and Prince Nikolai?"

"What do you mean?"

"Well, I know he was enamored with you. You just had to send him one of your come-hither looks, and he was at your side. But I'm sure if you were in love with the prince, you wouldn't be kissing Northam."

Roberta's gaze was direct. As if Olivia's answer genuinely mattered to her.

"Even if I wanted him to, he's not going to marry me

after everything that happened at Grantham. And you didn't help when you stole his horse."

Roberta tried not to smile. "Stallion, Olivia."

They turned into the mews behind Ashton House, and Olivia's voice was thoughtful. "Marrying the prince would be like trying to fit into a box that is completely the wrong shape. Ivo told me that once, but I didn't want to believe him. Now I know it's true."

"What about the others Grandmama has paraded in front of you? That old man with the caterpillar eyebrows? Will you marry him?"

"No. I thought I might, but…No."

"You know Grandmama will keep trying to marry you off to someone suitable until you tell her not to?"

Olivia frowned. "I suppose you're right."

"You'll just have to marry Ivo instead, and then she'll wash her hands of you," Roberta said, and yawned. "I hope we don't have to work too hard today, or I'll never stay awake for the ball."

Olivia was silent. Marry Ivo? As if it was that simple. And did she want to marry him? That was a question she couldn't answer. But one thing she did know was that she wanted to spend a night with him. She wanted to be his and for him to be hers. Was that wrong? Probably. Grandmama would say it was. But Olivia knew if she had to marry a sensible sort of man, a wealthy man, as the dowager wanted her to, then first she was going to experience what it was like to be with the man of her dreams.

One night together. Something to remember.

Would he agree to it? Could she persuade him? Or had he become too much of a gentleman? There was only one way to find out.

Chapter Twenty-Eight

J ustina's coming-out was a much smaller affair than the grand ball that had been Olivia's entrée into society. Being the second daughter had its disadvantages, but Justina didn't seem to mind. After a final visit to Madame Annabelle's, she had been both nervous and excited, but she said again that most of the people who loved her would be there to celebrate with her, and that was all that mattered. Gabriel and Vivienne had arrived from Grantham, although the younger girls had remained in Sussex with their governess.

"Antonia, Georgia, and Edwina were naturally upset," Vivienne said after their greetings. "I promised them a special afternoon tea party when we get home again."

Edwina would be happy with that. As long as her dolls were welcome.

The dowager had invited the usual crowd, as well as some other guests she felt could be relied upon to make an appearance. This far into the Season, every host or hostess was eager for as many guests as possible, just as everyone was hoping their event would be a huge success. Olivia was surprised that so many people had accepted what was a minor occasion on the social calendar. She couldn't help but think that the Ashtons' reputation for disgrace had played its part, and that tonight, their guests would be breathlessly expecting yet another scandal.

Well, for Justina's sake, she hoped they would be disappointed.

There was one addition Olivia knew was for her benefit. Viscount Carey, a plump gentleman with a round face and beaming smile who, when introduced to her, blurted out, "But you are so pretty, Lady Olivia! Why have we not met before?"

"My granddaughter was away for part of the Season," the dowager said coolly.

"Well, she is here now," the viscount said, smiling as if his face might split in two. "Will you dance with me, Lady Olivia?"

"I would be honored."

What else could she politely say? She suspected he was another suitor her grandmother had picked out for her, and any doubts she might have had vanished when the dowager waited until they were alone, and then whispered in her ear. "He is very busy socially, you would never be bored, and he is wealthy enough to indulge you. He has a house in the country, as well as a town house here in London. I think he is the ideal choice for you, Olivia."

Olivia wanted to object, but Grandmama looked so pleased with herself. Was Viscount Carey really "the ideal choice"? Perhaps she might have thought so once, but now all she wanted to do was ask her grandmother to please stop. Not right this moment though, it would be selfish of her to make waves during Justina's coming-out.

Gabriel and Justina danced the first dance, moving carefully about the room. Dancing had never come naturally to Gabriel, but he had practiced, and Justina was always graceful. Olivia found herself a little weepy at the sight of them. It brought back memories of her own debut and the overwhelming and rather naïve emotions of that night. She had expected so much, hoped for even more, and then Ivo had held her in his arms.

It occurred to her to wonder what she would say if the dowager introduced Ivo to her as "the ideal choice." She wouldn't be trying to come up with excuses to avoid him. She would probably happily agree. A pity that was never going to happen.

Soon, the orchestra started up again, and everyone took to the floor. The prince was Olivia's next partner, and she was rather surprised to find him so affable. She suspected that since the expectation of them making a match had been removed, they could both relax in each other's company. Nikolai must have been under pressure too, worried about his future. Olivia was sure they would have been at daggers drawn within a day of the nuptials. And while Princess Olivia of Holtswig had a nice ring to it, she was not sorry to set that burden down.

Charles Wickley was her subsequent partner. As usual, he was easygoing and charming, but she noticed the glances he shared with Justina across the room. It was obvious Justina had her heart set on Charles, and although Ivo seemed to find him good company, she was still of two minds about his character. Remembering their joint venture at Cadieux's, she asked him how the gaming club was going.

"Exceptionally well! I am thinking of hiring more staff."

"I wonder if Gabriel misses it," she mused. "It was part of his life for so long. A simpler life than being a duke, I suspect."

Charles agreed. "I think he has more than enough to do at Grantham, and now he is happily married, he naturally wants to be with his wife rather than adding up gaming debts."

"Is Mr. Hart here? He was supposed to attend tonight."

She had learned from Gabriel that Freddie was on some assignment. His fighting days were over, but although Charles had offered him a place at Cadieux's, as a stopgap, he had refused it.

"Freddie Hart is a law unto himself," Charles replied with a grin. "He has something highly secretive in the offing."

After Charles, Olivia danced with Harold Fitzsimmons, recently affianced to Lady Annette. Roberta had been allowed to attend tonight, just as Justina had attended Olivia's coming-out, and it was a surprise to see her dancing with the prince. Olivia could see her sister's mouth moving as she chattered on, while the prince wore a bemused expression, as if he didn't quite know what to do with her. At one point, he even smiled, before he assumed that politely blank look, as if she had shocked him. Olivia was relieved when their dance finished without incident.

Viscount Carey came to claim Olivia for another dance, effusive in his flattery with everything from Olivia's beauty to the supper selection. "The dowager duchess is a woman of refinement and taste," he added with one of his big smiles. "You are lucky to have her watching over you and your family."

Olivia supposed he was right, but sometimes she wished there was a little less watching and attention to detail on the dowager's part.

Viscount Carey bowed as the music came to a stop, and asked if he could call upon her tomorrow. Olivia floundered, trying to find a reason to say no, aware of her grandmother's eyes fixed on her from across the room. "Thank you," she said at last. "I'll be sure to tell Grandmama."

He smiled, raised her hand to his lips, and left her feeling unsettled and anxious.

"May I?"

She turned to find Ivo holding out his hand, his green eyes reading her face and—she was certain—seeing everything. She felt herself relax as she slipped her gloved hand into his, although there was that tingle in her fingers at the contact, and that familiar warmth in her belly.

"No ill effects from this morning?"

His quiet murmur in her ear brought goose bumps to her skin. He was as handsome as ever in his formal evening wear, his face freshly shaven, although he was yet to return to his Brutus hairstyle—she was secretly glad about that. She liked his hair a little long. Apart from the hint of shadows under his green eyes, she would never have guessed he had been up before dawn this morning.

"Ill effects?" She wondered if he meant their kisses. Just remembering them caused her blood to heat up a notch.

His mouth kicked up in a smile as if he'd read her mind. Olivia turned away so that he couldn't see her blush. "No ill effects at all," she said airily.

"So, do you want to do it again?"

This time when she turned to him, her confusion must have been evident.

He laughed softly. "I meant race me on Arrow."

Of course he had meant that. She schooled her features. "No, but thank you."

He squeezed her fingers in his. "I am teasing, Olivia. As exciting as this morning was, I am happy to wait until you recover before our next dare."

The idea of them indulging in another challenge was exciting, yes, but...*Marry Ivo*, Roberta had said. Why did those two words seem to be lodged in her head? As far as she knew, he didn't want her as his wife. The only time he had proposed to her was to "fix" a scandal he had created. Hardly a wild and desperate declaration of love. And yet when she remembered the park this morning and their passionate kisses, the heat between them, it couldn't be denied that their relationship had grown beyond friendship.

Miss Fenwick was here somewhere. She and Ivo had danced earlier, and Olivia had tried not to watch, but she couldn't seem to help it. The idea that he might marry Miss Fenwick felt real. It could happen. Any chance of one night in Ivo's arms was already slipping through her fingers, and suddenly, she couldn't bear it. Ivo arched his eyebrows. "What *is* the matter? You look quite green."

She blurted it out. "Grandmama has found another suitor for me. Viscount Carey."

Ivo's eyes narrowed. "Has she now?"

"She won't stop, I know she won't, and if I tell her I don't want to marry the viscount, she will only find someone else."

"Indeed." His gaze was watchful. "Why don't you want to marry Viscount Carey? He's a pleasant enough fellow, and he's seen everywhere. His wife would live a life of dissipation."

"Why don't you marry him then?" Olivia said sourly. "I'm just tired of being trotted out and shown off in the hope that someone with the right amount of yearly income will ignore all my faults and offer for me."

He leaned into her again, his warm breath making her want to shiver. Her skin felt so sensitive. She could feel the heat of his hands through their gloves. "I didn't realize you felt so strongly about it."

Perhaps this was the moment for honesty and boldness. She needed him to understand her feelings. She needed to encourage him to agree to her challenge.

"I worry that whoever we marry, we will drift apart. We won't be friends anymore."

His dance step stuttered. Ivo was never clumsy. "Olivia…"

She bit her lip. "And I worry that being friends precludes other things."

"Like?" But there was a spark in his green eyes, fixed so intently on hers.

Olivia took a rallying breath. "Kissing. Being with you in…in the bedchamber."

He opened his mouth, closed it again. She had shocked him into silence, but she couldn't stop now.

"You were talking about another dare," she said, her voice trembling slightly. "I dare you, Ivo. I dare you to show me how a man is with a woman."

He dragged his gaze from hers with an effort and, tucking her hand into his elbow, began to walk toward the supper room, only to diverge into the study at the last moment. He closed the door.

Olivia had taken a step back, a seesawing mixture of anticipation and trepidation humming through her veins. He was watching her, and there was a charge between them—like lightning flashing in a stormy sky.

"Come here," he said, his voice gravelly, and held out his arms.

All those doubts that had held her back slipped away. She went to him, and he folded her close. As he gazed down at her, she saw such tenderness in his expression that it melted her.

"Ivo, I want—"

"Hush," he said, and bent his head. Their mouths fused. Heat licked over her skin, and with a soft moan she tried to get closer, standing on her tiptoes. Her arms were wrapped around his neck, her fingers tugging at his hair in a manner that probably hurt, but he didn't complain.

He took a step toward the desk with her still in his arms, and then he was lifting her so that she was perched upon it. His hands slid down over her shoulders and her arms, until he was holding her hands.

"Don't only selfish cads kiss young ladies at private gatherings?" he asked, paraphrasing her words back to her from that painful day when he came to propose. There was a lift to his eyebrow that demanded an answer.

"Would you still be a cad if I had asked you to kiss me?"

He grinned. "Probably."

"I expect you have kissed a great many ladies," she said primly, but her heart was beating hard.

He smoothed a lock of her hair, tucking it behind her ear, and then brushed his lips across her cheek. "No one who matters," he said quietly. He kissed the tip of her nose, and then her eyelids, tenderly. He ducked his head and kissed her neck, making her arch upward with a shiver.

Olivia wanted to say *more*, she wanted to ask him how many women he had bedded, but she knew she would sound ridiculously jealous. She *was* jealous.

"I have never wanted to kiss any man but you," she said instead, her cheeks hot. "Well, any *real* man. I have fantasies sometimes."

He brushed his lips against her collarbone. "I'd like to hear about these fantasies."

"I thought you were going to kiss me. Properly, I mean."

He straightened and skimmed his lips against hers, a barely-there kiss. He paused and frowned. "This feels dangerous," he admitted. "I could lose control."

"I want you to," she whispered, reaching up for him.

With a groan, he sank into her, his mouth warm and desperate against hers. Olivia felt as if she was now caught up in the storm, being whirled and tumbled about. She tried to get closer to him, because this wasn't enough. What would his naked skin feel like against hers? His body heavy on hers? Her emotions surged up, and she knew that whatever happened to her and Ivo in the future, she wanted to experience this passion he was offering her. She was not going to change her mind.

"I want you to take me as a man takes a woman." The words rushed out of her. "I want you to show me what it's like to be with you."

He stopped kissing her and lifted his head. "Olivia?" he said softly, and it was a question.

"I dare you!" Her voice rose. She was shaky, but she meant it. The thought of lying in bed with Viscount Carey popped into her mind, and she was even more certain that whatever happened, whoever she married, it was Ivo she wanted as her lover.

There was a loud knock on the door, and guiltily, they sprang apart. Olivia hopped down to the floor and smoothed her gown with trembling hands. She wondered if her lips were as red and swollen as they felt. Before she could even say "enter," the door opened, and Roberta peered inside.

"There you are," she said with a knowing smirk.

"Is Grandmama—" Olivia began uneasily.

"No, she is too busy being astounded, as are we all. You will never guess what just happened."

Olivia and Ivo exchanged a glance. "What?" Olivia asked.

"You know that gentleman I saw with Mama in the park? He's just arrived, and she has introduced him to us as her future husband. What do you think of that?"

"She's getting married?" Olivia tried not to shriek.

"Yes. His name is Lord Harrowby, and he knew her before she married Papa…Well, not married, but you know what I mean."

"Why does something scandalous always have to happen?" Olivia wailed.

Ivo snorted a laugh, and Roberta chuckled as they followed her back to the ballroom.

She could see at a glance that it was in uproar. Humber was trying to create order, with the dowager at his side, while the guests didn't seem to know whether congratulations were in order or not.

"What on earth…?" Justina came to join them, gripping Olivia's arm painfully. "Why is she doing this? It's my coming-out!"

Evidently, Felicia had ascended the dais where the orchestra had been performing and was now hogging everyone's attention. She wasn't wearing one of her black widow's gowns, but a lemon-colored one that must have been made for her new, more slender figure. She had a smug smile on her face, as if she was pleased with the reaction to her announcement.

A gentleman stood beside her, his arm about her, frowning in disapproval at the cacophony. Roberta nudged Olivia, her face alight with glee, and Ivo looked amused too. It seemed to be only Olivia and Justina who did not think this was funny. "We are marrying at once, and then Lord H is taking me for a long honeymoon on the continent." Felicia looked even more satisfied with the uproar *this* caused. Of course, she could have told her family privately, prepared them, but instead, she had wanted to create an embarrassing scene. She did not care that it was her daughter's special day—but she had never cared about any of them.

The dowager was busy trying to undo the damage, coolly congratulating her daughter-in-law, as if she had been privy to the news all along.

"At least she won't be sneaking about Grantham, making trouble," Roberta said.

"I wonder who paid for her new dress?" Justina added.

"I did."

They turned to find Gabriel standing behind them, Vivienne at his side.

"She asked me, and I said yes. Told me some story about wanting to look her best for her darling Justina. I'm glad I did now. She would probably have appeared in her crow outfit and announced my pinchpenny ways to all and sundry."

Olivia noticed Viscount Carey looking on with that beaming smile, as if he was enjoying every moment of it. Not like the prince then, who had once more vacated the ballroom.

"There is never a dull moment with the Ashtons," Ivo said.

She met his eyes, and saw the sparkling laughter in their green depths. He was amused, but not *at* her. He was laughing *with* her, and suddenly, she felt better. If he was able to shrug off what promised to be a red-hot subject for gossip, then why shouldn't she?

"We aim to please," she replied.

He was still watching her, and it was as if they were all alone among the chattering and outraged guests. She was finding it hard to breathe, anticipation making her a little dizzy.

Olivia wasn't going to change her mind about their dare, and from the growing smile on his handsome face, neither was he.

Chapter Twenty-Nine

I t never ceased to amaze Ivo how shocking the Ashtons could be. He almost admired them for it. They could never do anything without making a scene. Olivia was forever worrying about being talked about, but she really should just accept that nothing she did was ever going to change her family. She needed to embrace it.

He watched as the three sisters huddled together, no doubt discussing how to contain this latest disaster. Roberta was smirking and Justina nodding, while Olivia waved her hands around rather wildly. Just moments ago, he had been kissing her.

The memory sobered him. He had tried so hard to be her friend, to subdue his careless ways, to be a better man. He had fallen in love with her but never told her because he did not want to drive her away. Seeing her dancing with that fool Carey and knowing he was the latest in the dowager's long line of "suitable" husbands for her granddaughter had made him unbearably jealous.

He understood that the pressures upon Olivia were profound. He had accepted that she was never going to marry him, so to have her hand him such an outrageous dare had left him reeling. But only for a moment. Despite the "better" Ivo informing him in a prissy voice that he must decline, he was damned if he was going to.

Maybe it was time he fought for what he wanted? Fought for Olivia? After all, what had he to lose that he wasn't going to lose anyway if she married Carey?

He wanted her. He had wanted her from their first moment. Remembering their heated kisses made him ache, in his heart and his groin. This was his moment, and he wasn't going to let it slip away.

The sisters had broken apart. Justina was returning to their grandmother, and Roberta was speaking to their brother. Olivia was alone, and this was his chance. He stepped up to her and leaned in, his voice low enough not to be overheard.

"I accept your dare."

She looked up at him in surprise, as if she had forgotten. "Do you? Are you…?"

"Sure? God yes," he said, heartfelt.

That made her choke back laughter.

He gave her a searching look. He had to ask, the man he was now demanded it. "You haven't changed your mind? I would understand if you did."

She shook her head. She had that mulish look that meant she was determined to see something to its end. "God no."

It was his turn to laugh. "Then I will send you instructions of where and when. Don't worry. I will be discreet. You are safe with me, Olivia."

She tried to smile, but her lips were trembling. "I know I am," she said softly.

Ivo bowed, and then went to join his mother and sisters. He could feel her gaze on him as he walked away. Soon, he would have her in his arms, in his bed, and once he had her, he was going to do everything in his power to keep her.

⃟

"No one will ever forget my debut!"

Justina was lying on her back on the bed, staring up at the canopy above. Olivia and Roberta lay on either side of her.

Olivia tried not to laugh. It wasn't funny. How could their mother take precedence over her own daughter? But that was Felicia, wasn't it? Selfish to the last.

Thank goodness she was going away for a long visit to the continent.

"I suppose she'll come back eventually," Justina said.

"Then we'll face it when the time comes," Roberta said.

She was being surprisingly mature, but ever since the horse riding lessons, Olivia had noticed her sister was no longer a child. She still behaved like one sometimes, but there were moments of real maturity.

"I suppose we could always go back to Grantham and hide. Imagine Mother strutting about the ton with her new husband!"

They all shuddered.

"I miss Grantham," Roberta admitted. "I love being there. Being free. But I am quite liking London too. There are exciting things to do here too. Especially when my sister races the Duke of Northam along Rotten Row."

Olivia couldn't shush her soon enough and Justina lurched up from the bed with a muffled shriek. "What! Tell me. Tell me at once!"

Chapter Thirty

I t was sheer luck that Olivia was able to attend the Longhursts' ball. When the invitation arrived two days after Justina's coming-out, the dowager was deeply involved with Felicia's wedding. Although it was a family affair—her wish to be married at St. James's Church had been rejected by Gabriel—Felicia had a great many wishes she wanted fulfilled, and the dowager, whether from a sense of guilt or a desire to see the back of her, seemed happy to comply.

"What is that?" the dowager had asked, seeing the invite in Olivia's hand.

"Another ball," she had said airily. "I may not go."

Her grandmother frowned. "You should take every opportunity to be seen. I wonder if Carey is going?"

Luckily, Felicia chose that moment to appear, informing everyone that the material for her dress wasn't the same as the one she had chosen. The dowager turned away to deal with this latest disaster, and Olivia breathed a sigh of relief. Hastily, she replied to the Longhursts' invitation, saying she would be at their ball, and dispatched the message.

She knew this was Ivo's doing. He had sent her a note the day after Justina's coming-out, informing her that he would see her at the Longhursts' ball and to wear a mask.

Then, on the evening, when she was preparing to set off, having ordered the coach, Gabriel almost put a stop to it. "What on earth are you wearing?" He was eyeing her mask warily.

"I am meant to be a Harlequin," she said self-consciously. The mask was painted in a variety of colors, and matched her yellow and red gown, which was hidden beneath her cloak. "Hidden" because the bodice was cut rather low—a task Olivia had achieved with the help of a maid who had been keen to earn some shillings by staying silent about her young mistress's plans.

"Where are you going?"

"A ball at the Longhursts'."

"The Longhursts? That rackety pair. Did your grandmother approve of this?"

"Of course. Carey will be there."

She was lying to him. She felt guilty, knowing he would never let her go if he knew the truth, but she couldn't explain to Gabriel how desperately she needed to meet with Ivo. It was a dare, yes, but that was just an excuse. And she knew how inappropriate the Longhursts' entertainments were for an unmarried young lady like herself. They were known for the sort of society parties where lovers met in secret. The company could get quite bawdy, but they were also known to be discreet.

"Will Justina be accompanying you?" Gabriel asked, and her heart sank. He was watching her closely, and if it wasn't for the mask, he would have been able to see the truth.

"She's with Adelina at the theater."

Gabriel narrowed his eyes. "I really don't think—"

"I'm going with her."

They both turned, both surprised to see Roberta

there. "You are going to the Longhursts'?" Gabriel made it sound improbable…because it was.

"Yes. There will be some other younger girls there to keep Lady Longhurst's daughter company. We will probably be playing silly games, but it's better than staying here with Grandmama and Mama." She rolled her eyes. "Sorry I'm not ready yet," she added, gaze fixed on Olivia. "I'll be quick." But instead of rushing away, Roberta hesitated, watching her sister.

Olivia opened her mouth but changed her mind before she spoke. "Hurry up then," she said.

Gabriel still looked uneasy about the matter, but he was a busy man, and soon, he was called away.

Olivia stood alone in her finery, wondering if she should just stay home. This was turning out to be far more complicated than it was meant to be, and now Roberta was coming with her—and wherever Roberta went, trouble followed. She was still standing there when her sister bounced down the stairs and joined her, rather breathless but looking respectable enough. She was even masked, although it appeared to be something she had dug out of the dress-up box in the nursery.

"You're not going to turn coward, are you?" Roberta demanded. "Come on, we'll be late."

Olivia let herself be tugged toward the door and the waiting coach. "How did you know…?"

"You've been so sneaky lately, and then I saw the invitation, although you tried to hide it. I could tell something was up. Please, don't make me stay home. I need something exciting to do, and I promise I won't get in your way. I'll sit in a corner."

"How did you know all that about Lady Longhurst's daughter?"

"I met her at one of those boring picnics for younger people, and I've heard gossip about the family. They are rather disreputable. Even more disreputable than us! No wonder Gabriel was worried."

Olivia ignored the last sentence. "I really don't think you should come. You'll only get into trouble, and I should be setting a better example for you."

"Oh please," Roberta burst out. "This is the most fun I've had since the horse race. Don't spoil it now."

"Robbie, I'm meeting Ivo."

Her sister's eyes widened, and she made a muffled shriek behind her mask. "Wonderful!" she breathed. "A tryst. Or is it a rendezvous? Hurry up, he'll think you're not coming."

Once they were inside the coach, Olivia leaned back and took a deep breath. She was trembling with fear and excitement, and now she had Roberta to worry about. What on earth was she thinking bringing her younger sister with her? And at the same time, what other option did she have?

"Promise me you'll sit somewhere safe and be good."

"Of course," her sister said airily. "I promise."

Olivia hesitated, but she wanted to do this. It was reprehensible but also rather wonderful. And when would she have another chance to make memories that were going to have to last her for the rest of her life?

❧

Impatiently, Ivo strode back and forth on the footpath in front of the Longhursts' town house. The windows were ablaze with candlelight, and the music ebbed and flowed, interspersed with the hum of many voices. Several couples had entered the building behind him, one woman giggling as her partner whispered to her. Olivia should be here by now, and the more time that went by, the more he wondered if this was a terrible mistake.

His thoughts were swirling around and around.

They would get caught, Olivia would end up facing another scandal, she would refuse to speak to him again, he would lose her forever. And so it went. Even though it had been she who wanted to do this, he still wasn't sure he should have agreed. The new Ivo, the better man, whispered in his ear: *You are behaving very badly.* At the same time, the idea of being with her at last was too marvelous to resist.

Ivo took a deep breath. The decision was out of his hands now. If she did not come, then they could go back to being friends. That wouldn't be so bad, would it? But he knew in his heart and soul that it wasn't what he wanted.

He felt her before he saw her, a warm tingle down his back. Ivo turned around.

Olivia stood behind him, and even cloaked, the hood pulled low over her head and a mask covering her face, he would have known her anywhere. He lifted his own mask—it had the pointed snout of a fox—and moved closer, his gaze fixed on hers, the scent of her soap as familiar to him as his own. "Take my arm," he murmured. "No one will question us. Everyone here is hiding something."

She took his arm, but he could feel her shaking.

"Have you changed your mind?" he asked her. If she had, then he would deal with his disappointment and do the right thing.

"No, I haven't changed my mind. There is a problem

however…" She glanced behind her, and for the first time, Ivo took his gaze from hers and saw there was another woman standing nearby.

"Who…?" he began before he realized. "Roberta?" He scrambled for something to say.

She gave him a mocking curtsy. "At your service, Your Grace."

"What on earth are you doing here?"

"It was either me come with her or she wouldn't have been able to come at all," Roberta informed him. "Gabriel was asking questions." She looked up at the town house. "Are we going inside?"

"What about…?" he began uneasily, looking from one sister to the other.

"Oh, don't worry about me," Roberta said blithely. "I'll be good."

"It is all very well to *say* that," Ivo replied. "But I'd feel responsible if anything happened."

Olivia squeezed his arm. "I'll make sure she behaves," she whispered. "And I can always send her home."

"And have Gabriel arrive and drag you out of wherever you are?" Roberta seemed to have ears like a bat. "I don't think so."

Defeated, Ivo turned and led the way up the steps into the house. He decided to just let matters unfold and hope for the best, although he wasn't at all sure this was a good idea, not any longer. He imagined him and Olivia trying to have their passionate moment, while Roberta made comments, and he gave a shudder. But they were inside now, surrounded by music and being handed glasses of champagne, and there were guests dancing. There were also couples seated on sofas set around the room, and it was obvious this was not the sort of ball Olivia was used to. He glanced at her sideways as she gave a little gasp. She had spied a couple kissing with a great deal of enthusiasm.

Was Olivia shocked? Roberta certainly wasn't. She was looking about her as if she had discovered the Holy Grail. Olivia turned to her and said sternly, "Go and sit in the coach and wait for me. This isn't the place for you. And not a peep from you, do you hear me?"

Roberta's chin jutted rebelliously, and she began to protest, but Ivo had spotted someone in the crowd and suddenly had a brilliant idea. "Wait here," he said, and headed across the room toward a plump, pretty woman wearing a great deal of rouge. A few words, and he was relieved to have the weight of Roberta lifted from his shoulders. He returned to the sisters.

"I have just spoken to Lady Longhurst," he said to Roberta. "She understands our dilemma. She has a daughter about your age, and although the girl is not allowed to attend these sorts of events, she is upstairs in her bedchamber feeling hard done by. Lady Longhurst is absolutely delighted for you to keep her company."

Roberta wriggled in delight. "I told you so!" she said to Olivia.

Olivia sighed and watched as her sister set off to accost the other woman. Ivo didn't wait to see what transpired. He wasn't at all sure how much time they had, and he wanted to make the most of every minute. He squeezed Olivia's hand, and she gave him an uncertain look through the mask.

"As much as I want to kiss you," he said, "I don't want an audience."

"No, that would be rather shocking," she agreed, sounding breathless. "What do you suggest then?"

He smiled. "Come with me."

Chapter Thirty-One

A servant led the way along a corridor, and Olivia and Ivo followed. From the brief conversation he had had with the man, it seemed that this had all been arranged. Candles flickered in sconces as they passed closed doors, the murmur of sound behind them. Olivia felt a little shaky, but she wasn't about to turn back. When Roberta had joined her, she had been prepared to call everything off. She would not allow her sister to be placed in peril. But now that problem seemed to have been resolved.

"Have you been here before?" she asked Ivo abruptly, the thought just occurring to her that he seemed to know his way around this place rather well.

"I have. Not recently," he added, glancing down at her. "Don't worry, you'll be quite safe. Even if anyone recognized you, no one here would dare to gossip about the other guests. They all have their secrets."

"The couple who were kissing…?"

"An unhappy gentleman who has found pleasure elsewhere. And if you are feeling sorry for his wife, she was there too, with her lover."

Olivia wasn't sure what to say about that. She knew such things happened, she wasn't a naïve fool, but to see it firsthand…No wonder Gabriel had had doubts. She was surprised he had allowed her out of the house, and at the same time, she was very glad he had.

The servant paused outside a door and opened it with a bow. "If you require anything else, sir, please ring for me," he said.

Ivo pressed some coins into his hand, and a moment later, they were alone.

It was a bedchamber, with the addition of a table set for two. A lantern softened the corners of the room and gave everything a golden glow. Olivia pretended to survey the food arranged on a platter, and the decanter of wine with two glasses. But in fact, all of her senses were fixed on the bed.

It was large enough for two, with comfortable-looking bolsters and a quilt sewn of green cloth with fantastical-looking creatures on it.

"Olivia..."

He had come up behind her without her hearing, and she jumped. She heard him sigh.

"Sweetheart, we don't have to do anything. We can eat our meal and drink our wine, and then we can leave."

She turned to face him. He had taken off his mask, and she could see him properly now. Ivo, her friend, who she knew would keep her safe. It felt at last as if they had gotten beyond the shoals of the past and were now sailing out into new waters. She reached up to touch his jaw, feeling the cleanly shaven skin. Her heart began to beat that tempo she recognized.

Desire. Need.

"I don't want to leave," she said. "I want to be with you for this night."

He smiled, but his eyes were serious. "You make it sound as if we will never see each other again."

She didn't think that was true, but Olivia knew her future and his were unlikely to head in the same direction. They would cross paths sometimes, only to part again. She told herself she was practical enough to accept that truth, no matter how much it hurt.

When she didn't answer, he carefully lifted the mask from her face and set it aside. She knew she wasn't naked, not yet, but she felt naked as his gaze roamed over her features. "You are so beautiful," he whispered. "I thought so from the first moment I saw you."

"Ivo," she breathed. "Kiss me, please."

His responding chuckle was rough, and then he bent, and his lips captured hers. The kiss was tentative at first but soon became passionate. Olivia felt her blood heating, her skin prickling within the confinement of her clothing. She was still wearing her cloak, and now she stepped back and undid the tie at her throat, so that the garment pooled at her feet.

Ivo's eyes widened at her gown's daring neckline. He groaned. He reached out to trail a finger across the swell of her breasts, before he lowered his lips to her throat, her collarbone. "May I?" he said, reaching around to the fastenings at the back of her gown.

She turned for him, and felt him unhooking and unbuttoning her, and then the sag of the loosened bodice against her skin. Her breasts ached, the tips drawn up into hard little points, and when he reached to cup her in his warm hands, she felt lightheaded.

His warm breath nuzzling against the curve of her shoulder made her shiver, before he turned her and looked where he had touched. His gaze darkened. "Even more beautiful than I thought," he said. Olivia closed her eyes as he leaned in and his mouth closed on the tip of one breast, rolling her nipple with his tongue. Her head fell back, and she gasped.

Every lingering worry left her, and all she could do was revel in these new sensations. This was Ivo, her Ivo.

"I want to see you too," she managed.

He lifted his head and smiled. "Your wish is my command," he said.

A moment later, Olivia was seated on the bed, while Ivo stood before her, removing his clothing, slowly and deliberately. It was as if he was seducing her, and she certainly felt seduced. The longing for him increased with every garment tossed aside, and when he stripped off his shirt, her gaze drank him in as if she was dying of thirst. The broad sweep of his shoulders and the smooth planes of his chest, with a trail of hair darker than she had expected running down over his flat belly. He paused, resting his hands on his pantaloons.

"Ivo," she whispered, and stood up. She had been holding her bodice up over her nakedness, but now it fell again, as she reached out to touch. His skin was warm, smooth apart from the hair, and she leaned in and kissed him.

The next moment, he was lifting her up into his arms, and she cried out in surprise, but then he was seated on the bed, and she was on his knee. The sensation of their bare skin pressed together was beyond words. She wanted this every day and every night. She ached to have him in her bed, in her life, forever.

Before she could begin to remind herself that such a wish could never be, he was kissing her again. Long, drugging kisses that made her body long for his hands, his mouth, and more. He pulled the pins from her hair, and it tumbled about them. He curled it in his hands and held her face at the exact angle for his mouth to take full advantage of hers. At the same time, her hands were on him, clasping his shoulders, caressing his skin, eagerly reaching down to where he was still clothed.

He was hard, and Olivia knew enough to understand it was because he wanted her as a man wanted a woman. When she ran her hand over the bulge beneath the cloth, he groaned and tipped his head back. "Olivia." His voice was deep and urgent. "If you have changed your mind, then tell me now."

She smiled. "Ivo, this is a dare. I never walk away from a dare, you know that."

He was looking at her now, returning her smile, but there was a question in his eyes. Did he want to hear how much she ached for him, how the place between her thighs was damp and hot and ready for him? She wanted to say those things, but she was suddenly uncertain. This moment between them felt more than physical. Her heart was engaged.

She loved him. And if she hadn't known it or wanted to admit it before, then she did so now.

Olivia reached to encircle her arms about his neck, pulling him down for more kisses. They fell onto the bed, facing each other, and the kiss went on. There was a sense of urgency inside her, a need that could no longer be denied.

"Should I take off my—" she began, but he was before her.

"Let me." He crawled down and knelt at her feet, removing her slippers and then reaching to lift her skirt so that he could untie her stockings. He smoothed his hands over her knees and calves as he rolled them down, and then he cupped her ankles. Ivo looked up at her, and there was something in his face, in his eyes, that made her think that this moment was more than physical for him too.

Still watching her, he ran his hands up her legs again to her thighs, and then he ducked under her skirts, and she felt his hot breath between them. She must have cried out in surprise, arching toward him, but it was so good. She could hardly bear it. And then his tongue was lapping at her, and even his teeth, gently, and oh God, it was too much.

Her body gathered itself, and suddenly, she was soaring.

When she was able to open her eyes again, he was still kneeling before her, watching her with an arrogant grin. Slowly, he began to unfasten his pantaloons, shoving them down over his slim hips, down over his muscular thighs. He wasn't wearing anything under them, which confused her briefly because she knew gentlemen wore underwear, but then she forgot all that when she saw him in his full, manly glory.

His arrogant smile had faded as he watched her eyes widen. "Olivia," he began, as if he was going to suggest they stop now, and she couldn't have that. She pushed herself up and reached for him, wrapping her hand around the thick heat.

Ivo groaned, and when she began to stroke him, he said in a muffled voice, "I'll spill if you do that."

Olivia stretched up to plant a kiss on his jaw, and then another, and then he was rolling her over on the bed, their bodies tangled in her skirts, and the ache inside her was growing again.

He was on top of her, taking his weight with his knees and elbows, but she felt his presence in a way that she never had before. He nuzzled against her throat, murmuring words she couldn't understand, all of her attention focused on his hand, now stroking between her thighs, causing them to fall open, and then she felt him pressing for entry.

"Sweetheart… want you…so much…"

For a moment, she thought he said he loved her, but she must have been mistaken, and even if he had…She reminded herself feverishly that people said things at the height of their emotion; it didn't mean they were serious.

Olivia arched against him, feeling the burn of his body easing into hers, the brief discomfort, before his fingers teased her into ecstasy. And then he was rocking against her, and she grasped his back, holding him to her, never wanting this to end.

Far away, a church bell rang, and she closed her eyes and imagined flying high over the city. She and Ivo, together.

Chapter Thirty-Two

S he was sleeping. Ivo had been asleep himself, briefly, but he didn't want to waste a moment of this time. They were lying on the bed, his body spooned around hers, with her back to his chest. He lifted his head and leaned over to kiss her gently on the temple, tucking her hair aside so that he could see her face. The pleasure had been beyond his wildest dreams, but he suspected that was because, for the first time, his heart was enmeshed, as well as his body.

He wondered how she could think they would only have this one night. It wasn't enough. He would fight for more, for her, with everything he had. It was either that or live with a broken heart.

"Ivo?"

He looked down. Her eyes were still closed, long, dark lashes resting against her pale cheek. "Yes, sweetheart?"

She smiled, the corners of her lips turning up. "I like it when you call me that," she whispered. "I've never been anybody's sweetheart."

That gave him a sharp pain in his heart, to think she had not been valued as she ought. He remembered how she had spoken about her childhood, the awfulness of it, and he swore to himself that if he won her, he would do everything in his power to make her life with him better.

"I will call you sweetheart forever now," he said, his voice rough with emotion.

Her smile dropped away, and he felt her body stiffen. Her eyes snapped open. She lifted her head and looked at him over her shoulder.

"I should get back," she said. "It must be late."

"Soon," he soothed. "We have a little longer."

She hesitated, and just when he thought she was going to insist, she snuggled down against him again.

Ivo pressed his lips to her nape, lifting aside her dark hair. She shivered, and he did it again, reaching around to cup her breast, gently squeezing the lush flesh. He moved his thumb over her nipple, feeling it peak. She was his perfect woman, he decided. His pocket Venus.

"Feels nice," she murmured, wriggling back against him, and he groaned at the sensation of her bottom pressing to his groin. "Can we do it again?" she added breathlessly. "Once more before we go?"

"God yes," he said. When he slipped his fingers between her thighs, he could feel the moist heat there, the beginnings of her arousal and the residue of their earlier lovemaking. His cock was so hard, he ached as he carefully pushed inside her, and then reached around to tease her. She was already gasping, arching back into him, and as he began to move, she did too.

He could wake up to this every morning for the rest of his life, and it would never be enough. Her soft curves against his hard muscle, the feminine scent of her on his fingers, in his nostrils, the sound of her cries as she drew nearer to her climax.

"Ivo," she gasped, her body trembling, her muscles tightening around his cock, sending them both into ecstasy.

They lay for a time, replete, but she was right. It was late.

Ivo rose and found the water and a cloth left by the servant. It was barely warm now, but it would have to do, he thought as he cleaned her lovingly. Olivia watched him through her lashes, but she did not protest. She seemed to enjoy his intimate attentions, and he remembered again her desolate childhood. He looked up at her. "You may be a little sore. I'm sorry if that's the case."

She bit her lip. "I am a little sore. But it was worth it, Ivo." They smiled at each other until her gaze slipped away. Then, as if pushing aside sentiment, she said briskly, "You won the dare. Congratulations."

He didn't want to think these heavenly moments had been part of a challenge. He suspected she had reminded him to try to distance herself, and he didn't like it. "Thank you," he said politely. "I will have to think of one for you."

She laughed uncomfortably. "No hurry. I expect my mother's wedding will keep me busy."

In mutual silence, they began to dress, Olivia turning to him only when she needed her gown refastened. He might have held her, kissed her, but she stepped away and reached for her cloak, quickly tying it before tucking her hair into the hood. The last thing was her mask, and when she had covered her face once more, Ivo went to open the door.

"Olivia," he said, "do you think—"

"I hope Roberta hasn't done anything disgraceful," she said quickly, interrupting him.

He let his words go. What was he going to say anyway? *I love you, please marry me?* She would only say no again. He had promised he would fight for her, but he needed some distance to regroup, to plan. This was not the moment to declare himself.

The scene in the ballroom was even more dissipated than before. Debauchery was everywhere. He hurried Olivia through, stepping over a single stocking tangled with a cravat, and asked for their coach to be brought to the door. Roberta was sent for and arrived, eyeing them curiously. As if disliking the silence that seemed to stretch between them, she broke into a monologue about the Longhurst girl and her collection of dolls.

"Next time, I will bring Edwina," she said. "She would enjoy a visit. For me, it was rather tedious. I am used to more exciting things."

Ivo was glad to hand them into the coach. For a moment, Olivia turned to him, but he couldn't read her expression behind the mask, and in the end, he bowed and let them go. The vehicle rumbled away over the cobbles, and behind him he could hear laughter from the Longhursts', but it was much more subdued than earlier.

He needed to go home. He needed to think. He suspected Olivia believed she had said goodbye to him, and that she was preparing to be friends again. She was foolish if she thought that. After tonight, "friends" could never be enough. Their lovemaking had crossed a line that they could never go back from.

From now on, for Ivo, it was either all or nothing.

Chapter Thirty-Three

W as it really that bad?"

Olivia jumped at the sound of her sister's voice, and then glared at her. "Be quiet."

"Ivo looked as if he'd swallowed a plum stone, and you are just as bad. If making love is that awful, I am never going to put myself through it, that's for certain."

"It wasn't awful. It was wonderful. It's just..."

Just that she was in love with Ivo, and now she would struggle even more to marry someone like Viscount Carey. She'd have the memories of this night, yes, but she had the lowering feeling that they would not be enough. Ivo would haunt her dreams, and she would relive their night again and again.

"It is just what?" Roberta said impatiently.

"Nothing."

Roberta huffed and folded her arms. "I'm never going to give my heart to anyone," she announced as they neared Ashton House. "I am going to live my life for myself, the way I want it, so there!"

"I wish you luck," Olivia said bitterly.

There was no one to meet them at the door. Everyone must be abed, so there would be no interrogation. Olivia hastened to her room, Roberta flouncing behind her, muttering about it being a complete waste of an evening.

After undressing, Olivia lay in bed and stared into the darkness. Although she shared the bedchamber with

Justina, her sister was still out at the theater and supper, and she was alone. She was too filled with uncomfortable thoughts to sleep, even though she knew tomorrow would be another busy day. The memory of the touch of Ivo's hands on her body made her ache all over again, and the expression in his green eyes when he told her she was beautiful...She would never forget it. But wasn't that what she had wanted?

Olivia knew now her dare had been a dreadful mistake. Because the memories wouldn't be enough. She was in love with a man who did not love her, a man she had sworn not to marry, and it felt as if she was being squeezed into a smaller and smaller space. What choice was left to her? Viscount Carey, probably. He had yet to ask her, but Olivia sensed it was only a matter of time.

A sensible marriage, with money enough to help her sisters and herself, and the opportunity to take her proper place in the ton.

No love match though. She would be just another young lady who set aside her heart's desire to focus on practical matters. And although there was nothing wrong with that, Olivia understood now that she was not that sort of girl. She wanted love. When Ivo had called her "sweetheart," it had been as if a door had opened before her, beckoning her through into a world where she could be somebody's beloved. Somebody's entire world. Somebody's sweetheart.

And it hurt a great deal to think she was going to have to close that door again.

As Olivia had foreseen, the following days were busy with Felicia's wedding preparations. It seemed even the tiniest detail was a matter for discussions and arguments, which her mother usually won. She had suffered when Harry's death had revealed the awful truth about their marriage, and she seemed determined to make the most of this second marriage. Lord Harrowby was very much in the background, and he seemed happy enough to let his bride have her way.

Olivia did not know him well, and those times she had spoken with him since Justina's coming-out, he had been reserved and rather stiff in his manner. But he seemed genuinely devoted to her mother, and despite all that had happened in the past, she was glad Felicia had found someone with her best interests at heart.

Not that she was feeling very charitable as she was sent running hither and thither, looking for anything and everything her mother needed for her wedding. The drawing room at Ashton House was to be decorated for the occasion, and Felicia insisted upon a bower of flowers that she and her intended could stand beneath as the minister performed the service.

The flowers were the problem. Every variety on Felicia's list was an exotic species and difficult to find. Expensive too. Gabriel was grinding his teeth by the time the day arrived for the actual ceremony.

It was a close family affair, which Felicia had only agreed to if there was a celebratory supper dance the next evening, to send the happy couple off on their honeymoon. As the vows were exchanged beneath the contentious bower, there were more than a few tears shed. Possibly more from relief than sentiment.

"It was quite moving," Justina said when it was over, and she flopped down onto the bed beside Olivia and Roberta. "Did you hear her thanking her beautiful daughters?"

"I had to look over my shoulder because I was certain she couldn't mean me," Roberta replied with a yawn.

Olivia yawned too. She was very tired from too many nights of little sleep, but that wasn't entirely her mother's fault. It was Ivo who strolled through her dreams, holding her in his arms, making her body sing, and sometimes telling her he loved her. She still wondered if she had heard him say that in the heat of their passion. Should she have told him that *she* loved *him*?

Carey would be at the supper dance tomorrow night, and Olivia had a queasy feeling he was going to propose. And if he did…?

"What would happen if I didn't accept Viscount Carey?"

The words startled her sisters. They turned to stare at her. Roberta grinned, and Justina looked concerned. "Nothing would happen," the latter said. "You should not accept him unless it is your wish to do so, Olivia."

"He is quite wealthy. He could buy me pretty dresses and gewgaws."

Roberta snorted. "Do you want gewgaws?"

"I thought I did." She stared into space, considering. "I could help both of you, and the other three girls. We will probably be paupers by the time Edwina comes out."

"You think too much about other people," Justina scolded her. "And why are you talking about this now?" she added suspiciously. "What has made you finally see the light?"

Olivia wasn't entirely pleased by the suggestion she had been walking around with her head in a fog, but she appreciated the sisterly concern. Should she tell them? She normally kept her secret heart quite secret, even from Justina, but she had been thinking and thinking, until her head ached, and quite suddenly, she couldn't think anymore.

"I am in love with Northam."

Justina's mouth dropped open, and Roberta rolled her eyes.

"I think if he asked me to marry him," *again,* "I would say yes." She put her hands to her face and groaned. "But how can I? He is in worse financial straits than us!"

Roberta laughed. "But think what fun you would both have!"

Justina was more circumspect. "I suppose that is a consideration, but remember he is a joint partner in Cadieux's. Charles says it is doing very well." She blushed, avoiding their eyes. "Not that you should only marry Northam for financial reasons alone. Do you really love him, Olivia? I wondered, seeing you together, but you insisted it was not to be."

"I tried not to let it be," she said with a sigh, "but yes, I do love him. I have probably loved him since the first moment I saw him. And now I sound like a character from Vivienne and Annette's novel," she said with a grimace.

Roberta had been watching them thoughtfully. "I think it would be the best thing ever," she said. "I have heard that Whitmont is a wild sort of place, with salt marshes and smugglers. Every day would be an adventure, just think!"

"For you maybe," Olivia retorted, but she *was* remembering Ivo talking about his home with such fondness. Was the thought of Whitmont so very bad? And how could it be, if Ivo was there with her?

"Marry him," Roberta said.

"If he makes you happy, then marry him," Justina added.

Olivia smiled, her eyes suddenly stinging with tears. "You have both forgotten one important point. He hasn't *asked* me."

Chapter Thirty-Four

T he first opportunity Olivia had to speak with Ivo was the supper dance the next evening. They had a house full of guests, and Olivia was charged with seeing that the food on the tables did not run out. She couldn't imagine an army demolishing what was laid upon the groaning tables, but she did her duty until she was able to slip away. She had not seen Ivo since their night at the Longhursts', and while she was looking forward to it, she was also dreading the awkwardness of it.

What did you say to a man who had lain with you and pleasured you? A man you had fallen in love with, seemingly against your will and your better judgment?

She discovered, when Ivo came to ask her to dance, that you made polite chitchat.

"Your mother must be pleased," Ivo said, looking about at the crowd.

"They're probably only here in case there's another scandal."

He laughed, but he was watching her, his green eyes mapping her features. He was thinking of their night together, and Olivia looked away, aware that her cheeks had heated and were probably bright red.

"Olivia," he whispered, "there's no need to be embarrassed. Not with me. I think you are perfect."

It was sweet. She looked back, and this time, she met his gaze. He looked as if he wanted to kiss her, and at the same time hold her fast in his arms, safe from the world. Her hand trembled in his, but instead of saying the things she wanted to, she blurted out, "Is it time for another dare?"

He frowned, and there was a moment of silence as they continued to dance. Perhaps he wasn't going to answer. A glance across the room showed Justina and Roberta staring at her meaningfully, as if willing her to speak the words that were burning the tip of her tongue.

I love you, Ivo.

"Ivo…"

"Olivia," he began, "there is something I want to ask you. Not a dare, exactly, but it could be if you prefer. Although you may consider it far too colossal to be considered a…Well." He laughed awkwardly. By now, the music had stopped, and they were standing in the middle of the room staring at one another.

"What is it?" she asked. Excitement burst like fireworks inside her. Was he going to declare himself? It felt as if he was. *Please, please, let it be so.*

His throat moved as he swallowed. "I know you said you could not consider me as a suitor, and I respect that. I understand. But lately, I have felt as if you might have changed your…That is, although you said no that time, I want to ask you again because I…"

As his words tailed off, she almost groaned aloud with frustration.

The words burst out of her. "Ivo, you're right. I did say no, but things were very different then. Now I…I think I…"

He must have read something in her face, because

his own lit up, and he leaned down as if he might kiss her, right here in the midst of the guests, with her family's eyes upon them. "I love you," he whispered. "So much, Olivia. I dare you to marry me."

It was a marvelous moment and typically Ivo. To ask her here and now. Her lips trembled as she smiled, her eyes filling with emotion. She wanted to scream "Yes," but it seemed worthy of more than that. She needed to choose her words.

But before she could speak, there was a scuffle at the door. Distracted, Ivo turned his head to look in the direction of the sounds, which were getting louder.

Olivia followed his gaze. She saw Humber, an expression on his face she hadn't seen since the night the prince's horse went missing. Behind him were several men in uniform. One of them was Freddie Hart.

Humber raised his voice above the music. "Gentlemen. This is inexcusable. If you would wait outside, I will fetch His Grace, and you can discuss the matter with—"

He was ignored. One of the soldiers brushed rudely past him, and Freddie followed. The music, which had been about to start again, came to a discordant stop, and everyone had turned to stare.

"We are here for the Duke of Northam," the soldier said in ringing tones. "Apologies if this is inconvenient, but we are on official business."

Beside her, Ivo had frozen. His gaze was on the uninvited guests, and he looked as shocked as everyone else. He had been holding her hand, and now his grip tightened almost to the point of pain before he abruptly released her.

"Ivo?" she breathed.

Gabriel was insisting in a gruff voice, "What is going on here? Freddie?"

Freddie bowed to the assembled guests, a regretful expression on his face. "Apologies, Your Grace," he said to his friend in a strangely formal manner. "I have been seconded to the Customs Office, and I am here at the behest of Lieutenant Harrison." He nodded to the officer beside him. "He and his men are revenue officers stationed in Kent."

Something unspoken passed between the two men. They had known each other since childhood, and Gabriel trusted Freddie with his life. But that didn't explain what was going on.

Lieutenant Harrison spoke up, loud and determined. "We are here to take Northam in for questioning."

Somewhere among the guests, Ivo's mother cried out, while there were gasps of surprise and demands to know what was happening. Olivia's head swung back to Ivo. "What is happening? Ivo?"

His gaze came to rest on her face, reading her distress and concern, but instead of explaining, she saw him make the decision not to tell her. "Nothing to worry about," he said in that infuriating way that men did when they thought they were being protective. Then he patted her hand in a brotherly fashion, and walked away. She might have followed him, she was angry enough to, but Charles suddenly appeared, and he prevented her by taking her arm in a firm grasp.

"You will only make it worse," he said with an apologetic grimace. "Freddie is there, and he will take care that nothing occurs that is outside the law."

"But what is happening?" Olivia looked for Ivo, who had now reached the soldiers. Justina slipped an arm about her waist, but even her calming presence did not help.

"Your Grace," the lieutenant's voice rose, easily heard above the chatter. "You are to come with us to answer charges under the Customs Act."

"What charges?" Gabriel challenged, looking from the soldiers to Ivo. "This is ridiculous! You are interrupting a private gathering for God's sake!"

"Bringing contraband into England. Smuggling." Lieutenant Harrison answered with a self-righteous look on his face. He reminded Olivia of a man at the end of a very good meal.

The murmur throughout the room rose to a roar as Ivo was surrounded by the soldiers and led from the ballroom. Crying out, the Dowager Duchess of Northam tried to reach him, but her daughters held her back, just as Charles had held Olivia back.

Olivia was shocked—Ivo arrested for smuggling?— and yet now that the moment of his arrest had passed, she was not as shocked as she should be. If anyone was going to be involved in such a risky venture, then it would be Ivo. He had even told her that Whitmont was an area famous for its smugglers, and that his family had been there for centuries. Of course they would be involved in smuggling.

Charles had followed the arrest party outside but soon returned. He went straight to Gabriel, and the two men conferred in quiet, serious tones.

"How dare they!" That was Ivo's mother, her daughters on either side of her, all looking anxious. "Someone must do something. Immediately!" She glared about her, as if expecting some knight in shining armor to step up and volunteer his services.

Gabriel would know what to do. Olivia hurried over to him, joined by Justina, who wanted to know what

Charles had heard from Freddie. When Charles turned to her sister, there was such a look of tenderness in his eyes...Olivia knew then that what was between them was more than an infatuation. They were a couple.

"Freddie says he can help a little," Charles explained, "although he has a position to maintain. The important thing is he's on the spot to make sure none of the revenue men overstep."

Gabriel frowned. "Do you think they will?"

Charles shrugged. "I hope not, but Harrison seems to have a grudge against Northam."

Gabriel considered this before adding, "Arnott might be able to help." That was when he noticed Olivia's presence, and his frown deepened. "I think the ladies should carry on with the dance. We should behave as if we have no doubt whatsoever of Northam's innocence, and that this is just an annoying mistake, which will soon be rectified."

Olivia opened her mouth, but Adelina, who was standing behind her, spoke first. "It *is* a mistake. He *is* innocent." She desperately searched their faces. "Isn't he?"

Gabriel responded reassuringly. "We'll do our best to see your brother released as soon as possible, and with the least amount of gossip." He looked about at the guests, who were agog with excitement, and his expression turned resigned when he met Felicia's outraged stare. "I'm sorry your send-off has turned into a circus."

After her mother's actions during Justina's coming-out ball, Olivia thought tonight was probably well deserved. All the same, there would be talk. She waited for the usual rush of dismay, that this was yet another nail in the coffin of her family's endeavor to be respectable. Another scandal that would sweep them back to seclusion at Grantham. But instead, to her surprise, the full force of it did not come. Even the uncomfortable vision of a cartoon of Ivo being dragged away only made her slightly uncomfortable. She would not allow strangers to rule her life, not anymore.

It was because she loved Ivo. He had been about to ask her to marry him! Yes, he might have broken the law, and Olivia might think him a reckless fool to have risked so much for a few bottles of brandy and a lace handkerchief. But she would wait until he was home, safe, before she told him that. Smuggling was not something she knew a great deal about, so she could not know how deeply he was involved. Could she marry a smuggler? Would he agree to stop if she asked him? She thought he would, but if there were decisions to be made, they would make them together.

Humber was lurking in the background, and Gabriel instructed him to fetch Mr. Arnott and inform him of the situation with the Duke of Northam. Humber pushed his way through the guests, who sounded like a hive of angry bees.

"We will soon sort this out," Olivia's brother said. Did he look at her a little longer, as if he knew…?

"I think Felicia has had her send-off." The dowager had arrived to join them. "And a memorable one it was too." Her dark eyes flashed. "Olivia, a word." She headed toward her favorite sitting room.

Olivia wanted to make some excuse. This was definitely not the time for a confrontation with her formidable grandmother, but when was the right time?

As soon as the door was closed, the dowager began to speak. "Viscount Carey has proposed to the Fletcher girl. You remember? The wallflower. Northam danced with her not so long ago. It seems he prefers a mouse for a wife."

She looked disgusted, and Olivia sat down beside her on the sofa. "I am surprised," she admitted. "We seemed to be getting on well."

"You didn't give him enough encouragement. Such a pity about Prince Nikolai," she mused. "I have tried to keep in touch, but lately, he has not responded to my messages. He has distanced himself from us, and I don't blame him. It is a great pity though." She smoothed the sleeves of her gown rather viciously. "I did my best to prepare the ground for you."

Olivia knew the time had come to be honest with her grandmother. She knew if she wasn't, there would be another suitor trotted out before she could draw breath. "I didn't want to marry the prince, and he certainly didn't want to marry me. We are too dissimilar, and I could never live up to his standards. I'm sorry, Grandmama. I know such a match would have meant a great deal to you and the family."

The dowager looked at her coldly, and Olivia awaited a tongue-lashing about ingratitude, but then the elderly woman sighed. She leaned back in her chair and closed her eyes. "You are probably right," she admitted reluctantly. Her eyes opened again, and she seemed to be staring into the past. "His father was just the same. High in the instep and thoroughly dislikable. Niki was brought up by his grandfather, and I had hoped he would take after him. Such a delightful man. But unfortunately, it doesn't appear to be the case."

"You knew his grandfather?" Olivia prompted curiously. She remembered the scandalous things Felicia had said, and wondered if there was any truth in them.

The dowager's dark eyes fastened on her, and she hesitated, but then seemed to decide *why not*? "Yes, I knew him well. You may find this shocking, but I was in love with Nikolai's grandfather. We had an affair." She waved a hand to stop Olivia replying, not that she could have. She was too surprised to say a word.

"You see, I was very unhappy at the time. My husband was more interested in his mistresses than me, and I already had my son, Harry, so I decided to seek my pleasures elsewhere. I even considered divorce. Niki's grandfather said he would take me to his country if I ran away with him. He painted a lovely picture of us together in his castle, with the fire roaring and the snow falling outside. I found it all very...tempting."

As the dowager reminisced, she looked younger and less tired. Knowing the difficult life she had had with her husband and then Harry, Olivia wondered why she had not left Grantham behind and run off with her true love. She almost asked the question, but her grandmother anticipated it.

"In the end, I decided I could not abandon my life, not after I had worked so hard to become the Duchess of Grantham. I had my son to consider too. I knew my husband would have been furious with me and would have taken steps to ensure I could never return. Did I really want to leave Harry in the hands of a disinterested father and possibly never see him again?" She smiled faintly. "You see, Olivia, when I married, I married the life of a duchess. It *was* my life. So I stayed and let go of my dreams."

Olivia imagined that turbulent time in her grandmother's life. "Did you ever regret your choice?" she asked quietly.

The dowager smiled. "Not at all. I am not one for regrets. I have lived my life as I chose, and he married someone far more suitable. It was a momentary madness that would probably have fizzled out and left us with no way of escape. Now I shudder to think of having been trapped in that castle."

Olivia had felt the same when Nikolai described it to her. She took a deep breath. "I admire you so much, Grandmama. And I have tried to be like you, to be guided by you. I thought that was what I needed to do. My— my destiny!" She smiled, and her grandmother nodded for her to continue. "But no matter how hard I try…It's as if something perverse inside me refuses to follow directions."

The dowager eyed her consideringly. "You are more like Harry than I thought. He was always headstrong. If there was a right way and a wrong way, he would always choose the wrong. I tried to counsel him, but he would never listen to me."

Did Olivia want to be more like her father? She wasn't even sure that was true. She could not imagine marrying one person and then forgetting about it and marrying another. And she would never squander a fortune on her own pleasures and leave her family in penury.

"Never mind the past," the dowager said, seeing Olivia's distraction. "Let's look to the future." She held out her hands, and Olivia went down on her knees at the old woman's side. Cold fingers wrapped around hers and squeezed reassuringly. "I expected too much of you. I thought you would take over the reins of Grantham when I am gone. You are a good girl, Olivia. You have looked after your sisters and shone when it counted, but you will go your own way when it comes to marriage." Her lips twitched. "Perhaps one of the others will be the one to shoulder the burden of the Ashton family?"

It was a relief to hear it. Olivia bit her tongue to keep from sharing her thoughts for her future. Her grandmother was being very generous, but she did not think her generosity would stretch to the Duke of Northam.

The dowager spoke again, in an affectionate tone of voice. "Whatever you do, I know you will do it in a way that makes me proud."

The praise was unexpected, and perhaps undeserved. Olivia felt her eyes well up with tears. Was her grandmother really setting aside the ambitions she had for her eldest granddaughter? Or perhaps she was just tired of fighting to turn her ramshackle family into something they refused to be.

When the dowager spoke again, she had shaken off her sentimental mood. "I will be returning to Grantham tomorrow."

The silence between them lasted a long time. Her grandmother's fingers relaxed in hers, and when Olivia looked up, she realized the dowager had fallen asleep with a smile on her lips.

Chapter Thirty-Five

I vo ran his hands through his hair and closed his eyes, resting his elbows on the table in front of him. His head was aching, but that was the least of his worries. He had been sitting in this cramped, untidy office for hours, since the crowded coach—did they really need that many soldiers to stop him escaping?—had brought him here to the new Custom House in Lower Thames Street. Harrison had marched him down a maze of corridors and into this room, then closed, and locked, the door. At first, Ivo had been furious and rattled the doorknob violently, but a voice on the other side had told him to sit and wait. He'd refused to obey, pacing back and forth, but eventually, his anger had leached out of him, and he'd thrown himself down on a chair and tried to think rationally.

His whereabouts weren't a secret. Someone would come, and hopefully soon. Charles? But his half brother and partner had much to lose by associating himself with Ivo in this situation. Harold then. His cousin would do his utmost to see Ivo set free, and then they would make Harrison pay for his presumption. Ivo tried to whip his anger back up again, but it was difficult to be furious and indignant when the charges against him were nothing but the truth.

He *was* a smuggler. And this might be the moment the full force of the law came crashing down upon him.

The expression in Olivia's eyes...He'd been trying not to think about that. She had been shocked. He had tried so hard to be better, and he had succeeded. And now, just when the past seemed behind them, and Ivo was seconds away from proposing to her again, Harrison had to arrest him. Would she have said yes? Ivo thought so, but whatever might have been, it was too late now. She would never say yes after what she, and all the Ashtons' guests, had witnessed tonight.

The sound of voices outside caught his attention. He'd been resting his head in his hands, but now he lifted it up. The lock on the door rattled as someone turned the key, and a voice he recognized demanded entry. When the door swung back, Gabriel Cadieux, the Duke of Grantham, stood frowning at him. Was he going to abuse him again for ruining the Ashton reputations? It was a moment before Ivo recognized concern in those dark eyes.

"There you are, Northam," Gabriel said. "Have you been harmed?"

"Only my dignity."

Behind the duke stood Harrison, face flushed, and mouth drawn into a tight line. He had the look of a man who had just received a tongue-lashing. Ivo hoped so. He knew how formidable Gabriel could be.

Another man brushed past Harrison, a slight man in neat clothing, who Gabriel introduced as Mr. Arnott. "My man of business and my solicitor. He is here to ask Lieutenant Harrison why he thinks he can hold you in this..." Gabriel scowled about him at the poky office and went with, "...place."

Freddie Hart also slid into the small room, which was already becoming crowded. His usually good-humored face was stern, and his red hair stuck up as though he'd been trying to tear it out. Ivo doubted Hart, good friend of Gabriel though he was, could help. He would be thinking of his own career and the repercussions of disagreeing with his superiors.

But Ivo realized he was mistaken when Freddie turned to him, and said, "Lieutenant Harrison does have permission to hold you here, Your Grace. That is correct. Although there are questions he must answer before he can ask any of you."

Harrison seemed uncharacteristically flustered. "I have good reason to hold the duke," he insisted. "I have a witness to his smuggling activities who is willing to give us incontrovertible evidence."

"Oh?" Freddie looked about him. "And has he? Given you this evidence?"

Harrison shuffled, nervously clearing his throat. "He has yet to give us the names of the smugglers. We have offered him our protection, but he is difficult to convince. And to answer your question, although he has said the duke is connected to this nefarious business, we cannot as yet prove it. The loyalty of his men is misplaced." He took a breath. "All the same, I firmly believe charges will soon be laid."

"Then you do not have evidence he is involved?" Gabriel repeated, in disbelief. "It sounds to me as if you have been the victim of a very bad joke, Lieutenant. What do you think, Arnott?"

Arnott took his cue. "Despite the lack of evidence, Lieutenant Harrison still went above his remit and insisted on Northam being detained. Now, from what I have learned, this witness has a great many questions to answer about his own involvement in the smuggling business. And he seems clever enough to have understood this and is now saying very little. Which means there is no reason to hold the duke. Indeed, it would be unlawful to do so."

Ivo had been listening in amazement. The witness, whoever he was, could not place him at the scene of the crime, and now was not talking at all in case he incriminated himself? It was Mystere, it must be, but who was Mystere?

"What is his name?" he demanded. "This witness of yours, who is he?"

Harrison looked even more uncomfortable. "I believe he goes by a pseudonym..."

"His real name!" Ivo insisted, daring the man to refuse. "I have a right to know. Don't I?" with a beseeching glance to the others.

Arnott responded. "If this ever came to court, which seems doubtful, the man's name would need to be given."

Harrison hesitated and then seemed to cave. "His name is Rendall."

Ivo sat down heavily. "I know him," he said shakily. "At least, I did. He has a grudge against me. Nothing he says is true, and I can prove it."

Could he? He wasn't entirely sure, but with Bourne's help, he'd do his best.

Gabriel turned to Harrison with a triumphant smirk. "Well, Lieutenant, what do you say to that? I believe Northam has stayed here long enough and that you are holding him without a shred of evidence. I insist you release him without delay."

Harrison was struggling to compose himself, clearly embarrassed by his blunder. "It won't be much longer, and my witness will—" he began, but Freddie stepped in for a quiet word in his ear. Whatever he said seemed to agitate the man even more. He swallowed before straightening up, and turned to Ivo. "You are free to go," he said, before adding in a threatening tone, as if he had to have the final word, "for now."

Ivo jumped to his feet, tugged down his waistcoat, and straightened his cuffs. He was still in his formal evening wear, cream breeches and a dark tailcoat, which made the moment feel even stranger than it already was. Had he ever thought the single-minded lieutenant was a reasonable man? He knew now how much he had underestimated the revenue officer's dedication to duty, and how shortsighted he had been to make a fool of him over a glass of contraband brandy.

"If you wish to speak to me again," Ivo informed Harrison, "you can do so through Mr. Arnott here."

Harrison bowed his head as if in deference, but it was obvious he was furious. Feeling a little lightheaded with relief, Ivo followed Gabriel and Arnott from the room. Behind them, he heard Freddie say in a steely voice, "A moment, Harrison," and then the door closed on them.

Ivo found he did not remember the way out of the place—his mind had been so occupied earlier that he hadn't noticed—but Gabriel and Arnott did. Finally, they were outside the building.

Ivo could smell the river, because of course the Custom House was beside the Thames. He could see that although the sky was clear and the moon was shining, at some point while he had been held prisoner, it had rained. The surface of the street was dark and shiny.

Gabriel had not spoken until now, but as a coach with the Grantham coat of arms rolled toward them, he said, "Harrison found out that you recently went into partnership with Charles. He knows there is a good chance you are supplying the club with smuggled liquor. I think that is why he acted precipitously tonight, because he believed his case was stronger than it was. Freddie says that until now, he was slated for promotion, and this blot on his record will rein him in. You were lucky, but you may not be as lucky next time."

Ivo took a deep breath. The air had never been sweeter. "Thank you," he said with simple sincerity. He still felt shaky. This had not been one of his better nights, and to learn how desperately Harrison wanted him behind bars was sobering.

"My apologies we took so long to get here," Gabriel went on as they settled into the comfortable seats. "Obviously, I needed Arnott with me." He leaned his head back against the padded rest and groaned. "I fear the gossips' tongues will be wagging tomorrow."

"They cannot blame you for my blunder," Ivo said wryly.

Gabriel grunted. "And yet once again, it happened at Ashton House."

He seemed rattled, and Ivo let his thoughts stray to Olivia. He had to ask, even if it brought on another of Gabriel's frowns. "Is Lady Olivia very upset?"

Gabriel narrowed his eyes. "After seeing you being marched out of the ballroom in front of everyone? I think she was as shocked as anyone there."

The coach was rumbling down the street, vying for position with various other equipages. Ivo noted they had left the river behind and were closer to Mayfair now. He would soon be home, and what had felt like a bad dream was nearly over. At least for now.

"You said you knew Lieutenant Harrison's witness?"

Arnott asked in his precise manner, turning his curious gaze on Ivo.

Ivo nodded. "He lived in Portside as a boy, but he left years ago. Bourne—my man in the village—tried to trace him when his name came up as a possibility but without success. Can I speak frankly?" He looked to each of them.

Gabriel's smile was without humor. "If you want our help, then frank is what you need to be. Whatever you have to tell us will not leave this coach. Arnott?"

"No, sir. You have my utter and complete discretion."

Ivo thought a moment, but there was only one way to say it. "I *am* a smuggler."

Gabriel's brows rose slightly, his dark eyes gleaming with amusement. "I think we already guessed that. You have been supplying my club with wine and spirits through Charles."

Ivo cleared his throat. "Yes, well…I have been a smuggler since I was a boy, and my father introduced me to Free Trading. We Fitzsimmonses have all been smugglers, back as far as we know. We have never had any trouble until Polgarth, the captain who brought my contraband in from France, was stopped off the coast by a revenue cutter and arrested. He had been informed on. The same happened to others along the coast. The only captain who wasn't arrested was a Frenchman called Mystere." He wiped his palms on his breeches.

"After Polgarth's cargo was impounded, Charles was in desperate need of supplies for the club—and not just Charles, I have other customers—so I decided to risk using Mystere. As far as we knew, everything went well. Mystere delivered the goods to my men, and they were passed on to my customers. No one complained. But then

Harrison was everywhere, and he was focusing his attention on me. He searched my house, harassed my men in Portside, even offering protection to anyone who gave evidence that could lead to a conviction. And now this."

He shivered, remembering that cramped room.

Gabriel and Arnott had exchanged glances during his recital. "Your thinking is sound," Gabriel said. "But my question is, why is this Mystere so eager to have you arrested and charged?"

"We think Mystere is Jacob Rendall, and he hates me because of something I did to him. He wants to revenge himself on me, and this is his way of doing it."

He wondered how he could have been so thoughtless as to insult the boy. His hurt and anger must have festered over the years, and this was the result. Yes, at the time Ivo had been young and his father had just died, but all the same, he felt he should have done better. It was as if all those instances of reckless behavior had come home to roost.

"Do you think Rendall will stop now? Keep silent to save his own skin?" Gabriel asked. "Charles is worried about the club, and if he's worried, then so am I."

Ivo imagined Charles *would* be worried. With the club in their joint hands, the last thing Charles needed was his partner charged with smuggling. The gaming club's customers would shy away, and the previous owner, Longley, would stir things up into a storm. Charles would lose money he could ill afford to lose. And Ivo would lose his freedom.

He wasn't sure he could survive prison and whatever came after—transportation to the colonies, or hanging, or simply languishing in a cell for years and years. He had always taken his privileged life for granted, and to have it taken away from him...No, he wasn't sure he would survive it.

The coach stopped, and Ivo looked up. They had reached his town house, and the windows were alight, unusual for the late hour—his mother was always early to bed. With a sinking heart, he knew his interrogation was not over just yet; he had to face his family. The front door opened, and Carlyon the butler stood there holding a lantern.

"My mother," Ivo began, a lump in his throat. Until now, the consequences of his arrest had not fully come to him.

Gabriel said sympathetically, "Your mother is understandably upset. You will need to set her mind at rest. Your sisters too. We will talk when we have both rested."

Ivo wanted to mention Olivia again. He had told her he loved her and had dared her to marry him! And he could have sworn she was going to accept. Well, Gabriel was unlikely to consent to a union between his sister and a felon. It was debatable whether he would consent to her marrying a smuggler either, although Gabriel was no hypocrite. But how could he take Ivo seriously after everything that had happened?

Ivo stepped down to the cobbled street. "Thank you again," he said sincerely. "I am in your debt."

"You are," Gabriel agreed cheerfully, and then the coach rolled off.

Ivo looked up at the moon and felt very alone. He could not remember ever feeling quite so alone. He wished, as he hadn't in years, that his father was by his side, to bluff his way through the coming interrogation. His father had always been a good liar. But then Ivo reminded himself that he was a better man than his father. With a deep breath, he started toward the house.

"Sir, your mother—" Carlyon began in a quavering voice, but he didn't finish.

"Is that my son? Ivo, is that you? Oh, thank God, I feared…" Ivo's mother was already coming down the stairs toward them. In the light of the lantern, he could see that her face was flushed and swollen from weeping as she stretched out her hands.

He hurried forward to take them, and then wrapped his arms about her as she clung to him.

"Ivo, oh Ivo, I was so worried! Tell me it is all some dreadful mistake!"

"It was a mistake, Mother, and see? Here I am, safe and sound." Over her head he could see his sisters had joined them, both looking apprehensive. "There's no need to worry. I am quite all right."

He led his mother into the sitting room, where there was a fire. As they sat on the sofa, her hands in his, it took some time to convince her that he really was fine. Every time he thought she was over the worst of her terrors, she would start up again. "Your father," she said. "He was…" Her eyes slid to his, and he was shocked at the misery in their depths. "He was mixed up in some dangerous business, but…I had hoped for better for you, Ivo. I know you idolized him, but when I pleaded with him not to lead you astray, he laughed."

It occurred to Ivo that they were having a truthful conversation. He had often wondered if his mother had so successfully erased the truth regarding her husband from her mind that she could no longer admit to it. But it seemed the truth had always been there, just well hidden, and the shock of Ivo's arrest had brought it out of hiding.

Eventually, he and his sisters persuaded their mother to retire with a dose of laudanum, and Lexy went with her. Ivo was left sitting, staring at nothing and feeling shattered. It wasn't until Adelina spoke that he remembered she was still there.

"You are, aren't you?" she said in a wavering voice that strove to be firm. "Involved in smuggling? Just like father and his father before him? Ivo, how could you!"

He wasn't sure how to answer her. "How could you" seemed to suggest it was something he had chosen, and he wasn't sure it was that simple.

"It was handed down to me by our father," he said. "Like my fair hair and green eyes. It just *was*, and it never even occurred to me to say no. When he died, it felt like a link that still bound me to him, and I wanted to make him proud by carrying on the family business."

And I enjoyed it. It was an escape from the tedium of running an estate drowning in debt.

Adelina heaved a sigh. "I know Mother can be frustrating, but it's the only way she can cope with the past, with our father. She pretends he was some dashing Sir Galahad who could do no wrong. Lexy and I go along with her because it's easiest, but we know that wasn't true. I remember very well the tears that were shed whenever she discovered he had a new mistress. I know I should have guessed about the smuggling, but perhaps I am a little like Mother and have my head buried in the sand."

For a time, they were silent. Earlier, Carlyon had served them coffee, and there was a decanter of spirits on the table. Ivo poured himself a glass and, with a glance at Adelina, poured her one too.

"The thing is," he admitted, observing the color of the liquid in his glass, "I don't know if I can stop. So many people rely upon me and the profits we make. Portside is a smuggling village, and the benefits are everywhere. Even Cadieux's has a part to play. How can I just end it?"

Adelina gave him a droll look. "If you go to prison, then you will have to stop. And you can always bail out of Cadieux's. I don't know why you agreed to be Charles Wickley's partner anyway. You don't owe him anything."

He hesitated. Was this the moment to tell her? It seemed to be a night for confidences. "Charles Wickley," he began.

Adelina fixed him with a puzzled stare.

Ivo continued. "He's our brother. Half brother. We have the same father."

Adelina picked up her brandy and swallowed it in one gulp, and then proceeded to cough violently. Her eyes were still watering when she finally spoke. "I did see the resemblance. I thought it was just one of those things."

"I've wondered for some time. Recently, I learned the truth from him. One positive thing is that he's not worried about claiming a share of the estate or anything ridiculous like that. Legally, he wouldn't be entitled. This is not the same situation as that of the Duke of Grantham. Though what does worry me is, if there is one bastard, there are sure to be others. Father had quite the reputation." He had dismissed Jacob's claim out of hand, but was he a half brother after all?

Adelina clenched her fists. "It makes me so angry when I think of what he put our mother through." Then, with a wide-eyed look, "You're not—"

"Certainly not!" Ivo responded sharply. "That is one trait I have not inherited from him."

Adelina relaxed. "I'm glad to hear it. And anyway, I rather thought you had a tendre for Lady Olivia Ashton. You did seem smitten."

Ivo laughed uncomfortably. "We are friends, but after tonight, she may never speak to me again." He wasn't going to discuss his deeper feelings for Olivia with his sister, no matter how good her intentions. Ivo yawned and rose to his feet. "I am going to bed. Thank you for…for everything."

He was at the door when she said, "Friends don't look at each other the way you and Olivia look at each other."

But Ivo kept on walking.

Chapter Thirty-Six

Charles was in his usual place, the office at Cadieux's Gambling Club. Ivo climbed the stairs, ignoring the interested looks of the staff. No doubt everyone had heard about his run-in with the Revenue Service. He knocked on the door and entered at Charles's invitation.

"Northam," he said and smiled. He was in his shirt-sleeves and wearing his usual colorful waistcoat—this one a sapphire blue—but it appeared as if he had been running his hands through his hair, because it stuck up in all directions. "Thank you for coming to see me at short notice. I had wondered if you were busy."

"Staying out of prison, do you mean?" Ivo replied dryly, closing the door behind him. "You said in your message that it was important."

"Yes, it is." Charles looked uncertain for a moment and then rushed into speech. "I am going to ask for Justina Ashton's hand in marriage."

Whatever Ivo had been expecting—a business discussion perhaps or the need for more French brandy—it was not this. "Congratulations."

Charles smiled thinly. "Well, I hope so, but there is an impediment to our happiness called Gabriel."

Ivo wasn't entirely surprised. He remembered their discussion at Whitmont, when Charles had told him

Gabriel was stuck in the past and did not believe Charles could be faithful to one woman. There was a time when Ivo would have believed that too, but he knew that since he set eyes on Justina, Charles had been a changed man.

"You thought that might be the case. Can't you talk him around?"

"I haven't tried. Yet. But there is something else, and that's the reason I've asked you here. I need to be honest with Gabriel and Justina. I need to tell them that I am your half brother."

Ivo considered this. Some months ago, he had been reluctant for the truth to come out, but now Adelina knew, and she had told Lexy. The three of them had discussed whether or not to tell their mother and decided not to. But he did intend to tell her eventually, when she had recovered from his arrest. Yes, she would be upset, but she was already aware of some of his father's worst traits, so he was sure she would recover from this one too.

"If you want to tell the Ashtons, then you have my blessing."

Charles looked relieved.

Ivo went on, feeling a little awkward, "Do you need me to be there? I have never had a brother before, but I believe that is the sort of thing they do for one another."

Charles's smile was back, and suddenly, it wasn't awkward at all. "Thank you. That would mean a great deal to me. I've told Gabriel I will call on him at Ashton House at seven o'clock, although he doesn't know why."

"I will be there."

Charles raised an eyebrow. "It may be a short visit."

Ivo leaned forward in his chair. "I'm sure he won't refuse you permission without listening to you first. You can persuade him, Charles."

"Perhaps. He is very protective of his sisters. This is a man who gave up his gambling club to take care of them. Even if he didn't still think of me as the rake I once was, he'd hem and haw about it, ticking off all the pros and cons."

Ivo considered his own situation. What would happen if he asked Gabriel for Olivia's hand? He'd probably be shown the door quick smart and told never to darken it again. He suspected Gabriel had already warned her to stay away from him, and honestly, he couldn't blame him.

Irritably, Charles pushed aside some of the papers on his desk. "Have you heard anything more from the Revenue Service?"

"Lieutenant Harrison is conspicuously absent, but that doesn't mean he's given up."

"You have friends in high places," Charles reminded him.

Ivo hoped that was true, but before he could answer, there was a perfunctory knock on the door, and Will Tremeer entered.

He stopped, gray eyes wide. "Oh, sorry," he said. "I didn't realize you were here, Northam. Have you come to check on your investment?"

Charles gave him a hard look. "Mind your manners, boy. Northam is just as much your boss as me. Do you want to return to Cornwall?"

Will shuddered at the thought but didn't seem too worried by the threat. "Apologies," he said, and gave Charles the information he had come to deliver.

Ivo stood up to leave. "I will see you tonight," he told Charles.

"It is seven o'clock," Charles reminded him, with an anxious look.

"On the dot."

Will followed him out.

"You are enjoying your employment here then?" Ivo asked him, just for something to say. He did not know Will well, but he found him a pleasant young man. He was certainly dedicated to the club, and Charles had come to rely on him a great deal.

"It's the best thing that's happened to me," Will confided. "Charles is the perfect employer. I miss Gabriel being in the office sometimes, but I still see him at home. And I'm grateful for both our sakes that he married Vivienne."

"I think he made the right choice," Ivo said.

Will beamed. "So do I!"

As he walked away, Ivo found himself mulling over Gabriel and Vivienne, and now Charles and Justina. He wished his own situation could end happily, but how was it possible when things were such a mess? He hadn't spoken to Olivia since that awful night, and although he had picked up his pen a number of times, the words would not come to him. Should he apologize? Should he tell her again he was a better man? How could she believe him now?

The sobering consequences of his many reckless actions, of his foolish mistakes, had truly come home with a vengeance when he learned Jacob Rendall was behind his arrest. He had realized just how far-reaching the consequences of his unthinking decisions could be. He must keep Olivia well out of it.

Whatever hopes he had for a future with her, he must put them aside.

Ivo was a little late arriving at Ashton House. Before he left, he had made the hasty decision to tell his mother about Charles, realizing that word might get out after the proposal. The truth was better coming from him than some malicious gossip. His revelation had brought on a bout of hysterics. Once his mother calmed down, and even seemed resigned to this fresh disclosure about her husband, Ivo left her in his sisters' care.

The Ashtons' butler informed him that Charles and Gabriel were together in the library, and Ivo hurried to join them. As soon as he walked in the door, he could see that Charles's request had not gone down well. Gabriel was frowning in an intimidating manner, and Charles had lost his usual even temper. In fact, they were leaning into each other as if they were about to start shouting.

When Gabriel looked up and saw Ivo, he barked, "What do you want?"

Ivo raised his eyebrows. "Charles asked me to come."

"You're late," Charles said quietly. "I told you seven."

"And I'm sorry, but I had to tell my mother. I'm here now."

Gabriel shot his friend a puzzled glare.

Charles ignored it. "I asked Northam to be present while I speak to you, Gabriel. In case you have any, eh, questions."

"Questions about what? I think I know you well enough by now, Charles."

Ivo couldn't help himself. "You may have known the child you lived with at St. Ninian's, Grantham, and your partner at Cadieux's, but this Charles is a changed man."

Gabriel looked even more unimpressed. "Is he indeed?"

Ivo took a steadying breath. Charles needed his help. After a lifetime of cock-ups, he was determined to redeem himself.

"Furthermore, I have the right to speak for him, because he is a Fitzsimmons. Charles and I are brothers. Well, half brothers, if you wish to be technical."

"Good God." Gabriel looked shocked, which was amusing in a way because Ivo knew how much alike he and Charles were in appearance. "Are you serious?" He looked from Ivo to Charles and back again, and then gave a huff of laughter. "I see it now. When did you find out, Charles, and why on earth didn't you tell me?"

Charles shifted uncomfortably. "I found out after the picnic at Grantham when I accompanied Northam back to Whitmont. There was a portrait there of his father... our father, and it was like looking into a mirror. I didn't tell you because it wasn't something Ivo had spoken about to his mother and sisters, and I thought it should be left to him. Not that I believed I needed to take out an advertisement in *The Times*," he added irritably. "It makes no difference who my father was to those who know me well."

Gabriel seemed to accept that, but he still sounded reluctant when he said, "Nevertheless, my sister—"

"Yes, your sister," Ivo interrupted, deciding it was time someone took control of what seemed to be a stalemate between the two men. "Charles wants to marry Lady Justina. He is sincere in his affection for her. I have seen that firsthand. Now he is a proprietor of Cadieux's, he takes his responsibilities very seriously. I think you are aware of that too, Grantham, or you would never have sold him the club. You trust him. I can't speak for your sister, but I assume she trusts him too, and is ready and willing to be his wife. Is that not so, Charles?"

Charles looked a little rattled by the turn of events. "She does...she is."

"Yes, I am aware of the affection you hold for each other." Gabriel's voice had gentled, but he wasn't giving in yet. "I had hoped it would pass." He must have heard how blunt that sounded, because he pulled an apologetic face at Charles. "Sorry, but I find it difficult to accept you are a changed man. I remember too well your nights on the town."

"We are both changed men," Charles retorted. "Why is it so hard to believe I could fall in love and want a happy life? Family, children, a home. We never had that, Gabriel, did we? Now you have it, and I want it too."

No one said anything for a moment. Gabriel mulled over his words, and then abruptly he held out his hand. Charles clasped it, and his relief was palpable. "You have my blessing," Gabriel said. "I will speak to Justina in private, and if she is content with the arrangement, then you have my permission to marry her."

Ivo watched them hug, pounding each other on their backs. He was very happy for Charles, but he once again suspected that, had it been he who requested permission to marry one of Gabriel's sisters, he would not have been given a favorable answer.

There was no point in thinking about it anyway, not when he was dealing with the matter of Mystere/Rendall. He couldn't even fight for Olivia, because who knew what would happen next? Ivo loved her too much to involve her in this dangerous situation. For now, he would keep her at a distance. That was safest, melancholy as it felt to be without her.

Chapter Thirty-Seven

O livia and Roberta had been waiting with Justina
ever since Gabriel and Charles closed the library
door. They had started off in the blue sitting room, but
Justina hadn't been able to remain seated patiently in her
chair. After Roberta came to inform them that Ivo had
arrived and gone inside to join the two men, the girls took
up a position outside the library. Olivia wasn't sure what
Ivo being here meant, but Justina wondered aloud if he
had come to protect his gambling club partner in case
Gabriel turned violent.

Roberta said that was silly. "Gabriel would never
hurt Charles. Although, he did get into fisticuffs when he
owned the club. I wonder which one of them would win?"

"Roberta!" Olivia reproved.

Justina wailed. "If they fight, Gabriel will forbid me
from ever seeing him again."

As the minutes ticked by, Olivia and Roberta did their
best to keep their sister's mind off the worst scenarios.

"A Christmas wedding," Roberta said in a falsely
cheery voice. "I don't think you should wait too long."

Justina stared at her with glassy eyes. "Or I might die
a spinster."

"Maybe you want a long engagement?" Olivia suggested, slightly desperate now.

"I don't care, as long as Gabriel lets me marry the man I love. If he says no, then I'll...I'll elope!"

As if on cue, the door opened and Gabriel led Charles out, with Ivo following. The men were smiling and looking pleased with themselves, and Olivia wanted to collapse with relief. Justina hurried over to Charles, and he then proceeded to lift her in his arms and swing her in circles. Gabriel snorted a laugh, and Ivo grinned.

Just then, his gaze found Olivia, his green eyes sparkling, and her heart leaped when he moved as if to come and join her. It was like the night at the Longhursts' all over again, and she could already feel his arms encircling her and his mouth covering hers. She had missed him so much.

Then, very deliberately, he looked away, and everything seemed to stop and then crash to the ground. He half turned his back, his shoulders stiff, his hands clenched at his sides. As if he was holding himself back from her. And she knew then that he wasn't going to approach her. He wasn't going to talk to her. He was cutting himself off from her, and from whatever feelings existed between them.

But those feelings still existed. Olivia *knew* they did. She loved him, and he loved her. She was almost certain he had used a dare to propose to her at the supper dance. Why was he doing this? Had Gabriel warned him off? But Olivia did not think Ivo was afraid of her brother.

Ivo was speaking to Charles and Justina, congratulating them. "I'm very glad for you both."

"Thank you." Charles's voice was hoarse with emotion, and his blue eyes filled. "And thank you for being here, even if you were late."

"You won't let me forget that, will you?"

Charles shook his head. "But you came. Not many people know what it is like to grow up in an orphanage and have no blood relatives."

"Hey, you had me!" Gabriel joked, but he was watching Charles with fond concern.

Charles laughed, but still looked very emotional. "I had you, and Freddie, but there is a sense of loneliness, of being alone, that never goes away. Until now." He wrapped his arm around Justina, holding her as if he'd never let her go.

Ivo leaned in closer and said something Olivia could not hear, before stepping back with the words, "I'll leave you to your celebrations."

"You won't stay for a glass to toast?" Charles asked. "Gabriel?"

Gabriel's smile wasn't quite as genuine as it had been. "Yes, please do, Northam."

But Ivo shook his head and waved a hand at them as he turned to the front door, where Humber was stationed. "Congratulations again!" he called. And then he was gone. Without even looking at her again, or speaking to her, or recognizing that she stood there, holding her breath and waiting. She felt bereft.

"Oh, for goodness' sake," Roberta muttered beside her, "go after him."

Stung into action, Olivia checked to make sure Gabriel and the others weren't taking any notice of her before she hurried toward the door. Humber was still waiting there. He seemed about to ask her what she was doing, but when she met his eyes, he wisely changed his mind. Olivia slipped outside.

Ivo was heading down the carriage driveway. He had evidently arrived on foot, and now that she thought about it, he did seem to do a lot of walking. He probably missed his salt marshes when he was in London.

Olivia paused at the bottom of the stairs. "Ivo? Why don't you stay and drink a toast? Gabriel is calling for the best champagne despite the expense."

He took another step, as if he wasn't going to stop, and then slowly, reluctantly, turned toward her. "I can't stay," he said, and he sounded as flat as she had ever heard him.

She crunched her way over the raked gravel to face him. "I'm not sure why you came." She sounded more hesitant than usual. Perhaps whatever he was feeling was catching. "Not that it wasn't very nice to see you, and I'm sure Charles appreciated your support."

Ivo stared down at her in the moonlight, as if he was considering his answer and whether he should speak it aloud. But he was taking a long time, and Olivia was tired of waiting. She reached for his hand, catching hold of it tightly in case he did something silly like pull away. Then, with a tug, she began to lead him across the driveway.

He resisted, dragging his feet, as they turned down the side of the house to a swath of green lawn surrounded by garden. When she didn't let him go, he sighed.

"I suppose it won't hurt to tell you. Soon, everyone will know."

"Tell me what?" she asked as their steps slowed and stopped. A moth blundered past as it made its way toward the lit windows. Her eyes were on Ivo.

"Tell you that Charles Wickley is my half brother. My father was free with his favors, and there was a woman in Portside. You can guess the rest. The baby was handed over to St. Ninian's to spare my mother. We only discovered the truth recently, although I have suspected it for some time. There is a likeness…You may have noticed it." His mouth twitched into an almost smile.

Olivia felt a jolt. Her grandmother had warned her that Ivo might be like his father and make her miserable, and although she did not think that was true, she now understood her meaning.

"Your half brother! That's…Well, that's wonderful. I wish you had both known sooner. Then Charles could have lived with you, and you could have been friends. Although he might not have been best friends with Gabriel then, and Justina might not have fallen in love with him." She was rambling, and her cheeks warmed with embarrassment.

Ivo didn't interrupt her, but his smile grew wider.

She finished on a positive note. "You have a brother, who is also your partner, and I think it is a very good thing."

He seemed to reflect on that before answering. "It *is* a good thing. Sometimes life can change in an instant. A chance meeting, a missed appointment, a glance across a ballroom…" He stopped. She saw him turn away before looking down at her again, his gaze cataloging her features as if he wanted to remember them forever. "And nothing is ever the same again."

This was the perfect setting for a romantic declaration. The shadows creeping in, and the air scented with clematis, while the crickets sang in the grass beneath their feet. It was a magical moment, and she was certain it was *their* moment. There would never be another one like it, and she must snatch it up with both hands and hold on tight. She searched for the right words, the perfect words, but Ivo spoke first.

"Olivia." He breathed her name as if he was bewitched.

She could see the intense longing in his face, and surely he could see everything she was feeling for him in hers. "Ivo," she whispered.

In an instant, he had crushed her to him, kissing her mouth as if he would die if he didn't. It felt as if they were both drowning as they sought to get as close as possible. Her fingers tugged at the hair at his nape, twisting in the soft curls, while his tongue invaded her mouth and twined with hers. This felt desperate and heartfelt. The culmination of a long, hard-fought battle between them.

When at last the need to breathe forced them apart, Ivo cupped her face in his hands and gazed down at her. His thumb brushed back and forth over her swollen lips.

"I've wanted to kiss this mouth since the first time I saw you," he said. "I made that stupid wager just so that I could, and I ruined everything."

She blinked. She was in danger of forgetting the questions she wanted to ask him, and the answers she needed before they took the next step. Her fingers trembled as she covered his hands with hers.

"Are you really a smuggler?"

His expression changed, hardened, and he dropped his hands and stepped away. She could tell it was the last thing he had expected her to ask him, and the last thing he wanted to answer. But Olivia came after him. She wasn't letting him go now.

"You can tell me anything, Ivo, as long as it's the truth. I want to hear it from you and not through the whispers of people I care nothing about."

He had stilled to listen, but she could see by the resolve in his face that his answer wouldn't be one she wanted to hear. "You say that now, but this business is dangerous. And it isn't over. I could end up in prison. Or with the hangman."

"Ivo, no," she gasped, because now it seemed very real.

"My family have been smugglers for generations, and when my father handed the business to me, I was so proud. I wanted him to be proud. Smuggling may be illegal, but it supports the people in Portside and brings in welcome income for us. For a long time, I didn't think about the consequences if I was caught, and it felt like a game. Now it's real, Olivia."

"I understand," she said softly. "I really do, Ivo."

"Do you? Then you should understand that I don't want to drag you into it. You were wise not to accept my proposal that first time. Until I met you, I don't think I ever really considered how my behavior affected others. Now I can't *stop* thinking about it. Your brother doesn't trust me, and he's right, because I'm not sure I trust myself when it comes to you. I need to deal with the situation in my own way, without worrying you will be hurt by it."

She stood like a statue. He really meant it. He wasn't going to change his mind. He was strong and determined, and he cared about her more than he cared about getting his own way. Was this the new Ivo or had this man with a steel core been there all along?

"What about what I want?" she said. "If I am willing to risk myself, then it should be my decision."

"No. I couldn't live with myself if anything happened to you. I've done a lot of foolish things, and this will not be one of them."

"Ivo!" There were tears on her cheeks. "You asked me…you *dared* me to marry you. Don't you want to hear my answer? Because it is yes. Yes!"

He seemed shocked, and then, with a groan, he took her hands in his tenderly, and raised them to his lips. "Sweetheart, you have made me happier than I have ever been. Truly happy. But…"

"A tête-à-tête in the garden. Why am I not surprised?"

The voice was mocking, and Ivo turned at the same time as she did. There was someone standing watching them, and Olivia's heart sank. Gabriel.

"I've warned you before, Northam," her brother said, and now his voice was a gruff growl. "You may be Charles's brother, and I may have to welcome you because of him, but know that if you cross the line one more time with Olivia, I will see you ruined."

He was furious. Olivia did not doubt he meant what he said, but she knew she couldn't let him send Ivo away. Not now. She stepped between them, even though her legs were trembling from the fury in her brother's voice. Gabriel loved her, she reminded herself. He was doing this because he loved her.

"Wait," she said. "Please, Gabriel, listen to what I have to say."

For a moment, she was sure he was going to refuse and everything hung in the balance, and then he seemed to collect himself. "Very well," he snapped. "But talk quickly, Olivia, because my patience is running thin."

Chapter Thirty-Eight

Ivo wasn't the sort of man to allow his ladylove to protect him from her angry brother, so he quickly stepped up beside her so that they could face Gabriel together. He understood why Gabriel was angry. He had caused Olivia's reputation to be compromised twice already, and in Gabriel's eyes, this was just another careless attempt on his part.

"I have asked Olivia to marry me," he said.

Gabriel's eyes widened. "You've what!?"

"And she has said yes."

For a moment, he seemed at a loss, but not for long. "You need my permission for that, and you don't have it. Marry my sister to a smuggler who is as likely to be in prison as hanged? What sort of brother would that make me? No, under no circumstances."

"Gabriel, what about what I want?" Olivia cried. "I love Ivo. I've tried to tell myself I don't, and that it would be better for us all if I married Prince Nikolai or Mr. Scott, or Viscount Carey, but I just can't. You told me once that I should not marry without love, and that you knew what it was like to be made to feel your choice was wrong."

At least Gabriel seemed to be listening to her, although Ivo did not know how long his patience would last.

"I know the smuggling is a problem," he began.

Gabriel snorted in disgust.

"But I am divesting myself of it. People depend on me, so it will take a little time. I must think of their welfare." He trusted Bourne to step into his shoes and keep everyone as safe as possible. "I can't help but feel guilty when I think of my father and all those Fitzsimmonses before him, and that it is me who will bring this legacy to an end."

"A poisonous legacy," Gabriel huffed.

Ivo spoke simply and sincerely. "I promise I will step away."

"Have you heard anything more from Mystere or Rendall?" Gabriel asked stiffly, but some of the fury had left him.

"Bourne had mentioned a strange ship seen lurking beyond Portside. He thought it was *The Holly*, the same ship that had brought the contraband from France the one time we used Mystere. But whenever they tried to intercept it, the vessel outran them. I feel as if he is not done with me yet."

"And yet you would put my sister in danger."

"No!" Ivo shouted. Then, trying to sound reasonable, he added, "No, I would not do that. I do want to marry her, but I want to wait until this matter has been resolved. I feel that Rendall will show himself again, and this time, we will capture him."

Gabriel stared at him, and then at Olivia. "What do you think of this?" he asked her. "To align yourself with a man who has fallen foul of the law and may do so again? Could there be a worse scandal for our family? Your sisters will feel the mortification just as much as you. How will they find husbands, Olivia?"

"I know it sounds bad," she said, and when he looked at her, Ivo could see tears spilling over her lashes. "But Ivo is changed. You heard him. He is stepping away from the smuggling that has been in his family for generations. He admits his faults. He has always admitted them. I love him for that, and I love the man he will become. *Has* become. Please, Gabriel, give him a chance. Give us a chance."

Ivo expected the worst. That Gabriel would slash him to pieces with some vicious home truths and order his sister inside. He could not hide his surprise when the duke began to speak.

"I want to say no to you, Olivia. And yet I respect your judgment, and the thought you have given to your situation. You have done your best for this family, to the point where I feared you were setting aside your own happiness for the approval of others. I have worried about you, if I'm honest, because I see myself in you. I had to follow my heart to be happy, and so do you. Unfortunately, your heart seems to be leading you to Northam here."

Ivo bit back a laugh. "Nicely put," he said.

"It is!" Olivia declared. "I love him, and I want to marry him. I know we will be happy."

Ivo felt his own eyes sting at her complete certainty. Her trust in him. After all that had happened, it humbled him.

"If I were to agree to this ramshackle union, and I'm not saying for a moment that I am," he warned, "what would you live on? I know for a fact that Northam's estate is hocked to the gables, and now that he will no longer be smuggling…"

Olivia shot Ivo a look, pleading for him to say something to satisfy her brother.

Ivo cleared his throat. He felt the weight of this moment, the importance of it, and he meant to do himself justice. "The club is doing well. Charles has asked me to be there more often, and we have spoken about partnering in another gambling venue. We are not rushing into things, we're taking it slowly, but I think it will work. I have been able to pay off some of my debt to the bank, and even set aside moneys for my sisters' dowries. As you know, Grantham, one must look after one's sisters."

Gabriel grunted.

"So although I am in hock, it is not as bad as it was, and I am confident it will get better. Whitmont is in good condition," *unlike Grantham* he thought, "and my business and my tenants will support my wife and any children we may be blessed with. I will do everything in my power to continue my climb out of the pit, I can promise you that."

Gabriel stared back at him consideringly, and then he threw his hands up in the air. "I can't believe I am going to say this. I must be mad."

"Gabriel?" Olivia was wiping her cheeks. She reached for Ivo's hand, and he grabbed hers, holding on tight.

"I will agree to an engagement." He held up a hand as they both spoke at once. "We will not announce it, certainly not yet. I want to see what happens with this fellow Rendall first, and whether your friends at Custom House decide to arrest you properly this time. Do you understand?"

His wave of giddy happiness subsided, and Ivo nodded soberly. "I understand. I concur."

"But if all goes well, if the situation is resolved to my satisfaction," Gabriel went on, "then you will at some point in the future have my permission to marry my sister."

This time, there was no stopping Olivia. She ran to her brother, embracing him, and Gabriel wrapped his arms around her. "See," Ivo heard him say, "I am not such an ogre after all."

Olivia tipped her head back to look up at him. "You were never an ogre. You saved us all, and I am always grateful."

Gabriel looked a little self-conscious, and Ivo tried not to laugh. He understood the man's behavior, it was all to do with protecting his family.

"Thank you," Olivia went on. "Even though we cannot share the news, I am so happy. So very happy."

Ivo held out his hand, wondering if Grantham would take it. "You have my eternal gratitude," he said.

Gabriel shook. "Very well. Now, Olivia, return to the house, and, Northam, be on your way before we have everyone out here asking questions."

Olivia went to follow him and then turned back to Ivo. She looked alight with happiness, and Ivo grinned back at her. Then he watched as she skipped away, more like Roberta than her usual self.

He was relieved and happy, but he reminded himself that this was only the beginning. Now he had to find Rendall and make sure he could never threaten them again.

Chapter Thirty-Nine

The Ashtons were making the long-awaited visit to Whitmont. The Fitzsimmonses had been adamant they host the formal celebration of Charles and Justina's engagement. Adelina had said that once the shock had worn off, her family united in enthusiastically welcoming Charles into their ranks. It didn't hurt that he was charming and grateful for their attention, and when they learned of the years he had spent in an orphanage, it was a done deal.

Although Ivo wished it could be the announcement of another engagement entirely, he wasn't about to encroach on his brother's happiness. Besides, Gabriel was still holding firm on the subject of any announcement.

As the guests began to arrive and disembark from their vehicles, a cold wind blew across the salt marshes and rippled through the shrubs at the edge of the driveway. It was a small event, with close friends and family only, and despite his resolution to be the perfect host, Ivo was hoping for some time alone with Olivia. *If* he could escape her brother's watchful eye. Gabriel couldn't, he told himself, be everywhere at once, could he?

Ivo's mother broke away from her family to greet the Dowager Duchess of Grantham, being helped down from her coach by Gabriel. Olivia was just about to step down herself when Edwina dived past her, almost knocking her over, and skipped toward Ivo.

One of the other sisters—Georgia?—pulled a face. "You should make her say sorry," she declared loudly. "She gets away with everything."

Olivia looked slightly frazzled, and Ivo imagined how it must have been, cooped up with the noise and bickering between her younger sisters.

Edwina dropped into a low curtsy and announced proudly, "This is my best ever. Do you like it? I can stay down for ages too, and with hardly a wobble."

"Exceptional," Ivo agreed seriously, hiding a smile.

Olivia had reached them and took her sister's hand, scolding her that she should have waited.

"Why?" Those big blue eyes turned on Ivo. "He doesn't mind, do you?"

"I don't mind," he assured her. "It is a pleasure to see you, and all of your sisters."

"Edwina!" Vivienne called, and the little girl ran off.

Olivia's smile had a wicked slant. "Should I curtsy too?"

Ivo glanced beyond her. "Your brother is watching."

"He can't be watching all the time," she said with a pout.

"Exactly what I was thinking."

"Perhaps you can find him something to do that keeps him busy for an hour or two?"

Ivo groaned softly. "God, don't tempt me. I am trying to be on my best behavior."

"There's no fun in that."

He wanted desperately to kiss her. Just at that moment, a gust of wind caught at her white bonnet, and sent it sailing across the driveway.

Ivo didn't think. He chased after it. The bonnet rolled several yards, until turning abruptly into the shrubs that bordered the driveway, where it was trapped. Ivo bent, plucked it out, and brushed it off. The white hat was made of stiffened cloth, with an uptilted brim, and was decorated in fashionable lace and satin ribbons, with a drooping feather.

"Thank you!" Olivia was right behind him, sounding a little breathless. "This is the first time I have worn it, and it would be a shame if it were the last."

She was holding out her hand, and he presented the bonnet to her. "I don't think it's damaged," he said.

She smiled, but did not replace it, holding it at her side where the wind tugged at it again. Ivo could hear the voices of the others, but they were a little removed over here. Olivia looked about her.

"Everything is just as you described it," she said with a sort of wonder. "The house and the marshes."

Ivo was remembering that day in the park when he had spoken about his home. "Whitmont is not to everyone's taste."

"I suppose not. At least you do not have holes in your roof. That is…I assume not?" she finished, making her eyes big. "One day, the east wing of Grantham will fall down, and I think it will be a relief when it does."

"I assure you my roof is intact," he said gravely.

Their gazes locked and wouldn't let go. It was as if there was so much being said beneath the surface, unspoken. Memories of the past and hopes for the future. She forgot whatever else she had been about to say as Ivo devoured her with his eyes as if he couldn't stop himself.

"I feel like a starving man. Starving for you."

"Why have you withdrawn from society?" she asked. "I don't see you anymore. I look, and you're not there."

"You know why. I need to put my affairs in order if I am ever to live up to your brother's expectations."

"But I miss you," she whispered.

Her words caught at his heart like a broken nail. He wanted to wrap his arms about her and hold her against him. "I miss you," he said. "Every moment of every day."

She might have touched him, but Gabriel called out for her. Her lashes swept down to hide her eyes, making dark shadows on her pale cheeks, and her expression turned melancholy. "He is the best of brothers, but I wish he would relent and at least let us announce our engagement once Charles and Justina have celebrated theirs." She glanced behind her. "I should go and see that Edwina is not getting up to any mischief."

He accompanied her back to the house where his mother was holding court.

"I have put the youngest three in the nursery. It hasn't been used for years, not since Ivo, which is a shame. Perhaps one day," she added with a smiling glance at Charles and Justina.

Ivo hadn't seen his mother so full of joie de vivre for years. It was as if she had been closed up, folded in on herself, ever since her husband died, and now she was opening out like a flower.

"Everything is prepared," she assured everyone. "You will find no fault with my housekeeping. Although there is that annoying thing with the bunches of holly that someone keeps leaving at our door."

Ivo raised his eyebrows. "Holly? It isn't Christmas yet."

His mother was distracted by the younger Ashton girls indulging in some pushing and shoving. "I wish I knew who was leaving them. There was another one there this morning."

Something cold stirred in Ivo. Jacob Rendall had him rattled. The holly could just be some childish prank, and nothing sinister at all, and yet it was the name of Mystere's ship, and that felt like too big a coincidence.

Dinner was a triumph. His mother reigned supreme. They had hired extra servants for the occasion—for the first time in a long time, Ivo actually felt they could afford the expense—and it was organized chaos as everyone sat down for the first course. He was glad to have Annette by his side, just like the old days, and her chatter filled in his own silences. She had arrived with Harold, and of course Viscountess Monteith, who was Ivo's mother's best friend.

"Justina says her grandmother is stepping back from her position as chatelaine," she said in an undertone, sipping her soup. "Vivienne is taking on more and more of the burden of Grantham. I don't envy her, but she is so capable, I'm sure she will soon have everything running smoothly."

Vivienne was conversing with her husband, her cheeks flushed as she smiled back at him. Her happiness shone out. Beside them, Will Tremeer said something that made Roberta roll her eyes in her usual unladylike fashion.

"You are very solemn tonight," Annette said, with a sideways glance at Ivo. "This isn't a funeral, you know."

"Charles and Justina will be very glad to hear it."

She wrinkled her brow. "You are becoming a sad case, Ivo."

"That's better than languishing in prison, surely?"

He had been thinking of Olivia and the wedding that seemed to be slipping further and further out of his grasp. And then there were the bunches of holly left by some unknown person. Should he be worried? Should he set someone to watch for the culprit?

Annette looked at him and sighed. "Of course it is, but there must be something in between. You can still be happy, can't you? Especially on a day like this. Your brother is about to be married, and you have welcomed him into your family. Look at him!"

Ivo followed her smiling glance. Charles did look happy. He was so much a part of the Fitzsimmons family now that he could barely remember when he wasn't. When Charles and Justina married, he would stand up with his brother and listen to him speak his vows, and perhaps in a year or so, his mother might have her wish granted about the empty nursery.

He looked down the table at Olivia and imagined a child of theirs. Dark hair like hers and his green eyes, or perhaps fair hair and blue eyes. It didn't matter. He would love it, and he swore to himself he would never, ever, teach it the art of smuggling.

At the resolution, she looked up, and he was staring straight into those glorious blue eyes.

Now Olivia was watching him. With Adelina leaning forward to share some amusing anecdote with Harold, Ivo had a perfect view of her. Her glossy dark hair was dressed simply, and she wore a rose-colored gown, the neckline only just covering her cleavage. Ivo remembered perfectly well the shape and the softness of her breasts. The jut of her nipple against his palm as they kissed so desperately. The clasp of her body on his as they joined together and became one in their ecstasy.

He shifted in his chair.

Bloody hell! The last thing he should be doing was ogling her like this.

But she was ogling him too. Her gaze was almost a caress as it slid over his formal jacket and snowy cravat, before her attention shifted to his cleanly shaven jaw. His mouth…She lingered on his mouth, and he wet his dry lips with a sweep of his tongue before he could stop himself.

Her eyes widened and shot up to his, before quickly returning to her plate. She did not look at him again. She ate her meal, and smiled at her companions, and agreed with something Justina said…Ivo knew all of this, because he couldn't look away from her. He thought he could watch her forever and still not be satisfied.

"Olivia looks lovely tonight."

Annette. He had forgotten she was there, but when he turned to her, she was observing him with amused interest. She always did know him too well.

"So do you," Ivo said smoothly. "When is your wedding again?"

"You know when it is," she scolded. "Next April. Plenty of time to finish my book."

Ivo snorted a laugh, but Annette looked serene. She was happy, so much happier than she would have been if she had married Ivo, and he was glad to see it.

Gabriel was proposing a toast to Charles and Justina, and they all responded.

"This should be you next," Annette murmured at his side. "I see the way you look at her." She nodded toward Olivia.

He wanted to tell Annette about Jacob Rendall and his continued presence. He wanted to explain that it wasn't just himself who was at risk, but more and more he was beginning to think anyone who meant anything to him might become quarry to the smuggler. His sisters and his mother, his new brother. Until his enemy showed them exactly what his plan was, they were all in the dark.

At least while he kept their love a secret, Olivia was safe.

Thankfully, the next course arrived, and the person on Annette's other side claimed her attention. Ivo was left in peace, for a moment at least.

"Ivo!" His mother was calling for him to make another toast to his brother, and with a smile, he rose to his feet.

Chapter Forty

Justina was blooming. Olivia smiled at her favorite sister and watched her send covert glances in Charles's direction, which he returned. She was overjoyed for them both. Her own emotional state was another matter, and not one she wanted to share because it would certainly bring down the mood.

Freddie Hart, seated beside her at dinner, had been telling her about his new job. "Very hush-hush," he said. As far as Olivia could gather, it was something to do with the government and foreign spies, but it did sound exciting. And at least it took her mind off Ivo.

Over the past weeks, there had been many more invitations to society events, and Olivia had never felt so welcome and so comfortable in her role as sister of a duke. It was as if all her societal hopes and dreams had come to pass. It just wasn't enough. There was a hollowness in her chest that she knew now could only be filled by one man. She understood why he was absent—he was dealing with his own troubles, trying to ensure they could be together. But she still missed him dreadfully.

With dinner over, they moved into the drawing room, and Lexy entertained them on the piano with the latest tunes. In an adjoining room, the older guests were enjoying quieter conversation over coffee or, in Grandmama's case, a snooze. Olivia liked to think her grandmother could relax now that Vivienne had taken on so many of the responsibilities of Grantham. That the dowager had put her full trust in Gabriel's wife boded well for a harmonious future.

Roberta was seated on a sofa beside Ivo. Olivia watched the two of them through her lashes, and wondered what they were talking about. At one point, Ivo raised his eyebrows and Roberta laughed, as if he had given her the reaction she'd wanted.

She let her thoughts drift. Maybe despite Ivo telling her he was trying to be "good," she could persuade him to slip away? Or she could find his bedchamber later? The idea made her squirm pleasurably.

"Psst!"

Olivia looked up. The hiss came from the direction of the door, which was slightly ajar. A curly mop of brown hair bobbed into view. Edwina put a finger to her lips and then beckoned.

With a long-suffering sigh, Olivia rose and went to see what her youngest sister wanted. "You should be in bed."

The little girl's big blue eyes were swimming in tears, and she stood barefoot in her nightdress. "I *was* in bed. Georgia took one of my dolls and threw it out of the window!"

"Then Georgia should go down and fetch it," she said, even knowing that would not happen. If anyone was going to fetch Edwina's doll, then it would be Olivia. "Which window was it?" she asked, resigned to her fate.

Edwina flung herself into Olivia's arms. "Thank you," she said, her face pressed into her sister's waist. "I knew you would help. You are the best of my sisters."

Olivia couldn't help but smile. As they made their way across the empty foyer to the front door, curiosity had her looking about. Whitmont was not as grand as Grantham, but it appealed to her, with its old furniture and oak paneling and more intimate rooms. It felt cozy in a way Grantham never could, and it was most definitely in better condition. As Ivo had promised, there were no leaking roofs or an east wing completely closed off. She liked it. From the golden brick façade, to the unlikely cupola upon the roof, to the flat salt marshes all around.

"My feet are cold!"

The little girl was hopping about on the cold marble. Olivia lifted her into her arms, and gave a theatrical groan. "You are too big for me," she said as her sister snuggled comfortably against her.

"But you're only little," Edwina retorted. "One day I will be taller than you, taller than all the others."

"I wouldn't be surprised, given the amount you eat. Now, from which window did this tragedy take place?"

They were on the front steps now, and Edwina pointed to the right. Olivia remembered from her visit earlier that the nursery overlooked this part of the property. It shouldn't be too hard to find the defenestrated doll and bring it safely back into her sister's arms. A cold gust of wind blew across the driveway, and with it came splatters of rain. The stars were hidden behind the clouds, and it was dark and dreary. Not the place for a small girl in her nightdress with bare feet.

"Go upstairs to the nursery and look out of the window, Edwina. You can direct me to the right place."

As Edwina padded back up the stairs, Olivia took a lantern from the table in the foyer and headed outside once more. Another gust of wind made her shiver. She wasn't dressed for this either, in her pretty gown and slippers, but needs must. Holding the lantern high, she descended the steps and crossed toward the side of the house Edwina had indicated.

At least it was more sheltered here, with a shrubbery to protect her. She could hear Georgia and Edwina arguing from somewhere above and in front of her. She kept walking, until she saw her sisters' pale faces peering down from one of the upper windows.

"Here we are! Olivia! Here, here!"

"I see you," she called back, biting her lip on laughter. "So where is this poor doll? Georgia, you shouldn't throw Edwina's babies from the window, you know that."

"They're silly," Georgia retorted in a sulky voice. "She'd rather play with them than me."

Ah, perhaps that was the real reason for Georgia's meanness. She was jealous. She wanted the attention Edwina gave to her imaginary companions all for herself. It was something to consider next time the two girls argued.

Edwina was pointing down, and after a brief search, Olivia found the doll. It looked unharmed, but it was hard to tell. Her sister's dolls were all well loved.

"Pardon. Mademoiselle?"

A quiet voice made her start. Olivia straightened, the lantern swinging wildly in her hand as she turned around.

There was a gentleman behind her in a plain jacket and breeches and, oddly, boots that came up over his knees. His dark hair was pulled back at his nape in an old-fashioned queue and he was watching her intently with brown eyes in a narrow face. Well, one eye. The other was turned outward and appeared more white than brown.

Her first thought was that he must be a servant, because if he was a guest, she would have known him. And she didn't.

"You are Lady Olivia Ashton?"

Now she heard his faint French accent. Had someone been asking for her inside the house? Had they seen her go outside and were worried? But that didn't quite make sense.

"You *are* Lady Olivia Ashton?" he repeated, watching her with that strange intensity.

"Yes, I am. Who are you?"

He didn't answer her question, instead saying, "Will you come with me, please?" in a polite but firm voice.

Suddenly, Olivia did not like the expression on his face. But before she could tell him she wasn't going anywhere, he had taken her arm in a tight, painful grip.

Fear overwhelmed her. "Let me go!"

"Olivia! Olivia!" Edwina was calling frantically.

"Tell Northam I have taken his woman," the stranger shouted up at the girls. "Now I will have my revenge."

"Ivo…" Olivia tried to understand his meaning, but her sisters' screaming, and the man's painful grip on her as he dragged her away, made it difficult to think. "This—this is because of Ivo?"

"He forced me to leave, and took what should have been mine. All of this." He gestured about him at the house and garden. "I thought to send him to the gallows, but his men are too stupid to speak against him. This will be better," he said with satisfaction. "To take what he loves most and leave him alive and suffering. Yes, this revenge is better."

Olivia knew she had to escape. Now. She opened her mouth to shout for help, at the same time resisting his pull. But before she could utter more than a squeak, he wrapped his arm around her, and his hand closed over her mouth. She could taste the saltiness of his skin, and her stomach lurched. He was thin but taller than her, and he had a wiry strength. She fought him desperately, the lantern swinging wildly until he took it from her.

And then, for a brief, ecstatic moment, she was free. Until she realized he'd only released her so that he could cover her head with something coarse and rough that completely blinded her. A sack? It smelled of fish. Her stomach heaved in earnest, and she only just managed to swallow back the bile.

He was tying a rope around her, binding her arms to her sides beneath the cloth covering, and although she kicked and squirmed, it was no use. At least her mouth was free, so she screamed as loudly as she could—which wasn't very loud with her face covered. Her cries were choked off when he gave a vicious tug on the loose end of the rope. She was falling, and with her arms bound, she could not save herself. Panic made her heart beat so loudly she could not hear anything else.

She didn't fall. He was holding her up, but only until she regained her balance again. Then he began to pull her along by the rope tether, leading her like an animal.

"Where are you taking me?" Her voice wobbled and broke. "Please, let me go!"

He didn't answer her, and he didn't let her go. But he *was* talking, a constant stream of muttering, and she felt her skin prickle. This man was not rational. She was in the hands of a madman.

Chapter Forty-One

Y ou have nothing to worry about as far as Lieutenant Harrison is concerned."

Ivo stared at Freddie. "What do you mean?"

"He's been transferred. As far away from here as possible. His superiors were unimpressed with his bullheadedness where you were concerned. They thought he had overstepped the mark, and I must admit," he said, looking smug, "I did not correct them."

Ivo wanted to laugh, but he reined it in. "There's still Rendall."

"Yes, there is," Freddie agreed. "You heard that they let him go? There was no reason to hold him."

"That is what worries me."

He had hardly stopped speaking when there was a high-pitched scream from the rooms above. Conversation stopped, and the guests looked at each other, not sure whether to be worried or amused.

"Edwina's high spirits," said the dowager dismissively.

But the screams were getting louder, accompanied by the thud of footsteps coming closer. Edwina burst through the doorway, with Georgia close behind her, and both girls were hysterical.

"Gabriel, Gabriel!" Edwina sobbed.

Instinctively, Gabriel dropped to his knees and the girls ran into his arms.

"It's all my fault!" Georgia wailed. "I threw the doll out of the window, and Olivia went to get it, and then the man took her!"

Ivo felt himself go icy cold. It was as if his blood froze in his veins. Gabriel was demanding, "What man?" while the others watched on, shocked and confused.

Vivienne took Edwina in her arms, and attempted to soothe her. "The man outside," the little girl hiccupped. "He said, 'Are you Lady Olivia Ashton?' and then he took her a-away."

"Who was this man?" Ivo's voice was loud.

At the same time, his mother shouted, "Carlyon!"

Georgia clung to Gabriel. "He said to tell you," she said, looking at Ivo. "He said—he said," she screwed up her face in the effort of remembering. "'Tell Northam I have taken his woman.' And then he said he would have his revenge."

Silence seemed to fill Ivo's head, as if everything had stopped. The room dimmed. *Olivia.* He blinked when Carlyon appeared in front of him, his old face wrinkled with concern.

"Your Grace? The lantern is gone from the table by the door. One of the servants saw Lady Olivia go out with it."

Charles replaced Carlyon in front of him. "Is it Rendall? Ivo?"

Yes, it was Rendall. He had no doubt. Finally, he had shown his hand—and it was even worse than Ivo had imagined.

"It's dark outside," he said, thinking aloud. "He'll need a lantern to find his way over the salt marsh. He'll have taken Olivia's. We'll be able to see the light!"

And he was gone, ignoring the voices calling after him, taking the stairs two at a time. His brain was churning with worry and fear, but he had a plan now. The cupola on the roof had been built for just such a day as this. The tower rose high above Whitmont, high enough to see all over the salt marsh. And if Jacob Rendall had the lantern, that was even better. Ivo would be able to follow him. He could find Olivia and bring her back. He would wrap his arms about her and never let her go again.

Charles was right behind Ivo as he reached the roof and flung open the narrow door that led to the ladder. Quickly, he climbed upward, and in a moment, he was standing high above the world, with only the dark, cloudy sky above him.

Ivo didn't know what Rendall meant to do, but he knew it would be nothing good. "Revenge," he had said. He wanted revenge, and he was going to take the woman Ivo loved. How had he known that was Olivia? He didn't understand yet, but right now, that wasn't important. All that mattered was finding Olivia unharmed.

"There!" Charles pointed. There was a light bobbing out in the darkness.

Ivo had a map of the marsh in his head. He knew it as well as he knew the layout of his own house. And with the tide coming in, Rendall was heading into the most dangerous part, full of quicksand and pools of murky water that were traps for the unwary, ready to pull him down if he put a step wrong.

He took a shaky breath. Rendall must know of the danger, given that he had grown up here. Perhaps he just didn't care.

Ivo centered his spinning thoughts. He needed to reach Olivia before it was too late.

Other voices were growing louder now. Gabriel and Freddie had followed him and were asking questions. Justina and Roberta, too, their eyes worried. Gabriel put his hand on Ivo's shoulder to capture his attention. He looked grim. "This is Rendall, isn't it?"

"Yes." Ivo didn't look away from the other man's face. He knew what Gabriel was thinking. *This was all Ivo's fault.* "I will get her back safely," he vowed.

Gabriel hesitated. "You'd better," he said gruffly.

As Ivo climbed back down the ladder, Freddie's voice echoed after him. "Good luck!"

A quick visit to his room, and Ivo threw off his formal jacket, changing it for a coat, then he changed his shoes for boots. When he stepped out into the corridor, he found Charles, who had done the same. He had never been more grateful for his brother. Downstairs, Carlyon was wringing his hands as usual.

"Hang a light in the cupola so it can be seen!" Ivo instructed him. "And send someone to Portside to find Bourne. Tell him what is happening. Tell him I need his help in the marsh."

"But what will that beast do to Lady Olivia?" Carlyon wailed.

The remaining guests were gathered now in the foyer, and their voices fell silent at the question. Ivo could hardly bear to meet their eyes. "I am going to bring her back," he said.

The dowager gave a gasp. "You," she began, and Ivo could tell she was about to blame him for everything. He knew he deserved that, and he wouldn't have stopped her. But he was grateful when Vivienne cut her short.

"Olivia is a clever and resourceful girl. She will stay safe until Northam reaches her."

Ivo prayed she was right.

Charles hesitated as they began to move away from the house. "Do we need a light?"

"No," Ivo said. He had reached the gate that led into the salt marsh, barely slowing as he opened it. "I know this place. I know it better than anyone."

It was true. Even as emotion threatened to overcome him, Ivo reminded himself that he had played here since he could walk. Even with the tide coming in, he had the advantage, not Rendall. All his years living and breathing the salt marsh had been for this moment. If anyone could save Olivia, then it was he.

Chapter Forty-Two

O livia stumbled again, and this time, her slipper sank into watery mud. She had not dressed for this, being stolen away by a stranger. The hem of her skirt was already sodden and clinging to her legs as she walked. Even through the sack over her head, she could smell the marsh, a wet, salty smell mixed with rotting vegetation. She was in that dangerous place Ivo spoke of with such fondness. And she could hear the lapping of water. The tide was turning.

Did that make the marsh more dangerous? She thought so. She stumbled again, and this time, her slipper sank deeper. She felt the suck of the mud around her ankle.

Her cries and efforts to free herself brought the man. He reached down and, with a grunt, pulled her foot free, but her slipper remained behind. She stumbled to her knees and stayed there, trying to catch her breath. There were hot tears on her cold cheeks.

"Let me go," she begged. "Please, let me go."

"Be calm," he said. His voice was close beside her, and she felt the press of his hand on top of her head. "You are safe."

That kindness gave her back her courage. "Why are you doing this?" She tried to steady her voice. "Why do you hate Ivo?"

"He knows why. I told him I was his brother, but he

laughed and rejected me. My mother was dead, and I had no one else, but he turned his back. All these years, I've sworn to make him pay for his cruelty."

Olivia hesitated. "I'm sorry. But couldn't you have made a life somewhere else? My brother was an orphan, but he didn't seek revenge on whoever had put him in St. Ninian's."

She heard him take a deep breath. "You don't understand," he said earnestly. "Yes, I did make a life in France for a time. I even married and had a child. But my memories wouldn't let me be happy. I had no choice but to come back and seek my revenge."

Olivia knew how grief and hatred could fester over time. Her own mother had been guilty of it. But even she had recovered and made a better life for herself. It seemed to Olivia that this man did not want to forget the wrongs he believed had been done to him. He preferred to wallow in them.

"Northam loves you," he went on, and chuckled. "I saw you both today. Your bonnet blew away, and he fetched it. The look on his face, ooh la la. He wants you in his bed. I am glad he will never have you. I am glad he will never have any happiness."

Olivia wondered if she should tell him that it was too late, that she and Ivo were already lovers. Then to her astonishment, she felt the Frenchman untying the rope. When it fell away, he removed the sack from her head. She rubbed her face, taking deep breaths of the salt marsh as she looked about her. He had set the lantern on the ground so that the area around them was visible, but everything else was dark. Water was running near a narrow path, bubbling and gurgling, spreading outward with the tide.

She didn't want to look at her captor, but she couldn't

help it. He was standing over her, and the light made hollows of his eyes and his cheeks, while wisps of hair had come free and were sticking to his damp face. One eye bored into hers, the other strange and blind.

"I am not a cruel man," he told her. "I will not take your life with my own hands. The marsh can do it. The tide will cover it soon, and you will sink down into it. Northam will search for your body as long as he lives. Hoping, hoping, and never finding." His smile chilled Olivia to the bone.

At least she was free now. She could try to get to higher ground and then find her way back to Whitmont once it was light. She could...

He wrenched her hands behind her back, making her cry out. Twisting, she saw that there was a thick post behind her, hammered into the ground, perhaps a marker to show travelers the way. He was already tying her hands to it, the rope biting into her flesh. Satisfied, he gave the bindings a tug, and stepped back to survey her.

Apart from the light of the lantern, there was nothing but darkness in every direction. Water soaked into her skirt where she knelt, swirling around her, and with a gasp, she scrambled to her feet, pressing back against the pole as if it would save her from the rising tide.

"You're going to leave me here?" she said. "Please. You can't."

He pulled a pitying face. "Alas, I can."

"Then please, leave me the light!"

"Alas, I cannot do that either."

As she watched in horror, he extinguished the lantern. Now she couldn't see anything, not even him. As she stood, shivering and afraid, his whisper reached her from the darkness. "Adieu, my lady."

His steps faded. She heard the sound of waves

moving through the deeper channels that crisscrossed the marsh. Louder and louder as the water encroached.

Olivia sank down, her legs no longer holding her up, aware of the appalling situation she was in. He had said he was not a cruel man, but that wasn't true. He was the worst of men to leave her here to drown. To die.

She twisted from side to side, trying to see something, anything. The water was rising quickly now, and even if she was free, it would be too late to find safety. Where was Whitmont? If she could just see the lights of the house, at least she would know how far she was into the marsh. And then she did see a light.

It winked and faded and then brightened again.

A sob rose up in her throat. "Ivo…" She knew there was no use feeling sorry for herself. If she was ever to see him again, then she had to try to escape and find her way back to him.

But her bindings were tight, and the more she struggled, the more they cut into her skin. The top of the post was high, two feet at least above her head. Could she reach up and bring her bound hands over it to free herself? Struggling up, she stood as tall as possible, and lifted her hands up. It was painful. Her shoulders hurt as if her arms were being pulled out of their sockets.

She tried again and again, but it was no use. Why had he not tied her hands in front of her? But she knew why.

Olivia looked again for the light, and that was when she realized it was raining. A short sharp shower passed by, drenching her, but once the rain was gone, the light was back. She kept her eyes fixed on it as if it was her salvation. Her mind began to go into all sorts of strange places.

Her sisters, and Gabriel. Her grandmother. Ivo— most of all, Ivo.

He would find her, and they would live a long and happy life together. Tears ran down her cheeks, feeling strangely warm against her cold skin. The water was gushing now. It was not just in the channels, but had spilt over onto the marsh itself. She could do nothing but stand there, a sacrifice, as it crept higher and higher. Soon, it was over her knees, and then to her waist.

When she heard the voices, she did not at first believe it. Could it be that the man had changed his mind and decided he could not do it after all? But...it sounded like Ivo! And Charles.

She called out. The water was slapping at her chin now, cold and deadly. Surely fate could not be so cruel as to drown her when help was so close?

Suddenly, they were shouting, and water was splashing up into her mouth and eyes, and Ivo's beloved face appeared in front of her. His hair was slicked against his head, and water was clinging to his eyelashes, but he was grinning.

"Olivia," he said, "my love. My sweetheart. I have you. Thank God, I have you." He looked around, and shouted, "Charles, the knife! Rendall has tied her up."

Then he had ducked down beneath the water, and she felt the ropes being sawn apart, her hands too cold by now to feel pain. She was free, and he lifted her—the water was up to his shoulders—and began to wade toward Charles, who appeared to be on higher ground. Wet and shaking, she tried to speak, but her teeth were chattering too badly.

"You're safe now," Charles told her. Then, urgently, "Ivo, please tell me there's a way out of here?"

"Follow me."

Ivo didn't put her down, he carried her as they walked across the marsh, back to safety. Eyes fixed on Whitmont's guiding light.

Chapter Forty-Three

Afterward, it felt like a blur. Ivo carried Olivia back to the house because she didn't seem to want to let him go, and he certainly didn't want to let her go. Charles followed carefully behind, not as sure as Ivo at making his way through the marsh that had been his childhood playground. The water had risen as high as it would go, and Ivo knew Olivia would have drowned if they had not found her when they did. But he had found her, and she was safe in his arms.

Back at the house, everyone was waiting, relieved, tearful, asking questions none of them felt able to answer. Ivo carried her through the front door and into the warmth of his house. He sat down close to the fire, still holding his love, and she pressed her face into the curve of his neck and clung.

"I'll see a bath prepared," Adelina said. "She must be chilled to the bone."

"Poor child!" his mother declared. "What sort of creature would do such a thing?"

"Rendall," Gabriel murmured. Then, his dark eyes fixed on Ivo. "Was it him?"

That was when Olivia finally spoke, lifting her head as she told them haltingly what she knew. About the man who turned his back on a happier life, on his wife and child, to return for revenge. She had barely finished when Carlyon's voice reached them from the door, saying that Bourne had arrived with two of his men, and they had news. Not wanting Olivia to have to be subjected to their stares in her sodden state, Ivo ordered for them to be told to wait in his study. Charles went out to them, followed by Gabriel and Freddie.

Ivo pressed his lips to Olivia's matted hair. "I need to speak to Bourne," he whispered. "Let your sisters take you upstairs."

Reluctantly, she released her hold on him. Vivienne slipped an arm about her, ignoring her filthy gown, and with Justina and Roberta, she moved toward the door. Once there, Olivia paused, and turned back to look at him, seeming to steady herself.

"None of this was your fault," she said, as if she knew he was already blaming himself. "He could have stayed and had a good life in France, but he came back instead. His revenge was more important to him than his own happiness."

When she had gone, Ivo put his head in his hands. No, it wasn't his fault, and yet his thoughtless actions had contributed to it. With a deep breath, he stood up, his body aching from the rigors he had put it through on the marsh. *Worth it*, he thought. He had saved the woman he loved. Another moment, and it might have been a different story.

In the study, Bourne stood waiting. "Your Grace," he said. "Rendall is dead. We saw him at a distance, and he saw us. He jumped into one of the deep channels and was taken under. We did not see him again."

"He drowned himself?"

"He was raving. Foolish words I will not repeat."

Ivo tried to imagine a man so twisted with hate he would do such things.

"He was never your father's son," Bourne added into the silence. "I knew his parents. His father died when he was a child, but Jacob was his image. It was all a fiction he clung to."

"And yet," Ivo said quietly, "I could have been kinder."

"If you had, he might have thought that was an invitation to latch onto you and your family." Bourne shrugged. "Best to let things go, sir. You have your woman back, and you are free of his threats."

"He is dead, you are sure of it?" Gabriel demanded. When he was assured of Rendall's demise, he seemed to relax. "It is over." His dark gaze found Ivo. "You have my gratitude, Northam. My sister would not be safe upstairs without you."

Ivo wasn't sure what to say. He opened his mouth to take the blame, but Freddie cut him off.

"Men like Rendall can't be controlled or their behavior predicted," he said firmly.

Charles clapped Ivo on the back. "She's safe," he said quietly. "I, for one, would like a drink to celebrate. And just so you know, don't ever expect me to set foot on that bloody marsh again."

Ivo snorted a laugh, and then they were all gathering around him, patting his back, encircling him in congratulations. When a glass was put in his hand, he raised it high.

"To my future wife!" he said.

Gabriel met his eyes and there was a pause, and then he raised his own glass in the toast. "To Northam and Olivia."

It was all the encouragement Ivo needed. His heart overflowed.

⁂

Olivia woke with a start. It was dark, apart from a candle left on a table by the door. She had insisted on it, not being able to face the night. The room was quiet, Edwina curled up on one side of her and Georgia on the other. They had not wanted to leave her once she had bathed and changed into her nightdress.

Olivia smiled to herself. She had been well looked after by her family and Ivo's, and she was grateful. But right now, all she wanted was him.

Cautiously, she rose, leaving the sleeping girls, and made her way to the door. The passage was empty, the doors to the bedchambers closed. She realized she should have discovered which room was his before she ventured out here. Silently, she made her way along the carpeted passage, holding her candle high, and it was only when she saw another slightly ajar door that she stopped. Could that be Ivo's room? She suspected he had left his door open on purpose, in case he was needed.

She peered inside—quietly, she thought—but she must have made some sound because whoever was in the bed sat up.

"Olivia?"

Ivo. "Yes, it is me."

She closed the door, but she could still see the shape of him from the light coming through the window, where the curtains were drawn back on a view of the garden and the starry sky. The rain had long ago gone, and all was calm again. It was almost as if none of it had ever happened.

She gave a shiver. She had been told that the man, Jacob Rendall, had drowned after he left her. He had not wanted to face the consequences of his actions. Was it wrong of her to be glad he was dead and could no longer hurt them?

"Olivia?" Ivo called again softly. "Are you well?"

She made her way to the bed and climbed up, crawling across the mattress to reach him. It was a very large bed. He reached out, caught her in his arms, and held her tight, breathing in the sweet scent of her clean hair.

"I needed you," she said.

"I needed you too, but you were too well guarded for me to slip into your room," he admitted.

For a time, they were silent. He nuzzled against her ear, then left a trail of kisses over her cheek and neck. She ran her fingers through his hair, enjoying the silky curls, twisting them gently around her fingers.

"What is it, sweetheart?" he murmured. "Rendall is gone. Bourne saw him go. There is nothing more to fear."

"I'm not afraid," she said. "Well, a little. The memories will probably be with me for a long time." The next words were blurted out. "When can we marry?"

He tipped up her face and kissed her gently on the lips. "Gabriel gave me his blessing. I suppose we'll have to wait a decent amount of—"

With a cry of joy, she climbed onto his lap, straddling him, her hands clasping his face as she rained down kisses upon him. Laughing, he seemed to bask in her attention. "I was worried too," he admitted. "I thought he might blame me."

She gazed into his eyes. "Do you know I told Rendall about Gabriel, how he hasn't allowed his beginning to darken his life and has gone on to be happy and success-ful? He didn't want to listen. He was set on his course."

Ivo grimaced. Then, "Enough about Jacob Rendall," he said briskly. "When do you want to marry?"

Olivia supposed "as soon as possible" wasn't the right answer, but it was the truthful one. If she had her way, she would marry him at once. It was partially to do with what had happened on the marsh, though that would pass with time. But it was also because she was deeply and irrevocably in love with this man. Attending social engagements, taking her place in the ton, would not be nearly as much fun if Ivo was not with her.

"Before Christmas," she said. "I don't want a long engagement."

He grinned. "Hmm, my mother will be over the moon. Two weddings to think about."

"I'm not sure what Grandmama will say, but after what she told me about her own marriage…At least I will be marrying a man I love."

He wrapped his arms about her and rolled her over onto the bed, his body on top of hers. Her nightdress had rucked up, and he slid his hand up her thigh, lifting her leg over his hip so that he could nestle closer.

Olivia felt the hard shape of him against her, and everything else flew from her mind. This last month without him had been a long one, and she could not wait any longer. Their lips clung, and their kiss deepened before he bent his head and found her breast through the thin cloth. He ran his tongue around her aching nipple, sucking it into his mouth so that when he stopped, the cool air on the damp material made her ache with desire.

"Do you want me to stop?" Ivo asked. "I can wait, sweetheart."

"No. *You* may be able to wait, but *I* can't."

He laughed softly as he slid down over her body, slowly, teasingly, until she was arching against him, urging him to reach the heated place between her thighs. When his mouth closed on her, she bit her lip to stop the cry, worried it would bring someone running. She was soon close to her peak, making the most unladylike noises, her body begging for release.

And then he stopped. Disgruntled, Olivia leaned up on her elbows to stare down at him. He gave a wicked grin and crawled over her, and she saw the hard length of him between them, nudging the curls between her thighs. She forgot about being peeved then, as he cupped the globes of her bottom in his hands, and lifted her to the right angle for his body to join with hers. Slow and careful, deeper and deeper, until she was gasping and clinging to him.

The world sparkled about her as she soared. Ivo groaned as he too reached his climax, and then his mouth was on hers as their kisses turned to murmurs, and then to replete silence. And they lay together, dreaming of the years to come.

Chapter Forty-Four

T he bells rang out at the Grantham village church, and despite the chilly weather Olivia had never seen so many smiling faces. Everyone said it was the most anticipated wedding in a very long time. Her family was there, even her mother and her new husband, and of course the Fitzsimmonses.

Ivo stood at her side, so serious as he repeated his vows, and then giving her hand an encouraging squeeze when she found herself choked up with emotion as they were pronounced husband and wife.

Her friend, her love, and her husband.

They had been on a long journey, and now they were at the beginning of another one, a life together, and she was so looking forward to it. When she left Grantham, it would be for the last time with it as her home. Whitmont would be her home now.

Grandmama, who had seemed resigned to the inevitable when told her granddaughter would be marrying the very man she had forbidden her to spend time with, had set aside her disappointment and organized a celebratory meal. As the wedding party arrived, Olivia sat down at the table. All about her were the faces of the people she knew and loved. Edwina was bouncing in her seat, particularly excited, having been a flower girl at last, her dream come true.

"Justina and Charles have asked me to be their flower girl too!" she said excitedly. Antonia laughed, but Georgia screwed up her face. Jealous, of course.

Ivo leaned closer and reached for Olivia's hand. "How are you feeling?" he whispered under cover of the chatter around them, his green eyes anxious.

"Better than I was earlier," she whispered back, and smiled.

Ivo was the only one who knew that their last tryst, the night he had saved her life on the salt marshes, had borne fruit. Olivia was excited to think that she was carrying his child, but a little daunted too. Just as well they were marrying quickly enough to muddy the waters of those who liked to count backward from a child's birth, although there would still be gossip.

There would always be gossip when it came to Olivia and Ivo. It was something she had come to accept.

Ivo had been quite overcome when she had told him about the baby.

"A child? *Our* child?" He had put his hand gently on her belly, and his eyes had filled with tears.

After they had held each other, and wept a little, Ivo had begun to tell her all the things he would teach their child. She'd given him a narrow look. "No, you definitely won't take him out onto the salt marshes."

Ivo's gaze had been too innocent to be believed. "Of course not, sweetheart. Not until he can walk."

"Or she."

"Or she."

Olivia had had to be satisfied with that. She trusted

him, believed in him, but he would always be a Fitzsimmons at heart.

She glanced up now and saw that Bourne was seated farther down the table, watching them. He had come to the wedding and the dinner in his capacity as Ivo's spokesman in Portside, but they had known each other for a lifetime. He smiled, his gaze shifting to Ivo, and she thought he was pleased to see that the wild boy duke was finally settled. Olivia had asked Ivo if he missed being a smuggler, but he had assured her those days were gone.

"There is enough excitement for me at Cadieux's," he had said. "And the new club. Charles and I are going to call it *Fitzsimmons*. Soon, I will have enough money to buy you whatever your heart desires."

Then she had teased him with more and more outrageous choices, but the truth was, she already had what her heart desired.

The servants were clearing the table for the next course. "Harrowby and I were in Paris." Her mother's voice rose above the clatter. "I think Ivo and Olivia should go there for *their* honeymoon."

"I want to come too!" Edwina cried.

Vivienne bent her head to the child, gently reminding her that flower girls did not go on honeymoons. Gabriel was watching them, a smile on his face, and Olivia wondered at the tenderness she saw there. Was Vivienne enceinte too?

"What are you scheming about?"

Ivo's whisper in her ear brought her attention back to him.

"How do you know I'm scheming?"

"You have that look in your eyes."

"Perhaps I am looking forward to when we can go to our room, just the two of us."

He kissed her in what was meant to be a chaste brush of lips but turned into something much less innocent.

There was an "oohh" sound from some of those at the table, and Edwina giggled.

"I was just thinking," Olivia said dreamily. She cast her gaze over her sisters. "I was wondering who the next Ashton girl will be, after Justina and me, to settle down."

Just then, Roberta gave a loud laugh at something Will Tremeer said. Was the world ready for Roberta Ashton to be unleashed upon it? Olivia wasn't at all sure.

Gabriel cleared his throat and stood up. "A toast," he said loudly. "To the Ashton family and all those they love, and all those who love them!"

The responding roar shook the rafters and threatened to turn the east wing into a pile of rubble.

Don't miss the next breathtaking novel from Sara Bennett, coming Fall 2025

About the Author

Sara Bennett is an Australian bestselling author. She has written books set in various time periods—medieval, Regency, and Victorian—as well as women's fiction under the name Kaye Dobbie. Currently, she alternates between publishing independently and writing for traditional publishers. Sara was a finalist for the RITA® award and the RUBY.

Sara lives in Victoria, Australia, in an old house in a gold-rush town, with her husband, two important cats, and a rescue poodle. She would love to spend more time in the garden, but there are just too many stories to be written.

You can learn more at:

Website: Sara-Bennett.com

X @SaraBennett16

Facebook.com/SARA-BENNETT

Forbidden Love x Risky Secrets

WHILE THE DUKE WAS SLEEPING
by Samara Parish

When Adelaide Rosebourne has to impersonate her mistress for a few days, it doesn't seem like a difficult task, even if her mistress's supposed fiancé is in a coma. All she has to do is wait until he awakens and then convince him to retract the proposal—thereby securing a tidy reward. She doesn't count on the arrival of the duke's brother and his damned inconvenient interest in her affairs. But does it really matter? She'll be gone before he finds out the truth…

MY SECRET DUKE
by Sara Bennett

Most ladies would be thrilled to receive a proposal from a handsome duke only weeks into their first season, but Olivia is not most ladies, and the circumstances are less than ideal. A scandal has left her family's coffers empty and its reputation on the rocks, which means Olivia must marry someone rich, with an impeccable pedigree. So a man with shaky finances and a taste for risky adventures is exactly wrong for her, no matter how charming his smile…

Forced Proximity x Scandalously Steamy

A GENTLEMAN NEVER TELLS
by Jodi Ellen Malpas

Frank Melrose is on the cusp of taking his father's printing business global, and the last thing he needs is the distraction of any woman, let alone the dazzling Taya Winters. A mysterious highwayman is causing havoc in Belmore Square, and Frank's under pressure from the newspaper to unmask the culprit, but his infuriating clashes with Taya keep slowing him down. What's more, he's sure that the highwayman is right under their noses—and that exposing their identity will not only end his story but ruin his family too…

Women's Fiction x Family Secrets

THE GARDEN OF LOST SECRETS
by Kelly Bowen

When Isabelle purchases a crumbling chateau in the French countryside, it's not just a renovation project—it's a chance to reconnect with her sister, Emilie. What she uncovers instead is an intriguing mystery about their great-grandmother Stasia, a children's book author who found herself one of the most hunted agents of the Resistance during World War II. As the siblings piece together the incredible truth, Stasia's exciting story of courage against the Nazis reveals an explosive secret that will change everything Isabelle believed about her family.